FOND & FOOLISH LOVERS

RICHARD BURNS

BLOOMSBURY

First published in Great Britain 1990
copyright © 1990 by Richard Burns

Bloomsbury Publishing Ltd, 2 Soho Square, London W1V 5DE

A CIP catalogue record for this book is available
from the British Library

ISBN 0 7475 0672 8

10 9 8 7 6 5 4 3 2 1

Typeset by Hewer Text Composition Services, Edinburgh
Printed in Great Britain by
Butler & Tanner Ltd, Frome and London

FOND AND FOOLISH LOVERS

BY THE SAME AUTHOR

A DANCE FOR THE MOON
KHALINDAINE
THE PANDA HUNT
TROUBADOUR
WHY DIAMOND HAD TO DIE

The day Jennifer Fox died, leaving no will, was the day her nephew fell for a married woman. In the course of seven quiet days of mourning, the lives and minds of those closest to Jennifer crisscross in a compelling and profoundly moving story.

As he tries to come to terms with his loss, Chapman, Jennifer's lover, uncovers a strange and sad story of doomed wartime love among her papers. Her nephew, Alan Gruafin, a poet and physicist, searches through her long-neglected book on Shakespeare. Her sister, to whom she hadn't spoken for years, carries on with her amateur dramatics while contemplating the likely proceeds from the sale of Jennifer's (and Chapman's) home. Meanwhile, her publisher sets off for the funeral with the manuscript of a bizarre collection of short stories to read on the train . . . Burns reaches the core of his novel from bold and unexpected directions, combining family histories, quantum physics, Darwinism, love and war; he spotlights the force of blood and the pull of romanticism. His novel is about love, life, death and literature and it is a very considerable achievement.

To Tina

CONTENTS

CONTENTS

Chapter One

TWELFTH NIGHT
or
WHAT YOU WILL

*In which Jennifer dies, Alan meets Wendy,
and Chapman reads some
Letters*

I

I conjure a black taxi in my head. It drives north along white roads. The early morning snow makes sense of Sheffield's post-war architecture, turning it monochrome, reverting it to the scaleless geometry of a draughtsman's illustration, but it leaves the road dangerous. The taxi driver, who is Pakistani, does not mind: this is a mercy mission; the client is on his way to hospital, visiting a dying friend; there is something pleasing about having a reason to drive hard on these white roads. His passenger cannot share this pleasure. He sits with his eyes closed, and his hands are useless on his lap. Were this an ordinary day he might even dismiss the taxi driver as a Paki, though on the other hand he might not, for even his practised prejudice is superficial and unconvincing. But this day he does not seem to have any thoughts or opinions at all, not even borrowed ones. It is as if his grief has fallen like snow inside him and lies like a layer over his emotions, obscuring them, so that he is aware only of the bleakness and not of its cause. Nor is this such a fanciful analogy, for after all this is an invented scene, and even the snow that lies on the road, slows down the taxi, gushes beneath its remoulds, has fallen only within me.

The taxi took him to the hospital door, where the driver refused a tip. The passenger climbed out. The snow that made the landscape fresh and pure made him cold, cautious, corrupt. He walked carefully towards Reception. Jennifer had asked he bring a book, and he carried it under his arm, while salmon pink grit stained the snow, melting it in untidy patches, and the warmth from the hospital cleared the steps. The doors opened in front of him automatically:

3

they were diligent but unfriendly, as though waiting for someone else.

'Gavin Chapman,' he said at the desk. 'For Jennifer Fox.'

It was before the visiting hour but the nurse showed no surprise. 'Which ward is she?'

'B5.'

'Upstairs,' she told him. 'Take the stairs through the glass doors or use the lift. It's only the next floor.' Chapman knew this already. He took the lift. Methodical signs, white lettering on blue, green and red, anatomised the hospital. The nurses' uniforms were blue and white, crisp and impersonal as new five-pound notes. He followed the fiscal nurses. He followed the dissecting signs. There was a stranger in Jennifer's bed: he looked alarmed, and a nurse saw this and led him to a private room.

'Here she is,' announced the nurse.

Chapman did not like the private room. It proved Jennifer was dying. 'Jennifer?' he asked.

She tried to sit up: the nurse helped her, bolstering the pillows with a thump. 'Hello Gavin,' said Jennifer. The plastic identification tag round her wrist seemed looser than before; the plastic had yellowed to the colour of discharge, the colour of decay.

He sat down by the bed. 'Don't let her get tired,' warned the nurse as she left.

'I'm already tired,' said Jennifer.

'Do you want me to go?' asked Chapman, anxious to do the right thing.

'No.' She smiled, almost. 'Of course not. You brought the book.'

He handed it to her, a paperbound collection of scholarly essays, the margin of its red cover faded to a dusty, sunlit grey, a memorial to the shelf and the smaller book it had pressed against. 'Yes.'

She took it and laid it on the bed beside her without opening it. There was a long silence. A bag of saline solution hung over the bed: clear drops fell like melting ice down the tube plumbed to her arm; she counted them as they fell. He watched her watching them and was isolated and afraid. 'This is fun,' said Jennifer at last. 'We must do this more often.'

He took her hand and found something trivial to say. 'It's nice they've found you a private room.' Trivia seemed safest.

It was not safe enough. 'The grave's a fine and private place,' she quoted. 'But none I think do there embrace.' She did not look at him. He wanted comfort, and she knew it and could not give it; she was dying, and it was too much to expect her to pity the survivors. 'Mary Tudor had a cancer,' she continued. 'In her belly. She was convinced it was a baby, and cherished it till it killed her.' Jennifer's cancer was in her cervix. 'A very female way to die.' The snow began to fall again, and Chapman had nothing to say.

A doctor came into the room: 'How are we feeling?'

'Minimal,' she replied, to be awkward. She disliked doctors. She disliked the way mystery was forbidden in their world. She disliked the way they reduced life and death to terms they understood and she didn't. She disliked the way they seemed certain of everything save how to save her.

The doctor ignored her professionally. 'It's the medication,' he said. 'Nurse'll be here in a minute and you can have a nice little sleep. Now, if you could just wait outside, Mr Chaplin.'

Chapman had met the doctor several times and had given up correcting him; he went into the corridor.

A nurse arrived, wheeling a tray of ugly implements to the door of Jennifer's room. 'Is Doctor with her?'

Yes.

The doctor's fingers probed Jennifer's womb. She shut her eyes to shut him out; she tried to make him more vulnerable and human by imagining how he must feel when he touched his wife, his lover, his mistress. She tried these things and they failed: the pain penetrated the medication and all she knew was agony till the injection that let her sleep.

Chapman was abandoned. He waited in the corridor, in the way, until he could squeeze in a word with a nurse. 'She'll be asleep for a couple of hours now,' he was told. 'Why don't you come back at visiting hour?' He walked away. He went outside.

These were the women's wards, irregular red-brick buildings older than him, uglier than him. There were drainpipes like varicose veins, some collecting, some melting the snow, and substantial fire escapes that sifted the flakes through mesh landings. He looked out over Sheffield but the snow was turning to sleet and the city turning to cloud, so he hunched up his coat, clutched his lapels, and started to walk.

Outside the maternity entrance was a wedding car, a white Rolls-Royce. Somebody's cutting it fine, he thought. The car was camouflaged, a different texture of white, and the ribbons that ran from the roof to the radiator were sodden and heavy. The snow had been cleared from the paths here, exposing the cigarette ends: brown butts declared bad nerves; hastily stubbed unfinished cigarettes signalled the triumphant moment of birth. Chapman had never had children, but he smoked there anyway, letting the inappropriate ritual salvage his sense of identity. Chapman had a taste for these second-hand conventions and, grinding the filter tip beneath his toe, he felt the comfort and companionship of those absent expectant fathers, and felt better.

Time was meaningless now, a mid-winter thaw, a saline drip into a corpse's veins. He found a canteen near reception and drank tea. The hot tea distorted the plastic cup, bulging it through the struts of its pale blue holder like four swollen bellies. He was cold, though the canteen was warm, and he was tired. He dozed, and when he awoke the visiting hour had begun.

The corridors were busy with children and concern now. He went to her ward. 'She's sleeping,' said the sister.

'Can I see her?'

'I'll see how she is. Wait here.'

The sister left him. He saw her open the door to Jennifer's room, step inside, step back out. 'Send for a doctor,' she instructed a passing nurse.

'How is she?' asked Chapman, but the sister did not answer. Chapman went into the room and the sister did not stop him.

The drip in her arm was still. Her eyes were closed. He moved towards her across the linoleum, but before he had reached her the doctor arrived. Jennifer had always appreciated irony: she would have enjoyed the fact that, though any fool could see it was too late for a doctor, none the less a doctor was needed, for only doctors can pronounce a patient dead. And she had always been unconventional: this was the visiting hour – the hour for dying came later, when the children were in bed – yet here she was, incontestably, incontrovertibly dead.

6

2

And who am I? Not in the pointless, philosophical way the question is asked by all save those of whom I'm afraid – men who place bets, tell jokes, carry large bunches of keys – but simply in reference to that stately black column of an 'I', that 'I' that is also an eye, with which this tale began.

Who am I?

3

Professor Jardine was late. 'Horrible weather, terrible traffic,' he told Chapman. 'Visiting hour's not over is it? Only I wanted a word before tomorrow's meeting. Pasmore's sure to press for his compulsory post-structuralism component in the Year One BA and I need Jenny's support.'

Chapman was baffled by life and by death, bewildered by the professor. 'Jennifer's gone,' he said, which was easier than saying she was dead.

'Gone home?' The professor saw Chapman's face. 'Oh. I see.' He wore no hat, took off his spectacles. 'If there's anything I can do.'

'Of course,' said Chapman.

'I'm awfully sorry.'

'It doesn't matter,' said Chapman, meaninglessly.

The professor searched the room for something to say and found the book Chapman had taken from Jennifer's bed. 'Ah! *Essays on Writers.*' Chapman said nothing. 'I recognised the cover,' the professor pressed on.

'Jennifer's,' explained Chapman. The only thing they had in common was Jennifer, and she was dead.

The professor replaced his glasses. 'I should go.' He wondered if Dixon, who had taken Jenny's classes while she was in hospital, was up to doing them full time. Thank goodness the new term hasn't started. But damned Pasmore'll get his way now. 'If there's anything I can do,' he repeated, 'just give me a ring at the department.'

'I don't think so.'

'And you'll let me know about the funeral? I'm sure there are many of us who'd want to pay our respects. Jenny was a fine scholar and a valued colleague.' Professor Jardine found he was speaking in the conventionalised language of the obituary columns, and rather despised himself for it, but could think of nothing else to say. 'Her death will be a terrible blow.'

They shook hands, two men in overcoats in the women's wards' warm lobby. 'I haven't thought about the arrangements yet,' said Chapman.

'No. Of course not.'

'But I'll let you know.'

'Fine. Thank you.'

'Thank you.'

'Fine. Well, I'll be off.'

'Well. Goodbye then.'

'Can I offer you a lift?' asked the professor.

'I'm fine thank you.'

'Fine. Well, goodbye.'

'Goodbye.'

'And shall I let the papers know?'

'Oh. Thank you. And goodbye.'

The weight of his grief was beginning to hurt Chapman's shoulders. The professor left, crossing snow that was diseased, eaten by dirt and the passing of cars; the soles of his shoes seemed to suck at the snow, and words Yeats had written came to his head in the rhythm of the slush of his feet:

Never to have lived is best, ancient writers say;
Never to have drawn the breath of life, never to have looked into
    the eye of day;
The second best's a gay goodnight and quickly turn away.

Yeats was the professor's specialism.

The car started at the third attempt; the professor switched on the wipers, the radio, the lights, and cautiously turned away.

4

It is after dark now. Orange streetlamps light a suburban street. The street is lined with trees and the trees are bare; the snow falling in front of the lamps is quaint and theatrical, something out of an illustrated Dickens, and the lighted rooms of the prosperous detached houses are warm.

This is a kind of reality. I know this street well. But it is an unreliable reality. For though the street exists it is peopled by my imagination. That man walking his dog, avoiding the icy pavements, preferring the rutted road, has been placed there to swell out the scene; likewise Ernest Gruafin, who is alone in number 17 not only because his son has moved to London and his wife is at the dress rehearsal in the village hall, but also to develop my plot. And because of the latter, when he answered the phone on the early evening of that fictional day when Jennifer Fox died, only he was surprised to hear Chapman speak.

'Is that Mr Gruafin?'

'Speaking.'

'It's Gavin Chapman here. I'm – I'm Jennifer's friend.'

'Oh, hello.' Ernest had known his sister-in-law's friend in the days when the sisters had been talking. 'Er, do you want to speak to my wife? Only she's out, I'm afraid.'

'It's about Jennifer. You see, she's dead.' Chapman had grown used to the word and used to using it, though he did not know yet all it meant.

'Oh dear.'

'Perhaps you could tell your wife?'

'Yes. Of course.' But this was inadequate. 'Er, where are you now?'

'I'm at the hospital still.'

'Look. Are you going home? Why not stop off here on your way back? I'm sure Bridget will want to see you. You are going back to Bakewell?'

There was a pause. 'I haven't a car.' It was an admission.

'Oh. But I could always fetch you. You're at the hospital? The Hallamshire?'

'The Northern General.'

It was further but Ernest could hardly withdraw his offer. 'Wait for me in the foyer. I'll be half an hour. You'll see the car. It's a blue Rover.'

'You're very kind. Thank you.'

'The least I can do,' said Ernest. 'I'll be with you soon.'

He went to his study to write a note for his wife; Chapman went to the hospital Gents. Ernest started to write, Chapman to read. 'Gone to hospital to collect,' wrote Ernest, then crossed this out. 'Jennifer dead. Gone to.' He crumpled the paper to a ball, dropped it in the bin. 'Gone out,' he wrote. 'Back soon. Ernest.'

Chapman looked at the graffiti. 'Suck my cock. Anytime. Leave date and password.' '12 inches. Clean. Nightshift only.' 'Sexy, sorry I couldn't make it. Same time next week? Dildo.' Between the lonely-hearted assertive homosexuals came more familiar messages. 'United Rool OK', 'Beware limbo dancers'. Chapman read them all, slowly, to avoid thinking, and returned to the foyer.

He sat down. The chair was low, its padding covered by bright orange plastic with an L-shaped split where it bulged athletically under the weight of his thigh. Someone had pushed a cigarette end into the split. He rested his elbows on his knees and rubbed his eyes with the heels of his hands. The air was tainted with hints of purpose. Antiseptic masked the taste of decay; lavender air-freshener blunted the antiseptic. The striplights stripped the walls and striped the ceiling. The heating-ducts hemmed the foyer. The atmosphere was the silence between the ticking of clocks. Nothing happened till he heard the scream.

Chapman looked up. A man was bleeding at the desk. Bright blood poured down his cheek as he struck and struck again at the small black nurse. 'Fucking coon! You'll not touch me, fucking coon!' His voice was thin with anger or fear. The nurse screamed again. Her face was bleeding too. Their indistinguishable blood spattered the tiles. 'Fucking coon!' She slumped, and he slumped too, falling to his knees and cradling her in his arms as though she were a lover.

The crowd gathered then, hiding the couple from Chapman's view. A policeman arrived. He pushed through, splitting the crowd, and led the man away. The crowd did not re-form. The nurse was helped to her feet and a woman in a housecoat mopped the spilt blood. The striplights jarred the floor where the mop passed.

Chapman rubbed his eyes again. His grief was an ache in his shoulders as well as a weight on his neck. He tried to ease himself in his chair and saw a man in an overcoat. The man stood by the desk. He looked out of place, ill at ease; he asked something of a porter and the porter shrugged. Chapman stood and walked over. 'Ernest Gruafin?'

'Chapman. Thank goodness I've found you.' Ernest looked to where the mop still swished the blood.

'It was good of you to come.'

'It was nothing.' The cleaner squeezed her mop into her bucket until the water dripped to silence and, picking mop and bucket up with one expert hand, left the foyer. 'Let's get to my car.'

They walked out. Bridget's husband, Jennifer's lover: they sought for something to share. 'Nasty night,' said Ernest.

'Not as cold as yesterday, I think.'

'No. Not as cold. But cold enough.'

'Cold enough.' Ernest was large, Chapman small: Ernest strode and Chapman was almost trotting to keep up. 'More snow coming, do you think?'

'We don't seem to get snow like we used to,' replied Ernest.

'No. That's true.'

'This one's my car.'

Chapman walked round to the passenger door while Ernest unlocked. 'It's open,' said Ernest before he got in. 'Central locking.'

'That's nice.'

'Very useful,' agreed Ernest.

They drove off in silence. The digital clock on the dashboard read 19.31, the year of Chapman's birth. They drove off in silence through the terraced car-parks and the imposing Victorian gates. The roads had been cleared. They passed demoralised terraces, community centres, caged video shops and launderettes, dropped through districts of students and immigrants, reached the brighter lights of the Wicker. T'Wicker where t'watter runs o'er t'weir: a stately railway arch and the all-night chemist where hunched youths pressed prescriptions for drugs. They reached the Don. Up the hill ahead of them was the city centre, flamboyant with Christmas lights. 'They really leave the lights up too long,' said Ernest, following the traffic signals left. 'They put them up in November; they could at least take them down now Christmas is over.'

The traffic system wound them round in a complicated loop, directing them back to where they had started. 'Isn't it Twelfth Night today?' asked Ernest.

'Is it? I expect it is.' Jennifer, author of *Shakespeare's Great Theme*, had died on Twelfth Night. It ought to mean something, and didn't.

'They really should have taken the lights down by now. No wonder the rates are so high.'

'At least she saw the New Year in,' said Chapman. Jennifer would not have found much consolation in this – second prize in a race between two – but she was dead and it was Chapman who needed such comforts.

'Yes, that's right,' said Ernest. 'And she had Christmas of course.'

Of course. Christmas Eve: the Falcon for a few drinks, a few too many. It hurts, Chap, she had told him. It really hurts. And the pain in her eyes and the sweat on her upper lip, bright fixed beads that did not jostle when she spoke, not even when she quoted *Macbeth*:

'Then comes my fit again . . .
I am cabin'd, cribb'd, confined, bound in
To saucy doubts and fears –
'Take me home Chap,
Take me home.'

Next morning it was clear her painkillers were no longer strong enough. They waited for the ambulance. He stood at the window, she tried not to writhe with the pain, and their Christmas dinner cooled in the oven.

Ernest stopped at a set of traffic lights. The lights changed – red, red-amber, green – and he pulled away. 'I'm sorry,' he said.

The ambulance had drawn up outside, flashing lights washing the room a cold blue. There was no snow that Christmas Day. The ambulancemen helped her into a wheelchair and took her outside. Their house was a house of illness, marked as if with a red cross on the door, or straw strewn on the street to muffle the horses' hooves.

The ambulance set off, past twitching curtains, festive houses. Jennifer tried to make some sort of joke about the ambulancemen working on Christmas Day, extra money, but it hadn't come out right and all they were left with was silence, her grey face drawn back and new lines round her mouth, the ambulanceman patting her hand and Chapman, sitting opposite, useless.

Ernest drove past the university. Odd lights were still on. He listened to Chapman's silence. I'm sorry, he thought. I'm sorry. But his sorrow was for Chapman's grief rather than Jenny's death. I ought to feel sorry Jenny's dead, he thought. I ought to feel sorry for her. But I hardly knew her, poor Jenny, poor dead Jenny, poor Jenny Horse-face. The sisters had never been close: Bridget had the looks and Jenny the brains, though that was more unfair on Bridget than Jenny. I hardly knew her, poor Jenny Horse-face. I can't feel sorry for her, only for this man in the car next to me who is also a stranger but is here, now, real. He's crying. He doesn't want me to know it but he's crying. Ernest felt the desire to cry too, but couldn't. To cry would be un-English. Ernest was half Jewish and therefore had learnt to be entirely English. And it wasn't his grief.

Chapman spoke. 'That was where she worked.' The university English department was a pair of Victorian semis up a cul-de-sac. 'That's her room.' But Ernest, steering his car and his thoughts, missed it.

Now they passed the old grammar school, Ernest's school, and the botanical gardens: respectable, sturdy, red-brick and stone, Brocco Bank and the Hunter's Bar roundabout, up Ecclesall Road to Banner Cross. Ernest made patterns of the journey. Incey-wincey spider, the Grand Old Duke of York. Marched them up to the top of the hill and down came the rain. Shops gave way to gardens then fields. A bus, a 240, a Bakewell bus, slowed them down. 'Would you mind?' asked Chapman. 'I think I'll take the bus. You don't mind do you?'

'No. Of course not,' said Ernest, wondering why he did.

'Thanks for the lift but I don't really feel like talking. I wouldn't be much company.'

'It's all right. I'm sorry I couldn't do more to help.' Ernest overtook the bus and halted by the next bus stop. 'And you will let us know? About the arrangements?'

The arrangements. 'Yes. Yes, I'll do that. Of course.' Chapman let the fresh night air into the car. 'Well. Thanks for the lift.'

'We'll see you again soon,' said Ernest. At the funeral.

'Yes.' At the funeral. 'Bye.'

'Goodbye.' Ernest pulled away. He resented the way Chapman had abandoned him to his borrowed grief, and regretted his resentment. He drove automatically off the main road, into the suburban village where he had lived for thirty years, reached his house. There were more lights on than when he had left: Bridget was back.

He got out, opened the garage doors, and parked his Rover. The air was cold and good. He stood, indecisive, at the edge of the drive. Come on. He closed the garage. The door was locked and he had to let himself in.

The hall was darkly furnished, mahogany and velvet. 'Bridget!' he called.

'Kitchen!' she replied.

He walked through. Bridget was at the kitchen table, reading her magazine. 'You're back early,' he said.

She ignored this. 'Where have you been?'

'I went to the hospital.' He knew his resentment of Chapman was unjust, but this was unjust too. It was not his bad news to deliver. 'The Northern General. Bridget, Jennifer is dead.'

His wife looked up. 'Is she?' she asked. It was the wrong response. It left Ernest with nothing to say. 'Why did you go?' she continued.

Ernest explained.

'You invited him here!' said Bridget. 'That seedy little creep!'

'I quite liked him,' said Ernest, and by this time he did. He and Chapman had been through something together, something Bridget had missed.

'You like everyone,' said his wife. 'I suppose he's getting the lot?'

'Sorry?'

'In her will. I suppose he's getting everything.' Bridget gave her husband a look that was part exasperation and part indulgence. 'I don't suppose you even thought about the will, did you.'

'It's not time yet, surely.'

'And what about the funeral? I'll give Alan a ring in the morning.

He's not seen Jennifer in goodness knows how long but he ought to know I suppose.'

'I'll ring now if you like.'

'Don't bother him,' said Bridget. 'It'll keep.'

And the will, thought Ernest, though he said nothing. Can't that keep? Or is her money all you can think of? He turned away from his wife, who watched him and knew his thoughts.

Money was not all she could think about, it was all she could talk about. Money is safer than emotion. Money can be counted, secured, saved for a rainy day. Her emotions were not so secure. She heard Ernest go upstairs. She heard without listening: the loose tread four steps up; the different sound as he reached the landing; the bathroom door opened and closed. She tried to think kindly of her sister. She tried to think of good times: she knew there must have been some. But Jennifer had been seven years older, and Jennifer's childhood had been peace; all Bridget could remember of childhood was war, rationing, Daddy in his ARP helmet, Jenny with important things to do and herself doing nothing, going to school, staying awake in the Blitz, hoping to see a bomb explode or a building burn, but, just as she had never stayed awake long enough to see Father Christmas, never quite managing it, until the war became as remote, as much a conspiracy of elders, as Santa.

Jennifer won prizes but was not pretty, did not have boyfriends like the other girls' sisters, could not be talked about or emulated. Maureen Taylor's sister brought home American airmen and clerks in reserved occupations who could get hold of coupons and coal; Jennifer had worn glasses and gone to university. Jennifer had not been normal, she had been special and gifted and seconded to war work which was secret and adult and enticing; Bridget, who was pretty and clever but never so special, grew up wanting to be like Maureen's sister and needing to be like her own, and somehow managing neither.

5

Dr Crabcalf leant against the back of his chair and linked his fingers behind his head. 'This is as probably as many as we can expect tonight, so let's begin. I'd like to welcome you to this year's first meeting of Crouch Poets and wish a Happy New Year to you all.' There were five Crouch poets that night, a ragged pentagon of grey plastic chairs in a corner of this North London school hall. 'I'm sorry it's so cold in this place. Wendy, you work here. Another word with the caretaker, do you think?'

'I can try.'

'Good. Well, before the workshop starts,' Crabcalf continued, 'there are a couple of announcements I'd like to make. Firstly,' he consulted a sheet of paper, 'I'd like to welcome a new member to our intrepid band, Alan Gruafin.' He pronounced the strange surname as Alan had requested, grew-*a*-fin; the others turned to look at Alan. 'Alan is already quite a success: Action Court Books have published a pamphlet of his poems, and a few years ago he won a Gregory Award. We hope he'll enjoy being with us – our aim is to create a sympathetic environment where everyone can develop their potential to the full. Not all of us have had Alan's triumph but I know we share his enthusiasm for poetry, and that's the main thing. I'll not introduce everyone, Alan, as it'd take too long, but I'm sure you'll soon work out that Wendy's the pretty one, Jim's the ugly one, and Ted's the only one left. Not a brilliant turnout tonight: numbers are usually higher.'

Wendy and Ted smiled at him; Jim leant over and took his hand. 'Jim Hamilton,' he said. 'Pleased to meet you.' His accent and beard were Scottish and thick. Dr Crabcalf was still talking. 'What else? Ah yes. I've asked Ursula Fanthorpe to judge the next Crouch Poets' Open Competition. As you know, Ursula is very busy, but I hold out hope. And finally, by next week the dance group will have finished rehearsals, so we can go back to our usual seven-thirty meeting time, which I'm sure everyone will appreciate: longer to discuss our work; longer in the pub. By the way, the drama group asked me to tell you that they'll be performing *The Widowing of Mrs Holroyd* on Friday, Saturday and Sunday nights this week, and there are plenty of tickets left.

'Right. Down to business. I think Ted has a poem for us.'

Ted, middle-aged, well-organised, handed out a photocopied sheet. Dr Crabcalf raised his eyes heavenwards when he received his copy; the others smiled and grimaced. 'This poem is called "The

Argument". Some of you have seen it before but I've made one or two alterations.'

Alan read as Ted spoke:

'My wife and I had an argument today
So I sit downstairs and watch the television
While she is listening to the radio in the kitchen.
The TV news is about the Lebanon
And makes no sense. Arguments never make sense
But at least my wife and I can patch ours up,
Go to bed, kiss and hug one another close
– With luck.'

There was a long pause at the end of the reading, and it grew longer. 'I like it,' said Alan. 'It's short and to the point and says something about the world and your relationship with your wife at the same time. Yes, I think it's good.'

'Thank you,' said Ted. 'And I hope you noticed the changes.'

'Well,' said Dr Crabcalf, slowly. 'I can't say I did. You said this was going to be a new poem, Ted.'

'They're in the second and third line. "Now" at the beginning of the second line has become "So", and the third line used to read "And she is in the kitchen listening to the radio".'

'But you said it was a new poem, Ted,' insisted Dr Crabcalf.

Ted looked up. 'A workshop is where you work up your poems, get them to be as good as they can be.'

'Absolutely. But you've been bringing the same poem to us every second session for months.'

'So? I'm still working on it.'

'But the changes aren't important any more,' said Wendy. She was pretty in a small, blonde way. 'We've already told you we like the poem; why keep bringing it back? Unless you want to hear us say it again?'

'But you're wrong,' said Ted. 'The changes do matter. Every word has to be right.'

'It's not *Paradise Lost* you know, Ted,' said Jim. 'It's half a dozen decentish lines. There's a limit to how many times you can change it.' He grinned 'There's a limit to how many times we can hear it.'

17

'But,' said Alan, 'you can't really argue with what Ted's said. The purpose of a workshop is to work on our poems. If Ted thinks things need changing he should change them. That's up to him.'

'True enough,' agreed Jim. 'But there comes a point where we lose interest. That's all.'

'We all enjoy this poem,' said Crabcalf. He linked his hands behind his neck again, brought his elbows together in front of his mouth, spoke into the cuffs of his jacket. 'But what we're trying to say is that we'd like to see something else from you now. We want to find out what else you can do. Wendy?' – he turned to her – 'You said you were bringing a poem for us.'

She shook her head. 'Sorry. No time.'

'No time!' said Jim. 'You're a bloody teacher! You're on holiday!'

She raised her eyebrows, drew in her upper lip. It was a pleasing gesture; it pleased Alan. 'The holiday finished last Tuesday.'

'What about you, Alan? Have you brought anything?'

'Nothing very new, I'm afraid. One of the reasons I came along to the workshop tonight was to see if it could get me writing again.' And something to do now Anne-Marie has gone, he thought.

'It'll be more new to us than Ted's poem,' said Jim.

'Please,' said Crabcalf. 'We'd love to hear whatever you want to read.'

Alan shrugged and opened the ring file in front of him. 'It's called "The Promise of Arrivals".'

'Has it been published before?' asked Dr Crabcalf.

'Not in this country,' he said, unintentionally impressive. 'I've no copies, I'm afraid. I'll just read it.

It's been our century, Dad,
and we did what we could,
dust settling on the books
and a conch for a bookend.

But it was trains not waves
when I held the conch to my head.
It was Buchenwald I heard
chalked above the running board

and the train, high silled,
European in style,
duns through the night.
All journeys are a promise

and we are the legacy of speed,
the timetabled sound,
the promise of arrivals
and the promises we made as we left.

This conch on your shelf,
it buttressed a fat weight of books,
but the books came tumbling down
when I held it to my head, Dad,

when I held it to my head like a revolver.'

Again the silence. 'Perhaps if I could read it?' suggested Dr
Crabcalf.

'I liked it a lot,' said Wendy. 'It seems so – dense.'

'A bit too dense for me,' said Jim. 'I'd need to read it to myself.'

'I'm sorry,' said Alan, handing the typescript over. 'If I'd been
well-organised like Ted I'd have made photocopies.'

'Really is bloody cold in here,' said Jim. 'Where're you from?
You're no' a Londoner.'

'I was born in Sheffield.'

'You can't have everything.'

'Have you finished with Alan's poem yet, Dr Crabcalf?' asked
Wendy. 'I'd like a look.'

'Mmmmm? A moment.'

Wendy turned to Jim while she waited. 'Have you heard from
Robert about your stories yet?'

'Not a word,' said Jim.

Crabcalf finished reading, handed the paper to Wendy and spoke
to Alan. 'A curious form,' he commented. 'Very economical, but
perhaps you should explain more about the connections between
ideas. Somehow the Buchenwald train doesn't quite tie in with the
train journeys you describe in the next stanza. You make the specific
general in a way, and I guess it's also about your relationship with

your father – well written too, certainly – but I'm not sure the ideas aren't jammed together too tightly. What made you choose to read this one?'

Alan thought seriously. 'Because it's not quite right,' he decided.

Jim nodded; Wendy smiled. Alan liked the smile. 'Anyone anything else to say about Alan's poem?' asked Dr Crabcalf. 'If not, I've a poem of my own I'd like to read. It's part of my sonnet sequence,' he explained to Alan. 'The others have heard many of the other poems involved. The leading persona is Eric, who teaches English literature at Boston University; it's a record of his thoughts there. This one's about – no, I'll let the sonnet speak for itself.

I stand upwards of the bay, Teiresias, hoping
that the maximum advantage of the soul
is taken with the words you found, and coping
with the sense of something whole and wholly whole;
Wittgenstein declared the best we're able
to do is say what's sayable, at least.
Of that, least that, I think perhaps I'm capable
for that is my desire and my release.
My grandeur in God's eyes and in my own
is recompense for silence in the heart.
In sex I have no mistress, and I hone
the feeling of the moment in my art:
impeded by the words that turn out wrong
I suffer into silence for my song.'

Rather than suffer the silence, Dr Crabcalf launched into explanation. 'I was a teaching assistant at BU in Sixty-eight. The sequence is part autobiographical, based on my experiences there. My experiences of life and of drugs. Eventually there should be three hundred and sixty-five sonnets, one for each day of Sixty-eight, dealing with sex, politics, the music and the drugs.'

'Wasn't Sixty-eight a leap year?' asked Jim.

Discussion was limited to anecdotes from Jim and Crabcalf about what 1968 was like, really like. Alan and Wendy were too young to remember; Ted seemed to have missed it. Ted, feeling the cold, mentioned the pub; Jim was keen. 'There's where the real work gets done.'

They had to stack their chairs before they left. Alan chose to stack his next to Wendy's. 'Is it always like this?' he asked.

'There are usually more people.'

'More poems? Three in an evening is hardly many.'

'Well. Dr Crabcalf always reads one of his sonnets, of course. And Ted's been working on his poem for ages. Jim writes stories and occasionally brings one. He's trying to get a collection published just now. And other people do bring stuff. Sometimes.'

'What about you?'

'Sometimes.'

Alan gathered his possessions in a Sainsbury's bag and they walked through the empty school to the playground. The playground was surrounded by walls, the walls were topped with broken glass, the glass was scratched with streetlight. They crossed the road to the pub. 'How did you hear about Crouch Poets?' asked Ted.

'I saw a poster in the library, gave Dr Crabcalf a ring,' Alan replied. He wanted to be friendly. He wanted friends. 'He was very encouraging. I suppose I want a bit of encouragement. I don't seem to have written much for ages.'

'Writer's block.' Ted nodded. 'I know all about it.' He held the door open for Alan and Wendy. 'It's so hard to keep your standards up.'

The pub was warm and tasted of smoke. 'What do you do?' Alan asked him. 'For a living I mean?'

'I work for Telecom. I'm the man who sends your bill.'

Alan could think of nothing to say to this. 'Oh.' Ted smiled roguishly, as though he was used to the effect his job had on others, as though he rather enjoyed being a pariah. 'What about you, Wendy?' asked Alan. 'You work at the school? What do you teach?'

'Yobs.' She showed small teeth in a smile. 'English. But I don't talk about it.'

'Ah, the old war wound. I teach too.'

'Really. English?'

'Physics. At an American college.'

'That sounds interesting.'

'I wish it was. It's all right. Bit basic. Kind of sub-A-level stuff really, though.'

'What do you want to drink?' she asked.

'Oh. Thank you. A pint of Guinness.'

She passed this on to the barman. 'And a half of lager for me.'

They sat down, the five of them round a table. Jim lit a pipe, Dr Crabcalf a cigarette. 'How did you enjoy your first meeting of Crouch Poets?' Crabcalf asked.

'Very much.'

'We're not all in your league, of course, as poets. But we try. That's what Valerie Eliot once said. Eliot and Stravinsky were going into a restaurant and the *maître d'* said, "The world's greatest poet and the world's greatest composer are dining here tonight," and Valerie Eliot said, "They try."' The Crouch Poets laughed dutifully.

'Are you working on anything now?' asked Wendy.

'Now? Not really,' replied Alan. 'I was just saying, I joined the group in the hope of inspiration. I seem to have stopped writing just at present.' And Anne-Marie has gone. 'I sometimes think I'd rather write a novel than poems.'

'Why?' asked Jim. 'I'm a prose man myself. A bit of a leper in this company, you know.'

'Maybe there's more room for ideas.'

'Surely the great vehicle for ideas is poetry,' said Dr Crabcalf. 'That's what I'm writing, always. Ideas, ideas, ideas.' He took a drink of his beer and turned to Jim, to 1968.

'I suppose you're right,' conceded Alan. Crabcalf wasn't listening.

Ted was, though he sat nursing his pint and seemed unlikely to speak. Wendy was listening too. 'I don't think I could write a novel,' she said. 'Too many words.'

'I don't know if I can either, but I intend to give it a try. One day.'

'What'd it be about?'

'The usual things I suppose. Life and love, birth and death.' The break-up of a relationship.

'How tedious.' She wondered if she was flirting with him, decided she was, decided she liked it. 'Tell me about yourself. Do you take sugar in your coffee – no, you wouldn't. Do you have a car? Do you read in bed?'

Alan wondered if she was flirting too, decided she was, decided he liked it. 'I've nothing else to do in bed.'

'How tragic.'

'Mournful,' he agreed.

'And what do you read?'

'I've just finished *Out of this World*, Graham Swift.'

'Overrated,' commented Crabcalf, overhearing.

'I didn't think so,' said Alan.

'And what else?' asked Wendy.

'I like novels with ideas.'

'Don't you ever read poetry?' asked Crabcalf.

'What novels?' asked Wendy.

'Not so much these days. And the Italians mostly: Calvino, Primo Levi, Cruso.'

'Stefan Cruso? That's a coincidence. My husband's meeting him tonight.'

'Husband?' Alan looked at her hand. Engagement ring, wedding ring: the first attractive woman since Anne-Marie left and ha bloody ha.

'He works in the publicity department of the Lanchester Press,' she said.

'I hope they're more efficient than the bloody editorial department,' put in Jim.

'Lanchester are looking at Jim's stories now,' explained Wendy.

'Balls. No one's looking at them,' said Jim. 'My manuscript was just the right size to prop up a rocking desk and that's where it's been since the moment it arrived.'

Alan laughed. 'You were talking about your husband,' he prompted Wendy.

'That's right. John's taking Cruso out for dinner.'

'That sounds fabulous. I'm sure he's a fascinating man.'

'My husband? No, not really. A bit boring really.'

'I meant Cruso.'

'Yes, I expect he is. I didn't know he was Italian. Perhaps he doesn't speak English. That'll be fun for John.'

'I think he will speak English: he used to teach creative writing in Australia. His last novel was set there.'

She finished her lager. 'I'd better go.'

Was it the reminder of her husband that was making her leave?

'Won't you let me buy you a drink?' asked Alan. 'You bought me one.'

23

'You'll be at next week's meeting, won't you? You can buy me one then.'

And so she went, petite, pretty, interesting and married, exchanging quick goodbyes and buttoning her coat as she went through the door. 'Nice girl,' said Alan, hoping they might talk about her.

'Yes,' agreed Dr Crabcalf. 'Now, tell us. How did you get your pamphlet published? I'm sure that's what we'd all like to hear.'

6

The bus bludgeons through the hills toward Bakewell. The hills are pied, nightblack and snow, above them steep clouds bubble round the haze of a slow white moon; inside the bus Chapman thinks about death.

His mind is finite, limited by his skull. This is appropriate. Life is finite; life ends with the skull, the rictus, the insolent grin of death. But despite his finite brain, which ought to cavil at infinity, he finds he can cope with infinity quite well. Infinity means there is always something more. It is the finiteness of things that troubles him.

Once upon a time North America teemed with bison, herds of which, caked with dried mud the colour of their droppings, passed endlessly in front of the gunsights; the sky was pregnant with their dust; the buffalo went on for ever, eternal, indestructible, ineffable. And because they were infinite they were killed. The killing was easy, careless, constant. Infinity is easy to conjecture. It is the finite — finite numbers of buffalo, the finite length of a life – which confounds us. Chapman can look at the sky and contemplate death; he looks at his hands, clenched in his lap, bony, familiar, smudged with liver spots and the blue pattern of veins, and cannot.

The bus gets to Bakewell; Chapman gets off. For a moment he is part of a crowd, then he is alone. The snow has turned ugly in his absence. He walks along the road between the sharp embalming scent of the fish shop and the shrouded humps of parked cars and turns down the street where he lives. He passes pisspot yellow pools of streetlight and dog pee and unlocks the door of his empty house.

He goes in. He is there. The house is still empty. Wearily, having nothing better to do, he puts the kettle on.

7

Wendy put the kettle on. The blind was up. Night lined the kitchen window like the backing of a mirror: she looked out at her neighbours' occasional lights, her kitchen, herself. The meagre mirror simplified her face, hollowed her cheekbones, silvered her fair hair. She put the kettle on, unhooked a mug from a cupboard, added a spoon of instant coffee.

The kettle boiled and switched itself off. Wendy poured in the water, poured in the milk, tapped in a sweetener from a plastic tube. She went into the living room. Wall-lights glared against cream-painted walls. A pair of cream two-seater settees faced one another across a glass-topped table. By the door, neatly framed, were their matching degrees from Durham. John had gone to Durham because he had missed a place at Cambridge; Wendy had gone to Durham because it was about as far away from her mother as she could get. At either side of the chimney was an alcove, and both alcoves were full of books. Many were first editions, many were signed. These were John's. Her books were paperbacks, Penguin Classics and Faber poets, Austen and Hardy and Larkin and Heaney. She looked at John's books. There were two full shelves of Lanchester Press publications. She ran her finger along the spines and found Stefan Cruso, *Aesthetics of a Gumtree*. Peculiar title, she thought, lifting her brows. There was a biography in the back: when he was born, where he had worked, what he had written, the prizes he'd won.

The other flap of the jacket contained a brief description of *Aesthetics of a Gumtree* and a number of reviews of the Italian edition.

A narrative of destruction by a master of despair, leading the reader through a single day in the life of Nick, a Greek Australian. We learn of his ambitions, his dreams, his reality; we also learn of Nick's father and his collaboration with the Nazis in World War Two. A tapestry woven of many threads, *Aesthetics of a Gumtree* is one of Cruso's most compelling books, combining wit and wisdom, humour and tragedy, to chilling and startling effect.

She sat down, took a sip of coffee, and opened the book at random.

Here I am standing on sydney harbour bridge thinking of dedalus soaring into the liffey, joyously, joycily. Joyous thoughts, essential puns: soaring, saw, seesaw, seesaw balanced between seen and unseen, seen and obscene; sydney doubling dublin or was it vice versa, versi visa? the veni vidi vici of looking down from a bridge and holding in his head all he saw, colonising the colony, making it part of his empire of words. Here I am he thinks and vice versa I am here, standing on sydney harbour bridge watching the opera, opera house, quartered onion squeezing its layers towards the bay, or baying trumpets, fanning fanfares, waving waves, great scalped scallops scaled like a cathedral, organised like an organ, an internal organ lung-lunging like a singer toward the high notes and the clapping cheering ovation of the waves. And then the triumph pales, the sentence fails, and he is standing on sydney harbour bridge, with fear.

Wendy stopped reading and turned to the title page. There was no translator's name. As the puns suggested, *Aesthetics of a Gumtree* had been written in English.

She turned to the beginning and started to read again. She wanted to like the book. She wanted to like it because Alan liked it. And because Alan liked it, in time so did she, so that by the time John came home, weary and over-fed, she was on page fifty-eight and fascinated.

'Christ, I'm tired,' said John.

'Hello. So what's new? How was your date?'

'Cruso. Not bad. Speaks perfect English, thank God.'

'What was he like? I'm reading him at the moment.'

'*Orchestra without Violins*? Oh no, the one before. Oh, not bad really. Like a lot of these continental authors he's a bit intense, convinced we live in a great age of the novel. I just nodded and let him get on with it.'

'I like this book.' Wendy liked many books, most books; Wendy liked books.

'Do you?' John rubbed his eyes. He had joined Lanchester Press straight from university; his job and his marriage had begun within a week of one another, in 1980. She had been in love with John, and in love with his career; he had been in love with Wendy, and in love with his career. But though they did not know it, they did not mean the same thing when they spoke that caressing word 'career'. For Wendy, John's career was literature, publishing, the dusty glamour of titles and proofs; when John talked of career he was talking about promotion and advancement. 'I've not read it myself,' he said.

'You never do these days. What do you say when you have to meet the authors and they ask what you thought of their books?'

' "I'm afraid I haven't had the chance to read it yet. But I'm very much looking forward to it." ' He was good at palming off authors, chatting with agents, hosting parties. He was good at telephoning literary editors and getting space on the book page. His job was professional enthusiasm, a praising of books over Groucho Club lunches and West End champagne; the work was easier if the enthusiasm was sincere, but the essence, even the vocabulary, of his performance was the same. Simply stunning, hugely talented; partly to compensate for these gushes, partly to justify them, he was cynical when away from his work.

'Is that really what you say?' Despite herself she was amused. 'Every time?'

'Every time.' He was tired of his job, tired of someone else deciding what books he had to like. Incorporated Publishers had made the first move: now it was up to him. So goodbye Lanchester Press, goodbye evening meals with intense Italian authors, goodbye pushing books that would never make their advance though their authors could write like angels. And hello Incorporated Publishers, hello ghostwritten memoirs, Hollywood trips, star names and star faces. He would not be expected to like the contents of Incorporated's books, simply to enthuse about past sales, advertising budgets, the author's appearance and public appearances. He felt there was more integrity to his new job, but he had not yet told Wendy he was moving. She would think he had sold out.

'Look, love, it's late, I've had a long day. Why don't you make me a cup of tea and we can go to bed.'

They lay in bed. John was looking forward to handing his notice in; Wendy was looking backwards over a long mixed day. John drifted into a peaceful sleep and Wendy stayed awake. John snored slightly. She used to find this charming, endearing. It wasn't an offensive noise, nearer a whistle than a snort, and he looked so innocent, so unprotected, so unaware, while he was doing it. She used to tease him about it; he teased back, told her she was making things up.

Now it irritated her. Intolerably. And now they never made things up.

8

The blade presses the bulge of Jennifer's vein. The vein is blue and the blade slices. The blood is red. The embalmer inserts a tube and the tube goes red. It drains down to a plastic bucket by his feet.

He makes another cut and introduces a second tube to her arm. This tube is paler, the colour of condoms or sweet wine. The blood vessels waste then swell again, and while this operation goes on the embalmer syringes fluid into her navel until her collapsed stomach rises.

He turns his attention to her face and hair. The hair is shampooed. Though we know the corpse can feel no pain we are surprised and perhaps shocked at how rough he is. He takes out her two false teeth, cleans them briefly with a damp vest and scouring powder, replaces them, and adds a piece of wadding to each cheek. The mouth is sewn: a strong needle stabs her gum, tugging a piece of gut; another stab and tug and the stitch is down. He makes six such stitches to stop the jaw lolling, applies lipstick carefully, and admires his handiwork. Comanche lines of wax-paint, numbers 5 and 9, are smeared and blended. Her closed eyes are shadowed and the lashes blackened. He is a craftsman.

Her blood has drained into the bucket by now. He turns off the flow of embalming fluid and unplugs her from the drip bag. He dresses her carefully: clean underwear, clean black dress. He towels the hair and then uses a drier on it, brushes it, flicks it. He checks the make-up has not smudged, sucking his lips in professional assessment before nodding. His mate takes the bucket over to the toilet and pours it down. The blood makes pale smears on the white pan, settles smokily, then makes the water red. The lad unzips his flies and urinates briefly, without malice. It is cold in the mortuary. His urine unravels as it falls and steams as it unravels. He leans over, pressing the flush. Her blood flushes away.

9

The kettle boiled dry, spat out the socket, woke Chapman up. He lifted his hands to his eyes and rubbed hard; he went through to the kitchen and, because he could think of nothing sensible to do, did nothing. The wall clock said quarter past nine. He wondered about going to the pub, but though he wanted a drink he did not want company. He took a tumbler, the soda syphon and the bottle of scotch from the cabinet and went upstairs.

He went to Jennifer's study. It already looked unused, abandoned in the dull light of a forty-watt bulb. The keys of the antiquated typewriter on the desk were dusty, the sheets of paper she would never use were desolate. He sat down at the desk, perching on the silly S-shaped chair she had bought, mail order, to improve her posture, and lit a cigarette. The ash-tray was full of paperclips.

He smoked. The room was cold. He stubbed the cigarette into the paperclips and stood. The night was bright beneath the moon. He closed the curtains.

The room was mostly bookshelf. Some shelves were expensive and glass-fronted, others were planks on DIY brackets. Chapman poured himself a glass of whisky, added soda, and looked at the titles, aimlessly, without interest. He had never had much time for books. He breathed out through his nose. People thought it odd, the two of them getting together. Well, perhaps it was.

Among the books, in fat brown filing boxes, were Jennifer's letters. She had a carbon copy of almost every letter she had written, preserved on flimsy bank paper, often overprinted where she had corrected the original. 'One day,' she had told him in the sardonic mood that came after cancer was diagnosed, 'all this will be yours.' He had found no reply.

He took one of the filing boxes down from the shelf and cleared a space on the desk for it. 'Somerville College, Oxford', he read. '15th March 1943'.

Dear Mother, Father and Bridget,
This is to demonstrate I can use the typewriter you so kindly bought me. I'm even making a carbon copy, like a good secretary should, so should I fail my degree I won't be unemployable. I hope everyone is well, and that Henry is eating again. All my love.

There was a blank where the name should have been, space for a signature, but who on earth was Henry?
He turned through the letters.

Dear Dr Foley,
Thank you very much for your encouraging comments about my work. After graduation, however, I feel I must make some contribution, however small, to the war effort, and therefore will not be applying for a fellowship this year. But thank you again for your confidence in me. Yours sincerely.

Another one, headed with an army box number.

Dear Mother and Father,
As you can see they have let me bring my typewriter. In fact, they are training me to use it properly, with all my fingers. It seems that, despite my First, I am going to be a secretary after all. Only a month left now before I get my posting. I hope it will be neither too far away, nor too dreary, but it isn't ours to reason why etcetera. Best wishes.

He saw a poem inserted in the middle of a letter.

Dear Mr Daker,

Thank you for your charming and encouraging letter. I hope you were serious when you asked me to send one of my poems. Of course, I shall never be a *poet* as you are, but writing poetry does give me a sort of pleasure. It is a sonnet, and is called 'After the Bombing: Sheffield 1941'.

The houses gone, the streets alone remain,
Threading through the broken walls and floors
Like the stitching on a counterpane
Without relief. There's no relief in wars.
I only walk the streets, though there're no laws
That keep me from the houses. I just feel
That crossing where the houses were would cause
Some injury to those who lived there, real
And vanished English people, so I steal
Along the pointless pavements 'twixt the piles
Of rubble and the bombholes time won't heal.
This extends my journey several miles
But though the homes are gone I do not care,
Without invitation, to walk there.

I suppose lots of people have felt like this, that to trespass on the ruins is to invade the privacy of the people bombed out, even though the real reason for keeping out is fear we might fall into a cellar or something. And I know that the poem isn't all that good, but I would be delighted to hear any comments you care to make. And thank you again for your encouragement.

Wondering who Mr Daker was, Chapman continued to leaf the frail sheets. Now there was no address at all to head the letters.

Dear Margaret,

Bessie gave me your address. I'm afraid I can't give you mine: it's a secret, believe it or not. But it's rather enjoyable and very interesting. It's good to learn I have 'the right sort of mind' for this kind of work – I always suspected I had quite the wrong sort of mind, too serious and blue-stockinged, to be much use to the war effort. But with most of our menfolk away it seems there's room for the sort of girl I am. It's an odd spot though, very home counties, quite posh, at the end of a long drive. Soldiers and civilians come and go all the time, but we've a decent-sized complement of regulars. The war dominates everything of course. The boffins are mostly able-bodied but the other men, apart from the guards, are all damaged one way or another. Damaged heroes. Some of them, especially the ones who've had burns, are rather disturbing to look at, but everyone seems friendly enough. We learn all sorts of interesting things, which I can't write about, naturally, in the course of our duties, but one thing I am sure I can tell you is that we're winning. Lots of love.

Jennifer had mentioned Bletchley occasionally. She had not talked about it much, and Chapman did not press, but he knew she had been unhappy there. He turned to another letter, dated December 1943.

Dear Margaret,
How are you and how is Godalming? Here in the Ministry of Fear everything is going swimmingly, though I stupidly burnt my finger a few days ago, while cooking. It still hurts. There is a man here – I can't give his name – whose whole face was burnt away in a Spitfire. They have made him a new nose out of what was left, but they cannot give him lips. He is like a man made of clay, botched and blotched, with just a slit for a mouth and a narrow pinched nose; he has no way of showing expression except his eyes, yet he has nice eyes. He was apparently at Cambridge before the war. He showed me a photograph of the Emmanuel Second XI: he was rather handsome then. No one could call him handsome now, but I think I am getting to like him. I wish I could tell you more about this place and what we're doing, but it's absolutely forbidden and with good reason. Give my love to Bill, and keep some for yourself.

Chapman refilled his glass. Jennifer was not unhappy yet.

TWELFTH NIGHT

January 1944.

Dear Margaret,
How are you? Great news about Bill's leave. I am seeing more and more of Stuart by the way. It's strange. When I first met him all I could think about was his poor damaged face, how ugly it was, and now I don't even notice it. We're all billeted in huts beyond the main building – they're really ugly but quite warm – and officially the men should never visit the women's quarters and vice versa. But we work strange hours, and anyway there are too many civilians for military discipline, so quite often after we've completed a watch we go back to someone's room for a drink. So Stuart and I are together a lot. I think I told you he was at Emmanuel, though he volunteered before he graduated. He was reading English, and sometimes when we talk I wish I'd read English instead of Greats. He's convinced his tutor, Dr Leavis, is a genius, and has given me one of Dr Leavis's books about modern poetry to read. He's also lent me a copy of *Prufrock and other Poems*. I'd read Prufrock before, of course – who hasn't? – but listening to Stuart talk about it – he has a lovely voice and even though he can't say 'p' and 'b' properly after his injuries he talks marvellously – I realise how little I understood. I always thought the poem was a sort of allegory, and its title was deliberately misleading, but now I see I was wrong: it's the story of a man on his way to meet the woman he loves at a party, wondering if he'll have the courage to speak to her and then, after a brief interlude at the party, coming home vanquished. As simple as that! And I know how Prufrock felt! Stuart and I discuss books wonderfully and I love his company dearly, but we never get beyond that. I don't know if he finds me attractive, or is afraid I might find him repulsive. I don't. I think he's a very nice man indeed. I think he's splendid. All my love.

February 1944.

Dear Mother, Father and Bridget,
Thank you for making my leave so pleasant. And Mother, you were right, I have something on my mind. I'm courting! Or nearly courting anyway – your blue-stocking daughter thinks she's finally fallen in love! But she's not sure if he loves her yet. I'm sorry I couldn't tell about it face to face, but I didn't want a lot of questions. You see, apart from anything else Stuart was one of the Few and was injured badly over Sussex. He's fine now, and

completely able-bodied, and I'm sure you'll all like him when you meet him. Give my love to Henry.

3 March 1944.

Dear Margaret,
I was so terribly upset to hear about Bill's ship. But 'missing' doesn't really mean anything, you know. Stuart says he's probably in some comfortable POW camp by now, sitting out the war in safety. Stuart's wonderful and nothing seems to worry him. I suppose he's been through so much. Anyway, I'm sure Bill will be all right in the end.

16 March 1944 (an original rather than a carbon).

Dear Margaret,
I'm sure it can't be so bad. You would have heard by now if Bill had been killed. And even if you're right and you are pregnant, it really doesn't matter. You should be proud to have his baby, and I'm certain Bill will be overjoyed when you get the chance to tell him. The war can't go on for ever. Actually, it's strange you saying you might be pregnant, because so might I. Stuart doesn't know yet – I haven't dared tell him – and there'll be all hell to pay if I am because it'll mean they'll have to train someone else to do my job, but really I'm quite excited. And it's funny to think that although Stuart's face is all burnt the baby's won't be. Actually, it occurs to me I won't be able to post this, because then the censors will know about the baby, but I'll carry on writing anyway, for myself if not for you. Because I really am tremendously excited.

16 March (a carbon this time).

Dear Margaret,
I'm sure it can't be so bad. You would have heard by now if Bill really had been killed, and even if you are pregnant I don't think anyone will mind. You should be proud to carry Bill's baby, and I know he'll be as pleased as Punch when he finds out. I've news for you as well but I can't tell it in a letter. Lots of love.

TWELFTH NIGHT

20 March.

Dear Mother and Father,
I had rather bad news today. My old friend Margaret, from
Somerville, has just written to say her husband, who was posted
missing weeks ago, is now confirmed dead. Apparently he drowned in
the North Atlantic, and I really don't know what to say to her. What
does one say? That I'm sorry? Of course I'm sorry, though I only met
him once, a nice-looking man in a blue lieutenant's uniform who took
us out for lunch in Oxford and spent the whole time talking to
Margaret and ignoring me until eventually I left them to it. That I
sympathise? She knows that already. Some platitude about how he
gave his life for his country maybe – some selected quotation, Horace,
Book 3, Ode 2? But she'll hear enough of that. I don't suppose you've
read Wittgenstein, and don't recommend that you should, because he
says the only things worth talking about are the things we can talk
about, and that's a load of tosh. The only things worth talking about
are the things we can't talk about. I expect Wittgenstein is still living
comfortably in Cambridge, ignoring the war. I also expect this
letter is incoherent, but I can't think straight. Poor Margaret. She
must be devastated. Best wishes.

22 March.

Dear Margaret,
I'm sorry I didn't write back immediately but I didn't know what to
say. I still don't. I'm so awfully, awfully sorry. All I can suggest is that
you treasure that baby inside you, love it, give it all the love you
would have given Bill. I know nothing can replace Bill, but at least you
will have the baby, which is so important. I have a few days' pass soon.
Let me know if you want me to visit you. I'll be glad to do anything I
can to help.

27 March.

Dear Margaret,
That's settled then. I'll be on the four-twenty. See you a week on
Monday. All my love.

6 April.

Dearest Stuart,

I'm missing you terribly but I'm glad to be here. Margaret is bearing up tremendously, and everyone's been so kind, especially now she's told them she's going to have a baby. Of course, there is a sadness here, despite the glorious weather. We drove out through the countryside this afternoon, into the Downs. I've been thinking a lot about what you were saying. I'm sure you're right about Romantic poetry. Romanticism couldn't last once man had invented the steam engine, much less the internal combustion engine. Romanticism depends on the idea that Nature is inviolate, eternal, but the whole idea of the industrial revolution was to tame Nature, make it do what man wanted. Artificial lights and vaccinations. So the whole Romantic idea became obsolete almost the moment it was stated – in fact perhaps it was really no more than the last desperate gasp of pre-industrial society, more nostalgia than reality. It's certainly all nostalgia by the time you get to Tennyson (and I agree with you completely, now I've read some more: Tennyson had a pretty way with words but didn't say very much). And so we get Realism, which as I see it was a way of showing satisfaction with reality. Nasty things were described, but with the intention of drawing people's attention to them so that they might be changed, like Oliver Twist and Dotheboys Hall. Everyone was convinced by Determinism – Social Darwinists and Marxists and Whig historians like Macaulay all believed the world would soon be a better place even if they couldn't agree about what adjustments needed making. But then came the Great War, and now this. Do you remember what you told me about the first time you flew: how it wasn't so much like seeing the world differently as seeing a different world, and how once you'd been in a diving aeroplane with the sky behind you and the fields racing towards you and no sense of our lovely friendly earth except as a tableau passing too fast for sense, how you could never believe in absolutes again? Do you remember that? I wonder if perhaps our whole generation, and maybe the one before as well, has felt something a bit like that, less extreme of course, but similar? That the world is going too fast? Even in Margaret's car – she drives herself you know – the world was outside and we were somewhere else, viewing it as though at a picture palace. Is this what modern art is all about, do you think, giving up on absolutes and realism because we have a different sense of reality? How do you paint a realistic picture of what you see from a moving car? The view changes before you've time to take it all in. I'm still not comfortable with modern art – I read Greats, after all, studied a world where nothing went faster than a horse (and no one ever tried painting on horseback!) – but I think I understand it better now. But am I right? Do tell me, dear wise Stuart. You don't have to write, though I'd be delighted if you did. But you must tell me when we're together again. I look forward to being with you again so much, so very much, and until then send you all, all, all my love and kisses my darling.

7 April.

Dearest Darling Stuart,
Thank you so much for writing, and for all the wonderful things you said, not only about books and painting and so on but especially about us. Do you really still have my brassière? I hadn't realised I'd left it – I must have been in a whirl that morning. I have nothing so intimate to treasure of yours, but I do have your letter in front of me, which I've read and reread a dozen times this morning already. Only three more days and I'll be with you. I know I shouldn't say it like that, but it is hard to be so happy in a house of death, and I am truly happy though missing you so much. And I have something to tell you when I get back, something wonderful but not something I want to put in a letter. I've talked to Margaret a lot about you, by the way, and she sends her love, but you mustn't take that too seriously or I shall get jealous. By the way, something rather strange and annoying has happened. A long time ago, certainly more than a year though I haven't my files here to check, I wrote to Andrew Daker to say how much I enjoyed his poetry. I mentioned I wrote poetry myself, and he was kind enough to ask me to send him one of my poems, which I did. It was a sonnet about how walking across the bombsites would be invading the privacy of those who had lived there – a rather silly notion I suppose, but I was younger then. I never heard from him again, but that wasn't so surprising as I enlisted shortly after. But now I find, in his new collection, *War Wounds*, a poem that is surely based on mine. If you see a copy of *War Wounds* have a look at 'Bombed Houses'. It isn't my poem, but it's certainly my idea. I don't know what to do about this; I don't even know if I'm offended or flattered. And now I must go because lunch is nearly ready and Margaret's mother is staying. With all my heart, my darling.

10 April.

Dear Margaret,
It was wonderful to see you, and wonderful you are bearing up so well.
I'm sure you are right and the baby will look just like Bill. And now you
know my news too! I still haven't told Stuart because I've only just got
back, and the first thing I had to do was write this. But I'll take your
advice and do it this evening, if we get a moment together. That's the
only problem with this place. Our shifts don't always coincide, and since
I've been away they seem to have introduced yet another roster. But I
know you're right, about everything. We'll have to get married terribly
soon.

17 April.

Dear Dr Foley,
Thank you for your letter. It is too early to be certain about the future,
but I am still interested in the fellowship. In answer to your other
question, no, I don't think I shall be getting married in the near future.
Margaret Williams must have misinformed you. With best wishes.
Yours sincerely.

The next letter was dated July. There was no reference to Stuart,
nor to the child. Chapman drained his glass. The bottle was empty
but he poured anyway. Two contemptuous drops fell. He continued through the file, reading only the dates of the letters. 1944
became 1945, peace came; Jennifer moved back to Oxford and took
up her fellowship. He lit a cigarette, drew on it, and stubbed it
clumsily out. Paperclips spilled like a broken chain. Turning the
pages faster, skipping many, he did not stop until, on 19 November
1951, he saw his own name. There were only three letters left in the
file after that, and anyway, that was a different story. Leaving the file
on the desk he stood up; he fumbled off the light and went to bed.

10

The bed lifts slightly as Bridget climbs out. Ernest, disturbed, hears her shuffle on her slippers and go through the door; a stair creaks as she goes downstairs.

He was not properly asleep, and now is not properly awake. He waits for her return. It seems strange to be in bed without her: he is always last to bed, first to rise. Being there alone reminds him of being ill; he stretches and finds he is more awake. What can she be doing? he wonders, and then: I hope she's all right.

He follows her down the stairs, stepping stealthily over the noisy tread. The house is dark but there is a light on in his study. He goes to the door. Bridget sits with her back to him. She is looking at a photograph album. He puts a hand on her shoulder. She does not move. Together they look at the photograph, a black and white studio shot of Jennifer at her first graduation, wearing her bachelor's gown and with her cap in her hands. The photographer's signature – Gratton of Cambridge – is in white in the bottom right corner. They do not speak. Jennifer's long face looks back at them. Bridget turns the page, past shots of her father and mother in a boat, their Fulwood house, Henry the labrador roistering on a beach, and stops at a family group. Father wears a dark suit, Mother a knee-length dress. Bridget, in her high-school uniform, looks defiantly at the camera. Jennifer, in the smarter, tighter uniform of a warrant officer, stares dreamily into space. 'Come back to bed,' says Ernest.

Bridget raises her hand to his. 'All right.' She stands. There are tears in her eyes that have not yet fallen. Ernest follows her up the stairs. Though there is no malice in him he feels happier now she is sad, which I understand completely. My nature is not so sweet as Ernest's, but I too am happier she is sad.

But who am I? Not in the pointless, philosophical way the question is asked by all save those of whom I'm afraid – big-busted women in market halls, women who arrange flowers in the church, those girls who chew gum on the bus – but simply in relation to that awkward intrusive 'I' that is also an eye and that tells you this tenuous tale as though it were profound.

Who am I?

Chapter Two

DAMAGED HEROES

*In which several Questions are posed
and a Few are answered*

1

'Who am I?' asked Jennifer, a week before her last Christmas, three weeks before she died. 'Well: I'm not you, and I'm not dead. Not yet.' She sat in a good chair overlooking their small garden. Autumn leaves turned to slime in the margins of the lawn, and she watched them as she spoke. 'Each of us can say this: not you; not dead. It's hard to say who we are, but at least we know who we're not. We're defined by negatives. Defined, distinguished, betrayed.'

Recently, Chapman had been making more effort to follow her thoughts, and nodded, though she did not look at him. She continued. 'Only fiction crosses these limitations. When I write, when I read, I'm no longer confined. I can experience something of what it is to be Pip Pirrip, Fanny Price, Anna Karenina, you, dead. We're defined by negatives, destroyed by what distinguishes us. But at least through fiction we can move in an era before our own, share experiences beyond our own.

'And that is why stories are so important. That is why stories are so necessary.'

2

Earlier, between the diagnosis of cancer and the day she had been forced to give up work, she had been giving a postgraduate seminar. The book was open on her desk. ' "Time's passing; time's passing," '

43

she read aloud. 'Which is of course true. Think of the familiar complaint you hear from people my age – "It was different in my day," "Time's not what it was," "Things ain't what they used to be." And things aren't. Though we can presume some common human ground, some essential and permanent human quality which runs through the history of all mankind, we are none the less far more remote from even our recent predecessors than we are from the most distant tribesman on the banks of the Orinoco. We can visit the Orinoco, and return; we cannot visit the past, and the past can never return.

'Given the ephemeral nature of life, what is the point of recording things? Time's passing; things are changing. Any work of art is, of necessity, full of contemporary references. The artist draws on all sources: the traditions and conventions of his medium, the perennial quirks of human existence such as love and death, and the temporal world which is his home. This is our century, our home. Why write a novel or a poem when, at best, only a fraction of what it meant will be discernible to those of a subsequent generation? Why write at all when everything changes?' She looked down at the book on the desk again. 'I'll read you what Denton Welch had to say on this question:

'Now as I lie in bed at quarter to eleven and hear the drunk soldiers sing and shout as they crawl back to their billet I am filled with satisfaction, for it is all passing, which is the only reason for wanting to preserve it.'

3

And earlier still, when the cancer was just a pain she tried to ignore. 'We agree that fiction is important for the reader. But what about for the writer? When studying literature we can either concentrate on the writer, in the way of the literary biography, or treat him – I dislike the grammatical convention that adopts the masculine pronoun for the human race, and dislike so much more the clumsy alternatives – simply as the vehicle for his ideas, as fashionable French criticism might encourage. Both views are current. One half of the community of critics devotes itself to increasingly detailed literary biography, the other to increasingly detailed textual analysis. This is more reasonable than it might at first appear. If you think about the authors who inspired all that criticism, you will realise that the writing of fiction lies in the tension between celebrating and negating the ego.

'I'll explain. On the one hand, the storyteller seems to make this claim: "I demand you look at my inventions; accept them; applaud them; I demand that you applaud me." Storytelling is a celebration of self: we are asked to take the author's fancies seriously; we are asked to pay to read the words he wrote. Yet at the same time it is a denial of self. As the same fictional writer of fiction might say, "I accept implicitly that my messy but tangible existence is less worthy of your notice than the imagined existence of imaginary characters."

'An author writes himself into your life; he writes himself out again.'

4

And who am I? I am an author, writing myself into your life, writing myself out again; I am neither you nor dead, and these parameters distinguish me and limit me, are my glory and my tragedy. This isn't much to work on, but it will do for the time being.

I do not use this word 'tragedy' loosely. I remember a conversation I had with Professor Jardine, a month or so ago. 'I sometimes think we should forget Aristotle and Wilson Knight and the rest of the commentators we've read,' I said, 'and start again with the plays, think about Macbeth for instance. At the beginning of the play he's a brave and ambitious man who loves his wife. This is his glory; this is what distinguishes him. Yet these same qualities, manliness, ambition, love for his wife, lead him to murder Duncan and start the chain of events that leads to his dismal death. He is destroyed, in other words, by what distinguishes him.'

'Certainly,' said the professor, a little impatiently, perhaps just a little pompously. 'No one would deny that. Least of all the commentators you've just dismissed.'

'And then there's King Lear,' I said, pressing on to the end of my argument, undeterred by his interruption. 'So noble and regal that he believes he can hand over his power and retain his authority. And Othello, who has just achieved the impossible: a black man with a beautiful, socialite white wife. Or Hamlet with his intellect and his ideals. Each is destroyed by what distinguishes him; the glory and the tragedy are one.' And then I explained about not being you, not being dead, about how we are all destroyed by what distinguishes us. 'Despite Aristotle,' I concluded, 'tragedy is not about hubris or catharsis. Tragedy is about the dynamics of each and every life.'

Now he was sympathetic instead of impatient, though I could see he was still unconvinced. After all, mine was a partial view. The walls were white, the floor was scrubbed, the sheets were crisp and clean. There was a venetian blind over the window, like a sheet of white foolscap, narrow feint, blank, between me and the rest of the world. There was; there is. I make words to fill the blank spaces, which is what a storyteller does. I make words to fill the blank spaces; I make patterns of the past.

5

She knocks at his door. 'It's open,' he calls, and she goes in.

His poor face tells her so little. He sits in bed, reading. His pyjamas are open at the neck; his throat and chest are a shocking white. 'Hello Stuart,' she says. 'Can I come in?'

'Of course.' She listens for warmth in his voice and hears none. 'I'm not disturbing you am I?'

He puts the book, face down, on the edge of the bed. 'Horace's *Odes "Vixi puellis nuper idoneus et militari non sine gloria."* '

She knows the ode; how might it be glossed? In love's wars I gained some glory? Is he being ironic? 'Stuart?'

'Jennifer.'

Their intimacy was a week ago and words exchanged in letters. It is neither here nor now. 'Stuart.'

'Come on,' he says. 'Out with it.' His tone is light enough for conversation, too light for what she needs to say. She wishes she had changed into her uniform; perhaps she would seem less a stranger.

'I missed you,' she tells him.

'I missed you too,' he says, but he is dismissive. Does he want her to go, or to say she loves him? 'Aren't you going to sit down?'

She sits at the furthest end of the bed, knowing she should sit nearer. Her embarrassed hands push her skirt between her knees. She studies them. 'Stuart. I think I'm pregnant.'

He does not say anything for a while and neither does she. Then: 'I suppose this is what they call a pregnant pause?' Is this bitterness? She looks at his ruined face, searching for a clue she knows she shall not find. 'Are you sure?' he asks.

'I think so.'

This is oxymoronic, and she would love him to tell her so. He doesn't. The gravity of her statement has sunk in and he has used up the last of his banter.

'I'm usually so regular,' she adds.

Their intimacy was a week ago and words exchanged in letters. 'How long?' he asks her.

'I've missed twice.'

'Oh,' he says, and she envies him his scars. She wishes she too wore a mask of boiled flesh and wasted muscle. His scars are a wall between them, like that between Pyramus and Thisbe, and this couple is as comic, as tragic, as they. 'What are you going to do?' he asks.

At least he has not questioned whether the child is his. 'I don't know. I suppose we should get married. For the baby's sake.' For my sake, she thinks, but she cannot say this. He does not invite this. He invites nothing.

'We'll have to think about it,' he says.

'Yes.'

'We'll talk about it later.'

'All right.' But it isn't all right. 'What's wrong with now?'

'We'll have to think about it,' he insists.

Their intimacy was a week ago, a lifetime ago; their intimacy never happened. 'I'd better go.'

'Yes.' He picks up his book again.

'Well, goodnight.'

'Goodnight.'

And she goes.

In the morning she is sick for the first time, but well by the time her watch begins. Each time the door opens she thinks it must be Stuart, though whether she wants to see him or avoid him she does not know. Each time the door opens she thinks it must be Stuart, but it never is. She sits in the darkened room transcribing inelegant bursts of noise for the cryptologists to decipher. She leaves for her meal. She leaves her meal. Someone complains she has made a mistake with a transcription and she pretends concern. There is a war on out there and every transmission may save a thousand lives. But a war demands courage, and she has none. She wants to see Stuart, she wants to go to his room, she wants to talk to him, love him. Instead she goes to bed.

She is sick again in the morning. There is a letter for her from her old tutor, Dr Foley, but she is late for her watch and must read it some other time. She goes into the darkened room, apologising, but everyone in there wears earphones and no one hears or acknowledges her.

And again she does not see Stuart, which is odd, for he should share this duty.

When the watch is done Captain Trelfall speaks to her, asks her if she knows where Stuart is.

'I'm sorry,' she tells him. 'I haven't seen him since Monday.'

'With both of you missing at the beginning of the watch – ' says Trelfall, then stops. She goes back to her room. Dr Foley's letter repeats the suggestion she should apply for a fellowship when the war ends. She wonders how the letter got through, but not for long. This war is being run by Oxbridge dons. I suppose Margaret told her I was marrying, she thinks. She writes back, trying to avoid bitterness. She is not marrying. The war will never end.

There is no sickness the next morning, and she has a late watch. She takes her reply, the envelope unsealed as regulations demand, to the post room, and turns towards breakfast. 'Warrant Officer Fox.' It is Captain Trelfall, looking serious. 'Colonel Gratton would like to see you.'

It is because I was late for my watch yesterday, she decides. Perhaps he will send me away from here. Perhaps this would be a good thing. She enters his office.

'Sit down. Jennifer.' He has never called her by her first name before. His room is pleasant though the furniture is old. He was a mathematician at Jesus before the war. This feels like a tutorial, and she has not completed her paper. 'I'm afraid I have bad news for you.'

The Blitz is long finished. She thinks: Surely my parents . . .

'Jennifer. Squadron Leader Jenkins is dead.'

'Stuart!' Outside the window a fuchsia, a bee in a fumbling flower. 'How? How did?' This is all wrong. 'How?' There must be some mistake, she thinks. Always we tell ourselves this: there must be some mistake.

'I'm afraid he hanged himself. He left you a note.' Colonel Gratton hands her a torn envelope. 'We had to read it of course.'

Of course.

My dear Jenny – By the time you read this I shall have abandoned you and abandoned all claim on your indulgence. Yet I beg your indulgence still, and your sympathy and gentle understanding. For despite appearances I do not believe taking my life at this time to be either selfish or cowardly; it is the inescapable consequence of our tragedy. And tragedy it is, in the high Shakespearean way: like Othello, I have found a woman who will love me, and whose love banishes my black and base looks. Yet your love has condemned me. Does this sound melodramatic? Perhaps it should. Perhaps melodrama is just a label we use that we may contain and thus despise the unacceptable and unapproachable, an aesthetic judgment born of a fear of life. Your love has triumphed over my hideousness, and yet love and the child we have made vanquish me.

Your pregnancy, you see, forces me to look to the future. Parenthood is aimed entirely at tomorrow, its obligations are to the future only. This is why we can turn our backs on our own parents, and despise them, without being despised ourselves, for our own children would do the same to us. Look at Shylock, at Lear. Look at Prince Hal. I have not spoken to my parents since my injuries, for my sake more than theirs. They would look after me, take care of me, and feel worthy doing it, but if I must go to hell let it be by my own road, my own hand.

The future. At present my face is acceptable, just, in this war and this place. The war justifies my injuries; Bletchley gives me an excuse for hiding myself away. At present therefore I can get by, live something approaching a normal life, share a joke, even have an affair. At present. But the future will be so different. It doesn't take much imagination to spot this. The war will not last for ever, and when it finishes my monstrous face will remain. Other men can take off their uniforms, put their medals in a drawer. I cannot. I will be at best a reminder to others of how lucky they were, and at worst a freak to scare the children. I am a monster, Jenny: even your kiss cannot turn me into a handsome prince; like Othello, killing myself, I die upon a kiss.

She is leaving the room. She is walking. The colonel speaks to her but his words are too far away.

She is walking down the carpetless stair, through the broad doorway. The clouds are fine and spread the light evenly over the day. She is walking. The white gravel that sprawls on the driveway, marches deliberately towards the barrack huts, hushes beneath her feet. Jays misbehave in the shrubbery. She is walking. She is carrying her baby and walking.

There are shouts behind her, and somewhere they stop her, taking her arm, turning her back. She does not resist. She can walk their way as well as any other. Someone tries to support her. She sees a shocked face staring down; following that stare she sees the dark patch on the lap of her dress, spreading, and the red on the gravel. Her blood is quite brilliant on the gravel.

She takes another step. She is walking. She is losing her baby. She is walking. There is a pain in her gut and lower, a pain and a pressure of pain. She is bent by the pain and the pressure of pain, bent to her knees and the trail of bright blood, bent to the blood she is leaving.

6

The winter sun has come out, poking layers of light between the plum-coloured shadows of the blind. I lie, on sheets my sweat has turned to mush, in a silence composed of small sounds, wheels and heels in the corridor, throbbing heating-ducts, rattling teacups and coughs. My eyes close on the past; they close like a stable door.

When I first came to write this, when I conjured that black taxi in my head and conjured the words to describe it, I wanted to be evenhanded and rational. I desired to describe death in careful cool terms; I intended a classical abstraction.

But since then I have seen Death's Angel, and must think the world anew.

Chapter Three

MEASURE FOR MEASURE

In which arrangements are made for a Funeral but no Will is found

I suppose the war was the most significant thing in the lives of all who knew it. It changed us, so that even now, nearly fifty years after Hitler invaded Poland, once I have thought back to it I cannot shake its memory. I cannot even shake its imagery, so that when I note that the day following Dr Fox's death is warmer I register also that it invades our mourning; when I record that the snows are melting I think of a stubborn resistance, a maquis of snow hiding beneath the hedges and retreating to the moors.

Chapman does not know of the thaw. He lies on his back, a small man made smaller by a bed too big for one, and his snores are as thin as the vapours of whisky. He sleeps late, and elsewhere alarm clocks go off, tidy buzzes to intrude messy dreams, a coercion, an awakening. Wendy, who has never known a war, still tightens her closed eyes against the Gestapo raid of day before opening them. 'Is it morning already?' John asks, neither expecting nor receiving a reply.

She drops her legs from under the quilt. Friday. The carpet is cold but soft. They sleep naked, approximately; increasingly, consciously, she wears her knickers. He is conscious of this too, this skimpy elasticated token of her displeasure. But he does not know why she is displeased, and is often too tired to care. Friday. Wendy goes to the bathroom. Her day organises itself in the shower. Double period with 4R, break, 1A's reading period, a period free, lunch. The regular routine. She turns the water off and steps out. John is shaving, scraping white foam off his neck. The apartment is small: as she edges behind him she nudges him, and a streak of red appears in the foam, is gathered, is washed down the sink. 'Thanks,' he says, but without malice. The regular routine.

53

She dries herself in the bedroom, rubbing talc under her small breasts, into her armpits and the narrow tuft of her crotch. Despite the central heating the day is cold. She hears John take his turn in the shower as she puts on clean underwear and selects a skirt. He comes out, a white towel round his waist, the black hairs on his chest a damp slick. He dabs at the cut on his jaw with a piece of pink toilet paper, which he holds in place with his shoulder as he fastens his watch.

She finishes dressing, applies careful sparse make-up – two strokes of lipstick, a little mascara – and leaves the bedroom. He dries himself too, pulls on a pair of boxer shorts, and stretches as far as he can. From the kitchen come the homely sounds of his wife brewing tea, and then the comfortable smell of toast. It reminds him of his parents' house, before his father died. He remembers his father knocking on his bedroom door at ten to eight – 'Time to get up!' – and his mother in her housecoat grilling toast. There was a bowl of cornflakes ready for him on the table, and milk in a blue-and-white striped jug. He remembers his surprise too, years later, when he discovered there were blue-and-white striped jugs just the same all over the country; he had always thought of such jugs as part of his home, and they wore the hooped colours of QPR, his home team. By the jug was the day's copy of *The Times*. There was a special discount for sixth-formers on *The Times* in those years and his parents made sure John always had his copy. He suspected his mother ironed it before he saw it. He still buys *The Times*, out of loyalty to his parents' aspirations for him, out of loyalty to his parents. He thinks back; he feels good. White shirt, pale green paisley tie, grey double-breasted suit, wool socks. His hair is still damp, smeared back, revealing the worrying thin patches above his temples that worrying only makes worse. He combs the evidence away, and still feels good as he follows his wife through to the kitchen. Pausing in the living room before the similiar spines of his Lanchester Press books he smiles. 'Toodle pip.'

On a plate on the kitchen table are two slices of unbuttered toast. He smears them with margarine without sitting down. It is still dark outside. 'Do you think I could take the car today?' he asks. 'I've lunch at the Groucho with Pam Ellis, and nothing after. I thought I might look around some houses.'

'Houses?' Wendy does not want him to take the car. If he has the car she will have to take the bus, ride back with the Friday-free schoolkids, decide what licence to give them, risk their Friday abuse. She hates that bus-ride. When she was a girl her mother picked her up from school. She never knew the glorious anarchy of school buses, the comradeship and the competition to sit at the back; she suspects she has missed something, and resents the loss, and resents it when John makes her travel by bus and face the loss. 'What houses?' she asks.

'I think it's time we moved,' he tells her.

'We can't afford to move.'

'I'm not so sure,' he says, and winks, which disturbs her.

'What's going on?'

'All in good time.'

She takes a mouthful of tea from her scarlet mug. If he wants to be childish he can be. 'We'd better get off.'

'There's no hurry. If I'm taking the car we can go straight to the school; there's no need to go to the station.'

'I haven't said you can take the car yet.'

'Pretty-please.'

She finds this irritating and slightly demeaning; to prevent him embarrassing them further she agrees. 'But if you're not doing much this afternoon you can pick me up.'

'All right. We could look at the houses together.'

'I don't want to look at houses.'

The blood on his face has dried; nothing can break his good humour. 'You want picking up.'

'Let's just go.'

They finish their cursory breakfast and put the crockery in the sink. We need a dishwasher, thinks John: we'll get one. They check they each have keys and lock the apartment, walk through the white-painted corridor to the door, let the block door shut on the Yale lock. A timorous light sprinkles the streets through dead trees. Their car is parked some way up the road because their flats have no parking of their own. They have a blue Fiesta, the sports model. John puts on a cassette, Dire Straits; Wendy prefers the news on Radio Four but John is driving.

They reach the school. Wendy sees the pub opposite as they turn into the yard. She thinks of Alan. Alan Gruafin: ridiculous name, but he was nice. She wonders if he'll turn up for their next meeting, knows she'd been flirting, knows that he will, and gathers her books from the back of the car. She gets out. No kiss. 'You'll pick me up at three-thirty?'

'On the dot.'

'Don't be late.'

He reverses the car round and leaves the school. 'Money for nothing,' sings Mark Knopfler, his voice gravelly but in tune. 'Money for nothing,' replies John, imitating the gravel, missing the tune. Alan lives closer to the school than Wendy. John drives past Alan's cold shared flat above the off-licence. The catlick tumble of Dire Straits makes open roads of the North London streets. John drives past and Alan sleeps on.

He drives into Bloomsbury. He thinks of Euston Road as passport control: once through you are in a different country, a country of one-night hotels and serious places, of the university, the museum, the publishing houses. Lanchester Press has offices on Bedford Square, facing the neat unnatural gardens, but John drives past to the underground car-park, leaves the car, walks back, buys his copy of *The Times*. The daylight has more confidence now, and though it is not term-time John still sees Arab students with expensive watches, duffle-coated research assistants, badly dressed lecturers with head colds. A derelict, a refugee maybe from the YMCA on Tottenham Court Road, sits against prim railings and stares beyond the passing legs. John does not dislike these veteran tramps, their beards the colour of cigarette butts and violated snow; he sees the choice they have made, freedom over comfort, independence over security, the bottle over everything, and feels he can understand it. It is the young down-and-outs who disturb him. He cannot understand them in terms of choice and individuality. The younger ones seem to have no choice. They are on the streets because they have nowhere else to go. Morality cannot dismiss them, nor notions of individualism. Only sociology and economics says why they are on the streets, begging, whole families sometimes, narrow, mean-featured women and ill-shaven, defeated young men, heart-rending children with tear-stained smut on their cheeks. They are there because of the system, and John, who has invested a fair proportion of his life in the system, would rather they were not there at all. So he tosses the tramp a round pound, which nearly preserves his good humour, and walks on, turning the corner of Gower Street and the square, entering the Lanchester offices.

The offices of Lanchester Press seem always full of builders. Clingfilmed radiators are stacked against a bleak wall; the reception desk, moved wholesale from a different building, has the robust inelegance of municipal housing; a poster for the work of Lanchester's best-known writer is slightly askew. John sees these things, and sees that no one else seems to. 'Is Robert in yet?' he asks.

'He's in his office. Shall I put a call through for him?'

'It's all right. I'll go up.'

He climbs the wide stairs. Robert's office, overlooking the square, is on the second floor. Some days the climb takes his breath a little, but today John gets there with ease. Today is a good day.

Janice types in the outer room of the office. 'Robert busy?' asks John.

'Shall I ring through?'

'It's all right. I'll go in.'

He opens Robert's door. 'Are you busy?' he calls.

'Not especially.' Robert is reading the *Independent*. He had turned to the book review and established it wasn't one of theirs; he had read the letters and the editorial on the same two-page spread; now he is glancing at the news, 'Good morning. What can I do for you?'

'Good morning. I'm handing in my notice.'

Robert nods. 'Moving on?' he asks. He is hurt that John is leaving.

John nods too. 'I think it's time.' He is hurt there is so little response.

'Certainly, certainly. You'll be staying in publishing?'

'Oh yes. I'm going to Incorporated Publishers, as a matter of fact.'

'Ah, the big boys.' Robert takes off his spectacles. 'The big-*time* boys. Headhunted, I suppose? No, I don't want to know what deal they're offering you; I know we'll not be able to match it. We'll miss you, of course.'

'And I'll miss you.' John speaks with a sincerity he had not expected. 'You've always been good to me.'

'You've always been good at your job. But the lure of the big bucks, eh? Big bucks, big books. Glossy film-star memoirs and the diet that worked for Di?'

'Something like that.'

Robert rubs his hands over his face, many times, like a fly washing, like a man used to defeats. 'A different world,' he comments.

John has no reply. 'I'll work my month's notice,' he says.

Robert speaks over him, beyond him. 'You don't know this, but a couple of months ago Incorporated offered to buy me out. Lock, stock, barrel. I could have been made for life. But I don't like their way of doing business. Writing isn't just a commodity you know.'

Here comes the lecture, thinks John.

'It isn't just a commodity,' Robert repeats. 'It's – I don't know – it's a record of the finest thoughts human beings have ever had. It's our record of the world and the way we respond to the world. Look at our lists. We're not big, maybe, but we're good. There are so many brilliant writers out there. So many. It's our job to encourage them, make it worth their while to be good. That's old-fashioned, I know, and Incorporated have a different philosophy. Push it, push it. They wanted to buy my backlist; they don't give a toss about the talented unknown writers. To start with, of course, they'd have paid more than I can afford for those writers' next books, and the writers wouldn't have been able to resist.'

John nods – writers love money, which justifies their careers in a world geared to price – and Robert continues. 'But then their books would fail to meet the advance, Incorporated would hassle them: "Frankly"' – he affects an American drawl, which is uncharitable, as Incorporated is an English company – '"we feel your product isn't mainstream to our image." They'd be talked into writing differently, or dropped out of hand, and that'd be the end of talent. It's a good way to run a business; it's a lousy way to publish books worth reading.'

John says nothing. He does not disagree, but he wants to share the good business. Robert puts his glasses back on. 'I hope you'll be happy with Incorporated,' he says, and John, detecting irony when only good manners were intended, says he thinks he will be.

'You'll serve out your month's notice, you say?' asks Robert.

'Naturally.'

Robert nods. 'Good.'

The interview is over and Chapman wakes up. He is used to being alone in their double bed. Jennifer was in hospital since Christmas. But then he remembers she is dead, a flat, meaningless thought that is urgent and means the world.

Some time before, when the cancer was first diagnosed, Jennifer bought him a book. *How to Cope with Bereavement*. He never read it. He never intended to read it. But this day, a dressing gown over his cotton pyjamas, he goes to her study, to her busy shelves, and finds it. His head is awash with whisky still and the whisky tastes like grief. He finds a sensible, factual book that documents each step he should take. Funerals? Jennifer wanted to be buried; she had reserved a plot in the local cemetery. 'Consult your mortician,' says the book, which is American. 'He will advise you on how best to carry out the departed one's wishes.' Wills? 'It is important you consult the departed one's attorney as soon as possible' – in this book people never die, they depart. 'Not dead but sleeping.' Chapman remembers headstones. 'Went to sleep . . .' Jennifer hated all that. 'Rather makes a nonsense of a perfectly good word,' she had said. 'What's wrong with just being dead?'

Chapman deliberately took her literally. 'Worms eat you,' he had replied.

She smiled. They used to make one another laugh. 'I doubt the worms mind what it says on the headstone,' she had said. ' "This one's not dead, it's sleeping; can't nibble *her* then." '

Chapman returns to the book. 'The will may be held in the attorney's office or in a bank; it is unlikely in this day and age that it will be kept in the home.' Newspapers? 'A notice in the departed's favorite paper is generally sufficient.'

But Jennifer was Jennifer Fox. Author of *Shakespeare's Great Theme*. Then Chapman remembers Professor What's'isname had said he'd let the papers know. It is a small relief, but important; it is the first relief of his mourning.

Jennifer's solicitors are Grigson and Mather. Chapman looks at the clock in the kitchen, realises the working day has long begun, and makes his telephone call. He is given an appointment for that afternoon, at three. Five empty hours until then. He goes back upstairs, back to her letters, and guiltily hunts his own name.

2

Ernest was cleaning the car, which took him out of the house. At twelve, it being Friday, he would go to the sports club for a drink and a couple of games of snooker. Meanwhile he cleaned the car.

Bridget was phoning Alan. 'Your Auntie Jennifer died yesterday,' she said. 'Are you going to make it for the funeral?'

Alan had stayed in the pub after Wendy had left. He didn't drink so much as a rule; he was bleary and feeling sick. 'When is it?'

'I don't know. That ridiculous man your aunt lived with is in charge. I expect he'll tell us soon.'

'I'm on vacation for another two weeks,' said Alan, using the American phrase his college used, not realising how it jarred with his mother.

'That'll be plenty of time,' said Bridget drily, thinking that if they didn't bury Jennifer in a fortnight they'd be nothing much left: the sisters were more alike than they had acknowledged; the same humour, the same disrespect. 'I'll put some sheets on your bed. If you come up tomorrow you can see me in my play. There are no tickets left but I'm sure we can manage something.'

'Good grief. Is it that time already?'

'We had the dress last night.'

'How was it?'

'Dreadful.'

Alan put down the phone, made coffee, burnt toast, before he realised his aunt was dead. He hadn't seen her in years, yet she was an icon. She was the literary side of his literal family; she was the ideal reader who had never, as far as he knew, read his poems.

He was twenty-seven, which was Hamlet's age. Crying was inappropriate, but in memory of Auntie Jennifer he wore black.

3

Siobahn wore black too. Always. It irked John but he didn't know what to do about it. Siobahn was another good reason for leaving. They shared an office, although she was his junior, and together they were the Lanchester Press's publicity department. Siobahn was lazy and clever; John was certainly not the former, and sometimes worried he might not be the latter. Siobahn often gave him things to worry about. 'Where've you been?' she asked.

'Talking to Robert,' he replied, though there was no need to justify himself. 'I'm leaving next month.'

'Cool,' she said, and John wondered what she meant. Cool for you that you're getting away; cool for me that I might get your job? Fuck her, thought John viciously, though occasionally and tenderly he had imagined doing just that. 'There's a man from Sheffield been on the phone,' she said.

'Sheffield?' He opened *The Times* on his desk. Uneven and obliterating, it lay across the piles of book proofs like a snowfall. 'What did he want?'

'One of our authors has kicked the bucket. He thought we might like to know.'

The day was going wrong. This needed attention. 'Who?'

'Jennifer Fox. You know, *Shakespeare's Great Theme*.'

John read the desultory headlines. 'God,' he said. 'I remember that book. I read it at university. Is it still in print?'

'Fuck knows,' said Siobahn. Even her name annoyed him: why couldn't it be spelt Shivawn, the way it was pronounced. 'I suppose you want me to check?'

'It doesn't matter,' said John. 'I expect I'd better let Robert know. Who was it called, did you say?'

'Bloke called Jardine. Professor Jardine. He said he was writing an obituary this weekend.'

'I'll tell Robert,' said John, and he picked up the phone.

'John?' Robert's voice, the Oxford accent making a fuss over the vowel. 'What can I do for you?'

'Seems one of our authors is dead. Jennifer Fox. She wrote *Shakespeare's Great Theme*.'

'I know what she wrote,' said Robert. He usually chided gently, but this was abrupt. 'How did you hear she was dead?'

'Man from Sheffield. Professor . . .' John looked across at Siobahn, who was reading a magazine. He fetched a box of paperclips from under the paper and chucked them at her. 'What was the Sheffield guy's name?'

'Oh.' She looked at the message pad. 'Professor Jardine.'

John relayed this. 'I don't know him,' said Robert. 'Did he leave a number?'

John passed this back to Siobahn, who nodded. 'Yes,' said John. He was bored with this already.

'Can I have it then?'

'Oh. Yes. Of course.' John put his hand over the mouthpiece. 'Pass it here then.'

'Say please.'

'Just do it.'

She peeled the sheet from the pad and passed it across. John read the number to Robert, who thanked him and rang off. 'Curious,' said John. 'Robert seemed quite upset.'

'They were probably lovers, years ago.'

'I can't see Robert having a lover.'

'Not even the author of *Shakespeare's Great Theme*?' asked Siobahn.

'Point taken.'

4

Ernest finishes rinsing the car. A hazy winter sun lies flat, a wafer in the sky, but the drive is in shadow and his hands are cold. Veins are a blueprint for the manufacture of fingers, and the flesh at the back of his hands is blotched white, fractured into scales. A white hair grows from each scale, except at the knuckles where the fracturing is deepest. He rubs his hands together, the back of one in the palm of the other, picks up his bucket and enters the house the back way, to avoid footprints on Bridget's carpets, while only a few miles away, in the same south-western segment of the same North Midlands city, Professor Jardine is in his study. His wife puts her head round the door. 'Coffee?'

'Please,' said the professor, and then. 'Don't go, Mary. Hang on.'

'Yes dear?'

Mary had been a nurse; Mary knew about death. 'It's Jenny Fox,' he told her.

'You shouldn't have agreed to do her obituary. You've enough to do without.'

'The obituary's a problem, but it's not that.' He tugged at his beard, making pimples of white flesh beneath the black and grey hairs; he took off his black-framed spectacles and put them on the desk. 'She was a strange woman. Do you know what she told me that time I visited her? That she'd seen the Angel of Death. "Death's Angel", she called it.'

'So?'

'She was serious. And seriously frightened.'

'She was dying and she knew it. Terminal patients . . .'

'. . . often see Death's Angel?'

'Well, not that necessarily. But their view of the world is different. What do you expect? Everyone knows they're going to die some day; terminal patients know it's going to be some day soon.'

He was unconvinced. 'I worked with Jenny Fox for eight years. She was the most rational woman I've ever known.'

'But you've known more rational men?'

He refused to be drawn. 'The most rational person. She'd no time for Yeats, never read him, said the mysticism and the hermetic system put her off and that *A Vision* was just silly.'

'You've said as much yourself.'

'Ah, but the poetry he made from that system!' His enthusiasm climaxed and passed. He picked up his glasses, opening and shutting the arms. 'Jenny once said, before she went into hospital, that she'd like to write a novel. She'd calculated she'd read three books a week, on average, for at least the last fifty years. Six hundred and twenty-five million words of fiction, she reckoned. Six hundred and twenty-five million. "I feel this gives me a certain expertise," she said.'

'And?'

'So she was going to write a novel. About her own death. Just think about that. She was going to imagine her own death and its consequences – "toss it like a pebble into the lives of my characters and watch the ripples spread forward, backward, sideways in time . . . a novel should be a shopping bag, full of the items that have caught the author's eye, its only integrity the author's vision". Hardly the precious exquisite modernist novel, though an identifiable part of the post-modernist tradition; serious novels, like poems, are getting longer again.'

'And?' She was used to her husband addressing her as though she were a tutorial, which did not mean she enjoyed it. 'You were telling me about Jennifer Fox's novel.'

'She knew exactly how it was going to start. Chapman, the bloke she lives with, would go to the hospital by taxi; they'd exchange a few words and then she'd die. "Without drama", were the words she used. "A nice rational death. After all," she said, "I need to rationalise my death. It's not so far away." And you know, I was going to be there too, after she died. And Mary, what makes this all so strange – '

'Is?'

'That that's how it happened. Exactly. I met Chapman at the hospital, just as she'd said would happen, and he told me she was dead.' He shook his head. 'Just as she'd said would happen.'

'Coincidence,' said Mary. 'Suggestion. Or maybe an accurate guess. I mean, you had to find out somehow.'

'I didn't remember about her novel at the time. It was only later, in bed, that I remembered this book she was going to write.'

'Is that why you slept so badly?'

'I didn't know you knew.'

She looked at him indulgently. 'Anyway, what's this to do with the Angel of Death. Death's Angel?'

'Oh, that. That was funny – wrong word – peculiar. She told me that originally it was going to be a very classical novel, a cool, hard look at dying, but that now that she'd seen the Death's Angel she knew classicism wasn't enough. She mentioned Goya. Apparently he'd seen Death's Angel too. She quoted him: "*Il sueño de la razon produce monstruos*"; it translates easily enough – "The sleep of reason brings forth monsters." It's the inscription to one of Goya's etchings. "But what if the monsters are really there?" she'd asked. "What then?"'

'Well?'

'She was saying, What if death isn't just an end, a straightforward result of the Second Law of Thermodynamics? "What if there really are monsters out there, beyond the limits of our perceptions, just as there are X-rays and microwaves and all manner of things we can't experience? What then?"'

'And?'

'"Then," she said, "no one can be sanguine about death."'

'She's right.'

'What do you mean, she's right? You're meant to tell me it was only the ramblings of a dying woman, that her ideas were a load of tosh.'

'Who knows?' She shrugged her shoulders. 'Why can't there be anything after death?'

'Because it doesn't make sense.' Jardine had a sudden wish to be taking a class on this subject, a class that would recognise his authority and his eminence; instead he was talking to his wife. 'When we die we stop. Period. No judgment, no afterlife, no nothing. Anything else is just superstition, either to make death seem less mysterious or, more commonly, to make the living behave the way their religious leaders wanted.'

'So? If you know all that why are you worried by Jenny Fox's death?'

He was cornered and didn't care. 'Exactly. Because I don't know it. Because I simply need to believe in my view of things, just as the remotest cannibal in Papua New Guinea needs to believe in his. And what's really worrying is that my view was Jennifer's view too. "We spend our lives looking at words, peering into the mouths of the dead as though we were dental pathologists," she once said to me: she could be a very bitter woman, but she was a realist, never a romantic. "Death's Angel!" I can imagine her saying: "Bollocks!" But then she saw the Death's Angel; Jenny Fox saw the Death's Angel and it changed the way she saw the world.'

'I'll go and make the coffee.'

Jardine shook his head. 'Sorry,' he said. 'It's just – I don't know – Jenny. She was so down-to-earth.'

'You're upset because a colleague is dead. Come on, how long is it since you had this conversation with her? Weeks, months?'

'A couple of months, I suppose.'

'Exactly. And why are you worrying at it now like a dog with a bone? Because Jenny Fox died yesterday. Death's like that; it's a shock, but it passes. We've all got to go some time.'

'Is that a consolation? I don't want to go like Jenny. I want to carry on believing, right up to the end, that I'll just break down into my constituent molecules and that'll be the end of it. Jenny was scared stiff. She'd seen the Death's Angel and was scared stiff. She trained as a classicist, you know. And she was always such a classicist in her teaching. "If you can't prove it, don't say it." That kind of approach. She didn't have a romantic bone in her body.'

The telephone rang. Mary answered it. 'It's for you,' she called to her husband. 'A Robert Winter of Lanchester Press.' Her husband came to the phone; she returned to making the coffee. Not a romantic bone in her body! she thought. Then why had she spent her life studying stories?

5

Alan is puzzling the same question; his notepad is crossed by dry jottings. 'Lifetime looking at books – bookish life – lecture halls and libraries.' He has the notion he should write something about Auntie Jennifer's death, something to remember her by, something to remember her with. He is a scientist as well as a poet: more even than Jardine his education has left no room for notions of life after death. He knows the carbon cycle, the beautiful symmetry of decay and regeneration; he understands the machinery of life too well to have time for some theory of death. The dead cease to exist, except as memories, and the only influence they have over the living is when they are remembered. Death is chemistry, poetry alchemy. He wants to record his memories; he owes her that much at least.

Yet her life has no interest for him. It seems arid, sedentary: she had lived with the same man in Bakewell for longer than Alan's life;

the couple never married, which was interesting, but the interest petered out at that point. He shares his mother's mistrust of Chapman, a small figure, military looking, with a neat moustache and swept-back thinning hair. There had been a game of cricket once, in the back garden of his parents' house, and Chapman had lost the ball. There must be a story about how they met, thinks Alan, considering the differences between them, but I can't imagine what it is. He was a bit of a jerk; she was a scholar who wrote books about books. There's no poem there. Yet he knows there is a poem to be worked from Auntie Jennifer's life somehow. Not a poem with Chapman in it, for sure, but a poem none the less. She spent her life with books, that was all, yet it had been enough to fascinate him, so that even when he chose his science A-levels, took his physics degree, he knew that books could matter too. Books were serious.

That was the word – serious. His auntie had been serious. Serious about books. He picks up his pen. His auntie had been serious about books. She taught him that words might matter. She was the ideal reader who had never read one of his poems. He writes this, then puts the pen down again. It doesn't make much of a poem. Looking for inspiration, looking for reassurance that he really can write, he turns back through the notebook and finds, as he knows he will, sketches for other poems, the Anne-Marie poems, the poems of departure and a different grief. He reads through one of these poems.

In a pub in Maida Vale
the day my girlfriend quitted
I drank Guinness and watched the absurd
stained glass the brewery had fitted
in an effort to give the place style.
I drank on my own and I heard

Irishmen boasting of how
history had made them sad
till my glass and the stained glass fused
my sense of the now and not now
and turned where I was to a mad
echo of places, a confused

memory of churches and meadows
where I had been half of an 'us'
until, though in a state of shock,
I knew this time for my worst.
The Irishmen mourned for past battles;
meantime my own past made mock.

I was busily ordering gin
when the black guy lugging an amp
entered the room trailing flex
and neatly lassooed a lamp.
Then the second black bloke came in
with the portable disco decks.

It's strange how strange things detain us:
the Irish talk turned to Gibraltar
while beneath the religious stained glass
the blacks assembled an altar
of frayed black plastic containers
as though they might offer a Mass

and I'd room in my undermined brain
to question the black men's motives:
were they hoping to make conversions
from the hard-bitten soft-centred natives?
The incongruous thing about pain
is there's room for incongruous things.

I watched the blacks and I followed
their diligent search for plug sockets;
I thought that we all should applaud them
as they stripped off their black leather jackets
and played a Republican ballad,
but the Irishmen smiled, and ignored them.

The incongruous thing about pain
is there's room for incongruous things:
it's strange how strange things detain us;
it's strange the comfort they bring.
I know nothing can entertain
like the company of strangers.

The poem is good, and Alan troubled. Does this mean the grief I felt over Anne-Marie's departure is greater than that I feel over my aunt's death? If so, isn't that selfish? Auntie Jennifer has died; she was probably in pain; she was probably fighting to the end. Anne-Marie left of her own accord. But I miss Anne-Marie more than I miss Auntie Jennifer, though Anne-Marie is still alive, and Anne-Marie makes me write better poems.

My grief must be entirely selfish then. It has nothing to do with the one who has gone; it's to do with the one who is left.

And Chapman, who is left, reads on, reads her letters and her version of their meeting and love. For he imagines that's what it must have been; it must have been love or they would have married, a curious equation that made a curious sense. They met in 1951. Living together had a terrible significance then.

He remembers her as she was when they met, serious – no beauty – a blue-stocking with a book to her name – forbidding. And Chapman had been so undemonstrative, so terribly conventional. She surely wasn't the woman he'd imagined for himself; he hardly knew her sort existed, with her competence and her profession and her financial independence. 1951 made pictures in his mind, Lyon's Corner House, the Hokey-Cokey, the Skylon and the ailing king. But she made him laugh, and she made him make her laugh. He finds a letter to a Somerville colleague.

Life in literary London is less exciting than you might imagine. Robert, my publisher, has arranged I should attend a series of dinner parties and receptions and so on, to meet people. But really you know I'm not sure I like people. They ask the crassest of questions: 'How long did it take you to *write* your book?'; 'Do you believe a woman can really *understand* Shakespeare?'; and my favourite, and favourite with those who've not heard of my book, 'Do you write under your *own* name?' So it was rather refreshing, last night, to meet a man who had not only not heard of my book but apparently had barely heard of Shakespeare. He was rather nice looking actually, obviously cared nothing for Eng. Lit. and (though in this classless overtaxed age it is heresy to say it) had clearly had a limited education, though he spoke well enough to pass muster. I feel I would like to know him better: an interesting *case*, and recently invalided out of the army: a damaged hero.

Later, lovers, they talked through their meeting. 'It still seems strange we met at all,' she said, splayed on her back beneath the sheets of his hotel bed. 'How did you know Jeremy?'

He lit two cigarettes and handed one to her, as lovers did in the movies, and charged coincidence with meaning, as lovers every-where do. 'I know. It was amazing.' He wanted to say: my mum used to take in washing; my dad worked in the docks when there was work to be had. And you; look at you: you're so special, so gifted; you've read so much, you know so much. And yet we didn't just meet, we fell in love. He was no philosopher; he characterised himself a simple man. But he liked the occasional flutter on the horses, and therefore knew, as a gambler, that because the odds against their meeting had been great the reward would be great too. He was certain he was in love.

She turned over towards him and he felt the resistant hair of her crotch on his hip. 'You still haven't told me how you knew Jeremy.'

'It's a long story,' he said, though it wasn't. He was just not a teller of stories; as a boy his accent was wrong. And thus he was so undemonstrative, such a terribly conventional man.

'Tell me anyway. I want to know.' I want to know because I want to know everything about you; everything that has a bearing on me; I want to know everything that hasn't.

'My parents lived in Wapping. I was an evacuee.' He had no way to convey what he meant by those simple statements, but images teemed in his head, high black tenements lurching against one another and the meagre sky between, cheap clothes slung across the street, hand-me-downs and stairwells where homosexuals loitered, the matt smell of stale sweat and the shiny stink of urine. And then the queue of children, the train, alien fields that basked in the hot summer of 1940, the indignity of being chosen by a family, which was better than the indignity of not being, and the large cream house they took him to.

'Poor you,' she said. 'Did you have to leave your parents? It must have been awful.'

'I suppose so,' he said. 'I was sent to Gloucestershire, and Jeremy's parents very kindly took me in.' He spoke in standard phrases that masked so much, masked what it was to be suddenly somewhere where sunlight reached indoors on to furniture chosen to please, masked the joy of smutless sheets that smelt of lye and meadowgrass, masked Jeremy's summer hols' mockery of his London vowels, masked his fear, at first, of the horses, and masked too the guilty ecstasy that was always with him: he was away – far away – from Wapping.

'I see,' she said. 'Jeremy's parents. So that's how you two know one another.'

'Yes.' Chapman's mind was full and charged. The necessity of every past moment was revealed. The twentieth century had borne him, moulded him, injured him. It had taken him to Jeremy's parents in Gloucestershire, pulled him to the South Bank to meet Jennifer, carried her to his bed. All history, all the turbulent tragic rage of the twentieth century, had conspired to bring him to Jennifer, to this place and this time, this bed. 'But I'd not seen Jeremy in years. I was in the army.' He had neither the will nor the power to fight so much destiny.

And she had seen the wound, a deep raw hole in the back of his calf that had taken most of the muscle. Damaged heroes. 'What happened to your leg?' she asked.

'A mine.'

'You could have been killed.'

'Four men were.'

'How did it happen?' And then, hurriedly: 'You don't mind talking about it?'

'It's all right,' he said, and it was, though he had always minded before. 'Korea.'

She waited for more but he was silent, so she thought he had finished and was surprised when he hadn't. 'There was a stream and a hill beyond, and a machine gun on the hill, facing us.' And a high evening sky crossed by squadrons of ducks, a scene like crushed leaves, a breeze. 'We had orders to advance up the hill, but this was a slow battle. Nothing to report except some Aussies to our right and the sound of the enemy gun. So we had time to go forward carefully, checking the terrain, giving covering fire.'

She wondered whom he was talking to. He seemed no longer to be talking to her.

'Their machine gun was badly sited. We got into position on the hill. They were lower than us and didn't know we were there.' The gunner wore a flat cap. When he turned to drink from a bottle I saw the red star. I waited. He put the bottle down and I shot him through the chest. He slumped forward. The loader turned the gun but a bullet took him through the neck. 'We took the machine-gun post quite easily, and then signalled to the Aussies. They'd been waiting for our signal and they came forward. We went down to meet them.' I heard ducks honking overhead, and evening insects in the undergrowth. 'We were quite close to the Aussies, about to join them and shake hands.' His hand was an inch from mine and cupped to a dimpled grin until – 'One of them trod on the mine,' said Chapman. Earth lurches. Soil rains down.

There is the screech of pain and the silence of the world.

Chapman looks up from Jennifer's letters. The dangerous memory of the event blends with the different memory of telling Jennifer until both are lost in the knowledge of her death. He remembers he has to phone the undertakers, and it seems a memory from further away. But he makes the call anyway. Leave it to us, sir, says a young voice, and Chapman is pleased to do so: Tuesday all right, sir? Oak has proved very popular, sir, and perhaps sir will find something suitable amongst our range of brass fittings in a variety of styles. Mourners, sir? Perhaps two cars will be sufficient then, sir? And we shall of course contact the vicar on your behalf if you so wish. You do. In that case, sir, we shall be in touch. When arrangements are complete. Yes, sir. And thank *you*, sir.

Chapman puts the telephone down. Tuesday. A hole that is six feet deep. Six feet: the height of a man and his depth. Except he is only five foot eight, and out of his depth.

He is hungry. He cannot face making something for himself. He puts on his coat and goes to the pub.

6

Ernest orders a sandwich. The bar is always quiet at lunchtime. Two wealthy local wives who've been playing squash drink self-consciously healthy orange juice, a few businessmen escape their businesses for an hour, a group of students enjoy their Christmas vacation, four pensioners like himself kill time. When Ernest first retired he hated the word pensioner. It was a word with a smell of its own, peppermint, mothballs and incontinence. But he is accustomed to the word now, and it is no longer sinister. It is a ritual, a series of routines. He has a quiz cut neatly from yesterday's *Daily Mail* in his pocket. He takes it out, straightens the creases, and it becomes a focal point for a small gathering of retired bankers and headmasters.

'"What is the capital of Bolivia?"' he reads.

'La Paz,' says the barmaid.

'Is that right?' asks Dennis.

The squash-playing squash-drinking women leave the bar. 'We'll find out when we get to the end of the quiz,' says Ernest. 'Question two: "Who wrote *Pictures at an Exhibition*?"'

'Rimsky-Korsakov,' says Dennis firmly.

'Rip-her-corsets-off,' agrees Peter.

'It sounds likely,' says Ernest. 'Do you know, Madge?' he asks the barmaid.

'Modest Mussorgsky,' she says.

'That sounds likely too,' says Ernest. He has read the answers already. 'We'll see. Question three: "What is the origin of the phrase 'A flash in the pan'?"'

'Gold-mining,' says Peter.

'No,' says Dennis. 'It's to do with old-fashioned guns.'

'Muskets,' says Rupert.

'I'm sure it's gold-mining,' says Peter. 'You know, panning for gold.'

'Dennis is right,' says Madge.

'There you are then,' says Dennis. 'Madge agrees with me.'

'Question four: "What is an aadvark?"'

'A South African ant-eater,' says Madge.

'Anyone disagree?' asks Ernest. 'All right. Next question: "What sport made Babe Ruth famous?"'

'Baseball,' says Dennis. The others agree. This is a sports club bar.

'And finally,' says Ernest. '"In which year did Edward VIII abdicate?"'

'Nineteen thirty-six,' says Madge, and again there is agreement. This isn't history, this is memory.

Ernest goes through the answers for their benefit. 'You did well,' he tells Madge.

Peter had been a headmaster. 'You read the *Daily Mail*,' he accuses.

She smiles, says nothing, polishes a glass.

'Quiet in here,' says Rupert. Someone says this every lunchtime; it is another part of the ritual, like the games of snooker and the quizzes from Bridget's newspaper.

'It is,' agrees Peter. Someone always agrees. That too is part of the ritual.

There are days when these routines annoy Ernest, and others when he relies on them. 'My sister-in-law died yesterday,' he says.

'I'm sorry to hear that,' says Peter.

'She'd been ill some time. Cancer.'

'Poor woman. Probably better off now.'

'I expect so.'

'Your wife's sister or wife of your brother?' asks Rupert. 'Sister-in-law could mean either,' he adds, as if worried he has been impertinent.

'I haven't got a brother,' says Ernest. 'My wife's sister.'

'I see.' Too old to be flippant about death, too young to be familiar with it, they can neither discuss nor avoid the subject. They look for things to say.

'An aunt of mine had cancer,' says Dennis. 'Went to the doctor complaining of pain, heard it was cancer, was dead in three weeks. Just gave up.'

'Jennifer didn't give up,' says Ernest with a little pride. 'We first heard about it last summer but she fought all the way to the end.'

Peter nods. 'Good for her.'

'I want my time to come when I'm making love to my mistress on my ninety-ninth birthday,' says Dennis. There is nothing original in the notion, but then most of the conversation in the sports club bar is unoriginal. It is that which makes it so reliable, so comfortable, so safe. Dennis has spoken the last word on death and the issue has been absorbed; Ernest orders another drink for himself – no one stands rounds in the sports club bar – and asks Rupert if he's taken down his Christmas decorations yet.

'Of course,' says Rupert. 'Twelfth Night was yesterday.'

This is reliable too. Reliable and comfortable and safe. Ernest sips his beer.

7

The last two periods of the day, of the week, are a double lower sixth. This suits Wendy. It's nice to be able to relax a little, forget about discipline. She had once written a poem suggesting her job was like that of the school nurse: by introducing fourteen year olds to books she was inoculating them against literature for life. It was a pleasing image, and Dr Crabcalf had praised the poem, but like many pleasing images it was inaccurate. These seventeen year olds were still interested in books, and she was glad. 'Where were we?' she asked.

'Act Three, Scene Two, miss.'

She turned through her abused Penguin copy. 'That's right, Stephen. Macbeth has just ordered the murderers to kill Banquo and Fleance. Why was it so important that Fleance gets killed? Tariq?'

'Because the witches said Banquo's children would become kings, miss.'

'Good. Because Banquo's children would become kings. Now, let's read on. Michelle, you carry on reading Lady Macbeth. Tariq, can you read Macbeth? Joanne, you be the servant. We'll read through the scene and then talk about it when we get to the end. Off you go, Michelle.'

'"Is Banquo gone from Court?"' asked Michelle.

'"Ay, madam, but returns again tonight."'

Returns again tonight. The class read *Macbeth* and Wendy half followed the familiar lines, but she was thinking about John. Did he really want to look at houses, to move? They'd already agreed there was no chance of moving this year: next year maybe, when the car was paid off, but not this year. So what was the point?

'"We have scorched the snake, not killed it,"' read Tariq. '"She'll close and be herself."' There was little poetry in the way he read, but he had a good clear voice and at least he took notice of the punctuation. Some of them just read it line for line, measure for measure. ' "Better be with the dead, whom we to gain our peace, have sent to peace, than on the torture of the mind to lie in restless ecstasy." ' Tariq wanted to be a writer; his parents wanted him to run the shop.

A little away from the rest sat Joanne. Joanne's sister had thrown herself, her UB40 and her unwanted pregnancy from the top of the multi-storey car-park in the shopping centre; she had landed messily on the pavement and died in the ambulance. And Joanne, the clever one of the family, had been at school, a fifth-former then, sitting in Wendy's GCSE class going through Philip Larkin's poems. That afternoon they had looked at 'Ambulances'. Joanne had read it to the class. Wendy remembered Joanne's voice, more confident then than today, working through the bleak beauty of the poem to the moment where the ambulance

Brings closer what is left to come,
And dulls to distance all we are.

The next day Joanne had been off school, but the news had come, shredded along the corridors and shared over staff-room coffee. 'Died in the ambulance.' She told John about the suicide and about Joanne reading the poem. 'A meaningless coincidence,' he had said. But it wasn't: she was forced to accept the coincidence but nothing could make it meaningless.

Tariq was reading the last speech of the scene now – 'Be innocent of the knowledge, dearest chuck' – and as always someone laughed at 'dearest chuck'; Wendy, following the lines about the great bond which keeps Macbeth pale and the crow making wing through the wood, decided it was again time to mention how frequently Shakespeare used images of darkness in this play.

8

As Chapman put the key into the lock to let himself back into the house the telephone started to ring. He knew life's little rules: when a telephone rings and I'm outside the door it'll always ring off before I can answer. But this time he got to the phone. 'Five Castle Walk,' he said, less disturbed by the caller's persistence than the breakdown of one of the rules.

'Mr Chapman?'

'Speaking.'

'It's Mr Cameron, Dr Fox's solicitor.'

'Oh yes. Of course. Right.'

'You made an appointment to see me about Dr Fox's will.'

'That's right.'

'There's been a misunderstanding, I'm afraid. We've no will here, and for certain we never drew one up for her. Perhaps you could try her bank?'

'Oh.' Chapman was nonplussed. 'I thought she had left her will with you.'

'We haven't even a record she made one.'

'She must have done,' said Chapman. 'The arrangements for her funeral were all made: she's a plot up the hill, everything. She'd hardly have done that and forgotten to make a will. Would she.'

'I'm not saying she didn't make a will, just that she didn't make it through us. Try her bank. Lots of people appoint the bank their executor.'

'I'm sure she said her will was with you.'

That 'I'm sure' deceived Cameron. He thought it a mark of uncertainty: 'I'm sure she said' is much less emphatic than 'She said'. And so the solicitor told Chapman that he must have misheard or misunderstood. But Chapman was *sure*. They exchanged goodbyes and Chapman put down the phone. It rang again immediately. 'Chapman,' he said.

'Ormond and Gullick, Funeral Directors. We've been in touch with the vicar, Mr Chapman, and ten-thirty next Tuesday morning would be magic.'

Chapman, bewildered, stared at the walls; John looked at walls, too, at walls and ceilings and fitted kitchens. 'A hundred and ten thousand?'

'That's right, sir. Though you could start at a hundred K. It's a buyer's market today.'

'So I've often been told.' The estate agent had a breezy, annoying

77

tone, half East End and half glib jargon; John looked around the house. It did not impress him. In theory he knew how much houses cost – £100,000, £200,000, £1,000,000 – and like most Londoners he had spent much of the previous few years watching the value of his flat increase, speaking with confidence of property values and appreciation, hearing with envy of those who left three-bedroom semis in Ealing and bought a castle in the Borders on the profit. Of course, the last six months or so had been different. The mortgage rate had gone up, more than once; the market had 'steadied'. But everyone felt so much richer.

Until the time came to move. He had not had the flat valued yet, but along the street similar properties were fetching £80,000; last summer two had changed hands for over £100,000, but John, unlike several of his neighbours, had no faith in that sort of price. His mortgage was for £24,000, which meant a profit of over £50,000 in six years. It was a paper profit, however, which would have to be sunk immediately into a new property, while to borrow the extra he would need scared him a little, stretched his pocket and his imagination. He was disappointed not to like the house more. 'I don't think so,' he said at last.

'It's a rising area,' said the estate agent.

'It's not for me,' said John.

'Convenient for the tube.' The responses were automatic and unhelpful.

'But I don't like it.'

'A very popular location.' Now they were unhopeful too.

'Then sell it to someone else.'

'You'll not find a nicer property at the price.' The estate agent looked at his watch.

'In that case I'd better stay in the one I've got.'

'As you like. And now, if you don't mind, I'd better be getting back to the office.'

John, dismissed, walks to his car as the estate agent locks up. He looks at the house again and shakes his head. Forget it, he tells himself.

John is good with company money. He is less certain of his own. He starts to drive. The estate agent suggested he knock £10,000 off the asking price. It seemed peanuts: the difference between £110,000 and £100,000 looks minimal. Yet £10,000 is the price of a new car, or ten good holidays, or fifty decent suits.

But the equation is not quite right. Money spent on a car, or a holiday, or a wardrobe full of suits, is money spent; money spent on a house is meant to be money invested. And if he spends £100,000 rather than £110,000 he would not save £10,000, to spend on cars or holidays or clothes; he simply would not have to borrow as much. And he gets tax relief on the money he borrows.

So because he wouldn't have that extra ten grand in his pocket, and because he would have the mortgage relief, he would not be very much poorer if he spent £110,000 rather than £100,000. This doesn't seem to make sense either, though, because £10,000 borrowed is around £100 to repay each month, and £100 a month is, for instance, eight bottles of malt whisky, twelve compact discs, nine hardback novels or two good meals out. So that extra £10,000 is important after all. But if £10,000 is important, what of £5,000, £3,000, £1,000? What of a saving of a hundred pounds, or fifty, on the price of a house? Sometimes they used the coupons that came through the door, fifteen pence off the price of a bottle of washing-up liquid or ten pence off teabags. But what about ten pence off the price of a house? Isn't that ten pence the same? Doesn't it have the same spending power, the same value? Hath not a Jew eyes? Hath not a Jew hands, organs, dimensions? But if everything is of relative value, ten pence on a house and a packet of teabags are not equivalents. Hath not a Jew hands, organs, dimensions, senses, affections, passions? But maybe those of a Jew are of relative value too. Not that I've anything against Jews, or blacks, or anyone. I went on the anti-racist marches when I was a student. I've no prejudice to speak of against anyone, he declares to himself: that's not the point. The point is that if something as tangible, as apparently fixed, measured and agreed on as money can be subject to relativity, then what of something as subjective as race? What measure to measure the measure?

He pulls up at traffic lights, first in the queue in the outside lane. Next to him a young man in an old Capri revs hard. John stiffens his mouth. The lights change. Racing furiously, the two cars pull away from the lights. They are side by side until the shopping centre, and then parked cars force the Capri to pull back. John smiles to himself, drives up to his house, and then remembers he was meant to pick up Wendy.

He is twenty minutes late already: bugger!

9

She knew she knew them, but still went through her lines. Ernest listened from the hall.

'How does my bounteous sister? Go with me
To bless this twain, that they may prosperous be,
And honoured in their issue.
   Honour, riches, marriage-blessing,
   Long continuance, and increasing,
   Hourly joys be still upon you!
   Juno sings her blessings on you.'

He chose not to join his wife in the living room. It still rankled with Bridget – and he knew it – that her drama group had chosen to do *The Tempest*, with only one real female role; it irked her still more that she had been given Juno, with seven lines, rather than Iris, who had forty-one. Moreover, Ernest suspected that those lines of Juno's were not among the Bard's best; 'upon you' and 'on you' was the sort of rhyme he associated with the Eurovision song contest. On the other hand, Ernest also knew that, when it came to literary criticism, he was not in the first rank. One night, soon after having been given her part, Bridget, with fine disdain, had read the adjacent pages of the play at him, and when he heard a famous line, 'Our revels now are ended', he had thought immediately of chocolates. Ah well, tonight was the first night, tomorrow the last. And then it would all be over. He did not look forward to tomorrow night – Bridget had bought him a ticket – but he looked forward to its all being over.

Bridget felt differently. She did not look forward to *The Tempest* with the same scared and sacred relish with which she had looked forward to *As You Like It*, five years ago now, when she had played Rosalind, nor to when she had played Lady Macbeth, in 1986, nor even as much as she had to *Othello* last year, for at least as Emilia, Iago's wife, she had decent lines to speak – but still she knew that nervy anticipation which rattled her guts, and knew too how empty she would feel on Sunday, with nothing to rehearse and nothing to fear.

And then there was the fact that Jennifer was dead. Jennifer, the author of *Shakespeare's Great Theme*, had never seen her sister play Shakespeare. Bridget had been cheated.

10

John apologised. 'Forget it,' said Wendy, but John knew she wouldn't. 'Let's just get home.'

Having nothing to say he said nothing. It had been a strange day, an anticlimactic day, and he did not want to end it with a row. Nor did he want to look at any more houses. Wendy didn't mention the houses anyway, so he supposed she'd forgotten about them, as she supposed he had.

They drove through the grainy January dusk; Chapman walks. His feet measure his way, organise his life. Walking is the first thing since Jennifer's death to make sense. Step for step, measure for measure. I suppose the rhythm of my heart is even more important, he thinks to himself, but it's the rhythm of my feet I'm aware of. He counts out beats. One two three four, one two three four, with a good sword and a trusty arm, a merry heart and true, King James's men shall understand what Cornish lads can do. He changes the count, one two three, one two three, and though the pace of the footsteps stays the same the emphasis changes. He hums 'The Blue Danube', da da-da-da dum, dum-dum, dum-dum, da da-da-da dum. And finally he tries one two three four five, one two three four five, and the Dave Brubeck song 'Take Five' which had been so popular once upon a time, but this defeats him. He does not mind. To have something to occupy him is enough.

He walks out of town and up the hill towards Monyash. He has no destination, nor any need of one; he is walking because the snow has gone and he has spent too long staying still; he walks because he needed a walk. Afternoon thickens to evening. He passes the church, its graveyard stubbed with statues, crosses, pointed gothic headstones. The undertakers call: Jennifer will be laid to rest at ten-thirty on Tuesday. Chapman no longer thinks about Jennifer's hatred of euphemism. 'Euphemism is to metaphor what sugar is to salt,' she told him: 'they look much the same but one sweetens and the other stings.' But now, as he grows used to the fact of her death, he grows used to the standard terminology which accompanies death. Jennifer will be laid to rest. She is departed and gone before. Phrases which once meant nothing, phrases which under Jennifer's tutelage had amused him, are now all the words he has left. And Chapman, a terribly conventional man, finds he prefers these words, for they are other people's words: they make her death less sinister; they make it no longer unique. She has gone before, as others before have gone, and her death is no longer unique. Her death is still a hole in his life, a hole the size of a grave maybe, and in time that hole will be filled, so that only the headstone, proud above the grave, moss grown and stained by the rain, will show, although, should he care or dare to dig, the remains shall always be there. Mankind is much practised in grief; we learn to accommodate death because one day death shall accommodate us. Monuments and rituals are euphemism and metaphor, ways of saying the unsayable, are sugar, are salt in the wound.

He reaches the end of the pavement, the edge of the housing, and decides to turn back. Below him Bakewell is a cluster of lights in the valley, its firm shapes already falling. He returns down the hill. Measure for measure, step for step, step you gaily off we go, heel to heel and toe to toe-oe, onwards stepping on we go, all for Marnie's wedding. In the anonymous dark, to the accelerated beat of his walk downhill, Chapman sings aloud. Step you gaily off we go, heel to heel and toe to toe-oe, onwards stepping on we go, all for Marnie's wedding.

Useless, cold, and unromantic as a morning-after hot-water bottle, what remains of Jennifer is filling a long chilled drawer.

Chapter Four

DEATH'S ANGEL

In which the World is seen anew

I

I place Professor Jardine at his desk, still working though his wife
has gone to bed. He will turn on his word processor and see the
screen go green; he will put in a disc and watch black lines cross from
the top, as though a Venetian blind were being drawn down the
screen, and then the screen will flash blank; bright green words will
appear, confirming the program.

The disc drive will fizz, Alka-Seltzer in a glass, and then the screen
will change to list the files on this disc. He has to wait for the fizzing
to stop before he can change the disc. The picture will change subtly,
to show files the professor has made: the files have curious
condensed names. DOVBEACH. NTE 7k, is seven kilobytes of notes
on Arnold's poem 'Dover Beach'; KEATSLET. CRE 4k is a selection of
quotations from Keats's letters on the subject of creativity. Jardine
will move the cursor over these and into the next column; file names
are briefly black on green as the cursor skims them, then return to
green on black. The next column contains some of his lectures,
written out in full because, despite the friendly scorn of colleagues,
he does not trust himself to speak impromptu. He stops at a file
labelled RMANTIC. INT 56k, a second-year 'Introduction to
Romantic Literature', and presses the E key, followed by ENTER.
The screen goes blank, then fills.

2

What do we mean by 'Romantic'? Two things, I suppose. First, there is the way the word is used generally: the left side of the brain is meant, so psychologists tell us, to be the rational side, whilst the right is intuitive; a romantic, in this and every age, is someone who trusts the right side of the brain.

The second meaning of the word is specific. 'Romantic', in the context of cultural history, refers to a certain period. It is always hard to date literary movements with any precision, but approximately at least we can think of the Romantic period as lasting from 1789, the French Revolution, until 1837, the beginning of Queen Victoria's long reign, though it has its origins in the work of writers such as Rousseau (1712–78) and exerted an influence on English poetry which lasted until the First World War.

English poetry is, of course, our main concern, but it is important to recognise that romanticism was neither exclusively English nor exclusively literary. There was a Romantic movement in music, which lasted rather longer than the dates I have given: Beethoven was perhaps the first and greatest Romantic composer, and his influence lasted for the whole of the nineteenth century, so that it is possible to speak of Bruckner, who was born in 1824 and died in 1896, as a Romantic, and likewise Tchaikovsky, who was born in 1840 and died in 1893. There was a Romantic movement in painting. Again, its greatest exponent was also its first – Goya, who lived from 1746 till 1828 – but other great Romantic painters include Delacroix, Géricault and Turner. There was a Romantic movement in architecture, too, but though it gave us the Houses of Parliament, St Pancras station and the Bavarian castle they filmed for *Chitty-Chitty-Bang-Bang*, I refuse to take Romantic architecture seriously.

None the less, if we are to come to some understanding of what romanticism means in terms of English poetry, it is worth examining what characteristics these manifestations of romanticism in various media shared. And perhaps the easiest way to understand romanticism is to look at what preceded it.

The era before romanticism, the era before the French Revolution, has gone by many names: the Ancien Régime, the Age of Reason, the Enlightenment. The last two titles are particularly suggestive. The eighteenth century was indeed the Age of Reason, insofar as, during that era, Reason was valued most highly of all the various human attributes, above imagination, vision, faith or love. Not that people in the eighteenth century did not have imagination, vision, faith or love, any more than the Romantics lacked reason, but that a higher premium was placed on reason than on any other human faculty.

To understand this we must go back even further in time, to the Renaissance, for in many ways the eighteenth century was the culmination of a movement which began at least two centuries earlier. The Renaissance was, self-consciously, an attempt to emulate the Classical civilisations of Greece and Rome. It was not entirely successful. For instance, Greek and Roman statues were painted, much like modern waxworks, but had, over the years, lost their paint. This was not recognised in the Renaissance. The 'Classical' statues of Michelangelo and Bernini would have seemed strange and unfinished to an Ancient Greek, but to us, used to the convention of representing the human form in natural stone, they are perfectly acceptable. Equally, and more significantly, the Greeks had a very different world-view to that of sixteenth-century Christendom. The Greeks perceived the universe as essentially arbitrary, governed by capricious fates. This is revealed particularly in Greek tragedy: it was accepted that humanity had a special place in the universe, but this was believed to be less a result of the capacity for rational thought than of our capacity for suffering. The idea, so central to the Renaissance, that the universe was governed by laws and divine justice was Hebraic and, despite Pythagoras and Plato, alien to the Greeks. This difference is largely theological. The Greeks had many gods and goddesses; there was no central authority. The Hebrews, and the Christians of the Renaissance, had one God who ordered everything. The tension in Greek tragedy is that of a servant trying to satisfy many masters – one thinks of Homer, whose works are the paradigm for almost all subsequent Classical literary endeavour, or of Euripides' *The Bacchae*, in which Pentheus is literally torn apart as he tries to assert his respect for the older gods in the face of Dionysus. In Hebraic thought the dilemma is how a human being, who is imperfect, can serve a perfect God; the Hebrew God can be inscrutable, and move in mysterious ways, but unlike the Greek gods He is never irrational or capricious. He tested Job's faith by reducing him to misery and poverty, but afterwards restored his fortunes and more.

This difference is important; another crucial difference between the neoclassicism of the Renaissance and its Classical model is manifested in one of the most important and influential theories of the later period – perspective. Perspective is the means whereby a painting in two

87

dimensions can represent three dimensions. The Greeks and Romans did not use perspective in their art; the rules of perspective are a fifteenth-century discovery. Perspective means that the illusion of distance can be created on a flat picture; it reproduces the way the world is seen by an objective observer and, four centuries before the invention of the camera, it produced results that can be called 'photographic', because it was based not on a subjective understanding of the world, in which kings were larger than peasants and victorious armies bigger than the vanquished, but on a relatively simple mathematical formula. And how we represent the world is a function of how we understand it: when mathematics denied a king's greater size, republicanism became a possibility.

The next three centuries were an attempt to find similar mathematical formulae to explain the rest of the universe. The great anathema of serious thinkers from the Renaissance to the French Revolution, and beyond, was superstition. It was during this period that the word 'science' was first used in the modern sense of an ordered and reasoned attempt to come to terms with human existence and natural phenomena. Just as the physical world was being explored and mapped by such figures as Magellan, Columbus and Cabot, so the history of science during this period is a process of discovery in which the areas of *terra incognita* were being continually reduced. Nicolas Copernicus (1473–1543) solved the problem of the way the stars and planets cross the heavens with the elegantly simple notion that the sun, rather than the earth, is the centre of the universe; Francis Bacon (1561–1626) proposed the important scientific belief that the laws of nature could be induced in advance of observation; René Descartes (1596–1650) provided a method for scientific enquiry based on observation and reason; Sir Isaac Newton

3

Professor Jardine will stand, stretch, and look at the clock on the mantelpiece. It is a quarter past twelve and he will not be certain why he is still awake, though he will know it has something to do with Jennifer Fox. He will pour himself a rare glass of port from the decanter on the sideboard and return to his desk, where the cursor winks insistently. He will press the page key repeatedly. Two hundred summarised years of human history will move up the screen and disappear, and then the cursor will stop beneath the thick green line that denotes a new page. Professor Jardine will sip his port fastidiously, as though testing it: he will taste the stout sweetness that warms his mouth and the bitter burr that vibrates on his tongue; he will swallow, and feel the warmth in his chest define the narrow line between his lungs. He will sip again, rubbing his tongue left to right across his upper lip to clean his moustache. And as his tongue moves left to right so do his eyes, starting at the top of the new page, working their way slowly down, while the cursor will sit obediently at the first letter of the page, blipping on and off and awaiting his command, illuminating that first letter, that otherwise insignificant lower case i, as a medieval monk might illuminate the initial letter of a manuscript.

4

An important contemporary English commentator on the French Revolution was Edmund Burke, whose *Reflections on the Revolution in France*, published in 1790 before the excesses of the Terror had taken place, nevertheless foresaw what was to occur.

Reflections on the Revolution in France was highly influential. Burke was self-consciously conservative, and his argument was simple. In England there was a system of constitutional monarchy which worked: rather than attempting to emulate the English model the French had thrown over the monarchy entirely, and in the process had thrown over rationality, liberalism and good sense. Yet though he argued from a position of moderation, Burke's language was far from moderate. 'Publick measures are deformed to monsters,' he claimed; the revolutionary leaders were 'suddenly and as it were by enchantment snatched from the humblest rank'; his description of the capture of the King of France is full of extreme and emotive description; his panegyric to Marie-Antoinette is justly famous for its immoderate eloquence. It was Burke's imagery, as much as his analysis, which formed English views of the French Revolution, and subsequent events – the Terror and the Revolution, and subsequent events – the Terror and the execution of

Louis XVI and Marie-Antoinette – endorsed that imagery and provoked new descriptions which were even more apocalyptic: 'Out of the tomb of the murdered monarchy of France,' he wrote in 1796, 'has arisen a vast, tremendous, unformed spectre, in far more terrific guise than any which have yet overpowered the imagination.' Though his politics looked backwards his literary style looked forward, refining the Gothic imagery of Walpole and Mrs Radcliffe and combining it with an intelligence of approach and seriousness of purpose that legitimised the Romantic sensibility as a viable and honourable alternative to Neoclassical reason.

5

Jardine, having found what he was looking for, will raise his eyes from the word processor. He will stare above the screen for a moment, then press the EXIT key; a series of choices will flash up on the screen: 'finish editing', 'save and continue', 'save and print', 'abandon edit'. He will choose the first: the exit options vanish and the words roll up the screen. A brief history of romanticism passes before him, too fast to be read comfortably, too slow to be ignored. Phrases catch the professor's eye. 'Coleridge's intellect envied as well as systematised Wordsworth's profound understanding of natural history'; 'Blake's greatness is undeniable but his contemporary influence was minimal'; 'as always, the burgeoning of artistic activity accompanies a period of intense political activity: the Chinese curse, "May you live in interesting times", would be a blessing to a dedicated poet'.

The screen will cease to unravel when it reaches the end of the file. It will sit still as the disc digests the words. This digestion is a noisy process and the Alka-Seltzers are all gone; as the machine chews over the conclusion to the lecture, so does the professor.

strange thing about Romanticism is that it had little real influence. The notion of progress, of the perfectibility of man, had been invented by the

Marquis de Condorcet in the late eighteenth century; it survived the French Revolution; it survived the Romantic movement. In the long run, all Romanticism did was widen the divide between science and the arts, and justify certain extremes of patriotism and sentimentality. But of course, and this must never be forgotten, it also gave us some great works of art.

Then the screen will return to the menu, and when the columns of file names have appeared the professor will take out the disc and switch his word processor off.

He will finish his port and take the glass to the kitchen. A certainty will be missing from his life. It will twitch like an amputated limb, a phantom limb. It is the certainty of his doctoral thesis and of his first book, *Yeats and the Romantic Imagination*; it is the certainty that romanticism in poetry was unable to survive the Industrial Revolution, and that Wordsworth's system extolling nature could not compete with the exploitation of nature in the nineteenth and twentieth century; it is the certainty that Yeats's mystical system – the Neoplatonism of Plotinus and Porphyry, the Theosophical cant of Madame Blavatsky, the whole superstitious nonsense of Cabbalism and Hermes Trismegistus and Orphism and the rest – was no more than an heuristic device Yeats had used to make music from the mechanical age, compared by Yeats himself to 'the cubes in the drawings of Wyndham Lewis and to the ovoids in the sculpture of Brancusi'. That is the certainty Professor Jardine will miss. I stand him at the kitchen sink. The curtains will be open. The professor will stare through the ghost of his reflection to the garden beyond, and know that too much can lurk in the dark. He will smile a little uncertainly, tug his beard below his ear, and go to bed. In the darkness beyond the window an owl shall swoop for its prey, a frost emphasise each grass-blade on the lawn, and death's dark angel shall stalk.

Chapter Five

THE TEMPEST

*In which Alan meets Wendy again
and travels to Sheffield,
where
Bridget performs in a play*

I

Jennifer Fox remained in a drawer; Alan made breakfast, toast and fried eggs. He watched the eggs change colour, consistency, form. The pan was not quite flat-bottomed, and the white formed a crescent around the edge. In the centre of the crescent were two yolks, bulging. This strip of white marked with two yellow circles reminded him of some pair of bizarre sunglasses or a bra for the gormless gaudy. He thought of abandoned bras, and of Anne-Marie who left her clothes on the floor, panties and stockings rolled together in a stylised figure of eight, skirt a loop or a zero, blouse bedraggled, arms spread, a π sign, an equation he had misunderstood.

The toast was jammed in the toaster. He used the point of a knife to ease the slices out. It was burnt on one side, pallid on the other, which was familiar enough. He used to scrape the black off; now he was no longer bothered. The crumbs on the kitchen side were worse than the charcoal in his mouth.

Cooking is chemistry. Heat affects molecules. The albumen turns white, hardens; the toast browns and blackens; the margarine becomes oil on the hot toast.

There had been a time he was fascinated by such things. Why does an egg get firmer when heated, yet margarine turns liquid? But by the time he knew the answer he had forgotten the question.

And water. Once water had captivated him, and particularly the way that, unlike other substances, water is lighter in its solid state than in its liquid state: he had seen in this quirk of chemistry, this exception to the rules of science, a suggestion of the hand of God.

For, if water were to behave like all other substances, were the solid form of H_2O more dense than the liquid, then life on earth as we know it – and in all probability life in any form – would be out of the question. Ice floats on water: if instead ice sank, as apparently it ought, the bottom of the seas would soon be a solid mass of ice. The property of ice which allows it to float also allows it to melt. Without this property, not only would the climate of the earth be irredeemably different, but the very source of primitive celled and multi-celled life forms would cease to exist. It was as if the process described in Genesis were in some way accurate: in the beginning God created the heaven and the earth. And the earth was without form, and void: and darkness was upon the face of the deep. And the spirit of God moved upon the face of the waters, saying, 'Ice shall float.' Water, the basis of life, was like humanity: it was singled out by God for special treatment, it obeyed God's special laws.

And then, in an A-level class in April 1979, he had discovered that the loose bonding between H_2O molecules traps minute quantities of air when it solidifies at low temperatures; therefore, instead of contradicting the laws of science ice was in strict accord with them, and God did not exist after all. Alan was not even disappointed. His faith in God was dislodged by his faith in science. It was as simple as that.

2

And Bridget bent over a jigsaw. The picture was an illuminated page from the *Grandes Heures* of Jean, Duc de Berry; she had completed the four edges, piecing together an even cream oblong, and was now trying to work out the complicated design of the decorative border. Certain of the edge pieces gave her a clue: along the top edge was what looked like part of a banner; around each corner were scrolls of gothic foliage; the left side of the picture was punctuated irregularly by birds and butterflies; luck had given her what looked like a medallion containing a shield with the fleur-de-lis in the bottom right corner, and lying alongside the medallion, contained within the joined edge, were several other pieces that also bore the symbol of the fleur-de-lis. Perhaps there's one of these shields in each corner? She assembled the shields, podgy affairs with the gold fleur-de-lis on the blue background of France, each edged with a scalloped red design that marked this as the arms of the Duc de Berry, and triumphantly fitted one into each of the corners. Now I'm getting somewhere!

Bridget liked jigsaw puzzles. Every Christmas she received at least two, and she always saved one for the numb Saturday between the first and last performance of the drama group's Shakespeare. In the past, when she had played larger roles, she had used a jigsaw as a release, a way of forgetting the tension of being Rosalind or Lady Macbeth, and a way of forgetting that by midnight on Saturday she would no longer be a character from Shakespeare but would revert, Cinderella, to being a suburban housewife, Ernest's wife, Alan's mother. But this year the jigsaw was simply an escape from boredom. The play had gone quite well the night before. She had Juno's lines committed to memory, she had nothing to worry about. This time the anticlimax had come early, in the choice of play and the casting; it was impossible to get worked up about her own part and she had exhausted her worries about the way the others would perform. So she concentrated on the *Grandes Heures* of the Duc de Berry, and was content.

It would be easy to find metaphors in Bridget's love of jigsaws, to see in her enjoyment of them her need for solutions, to find a parallel between them and her need for tidiness and order, and also her other need, thwarted except when she was acting, to be creative and even imaginative. It would be easy; it would not be the whole story.

The first jigsaw Bridget remembered, the first jigsaw with pieces that were delicate instead of childish, was of a country garden in summer. Someone had bought it for Jennifer, but Jennifer, hair freed from a bun and dangling on to the pages of her Latin primer, never completed it. Then Bridget had chickenpox and, recovering, scratching, had a week off school and nothing to do. Jennifer gave her the puzzle.

Each piece was a challenge and a triumph. She loved the picture she assembled, the long vista of the lawn edged with trees and herbaceous plants, the mysterious door in a mellow brick wall, the cream stone urn on its plinth. She made more than a picture that day;

she made a world. And this world was a present from Jennifer, an unasked for and unexpected confirmation that her sister knew she existed. Her parents came to her bedroom and praised her. She remembered her father, old-fashioned even then in the wing collar he wore for the bank, ruffling her hair and saying, 'That's lovely', and she remembered her mother in mauve, saying, 'We'll just have to get you another one.' And most rewarding of all was the memory of her father, signalling her challenge and triumph, saying, 'Fancy you doing it when Jennifer didn't,' as though what Jennifer did were the boundary of the possible.

She had been delighted with the picture, and delighted to have completed it, but even more delighted to take it apart. She slid the jigsaw off the tray and back into the box. The picture buckled and broke. In taking it apart she showed her independence from the picture; she showed her independence from the world she had made. In taking it apart she showed her independence from her sister.

She worked on the border of the *Grandes Heures*. Fragile entwining branches separated delicate illuminated cameos of swans on a pale green lake, brown bears waving bright pennons, mysterious monograms on a crimson field. All that was left in the box now was several hundred pieces of repetitive text, black gothic letters on a cream background, and other pieces that were temptingly coloured but made no sense as yet. She found herself working on a picture, framed within a border of its own, in the top right-hand corner. Pale architecture emerged, guarded by a haloed figure in a sweeping blue cloak. Jigsaws focus attention on colour. There was a red cloak too that surely fitted this part of the picture somehow, but then the telephone rang and she went to answer it. 'Gruafin,' she said. 'Cavendish Avenue.'

'Is that Bridget Gruafin? Gavin Chapman here.'

'Speaking.' She was curt. She was always curt on the telephone. She was always curt when interrupted. She was always curt to Chapman. 'Yes.'

'I'm not disturbing you am I? Only I thought I'd better let you know. About the arrangements.'

He was obviously finding this awkward; she offered no help. 'Arrangements?'

'For Jennifer. For her funeral.'

'I see.' She waited for him to say more, but the effort of the word funeral had apparently been too much for him. 'You were telling me about the arrangements for my sister's funeral,' she reminded him.

He heard 'my sister's' as though in italics: it was proprietorial; it laid claim to her share of the grief. But he said nothing of this for there was nothing he could say. 'That's right. Ten-thirty on Tuesday morning. If you could meet at our, my, at Jennifer's house at ten?' He did not assert any ownership of his own; he did not feel he had the right.

'Of course,' said Bridget. 'Is there anything else?'

'Er. "Flowers to Ormond and Gullick, Funeral Directors",' he said, reading the details off a card.

'Yes. I've got that.' Prompted by the malice of being interrupted, the malice of it being Chapman, she continued. 'We'll be travelling in the first car, I take it.'

'I'm sorry?'

'In the first car. We'll be travelling in the first car.' She had never trusted Chapman. She had never found anything in him to like.

'Good Lord. I don't know. I hadn't thought about it – I mean, yes, yes, of course. Yes, you'll be travelling in the first car. With your husband and young Alan.'

'And you?'

'Oh yes. Yes.'

'Thank you.' He was retreating; she pressed home. 'And when's the reading of the will?'

'Oh Lord.' Chapman sounded miserable. Misery was to be expected. His lover was dead. But there was misery in burying her too, a bureaucratic misery of arrangements to be made; this distracted from his grief and, because he recognised the distraction, made him more miserable yet. 'I don't know. I haven't, haven't found it.'

'What do you mean?'

'No, not yet.' It was time to put the telephone down. He looked for a way and found none. 'Well, I'll be saying goodbye then,' he said abruptly. 'I'll see you on Tuesday. Goodbye.'

'At the funeral. Yes. And you'll let me know about the will?'

'Yes, of course. Yes. Goodbye.'

'Goodbye.'

She felt she had humiliated him, and felt vindicated by this, as though by being humiliated he had deserved his humiliation.

Ernest had been sweeping leaves. It was too early in the year to start mowing, which was a pity, because he enjoyed the tranquil racket the lawnmower made, the relaxing concentration of making stripes on the grass. When he was mowing the lawn he was a noisy cocoon cut off from a noisier world. But it was too early to start mowing, and so he was sweeping leaves. He came in when he heard the telephone.

'Who was it?'

'That man Chapman. He really is a little twerp.'

'I don't know why you say that.'

'It's incredible! He tells me he hasn't even found the will yet!'

'That's strange.'

'Of course it is. I think he's trying something on.'

'I don't want to go into this,' decided Ernest. 'Not yet.'

'But what's he got to gain? The house I suppose; that must be worth quite a lot. Perhaps he hopes that if the will isn't read for a while we'll forget about it.'

'I don't want to talk about it,' insisted Ernest.

Her eyes were dark and dashed with light. 'This is your son's future we're talking about!' she told him. 'He's her only relative apart from me. Well, obviously I don't need the money. We're comfortable. I wouldn't take it. But Alan needs the money. It's time he bought somewhere of his own. It's time he settled down. What happened to that Anne-Marie girl anyway? I thought that was serious.'

'But can't it wait? Until she's buried at least?'

'That's what he wants us to do. To wait. I mean, what if he claims squatter's rights on her house?'

'I don't know. Jennifer probably left it to him anyway.'

'Then why is he being so mysterious?'

'Perhaps he really can't find the will.'

'And pigs might fly! People don't hide wills, they leave them with their solicitors. No, there's something going on. I can sense it. Anyway, we'll find out soon enough. We're meeting him before the funeral on Tuesday.'

'Oh. What time?'

'Ten.'

'Are you going to let Alan know? Give him my love.'

'Oh, there's no point phoning him. He'll be here this afternoon.'

'Oh. Right then.' Ernest, City Architect (retired), went back to sweeping leaves, and Bridget returned to the puzzle. The figure in the sweeping blue cloak, she realised, was St Peter holding the keys to heaven. He was stern; he looked almost angry, as though he too had been completing a jigsaw and had been disturbed by a knock on the gate. She went through the box again and found a piece, with a face on, that joined the fugitive red cloak she had made to St Peter and the pale buildings behind him. The supplicant waited at heaven's gate. Bridget knew it was imagination, but this face was a little like Jenny's.

3

Short words shine off the bathroom tiles, longer words linger on the enamel curves.

'I'll go without you then,' Wendy said.

'I didn't say I wouldn't come.'

'Don't be ridiculous.'

'I just need to get this finished.'

'For God's sake!' she said. 'You know what it's like in Sainsbury's on Saturdays. If we leave it any later there'll not be anything left. Why did you have to start it now anyway?'

'It needed doing didn't it?' asked John.

'It would've waited till this afternoon.'

'Well, I've started it now. I can hardly leave it.'

'I said I'll go on my own.'

'If you just wait.'

'There's no time.'

'All right. Go on your own if you must.'

'I don't see what else I can do.' She looked down at him from the bathroom doorway and asked: 'What are you doing for lunch?'

'What do you mean?'

'I just thought I'd eat out. Why don't you? Go to the pub.'

'I've to finish this yet.'

'I thought you were nearly done.'

'I am. Take no time.'

'Then don't be a bloody martyr. Have a pub lunch.' She turned away, still talking. 'You're the one decided it needed doing. I didn't make you. I'll take a key in case I'm back before you. And now I'm off.'

'You might wait.'

'Bye.'

'Goodbye.'

John returned to the wash basin. The water was off and so was the tap. The socket stared blankly at him like a damaged eye. He weighed the tap in his hand. He knew there must be a washer in there somewhere – when a tap drips it always means the washer's gone, doesn't it? – but he didn't know how to get it out. If I'd picked up Wendy on time yesterday she'd have given me a hand. We'd have laughed about it. He knocked the tap against the sink side to see if he could dislodge the washer. Nothing happened. She'll never forgive me if I don't sort it out now. I can imagine the lecture: 'You should've left it alone if you don't know how to fix it. Why didn't you call in a plumber?'

'Anyone can fix a dripping tap!'

'Anyone except you, it seems.'

He had to fix it before she came back.

4

Alan bundled his washing in a holdall, picked up the soap powder and went downstairs. He used to take dirty washing to his mother's. These days he preferred to wash it himself.

He bought a copy of the *Independent*. He only bought the *Independent* on Saturday, for its colour supplement and review pages; the rest of the week, if he bought a paper at all, he bought the *Guardian*. On Monday he bought it for the 'Creative and Media' job advertisements, on Tuesday for the 'Education' advertisements, and the rest of the week mainly for the answers to the Quick Crossword.

The launderette was humid, oriental. Veils of steam danced from the machines, clothes in the driers bowed in a cycle of everlasting prayer, fluorescent lights made scimitars and crescents in the scooped glass doors of the machines. Alan put the soap powder and the *Independent* into his holdall, put the holdall on top of his machine, and left the launderette.

He had not decided which train he should catch. An early train would give him plenty of time before his mother's play in the evening, and would put him in her good books; a later train would mean he would not have to hurry. Well, he asked, what else needs doing? Washing's sorted; can't finish packing till it's done. He crossed the road. I'll need some lunch: I could do with a loaf. Sainsbury's then; bottle for Dad and some chocs for Mum while I'm there.

Their branch of Sainsbury's was no place for pedestrians. He walked down the driveway. The cars splashed him as they passed, chucking handfuls of drops at his legs and shoes. In the air the drops were the colour of winter; they were dark and degrading on his clothes.

5

The garden was bleak, razed by the winter, reduced to the stubs of shrubs and cumbrous evergreens. Colours were few, a beech hedge the hue of old newsprint, the peeling white bark of the silver birch, the scarlet handle of his rake, the gentle yellows and browns of dead leaves. Ernest raked the leaves into an ochre heap and lifted them into the wheelbarrow. He never managed to get them all, and left rings of them torn on the lawn where the piles had been, which he then had to rake to his next heap, but he did not mind. He enjoyed watching them tumble as he tugged them with the rake; he enjoyed their colours and shapes. Sometimes the dead leaves turned to powder and he was left with a veiny framework, two-dimensional, like the trees he had drawn on to his architectural elevations, but other leaves remained firm, almost white on top, slimy and darker underneath where they had lain on the grass, and these curled prettily, coyly, when he raked them.

His shoulder was stiff. There was an ache at the base of his neck which rubbing did nothing to ease, and sometimes the ache was a pain. He rested on the scarlet handle of the rake. No point overdoing it. And when he rested he noticed another ache, harder to pinpoint, somewhere at the base of his left ribs. Probably nothing, he told himself. Indigestion. Stitch. But at my age you can't be too careful. He waited to see if the ache went away, or got worse. It did neither. Indigestion, he assured himself, and anyhow it's time for a cup of tea.

Bridget had finished the inset picture of St Peter at Heaven's Gate. St Peter still looked grumpy. The supplicant, probably the same Duc de Berry who had commissioned this book of hours, stood there with his red cloak and Jennifer's face and waited to be let in, but St Peter offered no encouragement. Behind the duke were other figures, a retinue perhaps or a queue, one of them in a long green outfit patterned with whirls of gold plants, the others more soberly dressed. These looked like academics, teachers, but unlike the duke they all wore beards and none of them looked like her sister. Bridget was enjoying this puzzle more than most. It was superbly intricate, and its patient reconstruction from a myriad cardboard parts gave her time to study it. The picture was reproduced on the box lid, of course, and though, like any jigsaw puzzler worth knowing, she never referred to the lid, she knew she was re-creating a sheet of parchment, illuminated and bearing many lines of Latin. But looking at the completed picture on the box had given her no idea of the complexity, the beauty, of the original; it was only now, piecing it together, that she saw what a wonderful thing this page really was. What on the box had been a pretty picture was transformed by an act of concentration into something serious and important. The border, for instance. There were thirteen medallions. The four in the corner bore the red-edged fleur-de-lis of the Duc de Berry; two others the red-backed monogram EV or VE; four were swans; three were bears. Thirteen. An unpleasant number. Friday the thirteenth; thirteen men at the Last Supper; if thirteen sit down at a table one shall be dead before the year is out. Linking the medallions, entwined in the decorative foliage, were scrolls. On each scroll something was written. Jennifer had won a scholarship to the high school, and been top of every class; Bridget had gone to a grammar school and had learnt a little Latin, but Latin had been what her sister did, and anyway it was a long time ago. Still she tried to read what it said on the scrolls, but the Latin and the angular gothic script defeated her. I expect Jennifer would know, she thought. And then: I keep thinking of Jennifer. And then: It was Jennifer bought me this puzzle.

She breathed out a soft snort through her nose. Bridget knew how to be sardonic. You gave me my first puzzle, and this'll be the last, and I have to admit it's the best. But you always were good at that sort of thing, weren't you. Good at leaving things behind so people couldn't forget you. Those letters you sent us from university, that Dad used to keep in a drawer. You weren't there when he died, were you. You were in Oxford writing your famous book about Shakespeare. Dad used to love getting your letters, even then, even when he was lying in bed with his kidneys a mess and his heart packing up. He used to make me read them to him. I was courting Ernest then, and he liked Ernest, but it was never me and Ernest he wanted to know about. It was always you. And they were so boring, your letters, so dry, full of scholarships and fellowships and lectures you'd been to about God knows what. No mention then of Chapman. Oh no. He was your dark secret. You saved him till after Dad died.

I'll be fair. You left Oxford after that, came up here to be near Mum. But it was never Mum, was it, Jennifer. It was always Dad. You and Dad; Dad and you. All those books he'd bought second-hand, Everyman editions of the classics, that he'd discuss with you. And the Latin he'd learnt in the evenings, learnt while you learnt it at school, so he could go through it with you and discuss it with you. He was a bloody good father to you. And you stayed away while he died. You stayed away while he died.

And what was the story anyway? There *was* a story. There was a story I never learnt. Something happened to you in the war, at that secret place you were at, and I never learnt what. But it hurt them. It hurt them both, but it hurt Dad most. Whatever it was he never got better. He was always ill after that. First his kidneys, then his heart. Breaking up bit by bit from inside because of something that happened to you, and then making me read him your letters even when he was dying. There was something unfair about that. You killed him, and even though you killed him he still wanted to hear your news, still kept your letters in a drawer. I burnt them. You didn't know that, did you. I burnt them after he'd gone. All of them. All your bloody letters. I burnt them after he'd gone.

Bridget stared at the picture of St Peter's gate and Ernest looked in at the door. 'Fancy a cuppa?' he asked.

'Thanks,' she said. She looked up and smiled, gratefully, but he was already gone.

6

Sainsbury's was a jostle, bright clothes and bright lights. Wire trolleys were humping in a line and Wendy pulled one free. Coitus interruptus: the redundant plastic child's seat flapped as she pushed toward the automatic barrier. There was the maternal scent of fresh bread by the door, odd because it could not be smelt in the shop, mysterious because the bakery was in the opposite corner, and then she was amongst the greengroceries. She selected automatically. A galia melon for Friday night, a bag of potatoes, a bag of onions, two sweetcorn heads clingfilmed together in a polystyrene tray, a carrot for Wednesday's bolognaise. Then it was the cans, tomatoes and chinese vegetables, soup for a late-night snack. At the head of the aisles was the cheese counter, crowded as always. She chose a wrapped hunk of white cheddar, larger than she wanted but the smallest piece left, and saw Alan.

7

Chapman checked in *How to Cope with Bereavement*. 'In the event of intestacy, the property of the deceased passes to the next of kin.' Who was that? Bridget? Alan?

He remembered a Christmas. He was not sure which year, but it must have been at Jennifer's mother's house, and she'd died in 1964.

Alan had been there too, a rather pretty lad with thin blond hair that still managed to curl. He was walking, after a fashion, and able to reach the low tables in Jennifer's mother's house, stealing coasters and ash-trays and offering them tantalisingly to his embarrassed father, his annoyed mother, before taking them back. Chapman had liked Alan. He had always wanted a son. But of course Jennifer couldn't have children, that was certain by then, even though they never did go to the specialist their doctor had recommended, and anyway he had a feeling she didn't want them. He remembered going on to his knees, talking to the child, recovering the stolen coasters and returning them to the table. Alan had liked him back.

And then, later, there had been a birthday party, Alan's tenth was it? Jennifer had insisted they drop in, though they hadn't been invited. 'He's my only kith and kin,' she had said. 'Let's see how he's getting on.' She had bought him a spirograph. He had one already. Alan was on the lawn, playing cricket with his friends. He had a new Jackie Hampshire bat and a ball. Ernest invited Chapman to play and Chapman, happier watching than playing, hit the ball over the fence. 'Don't worry,' said Ernest. 'Nothing broken. We'll soon have it back.' But then it was time for the children to eat, and Chapman had spoilt their game.

8

We are not made fools by love, but rather by trying to be loved.

9

John's favourite book as a child was *The Wind in the Willows*. Mole had been working very hard all the morning, trying to fix up his little home. First with a wrench, then with a screwdriver; then with cloths and towels and old rags, with a mop and a bucket of floor cleaner; till he had an irritation in his throat and eye, and damp callouses on his hands, and an aching back and weary arms. Spring was trying in the air above and the earth below and the bricks around him, penetrating even his dark and one-bedroomed little flat with its spirit of divine discontent and longing. It was small wonder, then, that he suddenly flung down his wrench on the floor, said, 'Sod it!' and, 'Oh bugger!' and also, 'Damn this bloody tap!' and bolted out of the bathroom without finishing the job. He went to the kitchen to make a cup of tea, tried to fill the kettle and realised the water was still off.

He went back into the bathroom. The old washer, looking worryingly like the new one, sat on the white basin like a lifebelt on a liner; the new one was imperfectly wedged in the tap; the tap sat on its side, mockingly useless, its spout made limp by this unfamiliar angle.

Mole gambolled in the great meadow, met Ratty, heard the Piper at the Gates of Dawn; John had a wife to think about. He could not face the tap any more, was prepared to accept it had won, but could face Wendy's scorn even less. I just wish I could remember how I'd got the damn thing off. But there had been no system: he had struggled until it had come free. Now he had to get it back on, and he was buggered if he could work out how. I'm buggered anyway, he decided.

He had a feeling he needed two spanners, one to hold the bolt at the end of the waterpipe, the other to tighten the nut that fastened the pipe through the wash-basin to the tap. He had another spanner but that was in the car, and the car was in Sainsbury's car-park. I suppose that's an excuse: I could wait till Wendy gets back because I need the spanner from the car. But what if I can't fix it then? If I've to wrestle with this sod I'd rather do it when she's not here.

His father would have known what to do. Dad was good at this sort of thing, fixing taps, putting up shelves, growing tomatoes in his allotment by the canal. It was quiet at the allotment. The noises of cars and lorries passing on the flyover were no more troublesome than the sounds of bees, a whirling background that emphasised the stark silence of half a dozen men digging the soil or tying string round their canes. Dad had a good spot. The shadow of the concrete piles had passed by noon, and he always grew sunflowers to take advantage of the afternoon sun. The sunflowers were alien there, a silly decorative quirk among those purposeful rows of onions and peas. Sunflower seeds have their culinary uses, but not in John's family. On the allotment the sunflowers were a flourish. Taller than a man, grinning on a fine day, their necks bent as though with age. John loved them. For him they were the reason for the allotment, pennant and symbol of Dad.

Dad would know what to do. But Dad had been dead ten years. John struggled again with the pipe, and surprisingly, healthily, the two pieces suddenly seemed to join. He tightened them carefully, mopped up the last of the water, and put his tools away.

'Thanks, Dad,' he said as he left.

10

Alan looked puzzled. He hasn't seen me yet, thought Wendy, and turned away. She regularly avoided those she knew. She especially avoided those she worked with when she met them out of school. It was a way of preserving her privacy, preventing the working week encroaching on her free time. It meant missing those preposterous conversations that start, 'Well, fancy meeting you here' and end, 'Well, I must be off then' and have neither sense nor substance between. It meant not having to remember her colleague's husband's name. But it was not only colleagues she avoided. Never more than twice a year she went to stay at her mother's house in Felpham, a middle-class suburb of Bognor Regis where once William Blake had lived. John seemed to like Felpham. Its front is a shingle shore. The English Channel, beaten pewter, is grey to a grey horizon and climbs to a thin grey sky. Stolid black groynes defend the beach. Houses overlook the sea. John liked Felpham, but evenings at her mother's house were awkward. Wendy and her mother spoke in short encoded bursts, brief messages that condensed a history of mistrust. 'Do you have to do it like that?' 'If you've nothing constructive to say, don't say it.' 'You haven't changed.' After dinner, after John had washed the dishes and Wendy vengefully dried them, he would suggest going out for a walk. 'I always like to see the sea.' They went down to the beach. Apologetic shingle shuffled underfoot. Sometimes the tide was out. Sometimes someone walked a dog. Wendy and John did not talk. He wondered why Wendy disliked her mother so much, wished the two of them could patch it up. Wendy wished the same, then felt a traitor to her father for the wish. 'Let's get a drink,' John would say, and they would go into the village, tight streets that Blake would have known at the heart of the desirable detacheds, and into the moist warmth of a pub. They sat at a table. John drank bitter; Wendy sipped Campari and soda while people who had known her all her life went to the bar for drinks. She acknowledged no one. Avoiding the people she had known was a way of avoiding her past.

And perhaps there was more to it. Avoiding the people she had known was a way of disowning her present. It hid the fact that John was a success and she was a schoolteacher, hid it even from herself.

'Wendy!'

'Hello,' she said. 'I didn't see you there.' Alan's eyes and voice were warm; his face was rather nice; his poems had achieved some success. She felt guilty and stupid for having tried to avoid him. 'Shopping?' she asked, aware she was voicing both guilt and stupidity.

'Bits and pieces,' said Alan.

'Well.' She could think of nothing more to say, nothing that would prolong the conversation and assuage her guilt. 'Well. I'd better push on. I've the whole week's shop to do and I'm on my own.'

'Of course. I mustn't stop you. I'll see you at the meeting on Thursday.'

'Yes. See you Thursday.'

She pushed the trolley down the aisle, between the cereals and the soups.

Alan looked at the prophylactically wrapped cheddars and the Austrian smoked in its brown condom and tried to remember what he wanted to buy: chocolates.

He set off down the next aisle; she rounded the corner, pushed her trolley back towards the cheese counter, and met him again.

'Small world,' she said.

'Big shop,' he replied. 'Do you know where they keep the chocolates?'

'Chocolates? You know, I haven't the faintest idea. Do Sainsbury's sell chocolates?'

'They must. They sell everything.'

'I suppose,' she agreed, and showed him the smile he enjoyed. 'Oh well, best of luck.'

They set off in opposite directions, went round opposite ends of the aisle, and met as they knew they would. 'We'll have to stop,' they began together.

' – meeting like this,' he finished for them.

'No luck with the chocolates?' she asked.

'Not yet,' he admitted. 'But I'll persevere.'

'Aren't you shopping for anything else?' she asked. She felt comfortable with him. 'You know, bread, meat, the staff of life?'

'I do need a loaf, actually. And a bottle of something.'

'Something alcoholic?'

He nodded.

'I thought as much,' she said, impressing herself with her eloquence, impressed he could inspire it. 'Only a dipsomaniac would live on a diet of bread and chocolate. Only a dipsomaniac could!'

'The bottle and the chocolates are presents for my parents,' he said, the words defensive but the tone light. 'And I'm only getting a loaf so I've something in when I get back.'

'You're going away?' Well done, Miss Marple, she congratulated herself.

If he found the question as crass as she did he was admitting nothing. 'To Sheffield,' he said. 'For a funeral.'

'Oh dear. I'm sorry.'

'My aunt.'

Her face must have asked the question but she did not want the reply. 'Cancer,' he said.

'Oh, that's terrible.'

It was certainly a terrible subject for a conversation, he thought, but could think of nothing else to say. 'Meet you on the next aisle?' he asked.

'Why not? Unless you want to come my way?'

'As long as you haven't already passed the chocolates.'

'I've not noticed them.'

'In that case,' he said, 'I would be honoured to accompany you.'

They walked together. She steered the trolley, halted it, loaded it. They talked to this broken rhythm.

'I enjoyed the poetry meeting,' said Alan.

'Did you? That's good. Do you think I ought to get a three-pound bag?'

'That's up to you. Have you been going long? To the poetry group?'

'A year, I suppose. It's something to do.' Her trolley bumped another. 'Sorry.'

'You don't sound all that enthusiastic.'

'Sorry,' she said again. 'I was trying to remember if we needed minced lamb.'

'I'm glad you let me walk round with you,' Alan said. She waited for a compliment. She hoped for a compliment. But she was glad when he said only: 'I was running out of things to say when we met. I think What's a nice girl like you doing in a place like this? would have been next.'

She reached over the frozen meats, trays of unrecognisable animals crusted in frost, for a packet of stock cubes. 'You're coming to the next meeting?'

'I think so. Everyone seemed very pleasant. You know, Ted and Jim and Dr Crabcalf. It depends how long I'm going to be away.'

'I hope you do come,' said Wendy. 'Jim's not a bad writer. Some of his stories are really rather good. And Julie Forrester, whom you've not met, she's good too. But most of us are pretty awful really. We need someone like you, with a bit of real talent, to raise the standard a bit.'

'I hope you're joking,' he said. 'I'm no earthly good at all.'

'False modesty, Mr Gruafin? You're nearly famous. By Crouch Poets' standards you *are* famous.'

'I can't write poetry. Not any more. I'm probably getting too old. By the time Keats was my age he'd been dead two years.'

'Then he wasn't writing much at your age either, was he. How old are you anyway? Twenty-seven? And can you pass me a packet of bacon? No, the streaky. John likes his cholesterol.'

'Twenty-seven, that's right. Is John your husband?'

'For better or worse. And twenty-seven is young, believe me.'
They negotiated separate ways around a straggling family group.
'I'm thirty,' she said: 'I should know.'

'Really? I thought you were about twenty-six.'

She was pleased. 'What a kind man you are, dear sir,' she said.

They walked another aisle. Alan's compliment had made them
aware of one another, aware of the intimacy of shopping together.
Around them were couples and families, nuclear units bonded
together by affection and familiarity and loyalty, post-coital couples
who washed their underwear together and squeezed one another's
blackheads. 'It must seem strange to help someone shop for food
you'll not eat,' said Wendy, and this was so near Alan's own
thoughts it shocked him.

'Yes,' he said. 'Yes. It's a while since I was shopping with
someone else.'

He was single, attracted, unpushy, so she was in control. She was
in control and excited. The future was her decision. The future was
her decision and because she had made no decision the future was all
possibility. She smiled at him her best smile.

11

The tiled floor was damp and patterned with footprints. 'Wogs out'
was sprayed clumsily on the wall. Chapman watched his piss hit the
enamel and spread in a gothic arch. He felt unsteady, though he had
not drunk so much; he closed his eyes and waited for the faintness to
pass.

He rinsed his hands under the tap and wiped them on his handker-
chief as he walked back into the saloon bar. In the evenings the bar
smelt of tobacco; at lunchtimes like these it smelt of fried onion and the
décor was gaudy in natural light. He returned to his seat. Behind him a
couple talked tipsily.

'Never known a winter so mild,' the woman said.

'Greenhouse effect,' the man replied. 'Burning the rainforest like on
Panorama.'

'I don't think I saw it.'

'Night Harold phoned.'

'I'd've been on phone then, night Harold phoned.'

'That's right, on phone. Anyway, they're burning trees, millions of them. Stands to reason it makes the earth hotter.'

'I'd read it was the world was moving.'

'How do you mean, moving? Course it's moving. Otherwise we'd fall off.'

'Not round and round. Like, *tilting*,' she said.

'No,' said the man. 'It's the rainforest.'

Chapman wondered if the earth were tilting. How would you tell? There must be dedicated scientists somewhere, watching as the sun rose and set each day, recording its position. It would change position every day, of course, as the days got longer or shorter: solstice, he thought, and equinox, and he relished the handsome words. So you would have to check its position not against the previous day's record but against those of the previous year. It must be a good thing to do, watching the sun come up every day. And at night they must watch the stars.

One Christmas, long ago, Jennifer had bought him a children's edition of the *Iliad* and *Odyssey*, a lovely book with many illustrations. 'Chapman's Homer', she had called it, and shown him the poem by Keats:

Then I felt like some watcher of the skies
    When a new planet swims into his ken;
Or like stout Cortez when with eagle eyes
    He star'd at the Pacific . . .

He had a sudden sad wish to be a watcher of the skies, an observer of the dawn, to record each day the earth on its path. It seemed a worthwhile, unheralded thing to do. An unexpected vision came to him. He saw the earth, blue, mantled by cloud, silvered by the distant sun. But this wasn't the famous view of the earth from the moon, the Apollo 11 picture. This was even more unnerving: the blue and silver globe voyaging endlessly through the blackness was lonely. He felt pity then. The earth bore us, fed us, sheltered us, but we can't even provide it with decent company. We just mess with it, tear up the soil and burn the rainforest.

And that's why I'd like to be a watcher of the skies, thought

Chapman: I'd like to help navigate the earth through space, keep it company, show I care and appreciate and love it. He stood and ordered a drink, as elsewhere so did John. 'And a lasagne.'

'Three eighty-eight please, mate.'

John recognised no one in the bar. He sat down, opened *The Times*, and waited for his meal.

12

They loaded her car and had coffee in a teashop off Hornsey High Street. Condensation made the window useless. They spoke cheerfully enough of the distant past, the time before she met her husband; they exchanged telephone numbers on sheets torn from Alan's notebook and pretended this too had no significance.

In some places the condensation was too heavy. It trickled down the glass, peeling off a strip of grey. Wendy paid for the coffee, 'To thank you for your help,' and they left. The world beyond the window was also grey.

They stood on the pavement. Damp litter was pressed on the flag-stones. They picked up their conversation. 'I don't know mine would go that far,' Alan was saying. 'But she used to make me go to cubs.'

Wendy laughed. 'I know what you mean. My mother used to send me to dance classes.'

'And she always gave me cheese and pickle in my sandwiches for school.'

'She let you stay sandwiches?' Wendy feigned incredulity. 'I used to dream about sandwiches. *My* mother made me stay school dinners.'

'Ugh. But I bet you didn't have to clean your football boots in the back garden, *even when it was raining*.'

'I can see you're really looking forward to going to stay with them.'

'Dad's all right.'

'My dad was all right too. He's dead now, God rest him.'

'I'm sorry.'

'It was a long time ago.' But why Lanark? What was he doing in Lanark? 'Hey, you'd better get off if you want to catch that train.'

'I suppose I had,' he agreed. 'Well, it's been nice talking to you.'

'You've got my number. You'll give me a ring when you get back?'

'If you're sure.'

'We can go for a drink.'

'It's been nice talking to you,' Alan repeated.

'Get off before it's too late,' she advised. 'I'll see you soon. Bye.'

'Bye.' Her advice was good; there was nothing he could think of to say. 'And thanks for the coffee.'

'Thanks for the help. Hey! Did you ever find the chocolates?'

'Oh, damnation.'

'You'll be able to get some at the station. And now get off, before it's too late. Bye now.'

She turned back towards Sainsbury's; he returned to the launderette. She got in the car and turned over the engine. I wonder if John's had lunch, she thought: I wonder if Alan will phone.

Someone had taken Alan's clothes from the washing machine and dumped them in a pink plastic basket, but at least there was a drier free. He loaded the drier and put in his coins. The clothes, still weighted with water, turned clumsily, climbing the perforated walls and rolling down.

13

When my parents died, thought Chapman, I suppose I must have felt grief. It was a long time ago. He was in Palestine when his father died, dropped dead in the kitchen; he missed the funeral.

He was given compassionate leave. He went to his mother. She was in the kitchen making tea. 'You're too late,' she said.

'I know.'

'Don't suppose it matters,' she said. 'It wasn't much of a bash. But you'd have looked nice in your uniform.'

'I'm sorry.'

She looked at him. 'If you say so,' she said.

And later she had died. It was summer. The day of the funeral was hot. His mother's family was there. 'I'm living in Bakewell,' he told them, explaining nothing. A woman from the nursing home handed him a carrier bag. 'Your mum's things.' The sky was blue. It was a day for weddings. 'I can't stay,' he told Uncle Bert. 'I've got to get back.'

He took a bus to the station. He opened the carrier bag. A pair of spectacles, a cheap locket, a paperback Agatha Christie. Her family must have taken the rest, he thought. He imagined them round the death bed, opening cupboards, trying on her clothes, dividing the valuables. The picture made him feel better, made staying away seem honourable. He didn't mind her family taking it all. It was better than thinking this might be her lot.

He returned the items to the bag. A pair of spectacles, a cheap locket, a paperback Agatha Christie. It was better than thinking this might be her lot.

He finished his drink and stood: I suppose I must have felt grief.

14

Wendy opened the lock. 'John?' she called. There was no one there. She carried the shopping bags through to the kitchen and unpacked, the frozen food first. She was annoyed John was out because she had to unload the food on her own. She was pleased John was out because it gave her time to think. She wanted to think about Alan.

She had no doubt they had got on well, but neither was she fooled. When they had talked of their childhoods, for instance, Alan's complaints had been the routine niggles of adolescence. She had been impressed by a passage in *Aesthetics of a Gumtree*:

We were born, as it were, into Myth: mythic parents towering over our cradles like Saturn, and the dynamite brightness of the world. And from the chaos comes the Creation, that first loud 'I AM' which orders the chaos around us. An island seems to order the waves so that wherever you stand on that island the waves still come towards you. 'I AM' is such an island. And then there is the Age of Heroes, parents and talking bears, demons under the bed. And finally disillusionment, a sort of perspective, so the more you see the more insignificant each detail becomes, and with this the knowledge that the great 'I AM' which organises your world and stands in the face of entropy will one day cease to be.

It is part of the nature of things that we each assume our own myth to be special, either the most typical or the most different of all the myths there are. As far as Wendy was concerned Alan's was the ordinary myth, of everyday life and the passing tensions of being a child; her myth was different. 'Wendy,' said her father: 'I'm not going to live with your mother any more.' 'He's not just left me,' said her mother. 'He's left you. And I want you to remember that.'

And then she came home from school, only two weeks after he left. 'Wendy,' said her mother. 'The police have been on the phone. Your father's dead.'

Incomprehension. To lose him twice in a fortnight. And mother still talking. 'He was run over. In Lanark. He was hit by a delivery van in Lanark.'

Why aren't you crying? Wendy wanted to know. And why Lanark? What could he have been doing in Lanark?

Wendy was twice as old now. She knew why her mother wasn't crying. Her mother had been deserted. Her mother had cried when he'd left. Her mother cried later that night. No one had told Wendy that there was another woman, but as time went on she learnt about marriage and learnt few people leave unless they have someone to go to. Wendy understood that her father had left of his own accord, had left her mother, had left her. She understood the whole story without being told, how he'd betrayed them and gone, yet the myth persisted and informed her life. Mother drove father away in the myth: father left and was run over in Lanark. Mother killed him.

She could forgive the arguments and the separation. She could forgive her mother the facts. She never thought to forgive her the myth.

Wendy went back to the car, collected more bags, locked up. The bags sagged on the pavement. She picked them up and her arms ached. The handles stretched and cut into her arm. I wish just once I could park outside the flat instead of halfway down the road, she thought, and then: I wonder if Alan made his train.

15

For a while the railway runs alongside the motorway, racing Volvo trucks and marketing executives, and then heads off through fields and past the ceremonial chimneys of the London Brick Company to travel north through Luton, Leicester, Loughborough, Long Eaton, an alliteration of comfortable towns. More people get off than on.

Coleridge understood the mind very well. According to his theories, the mind is above all an organising organ, processing the shapeless information that comes in through the eyes and ears, nose and nerves, making sensation make sense. Alan sits in the standard class. His seat faces forward and he is by the window. The seat next to him is empty and opposite him across the steel-rimmed formica table a young man with pimples listens to his Walkman. There is a hierarchy to perception. Alan reads the copy of *The Oxford Book of Travel Verse* he picked up from a remainder shop. At the moment this occupies the bulk of his mind, is a first-order sensation, but he is aware of other things. The Walkman exudes a tinny rhythm – Outside are rapid towns and spaces between towns; the foreground is breakneck and the horizon stately – The wistful fragrance of a perfume drifts by – Spoken words stand proud for a moment above the sounds of the train like rocks exposed by the sea: 'What college you at then?' 'Put it down Mark!' 'And I thought if he's going to smile at me like that I'll give him one where it hurts': the sea swallows them again. These are second-order sensations, acknowledged, but acknowledged as unimportant. Finally there are the third-order sensations, which are not even acknowledged though undeniably present, the gentle pressure of his clothes on his flesh and the weight of his flesh on the seat, the font in which the words he reads is set, the tremulous flicker of the lights.

It grows dark outside. On the roads the marketing executives turn on the lights of their cars, and the clouds and the sky become the same colour.

The hierarchical function of the mind edits information, but there is another function, which Coleridge called the esemplastic, which arranges that information into a sequence. A computer processes information according to algorithms; an algorithm is a series of mechanical operations. The mind is not a computer and doesn't seem to work like that, or at least not exclusively. The same algorithm can be performed on a different computer but will produce the same result; human thoughts pass through the filter of identity and are conditioned by who we are. The mind *can* perform algorithmically, solving problems of maths or chess, and in these areas the average mind is noticeably inferior to a computer, slower and less precise; in contrast, the computer *cannot* perform esemplastically.

But what is esemplasticity? Alan is dozing now. Under the bright artificial lights the pages of his book seem fierce and the words stop making sense: his eyes see violet ghosts that shadow each letter, and the letters become fluid; words curl at the edge of the page as though peeling away from the paper. He blinks the book back into focus then closes his eyes and falls asleep. Sleep illustrates best how the esemplastic mind works; it demonstrates the elegance and accuracy of Coleridge's notion.

Sleep isolates the mind from the senses. It does this imperfectly – a sudden sensation, an alarm clock or a shake, wakes us – but effectively enough for us to be mostly unaware, while we sleep, of what is happening around us.

We recognise that the heart and liver continue to work while we sleep, pumping oxygenated blood through our arteries, regulating the chemicals in the bloodstream. Likewise the esemplastic mind continues to process our thoughts. Only now it has no direct sensory experiences with which to work: instead it plunders the lumber rooms of the mind.

There are several levels of sleep, and Alan's is not particularly deep. He is dreaming none the less. Dreams make sense while we dream them. Alan's dream starts from conscious thoughts about the book he was reading. He had been surprised to see it remaindered – a 1986 edition, hardback, attractive – and pleased to buy it cheap; his pleasure in the bargain, his sense of making a good purchase, had kept him loyal until this journey. But the journey has made the book unsatisfactory: it is not a book about travel, he has realised, but a book about places; it is not about journeying but arriving, and the rhythm of the train, which is seen as well as heard, emphasises its failure. He wants to read about travelling itself, about the process and the progress. He does not want to read of destinations.

So he dreams about the comfortable suburban house where his parents live. His impatience with *The Oxford Book of Travel Verse* is due to a feeling his conscious mind has refused to entertain: he does not much want to arrive. He dreams about his parents' house, the house he calls *their* home and still thinks of as his. He does not much want to arrive because he cannot rid himself of the sensation that somehow his mother has arranged Auntie Jennifer's death and the funeral just to get him to see her play. In the dream the house has grown large, and though he thinks he recognises each room he cannot find a way out. But the house he dreams is clearly not his parents' house, the house in which he lived for more than twenty years; it has features of his parents' house certainly, to which other features, drawn from that lumber room of the mind, have been added. It is his esemplastic mind which unites these disparate images and gives them the semblance of coherence.

For this is the function of esemplasticity. Asleep or awake, it makes sense of the available information, editing it or amplifying it according to the model we have of the world, turning sensation into sequence. The dream flits bizarrely from scene to scene. Alan is teaching now – another situation in which he often feels trapped – and the entirely unreasonable transition from his parents' house in Sheffield to a laboratory in London is achieved without a jar: his esemplastic mind, which when awake is constantly smoothing the rough edges of experience, does exactly the same thing as he sleeps. He is standing in front of a class. Quantum theory fascinates him, yet he hates teaching it. He knows why this is. He works in a liberal arts college, and most of his students take his course because they need credits in science before they graduate; they have no grounding in mathematics, and quantum theory is essentially mathematical. He therefore has to translate an elegant mathematical description into a rather imprecise verbal one. His students, mostly Americans and Arabs, are enormously respectful. They pay large sums of money to listen to what he has to say; they sit with their writing pads open and their pens at the ready. Alan finds himself at the front of the class, by a glossy white board that covers half the wall. 'The German physicist Max Planck worked out that atoms don't lose radiation in a regular way, the way water runs out of the bath,' he is telling them. 'They lose it in "quanta", little electromagnetic bursts.' Alan draws a circle with a felt pen on to the glossy white board. This represents an atom. He draws crude wavy lines coming from it to show these bursts. 'Planck also noticed that there is a direct correspondence between the whole energy E and the frequency v. This correspondence is roughly 6.6×10^{-34} Joule seconds, and is called Planck's constant, h.' He writes the famous equation $E = h v$ on the board. 'E is the whole energy; h is Planck's constant; v is the frequency of the oscillations, the bursts of energy.' The students take down the equation. A hand is raised: 'Sir, what's the value of h again?'

The value of h is irrelevant: 6.6×10^{-34} Joule seconds means nothing to his students; the important thing is that the energy is emitted in packets which are dependent on the value of E. Yet he dare not discourage a student who shows an interest, so he writes this meaningless value on his board. He is in a double bind. On the one hand his students are mathematically ignorant; on the other they respect what he has to say only if he can justify it with numbers and equations. In fact, he has noticed, they prefer complicated equations: $E = h v$, so elegant to a mathematician, lacks impressive Greek letters or abstruse symbols. The students respect his equations not because they do understand them but because they don't: he could make up equations, $E = H_2O$, and no one would be any the wiser. They have an equation of their own in their heads, thinks Alan, which says that equations are serious and education is serious and therefore equations equal education. These are children of the Reagan years, after all, and the education equation goes further: education = qualifications = job = money. These students have to pay to be at the college, \$13,000 a semester. They want a return for their investment. So he writes down the meaningless value of Planck's constant, to give them value for money, and finds he has written $E = \$$ on the board. The students take this down. In his sleep, Alan is amused. He starts to play the piano.

16

Do I dwell too much on this dream? Other people's dreams are boring; dreams, moreover, are a notoriously clumsy authorial device. Wendy is sick to death of stories from her pupils that end 'Then I woke up and it was all a dream'; even in the more sophisticated writing that Robert and John deal with, dreams are rarely handled well. But I justify the inclusion of this dream on several grounds. First, it says something about the way Alan thinks; secondly, it tells us something about the way everyone thinks. But mostly it says something about me, in my bed between sterile walls. The string to open the blind is out of my reach. Dreams and this book I write make some sense of my time. This book is about several people, and one of them is me. I write myself into your life. I write myself out again.

17

There is a mystery about dreams, but that mystery has less to do with their mechanics – Coleridge's esemplasticity explains that well enough – than their function. Some dreams are doubtless about anxiety, but others seem to be dreamt just for the kick of going into the lumber room, sorting through old files and old photographs, making a specious sequence of unrelated events. Dreams often amuse: perhaps they are a way of entertaining us in the dangerous time after dark, a way of persuading us to stay in one place and conserve our energy. Alan starts to play the piano, and this seems reasonable to him because the regular rhythm of his left hand corresponds, in this dream, to the electromagnetic oscillation described by Planck. He plays a simple piano boogie – a broad chord of dotted quavers on the tonic and the fifth, followed by dotted quavers on the tonic and sixth, with the semiquavers behind the dotted notes giving a syncopated variation to the beats, so that it goes da da-di di-da da-di di – and this, which derived from the rhythm a train made in the days when tracks were made of short lengths of steel, takes him back to the train he is on, and he stirs. *The Oxford Book of Travel Verse* is still on his knee, and the boogie-woogie in his head becomes the dactyls of Auden's 'Night Mail'. Sleep is slipping away but has left its mark, and Auden's lines alter in Alan's head:

This is the nightmare crossing the border
Between what's sane and what's mental disorder.

This too amuses him; he smiles and is fully awake. He cannot remember his dream.

A steward wheels a trolley along the carriage. Alan orders a coffee, black, no sugar. 'Forty-five pence, sir.' It seems a lot for a fix of caffeine in a cup of dirty water. He is handed his plastic cup and his change. Decaffeinated coffee is even more bizarre, thinks Alan: that's only the dirty water.

The caffeine does its duty. He looks through the window. It is quite dark now and he sees himself looking back. The trouble with black coffee is it stays hot too long. Occasional lights outside suddenly start to thicken, to congeal, and the train is reaching a town. Silhouetted against the sky, black against a navy blue, caught in inadequate pale floodlights, is the familiar twisted spire of Chesterfield's famous church, and Alan knows he is almost home.

Local legend has it that a virgin had once married in the church, and the spire was so astounded it bent down to have a look. The truth is more prosaic. The wood that held up the spire was inadequately seasoned and had warped. But, thought Alan, the chances of the wood warping as much as it clearly has without the spire falling down must be tiny. If it wasn't that the spire looks ugly and almost obscene now it's bent you might suspect God had a hand in it; as it is it's the devil's work, and the phallic tendencies any spire has are emphasised by the asymmetry.

They pass through Dronfield, grey in the failing afternoon, grey at any time, and into the Bradway tunnel. Around him people start packing their belongings, ready to get off in Sheffield. All Alan has to pack is his book, and there is no hurry. He knows from experience that the train always stops before it gets to the station, to give visitors a chance to savour Arnold Laver's woodyard and the Queens Road bus depot.

He is thinking, though he does not know why, about Planck's notion of quanta, a simple notion really: in a world where matter comes in lumps, energy must come in lumps too. On the day Planck made this discovery he took his son with him on a walk. 'I have had a conception today as revolutionary and as great as the kind of thought that Newton had,' he said.

Alan would like to have such a thought.

Alan would like to have a son.

18

Chapman was walking again, but now walking brought no relief. He crossed Bakewell bridge. The dark waters of the River Wye tugged at the sunken weeds, regimenting them into lines that disappeared beneath the dark arches. I'm going to lose my home. The water-weed was well rooted and bent with the flow. I can bend with the flow as much as I like, thought Chapman, but I'm going to lose my home.

He was fifty-eight years old. He had a small invalidity pension, no skills, no savings; a pair of spectacles, a cheap locket, a paperback Agatha Christie. Naked we come into this world . . . A plastic cup, its sides split and flattened to a crude star, was bumped and bothered downstream. That's me, he thought, a paper cup. A paper cup on the stream of life.

It was a lousy image. It was such a lousy image he raised his head as he walked.

19

Ernest had a son, and the son was late.

'I know,' said Alan, leaving his bag at the foot of the stairs. 'I'm sorry.'

'Your mother's already left. I hope you had a bite on the train; we'll have to get out again straight away.'

'You got a ticket then?'

'Afraid so,' said Ernest, and they laughed. They were closest when they conspired. 'Anyway, get a move on. Starting soon.'

The car fitted snugly in the garage. 'I'll back out.' Ernest worked his way to the door and let himself in.

The engine fired and red light glowed on the drive; Ernest reversed and the red light was trounced by white. Alan opened the door and folded into the passenger seat. 'It's almost warm tonight.'

'Ridiculous for the time of year, though we did have snow. A couple of days ago. The day your aunt passed on.' Ernest backed on to the street. 'It didn't last. Did you have a good journey? I don't suppose there's been any snow in your part of the world.'

'None at all. The journey was fine,' said Alan. 'I'm glad I missed the Christmas rush,' he added, a covert apology for his Christmas truancy.

'It was quiet at home over Christmas,' Ernest told him, meaning I forgive you but your mum may have other ideas.

'How is Mum anyway?' asked Alan, hearing what was left unsaid.

'She's fine,' said Ernest, then remembered that Jennifer was dead. 'I mean, she misses her sister of course.'

'Of course,' said Alan, but the sisters had never been close.

'She's taking it well,' Ernest continued, 'but I'm glad she only had a small part in this year's play.'

'Yes. That's a good thing,' said Alan.

It was a short drive, past the old school and the Hare & Hounds, the ugly white rendered façade of the garage and its old-fashioned tombstone pumps, the post office and the chemist. Cars spilt from the village hall car-park and on to the road, making driving awkward and parking worse. 'There's a cast party afterwards,' said Ernest. 'At Susie Mayfield's.' He drove past parked cars until he could stop.

'Are you going?'

'No. I don't think so. Not with your aunt so recently gone.'

And Mum's bit-part in the production, thought Alan. 'There's a space up there,' he said.

'Good. We might stay a bit of course. It depends on your mother.'

'It's all right. I'll walk home. I've got a key.'

There was no one on the door and it was already dark in the hall: the seats were not numbered and there was no one to show them where to sit. The village hall had a proscenium arch but the drama group was using a space on the floor in front of the stage as well. The only free seats they could see were at the front, raw and exposed. As they sat dim lights were raised on the acting area, and on them as they shrank to their seats. Thunder clapped. The wind howled. Figures came on from doors either side of the stage. 'Boatswain!'

'Here, Master! What cheer?'

'Good, speak t'the mariners. Fall to't, yarely, or we run ourselves aground . . .'

It was well done, thought Alan. The crew brought masts with them, assembled as if for shelter beneath them, swayed in co-ordination to represent the yawing ship. The villains, Antonio and Sebastian, bitched wittily against the noise of the storm, and temperate old Gonzalo could only suggest prayer against the anarchy of the storm. 'The wills above be done,' he cried, 'but I would fain die a dry death.' Ernest, unfamiliar with the play and the language, was unsure what he had seen, and this worried him; Alan decided he might enjoy this after all.

And then the storm was over, replaced by brighter lights, pink and pale blue, and Prospero entered. The good magician, his beautiful daughter at his side, his cloak of many spangles wrapped around his shoulders, stood directly in front of Ernest and told his daughter his tale of loss and betrayal, while Bridget smoked a cigarette.

They called it the Green Room. Two of the mirrors were ringed with bulbs and the mariners queued to change their make-up, for they would be spirits later. A tannoy relayed the lines from the stage: Antonio's treachery, Gonzalo's loyalty and Miranda's pity lost their timbre through cheap speakers.

Ariel entered from the proscenium. She had good legs and a skimpy costume; the faint eroticism, born of the costume and the knowledge this girl was an amateur, a local, gave an edge to Alan's enjoyment.

Bridget had nothing to do until after the interval. Juno's wig, narrow strands of tin-foil, rested on her lap like a survivor of Christmas. Caliban, the village policeman, practised his scowl and was bustled into the wings. Bridget yawned a twist of smoke.

Alan was less impressed by Caliban, whose costume seemed to be scales of overlapping green silk stitched to a leotard. He was glad when Prospero dismissed his slave and Ariel returned. This was a potent Prospero, tall and bearded, dominating the stage. Ariel sang to Ferdinand: Full fathom five thy father lies . . . These are pearls that were his eyes. Alan thought of Eliot, of Phlebas the Phoenician a fortnight dead, of death by water, of his father, his aunt. Fear death by water. Fear death. Ferdinand and Miranda fell in love. Miranda was less exciting than Ariel but looked a little like Anne-Marie.

Bridget lit another cigarette. She was not a heavy smoker. She had one in the morning with her coffee, which she excused to herself because she found it opened her bowels, and maybe two or three in the evenings in front of the television. In the Green Room, though, she always smoked, a comfort like saying 'Break a leg' and referring only to 'the Scottish play', a ritual and a nod towards their notions of professionalism. The smoke clung to the back of her throat. She blew it through her nose and it ruffled the silver wig on her knee; she released a last wisp through dead lips. Jennifer had given up smoking ten years ago. Jennifer had died of cancer. Bridget drew in more smoke and stubbed the cigarette into the ash-tray. The ash-tray was damp and stung the hot ash.

The lights went down between acts. 'It's not bad is it,' said Ernest as they clapped. The clapping was replaced by shuffling and coughing, on stage as well as off, and the lights came up again on figures on the ground. The shipwrecked courtiers conversed; Antonio and Sebastian plotted the death of old Alonso, King of Naples, the death that would make Sebastian king, and Ariel thwarted their plot. Alan was enjoying himself. It was easier to watch when his mother was not on stage, easier to enjoy. Prospero, the old alchemist, was weaving his spells, converting tin-foil to gold, and though the performances were uneven the poetry carried them through.

Ernest did not think in terms of enjoyment, but he was doing his duty and his duty was not too painful. He was beginning to understand who some of the characters were: Prospero, Ariel, Miranda and Caliban were easy, and Ferdinand was all right, but the courtiers blurred for him, their identities and motivations indistinguishable. And then Stefano and Trinculo came on, swaggering drunkenly, and though Ernest had no idea at all who they were he enjoyed watching them.

' 'Ban, 'Ban, Ca-Caliban
Has a new master. – Get a new man!'

The scene shifted. Miranda fell for Ferdinand and Prospero watched and smiled while cursing the young prince; Caliban led the drunkards round the island; the courtiers were bemused by Ariel and the spirits. Alan looked for his mother amongst these spirits but her part came later. He was glad. He could let his mind wander a while.

Prospero is a magician in the hermetic tradition. Hermetics is mystery; hermetics is alchemy. Hermetics is the study of things-beyond-science, and it takes its name from Hermes Trismegistus, thrice-honoured Hermes, who was the Greek equivalent of Thoth, the Egyptian god of the moon. Thoth has the head of an ibis, or sometimes a baboon, and is master of laws and languages, writing and the calendar. At the judgment after death Thoth weighs the heart. The Roman Hermes is Mercury, quicksilver, the alchemists' friend; Mercury is bearer of the staff of winged serpents, the caduceus; Mercury signifieth subtill men, ingenious, inconstant; rymers, poets, advocates, orators, arithmeticians, and busy fellowes.

The word of Hermes Trismegistus is contained in the hermetic books, the forty-two books of Alexandria which form the basis of Neoplatonism. Using the hermetic books, Plotinus, Porphyry and Iamblichus, in the third century after Christ, reworked the mysticism in Socrates and Plato. The universe according to Plotinus is a hierarchy rising from matter to soul, soul to reason, reason to god, wherein god, pure existence without body or form, is the final abstraction.

Soul is a meaningless concept to me, thought Alan, but psyche, the Greek word, has connotations of the mind and thus perception. This would give a different hierarchy:

god

↑

reason

↑

perception

↑

matter

Which makes a kind of sense, thought Alan, as long as god remains pure existence rather than some anthropomorphic figure with an old man's prejudices.

The other source for Neoplatonism is Pythagoras, who sought the explanation of the universe in numbers and their relation. The universe can be decoded, according to this view; everything is there to be explained for the person who has the key. Prospero has the key; Prospero carries the magic staff.

Ernest's mind wandered too. He had unravelled the courtiers a little, learnt Antonio and Sebastian were villains, understood they were plotting, and this made him think of old Ryker. Ryker had been City Architect when Ernest was new to the department, fresh from private practice, an experienced architect inexperienced in the ways of the Town Hall. When the auditors had asked about Ryker's honesty Ernest had first been loyal, then disloyal. No, Ryker wasn't always visiting sites when he said he was; no, the visiting Russian architects hadn't been given special commemorative plaques despite Ryker's receipts; no, the visit to Strathclyde hadn't been necessary. Ryker had been corrupt, no doubt, thought Ernest, but I needn't have been the one to say so. Yet I did: I told them all they asked me and more, and Ryker was dismissed and I was promoted. I did the honest thing and they rewarded me, and I can't forgive myself their reward.

The lights came up for the interval, for relief, for an easing of buttocks and minds. The audience clapped. 'I'm going to see if I can get a programme,' said Alan, wanting the name of the girl playing Ariel. 'Do you want a coffee?' Ernest did, and the Green Room was bustle and comment. I thought I'd forgotten my lines. Did you hear what Jerry said? I nearly died. Susie Mayfield, the director, stood and spoke: 'You were wonderful darlings!' she said, and her darlings glowed with pride. 'But now you've got to really sock it to them! I'm off to check Kev, see the effects are working. But keep it up! And break a leg!'

Her amateurs enjoyed the gush. This was a place where embarrassment was outlawed; this was the magical isle, though the coffee was made with milk and filmed with grease. Alan bought a cup for his father, decided he couldn't face one himself. There was a pile of programmes on a table by the door, and an ice-cream tub full of

money. Alan guessed the price and put ten pence in. 'Two sugars?'
he asked Ernest, returning with his programme.

'One,' said Ernest, too late.

'Sorry.'

'Doesn't matter.' Alan sat down. Ariel was played by Samantha
Crowshaw. The name meant nothing. Juno was played by Bridget
Gruafin.

The interval ended. Kev turned down the lights. Bridget waited in
the wings of the stage. The dimming lights were an indrawn breath.
Prospero and Ariel stood below her, ready to enter the acting area in
the auditorium; Ferdinand, Miranda and Iris were opposite. The
dimming lights were an indrawn breath. 'If I have too austerely
punished you,' began Prospero, walking on to the acting area, 'Your
compensation makes amends.' She could not see the action. It was
cold in the wings. She followed the rehearsed moves, breathed
slowly and carefully through her nose, and listened for her cue. She
was anticipating the action rather than following it, and Ariel's
forthcoming lines ransacked her head. And with her sovereign
grace; and with her sovereign grace; and with her sovereign grace.

'Be silent!' demanded Prospero from on stage, and Kevin let off
the first of his effects, a firecracker in a bucket that had needed Fire
Department approval.

'Ceres,' began Iris, addressing Ariel because the text is confusing
here; Iris emerged through smoke, and Bridget, moments left now,
became Juno, queen of the heavens, taller with each inhalation:

'the Queen o' th' Sky,
Whose wat'ry arch and messenger am I,
Bids thee leave these, and with her sovereign grace – '

Kevin's second effect, a kind of sunburst, a brilliant light on a
sheet of polished gold foil, announced Juno. She stood against the
brightness, a triumphant silhouette, and Iris continued:

'Here on this grass-plot, in this very place,
To come and sport. – Her peacocks fly amain.
Approach, rich Ceres, her to entertain.'

Ariel flashed her lovely legs; her nipples prodded nylon as she spoke.

If the lines were unnatural so was Bridget's pose. She stood on the stage above the action, one hand open in a gesture of generosity, the other on her hips, forthright and determined. The position was strained but Alan saw his mother in it, his mother magnified and writ large.

'Great Juno comes,' announced Ariel: 'I know her by her gait.' And Alan knew her too.

Stately, impressive, his mother approached. 'How does my bounteous sister?' she asked, and no one knew Jennifer was dead:

'Go with me
To bless this twain, that they may prosperous be,
And honoured in their issue.'

And then she spoke to Alan:

'Honour, riches, marriage-blessing,
Long continuance and increasing,
Hourly joys be still upon you!
Juno sings her blessings on you.'

Alan, wifeless, childless, was chastised. 'You're just going to live together then,' Bridget had asked over the phone when he had told her about Anne-Marie.

'We feel more comfortable,' he had said.

But it was not true. Not exactly. Anne-Marie had felt more comfortable unmarried; Anne-Marie had upped and gone.

The seat, plastic, unsympathetic, was hard now and Alan rolled his shoulders to relax his spine. His mother moved from the centre of the stage. Other spirits appeared, joining her, joining her joyful dance until Prospero turned to the audience, confessed he had forgotten Caliban's conspiracy, and dismissed the spirits in confusion; Juno rushed with the rest, removed her wig in the Green Room, and lit another cigarette. 'Our revels now are ended,' said Prospero through the tannoy, and Bridget, agreeing, fished a damp cloth circle of make-up remover from the box by the mirror.

By now the play was only loose ends to be rapidly retied. Antonio's treachery was revealed; Sebastian's attempt on the life of his brother the King of Naples was shown too. Yet all was forgiveness, and when Trinculo and Stefano staggered in with Caliban, doubled under the cramps Prospero inflicted, they were comedy only, sobered and chastened.

The stage was abandoned. Prospero alone remained. He waited a long while, then spoke in unexpected tetrameter:

'Now my charms are all o'erthrown,
And what strength I have's mine own,
Which is most faint. Now 'tis true
I must be here confined by you
Or sent to Naples.'

Ernest listened, ignoring the cold milk-made coffee, its too many sugars and chewy richness. He understood: this is how Bridget feels when the run ends. Alan watched Prospero put aside his staff, his magic, his knowledge. The world has no place for such knowledge; Prospero put aside his staff and became an actor, slightly tawdry, soliciting applause:

'But release me from my bands
With the help of your good hands.'

Tonight, Ernest knew, and knew Bridget knew too, the applause would not be for her and for Juno. As Rosalind or Lady Macbeth Bridget had been released, satisfied, sated, but as Juno, bit-part, she would be given no liberty, would be trapped, would be forced to let herself down slowly. Ernest discovered he knew how. His wife would assume a fresh role, replace Juno with the part of the grief-stricken sister.

'And my ending is despair
Unless I be relieved by prayer,
Which pierces so, that it assaults
Mercy itself, and frees all faults.'

Jennifer's death would prolong Bridget's performance and, because he felt he must love his wife, Ernest hated to have to understand her as well. The world has no place for such knowledge.

'As you from crimes would pardoned be,
Let your indulgence set me free.'

The play was done. The stage was plunged to black. And then the clapping began, partisan clapping that had little to do with Prospero's plea but said daughter, husband, sister, lover.

The clapping continued. The characters came back on stage. Some had taken off the thick of their make-up. Alan saw his mother in Juno's wig yet her own face. Someone gave flowers to the director, and to Miranda. She's not really like Anne-Marie, thought Alan. Ariel gave a bow of her own; Alan checked the programme again. 'Samantha Crowshaw' still meant nothing. Caliban, Stephano and Trinculo won particular applause.

Alan was tiring of clapping but still it went on. He felt the same at classical concerts, everyone clapping for ever to show how appreciative, how educated, how clever they were. It was boring. But not as boring, he conceded, as showing cleverness by ridicule. And the performance had been good. So he gave one final burst of cup-handed claps and at last the players left the stage.

There was a metal dustbin at the Green Room door. It was circular and olive green, empty except for a few cigarette butts and a lettuce of balled paper. Bridget took off the wig and dropped it in. The Green Room filled with compliments and relatives. 'Everyone was absolutely splendid!' announced Susie Mayfield. Alan and Ernest came in, looked round, found Bridget. 'It was really great,' said Alan.

'Wonderful,' Ernest agreed.

'You noticed my part?' asked Bridget. 'I was easily missed.'

'Don't do yourself down,' said Alan. 'You were great too. So – *imposing*, if you know what I mean.'

'If you say so,' she replied. 'Are you two coming to the party?'

'Do you want to?' asked Ernest.

'We may as well,' she said. 'You?' she asked Alan.

Ariel sat on her boyfriend's knee. 'I don't really know anyone. I'll walk home,' he said.

'Have you got a key?' his parents asked together.

The Gruafins laughed. 'I've got a key,' he replied.

He stopped off at the Hare & Hounds. Jill Daniels, whom he had fancied at school, worked behind the bar. 'Still here?' he asked inanely.

'Nearly ten years,' Jill agreed. 'It's money, isn't it,' she explained. 'You living round here still then?'

'No. No, I live in London. Just here for a few days. Parents.'

'That's nice. Hang on, I've got to serve.'

She was busy after that but he did not mind. Already Wendy had taught him to look for rings on alluring hands, and he suspected that one day she would teach him much more. Jill wore significant rings. Not Jill Daniels now she's married then? I wonder who.

He walked the rest of the way home, along familiar streets, past unfamiliar infill houses. The night was still mild. Alan let himself in.

The house had not changed much despite him. The hall was still a little too dark, light failing to reach the corridor by the stairs; he turned on the living-room light and saw the new carpet, but the furniture was the same, arranged in a pattern around the television, with the coffee table still in the middle of the suite. One of his father's redundant drawing boards was on the table, and there was a jigsaw puzzle on the drawing board. He saw the perimeter of an illuminated page, with an inset picture in the top left corner and an illuminated letter just below; he saw a piece that would fit in the crux where the letter met the cameo picture, and added it. As a child he had sometimes stolen dried fruit from the jars in the kitchen cupboards. Will she notice? he had wondered then; Will she notice? he wondered now. He saw another piece that would fit, extending the illuminated margin between the columns of script. Better not, he thought, but pieced it in. Another piece fitted next to that.

He felt foolish and furtive. To avoid doing any more of his mother's puzzle he went to the bookcase.

The books were familiar. Bookclub editions of unfashionable books, *Kingfishers Catch Fire* and *Katherine*, paperback du Mauriers and Agatha Christies, the incomplete works of Jennifer Fox. *Shakespeare's Great Theme* had gone through several editions, and the first and second were represented here, as was *Literature in the Age of Certainty.* There was no copy of her most recent book, *Literature in the Age of Uncertainty.*

Alan had never read any of them. They belonged on the shelf, with Osbert Sitwell's four-volume autobiography and the conch shell that served as a bookend. But Jennifer Fox was dead. He eased *Literature in the Age of Certainty* from the shelf. There was a dedication – 'To my mother, April 1964' – on the title page: Granny's book, then, inherited like the Swiss music-box that played Brahms's lullaby and the chess set without a white queen. Alan sat down to read. He avoided looking at the jigsaw puzzle again. The mantelshelf clock struck twelve.

20

John turned off the TV. 'Are you coming to bed?' he asked.

'Later,' said Wendy. 'I'm reading.'

'Come on,' he said. 'It's late.'

'I'm reading,' she said. 'You go.'

'All right,' he said. 'I will.'

He went to the bathroom first, washing his face with Body Shop Mostly Men face scrub, a squirt of grey lotion that concealed refreshingly abrasive chunks. But the tube was almost empty and it farted when he squeezed.

He looked in the mirror. A single dark hair dangled from his left nostril. He had always been hairy, but now hairs were sprouting in new places, on his ears and from his nose, bothersome hairs he resented. He took the tweezers from the bathroom cabinet, trapped the stray hair and pulled. The hair tugged loose and he sneezed. The sneeze was enjoyable. He used his fingers to loose more hairs and the tweezers to pull them out, but somehow could not sneeze again, which was mildly disappointing. He cleaned his teeth. His toothbrush was an Oral-B with a shaped head to reach the hard corners, but he scrubbed mostly the teeth at the front. He went to the bedroom and undressed. The bed was cold. He was tired but did not sleep till Wendy joined him much later.

Chapter Six

THE DESCENT OF MAN
or
UP AND DOWN

In which Man evolves from the Apes

The possibility of evolution as opposed to creation was first raised around the turn of the nineteenth century: Erasmus Darwin, Charles Darwin's grandfather and a notable scientific inquirer in his own right, examined the question in the last years of the eighteenth century; Lamarck's *Philosophia zoologique* first appeared in 1809. Contemporary developments in geology and archaeology both stimulated and lent credence to the evolutionary argument. Biblical exegesis had reckoned the date of creation to be 400 BC, but the geological evidence assembled by Sir Charles Lyell in *Principles of Geology* (1830) suggested that the world was much older; the Bible claimed that God had created the earth's creatures in the form that modern man knew them, but fossilised remains suggested that world had once been inhabited by creatures very different. Tennyson's '*In Memoriam*', published in 1850, refers to the disruption of the established view of a divinely ordained and permanent natural order, particularly in section 56:

> 'So careful of the type?' but no.
> From scarped cliff and quarried stone
> She cries, 'A thousand types are gone:
> I care for nothing, all shall go.'

Man, instead of being created in God's image, is merely *primus inter pares*, subject to the same capricious laws that killed the dinosaurs. But, despite this questioning of the biblical account of creation, it was not until 1859, when Darwin published *The Origin of Species*, that evolutionary notions began to gain general acceptance.

Darwinism is not a synonym for evolution – it is the mechanism by which evolution occurs. This mechanism he called 'natural selection':

139

creatures occasionally mutate; the majority of these mutations are useless but some give rise to modifications that increase the creature's chances of survival; the effective mutant reproduces successfully and a new species thereby evolves. Modern genetics allow us to understand the process better, but the principle is unchanged.

An essential feature of Darwinism is that the animation for this process is arbitrary: far from endorsing the notion of the inevitability of progress, Darwinism works without blueprint or grand design; the mutations occur at random, and whilst it is certainly true that evolution generally occurs only if the mutant gene confers some sort of advantage on the subject of that mutation, the ultimate benefits are often dubious. Imagine this situation. One out of a species of predators runs faster than the rest. He is able to catch more food therefore, and his offspring not only inherit his genes but are also better fed than the other families in that species. His family prospers; his healthy, speedy offspring are equipped not only to catch food but also to attract mates, and eventually the whole species – perhaps now sufficiently different from the originals to warrant being called by a different name – will run faster. This seems to be an improvement; it isn't. Improved muscle development requires improved nutrition: the total amount of time spent hunting will probably not change, though the modified species will take more prey. And in time either the hunters will become so efficient that they wipe out the food supply, or one of their potential victims will also develop the ability to run faster. The disadvantages of the former are self-evident, while if the latter occurs then the faster prey animal will have a better chance of survival, will breed more successfully than his slower relatives, and much the same process that occurred in the predator will occur in the prey: the net gain to either side will have been nil. In short, evolution is not about improvement, it is about adaptation. Significantly, however, that is not how it was understood. In the popular imagination of the late nineteenth century Darwinism was indeed a blueprint for improvement, the enshrinement, justification and mechanism of progress.

Progress was a dominant theme of nineteenth-century thought. From Karl Marx to Samuel Smiles, philosophers of varying degrees of ability and subtlety looked favourably at the way the world changes. Their concepts of what Utopia might be like, and how it might be achieved, differed enormously, but there was a general agreement that Utopia was possible. Certainly industrialisation and urbanisation had brought tangible benefits, albeit of a limited kind, in health care and sanitation; more important, they had weakened the hegemony of nature. Post-industrial production was no longer dependent on the seasons – a spinning jenny spins as well in January as June – and artificial lighting regulated the length of the working day. A poor harvest might still increase the price of bread, but it did not affect the smelting of steel. Wet weather might have hampered horse traffic, but the railways were impervious. Nature, the Romantic artists' most significant deity, was in retreat.

Literature in the Age of Certainty, Introduction, pp. ii–iii

2

Darwin's second major work, a study of the origins of *Homo sapiens*, was published in 1871. It is tempting to think that Darwin was warning against any overly optimistic interpretation of his theories when he called this book *The Descent of Man* – 'descent', after all, has implications other than the genealogical – but if this was the case he was being too subtle. And, brilliant man though Darwin obviously was, to assume that he was concerned by the misinterpretation and misappropriation of his theories is perhaps to assume too much. Darwin had remarkable assistance in the dissemination of his theories, most notably from T. E. Huxley, John Tyndall and Herbert Spencer. It was Spencer who coined the phrase 'survival of the fittest', in his book *Principles of Biology* (1865), and Darwin was happy to admit the usefulness of this term: 'I have called this principle, by which each slight variation, if useful, is preserved, by the term of Natural Selection', he wrote in *The Origin of Species*; 'The expression often used by Mr Herbert Spencer of the Survival of the Fittest is more accurate, and is sometimes equally convenient', he admitted later. Yet no phrase has caused more misunderstanding about the true, and arbitrary, nature of Darwinism. For to speak of the survival of the fittest is to encourage all sorts of notions that have no place in either Darwinism or human society. If the survival of the fittest is the law of nature, then almost anything, bullying, National Socialism, genocide, is justified. Indeed, Spencer recognised this, and in the concept of Social Darwinism he proposed, carelessly and perniciously, a construct that permitted those in power to do any number of unnatural acts within the jurisdiction of natural law. No single set of ideas, Macchiavelli's *The Prince* notwithstanding, have done as much damage to humanity as did Social Darwinism: in this climate, is it surprising that poetry was impotent? If it took a world war for poetry to free itself from the constraints of 'progress', it took two world wars before society at large could admit that Spencer's corrupt Darwinism had been wrong.

ibid., Ch. I, p.9

3

The novel, literature in prose, is a far more international medium than the poem. After all, as Robert Frost remarked, poetry 'is what gets lost in translation'. A novel can be translated far more faithfully. It is therefore reasonable, even in a discussion of English literature, to acknowledge achievements in other languages. The nineteenth century produced Balzac and Stendhal, Dostoevsky and Tolstoy, as well as Dickens, George Eliot and Hardy. Whilst – for temporal as well as geographical reasons – it is unreasonable to suggest that each was conscious of the other's activities, there can be little doubt that the influence each of the above named exerted extended beyond their country of origin. Certainly, there were themes and motifs that each of these writers shared, which can only be understood as manifestations and concerns of the era: principal among these is the influence of the Last Will and Testament.

The importance of wills in nineteenth-century literature is often overlooked, but cannot be over-emphasised. The will is a major determinant of plot in an inordinate number of nineteenth-century novels; in twentieth-century fiction it fades into complete insignificance, revived only occasionally by tired authors of detective stories.

There are perhaps three reasons for the emphasis on wills in nineteenth-century fiction. First, and most technically, it is an excellent plotting device. It should never be forgotten in criticism (and frequently is) that among any writer's concerns, one of the most important is to provide the impetus that will lead the reader to finish the book. In most fiction, this is the function of plot: plot is the lure which leads the reader on. Generally, the only suspense in a book is the question 'Which of the tried and trusted alternatives will the author choose?'; fortunately, although the alternatives are limited, the permutations are many, and this suspense is usually enough. None the less, it is always convenient for an author to have another variation available, and in the nineteenth century the will was undeniably one. The will was a conventional manipulator of plot and character.

Secondly, the elegiac qualities of Tennyson's verse have already received comment: death, and its environs, was another acknowledged convention in nineteenth-century literature. Despite improvements in medical practice, many people died in their prime, and it is reasonable that literature should acknowledge this. Indeed, in a time of improving medical standards, such a death, though not unusual, is given an extra poignancy. Death was a theme of nineteenth-century literature in a way inconceivable now. There has almost been an exchange of taboos: in the nineteenth century sex was signified by three dots on the page; in the twentieth century we can write freely about sex. But in the twentieth century death has been marginalised; a modern '*In Memoriam*' would seem grotesque. Yet even as early as *Oliver Twist*, Dickens had no compunction about describing not only the funeral rites Oliver participated in, but also the sordid death of Oliver's mother; Queen Victoria spent the last forty years of her life in mourning. Death was a registered and acknowledged aspect of the age. The Victorians may have been reluctant to discuss the facts of life, but they had no such inhibitions about the facts of death. It is therefore inevitable that the will, as a concrete manifestation of death, should appear in so many novels.

And there is a third reason. The will is the operation of the dead on the living; it symbolises the role of the past in the way present and future develop. In Trollope's *The Warden*, in Eliot's *Middlemarch*, in Dickens's *Bleak House*, the will is not only a structural device, but also a metaphor for the dead hand of the past. And these are only a few examples from many: readers can supply their own. This metaphorical function is paramount. Novelists of quality do not necessarily accept the conventions of their society; it could be argued that a function of the creative artist is to provide a critique of the society in which they flourish. None the less, they are part of that society, and their quality can be measured not only by the skill of their writing and the accuracy of their characterisation and description, but also by the degree to which, consciously or unconsciously, they expose their period. The nineteenth century was a period in which temporality assumed great importance. The future was full of possibilities; the past was a path that led to Now. In Macaulay's history of England, the works of Marx and Engels, the conclusion to *War and Peace*, or popular interpretations of Darwinism, this awareness of time, of past, present and future, is at the fore. The will was a convention by which nineteenth-century novelists could incorporate this awareness into their fiction.

ibid., Ch. V, pp. 85–6

4

But ours is an uncertain age, and Jennifer Fox left no will.

Chapter Seven

LOVE'S LABOUR'S LOST

In which,
it being Sunday,
nothing much happens at all

In that refugee state between sleep and wakefulness Wendy put her long dressing gown on and walked to the bathroom. She turned on the light, sat down, released air and pee together. She dried herself and went to the sink. The floor was shockingly cold; the floor was shockingly wet. 'Bloody hell!' The hem of her dressing gown had soaked up some of the water, which made it heavy, clammy against her legs as she went back to the bedroom. 'John!'

He stirred a little. 'What time is it?' he asked, looking towards the clock.

It was eight. 'I think you'd better get up,' she told him.

'It's Sunday. Isn't it?'

'Just get up.'

Bewildered and naked he got out of bed. 'What's the matter?' He sat on the side of the bed and turned on the light.

'The bathroom floor's covered in water.'

'Oh shit.'

He stood and went to the door. She saw the whorls of dark hair on his shoulders and buttocks, the knobbled shadow of his spine. She got back in bed and heard him barefoot on the lobby carpet, feet slapping noisier on the bathroom's vinyl, a sucking sound as he trod in the water. 'Oh shit,' he repeated.

'That's right.' She picked up her book from the bedside table.

'I can't have tightened it enough,' he explained. 'I'm sorry, love. I'll clean it up.'

He was awake now and expecting her to ask what good cleaning up would do while the tap still leaked.

147

He was relieved she didn't.

He was worried she didn't.

He fetched a floorcloth from the kitchen and mopped at the edge of the spreading pool. She heard him moving about, irritating noises, and then he came back into the bedroom. 'I need the second spanner. From the back of the car.' She looked at her book, turned a deliberate page.

He found underpants, trousers, shoes and a shirt. He went outside. The streetlights were still on. The paperboy pushed his bicycle up the hill, rested it against a garden gate, walked up the short path to a neighbouring door and began pushing newspapers through the inadequate letterbox. John opened the car's hatchback. The metal was cold. The tailgate swung out and over his head. The paperboy climbed over the low wall to the next house, his awkward bag banging at his hip. Cold air fixed the morning, hugging sounds and smells to the earth. The toolbox was under the carpet, in a cavity with the spare wheel. John yawned a tuft of warm breath and wished he was wearing a jumper.

Wendy heard him come back in. She turned another page of Cruso's tale of love and deception:

Last night the storm, the bilious bulk, the bulge of the storm, deliberate, a skyful of portent, potent, power & glory. And: rain in the east; flash, dash, crash of cold lightning; chunder of thunder bundling the bellying clouds and then dark. Whilst today, in the dawn, the glutinous flat light, more frightening than lightning, more terror than tempest. He was stormed out, believing he had nothing for his father, not even anger.

John knelt on the cushioned vinyl floor and mopped up the water. He thought about his guilt and the way he had let her down. She did not seem to care he had let her down. She seemed to expect it. Perhaps he hadn't let her down. You can only let down someone who has faith in you. Perhaps she's lost faith. He squeezed the water down the lavatory bowl and went back to mop some more. He noticed the vinyl was curling at the edges beneath the pedestal of the sink and the paint on the pipes was bubbling and chalky. There was a rough aroma at floor level, a curry and human scent like cumin, the unnatural heaviness of pine disinfectant. He squeezed more water from the cloth. I must tell her I'm leaving Lanchester, he thought, as though to grab her falling faith.

And Wendy continued to read. Cruso's style was sometimes unnerving. Perhaps because he was not a native user he took especial pleasure in the textures of English, sheer sounds of words and their shapes. They were in the boy's room now:

Pinned to the wall: New York Yankees pennant, magazine photograph of Bondi Beach and the bondi blondes posing before the breakers, reproduction of Warhol's Monroe. The last stranger than moonbeams, Warhol's reproduction of Marilyn's artifice, thrown together after she was dead, reproduced again in offset litho, no screenprint blowjob here. My symbols, the boy thought, clashing like cymbals. And what use the cymbals without the orchestra? Reproduced Marilyn, Marilyn of the legendary abortions, Marilyn who never reproduced, Warhol's image more real than flesh for what was flesh? No tune he thought no tune.

She wanted to ask Alan about the book. She tried to characterise it, organise her thoughts for when Alan and she next met. There's a sort of clumsiness to the finish, like he's throwing all these words down and leaving the surface rough. She thought of a Rodin statue, the bronze still showing the worked crests and smears of the clay original. A Rodin statue is like a physical encounter, she decided: there's always violence there, the violence of the way he lumped the clay together. But against that there's the precision of the finished thing. The surface may be rough but the statues are recognisably finished. The thumb-prints for eyes, they're not mistakes nor carelessness, they're a necessary part of the statue. And Cruso's wordplay, his way of piling word on word, thought on thought, is the same sort of thing. The surface is rough but the form is complete and itself; the form has a sort of integrity.

She was pleased with this. She wished Alan was there. She wished Cruso was there. It was ridiculous. John had spoken with Cruso, gained nothing. God, she thought, I'd love to talk to Cruso, and John did and got nothing out of it. John's a jerk.

And then again: John's a jerk. The thought was numbing in its comprehensiveness. John's a jerk. She had never characterised him this way before. John's a jerk.

She heard him in the bathroom, mopping the floor. Water dripped into the toilet bowl from the cloth, a polyphonic variation on a familiar sound. John's a jerk. Love is sometimes like credit. Credit can be extended to cover all sorts of embarrassments; it can be withdrawn, be re-categorised, become a debt. John had no credit left with her. He was exposed and vulnerable. He was bankrupt. He was a jerk.

2

The house is tidy. I knew it would be. Chapman wanders between aimless rooms, straightening pictures and polishing small tables, but this is unnecessary work, work for the sake of working, and he understands this. The house is tidy. He makes a cup of coffee and lights a cigarette, then sits in the living room; he looks out through french windows at the small terrace and the lawn, the brick wall beyond and the trees. There is a grave beauty to the winter trees. The garden looks nice, he thinks, and: I was a lucky man.

After the war was over, in the aimless ration-book peace, he was returned to Wapping. He did not stay long: he joined the Junior Leaders' regiment, wore their braided coat and their busby, and then the infantry: Palestine, Borden Camp, Korea. I liked Palestine, he thinks, enjoyed the climate and the people. It felt like a job worth doing, a policing role, and I never felt unwanted there. Borden had been boring; Korea had been nasty. And then of course I was invalided out, and he flexes his toes involuntarily, as the physiotherapist had taught him, to keep the damaged muscle alert.

Jennifer was next, for I was a lucky man: two years in an Oxford boarding house while she lived in college, one furnished room and the weekends to look forward to, a drive in Jennifer's Morris, Cotswold hotels, Mr and Mrs Chapman in the register or sometimes we took other identities, Dr and Mrs Hare though she was the doctor, Mr and Mrs Clarke, and once, sheer bravado, Lord and Lady Fox. He could barely remember the house where he had boarded for two years but he knew the two-night hotels, the Plough at Cutsdean, the Queen's Head at Broadway, that place – what was its name? – on the A40 where water was fetched from a pump. He had a job then, selling motor cars for Finches of Cowley. Outside, a winter robin lands on the terrace, cocks its head, at him or its reflection in the french windows, and puffs up its chest.

He had enjoyed Oxford, but when Jennifer decided to move north, to be nearer her widowed mother, he had been happy with that too. Living together, setting up home, buying unfashionable old furniture and watching fashion catch up: it had been good. For years and years it had been good; I was a lucky man. Yet Wapping was always in mind, grey tenements that grew from grey streets, an ugly crop not worth the harvest. It makes no difference to him that the slums are pulled down now, replaced by des. res. or council flats, offices and printworks. Wapping is a place of the mind, a place so solid, so dense, he knows its gravity will one day pull him back. Everything else, even this seventeenth-century house, this medieval market town, is temporary in comparison. It's no real surprise I'm losing this place, he tells himself: it isn't even a disappointment. I have used the last of my luck.

He puts out the cigarette, takes the ash-tray through to the kitchen, drops the stub in the bin and rinses the ash-tray under the tap; he dries it and, as he had done for thirty-five years, puts it away. It is Sunday: he goes to the paper shop.

I like Chapman. I want to describe him. I want to describe him neatly, economically, which is the way he folds towels in the airing cupboard or knots his conservative ties.

The shop is on the corner. He visits every day. Ten Park Drive and an *Express*. Over the years the shop had changed hands and, though he does not know it, promoted him in ways the army never did. When he arrived in Bakewell, a warm welcoming day in 1954, white clouds wandering lonely as a poet over the wooded hills of the Haddon estate, brightness between the shadows of the streets, he was an invalid infantry sergeant, but the shop soon knew him as the Captain; when the Harpers took the shop over in 1962, and Chapman was older, more distinguished, he became the Major; to the Prakash family, who now run the shop, he is the Colonel.

He is unaware of this. He does not know people talk about him, is vaguely surprised to be recognised. He is Jennifer's guest, her friend, and she is dead; only in private was he ever her lover. He kept house for her, prompted by his army training, his respect for Jennifer's work, his gratitude he was there at all. His routines were governed by Jennifer's day. He made her breakfast before she drove into Sheffield; he made dinner for her when she returned. He did the washing on Tuesday and the ironing on Wednesday; each afternoon when the weather was fine he worked for an hour in the garden. Monday is market day in Bakewell, livestock mostly but with a motley camp-following of general stalls, clothes and fresh veg., olive green canopies on metal poles like an anarchic army camp, and he shopped there and in the local shops. He is popular, in a gentle fashion. He is a gentleman. He is that nice-looking gentleman in the tweed jacket with the military bearing, the striped tie, the striped shopping bag. When he had first arrived in Bakewell he had been exotic, but that was thirty-five years ago. He still thinks of Bakewell as Jennifer's home, he as her guest, but he lived there where she only slept. He still lives there; she is not sleeping but dead.

And though he has reached the rank of Colonel at the newsagents, he will never make it to General. For, despite his straight back and David Niven looks, he lacks the authority a General requires. He returns to the empty house. Black crows cross the open sky. Their wings beat open and shut, on and off, a semaphore, and brown leaves bustle in the gutter like a gust of brittle animals. It is warm for the time of year. The sky is inconsolable.

3

Alan awoke to an earlier year, to the desk where he had sat to revise for exams, to the models and books on the shelf. He was in his bedroom at his parents' house; he was in a museum to his youth and, like the things he saw, those he heard seemed to come from his past. Central heating gurgled gastrically and from the kitchen below was the echoed gush of a kettle being filled at the tap.

He got up, drew open the curtains and looked out, south, over the same flat sky Chapman saw. On the windowsill was a Panzer tank,

1:48 scale, impossibly small. Everything this museum preserved was a memorial to his last summer in Sheffield, the summer of 1979, the summer before London, university and work. Alan rotated the Panzer's turret, testing his emotions. Every time he came home, for weekends, for each Christmas up to the last, he felt these same sensations, the gratitude nothing had changed, for the world was unreliable but his room and his past were fixed, and the terror, as though this too tangible past might claw him back, fix him, ossify him. It was easy to imagine being ill here, AIDS, brain damage, dying in this shrine to himself.

The warmth from the radiator below the window was not quite adequate. He turned to get dressed. There were black-spined Asimov paperbacks on his shelf, *Foundation, Foundation and Empire, Second Foundation*; the series had been continued, but Alan's collection stopped there. Next were selected works of Michael Moorcock, enticing titles like *The Runestaff* and *Behold the Man*, and a couple of Fleming novels with even better titles, *The Man with the Golden Gun* and *From Russia with Love*. Bronowski's *The Ascent of Man*, large and illustrated, hard-backed, dwarfing the other books, was a present from his parents in the Christmas of 1976. And there were quainter exhibits: models of Spitfires and Mosquitos, a Churchill tank and a German armoured personnel carrier, 1:72 scale, even smaller than he remembered, as though he had continued to grow after leaving. Which, he conceded, in a way I have. He pulled on underpants and jeans. His socks, rolled into one another, held a spongy dampness so perhaps he hadn't dried them long enough. He picked up his toothbrush and went to the bathroom, finishing the inventory in his head.

He considered the records, tidily arranged, *Genesis* and *Yes, The Eagles* and *The Damned*, forgotten tastes and half-remembered times. He thought through the files of A-level notes on the desk, physics, chemistry and maths, photocopies of the periodic table neatly hole-punched, pages of calculus and circuit diagrams, friendly red ticks in the margin and the occasional glum cross. In the desk cupboard were other relics, a lacquered box from his grandmother's house, a box of plastic Airfix soldiers and a heap of old Airfix magazines, a pile of unlabelled cassettes. Somewhere in there too was a map of the land of Doria. The toothpaste was sharp and refreshing. The map was neatly drawn in red and black India ink, exotic ink for an exotic country, though Doria was based on this suburb of Dore where he had lived for eighteen years. He had been the Lord Alanstrøm and this house, number seventeen on the street, the seventeenth Mansion and Castle Gruafin. Causewayhead Road, the main road through the suburb, became the River Cassavé; his school was the Land of the Evil Eye from which only heroes return unscathed. Cruso was right, childhood is its own mythology. Alan spat toothpaste down the sink.

He went back to the bedroom. 'Is that you, Alan?' called his mother. 'Are you up?'

'Coming,' he called back. It was easy to imagine the last ten years gone, wished or washed away, lost in some irruption of the fabric of four-dimensional spacetime, his mother preparing breakfast downstairs and Dad having a shave, the Sex Pistols on the turntable but the stereo off, homework complete on the desk, Michael and Richard calling, lift to school in Dad's car. It was easy to imagine, and tempting too. The present cannot compete with the certainties of the past. *Literature in the Age of Certainty* lay face down, open, on the bedside cabinet. Perhaps, he wondered, Auntie Jennifer was wrong to characterise the nineteenth century as the age of certainty and this as the age of uncertainty? Her characterisation said less about those centuries than about the way each life is lived. Alan was no historian but he had a shrewd suspicion that the nineteenth century, the era in which God died, seemed at the time a most uncertain age; he could imagine a Victorian looking back to the eighteenth century, before the disruptions of Darwin and the French Revolution, with nostalgia. For the past is always simpler than the present. The past has been observed and fixed. Alan was a physicist. He pulled on his sweat-shirt and sat on the bed. 'Observed and fixed?' It was a phrase from quantum physics. Left to its own devices a sub-atomic particle behaves like a wave. A wave is indivisible: an electron orbits a nucleus, and were that nucleus the size of the sun the electron would simultaneously occupy an area larger than the solar system. But when we measure the electron it behaves differently: instead of being a wave it is a particle, in one position only; the wave, which contained the potential of all possible outcomes of the measurement, disappears; in the terminology of the discipline, the wavefunction collapses. This is patently bizarre, yet incontestable. The wave/particle duality does not accord with common sense or the way we perceive the world, yet it unerringly explains events at a sub-atomic scale. And though sub-atomic particles are mindbendingly small, they are the stuff of which all matter, you, me, Alan, the stars, the very light that comes from the stars, is made. A sub-atomic particle may be tiny, but the implications of its behaviour are vast.

Alan drew the obvious analogy – an observed electron is a particle, but an unobserved electron is a wave; the past is observed, but the present, unobserved, contains the potential of all possible outcomes as it orbits – and then let his thoughts carry on. For another bizarre characteristic of quantum theory is what is known, famously, as the uncertainty principle, according to which, although it is possible to measure either the position or the momentum of a sub-atomic particle, it is impossible to measure both. According to Heisenberg, author of the uncertainty principle, the more accurately the position is measured, the less accurately can we know the momentum, and vice versa; the possibilities are fixed, so that if for instance we could measure its position with infinite accuracy we would have absolutely no idea at all about its momentum. Nor is this an inadequacy of our measuring devices. Heisenberg deduced that uncertainty is inherent in the act of measurement itself, and no known or potential measuring device can overcome it; not a single experiment has been devised, much less performed, to dispute this.

'Your breakfast is on the table,' called his mother.

'I'm on my way.'

He looked at *Literature in the Age of Certainty*, face down on the bedside cabinet. That title may be simplistic, he thought, but I can't argue with the title of the companion volume, *Literature in the Age of Uncertainty*, for this is surely the age of uncertainty, and I have seen the equations to prove it. He went downstairs.

4

Wendy and John sit in the living room, reading separate sections of their Sunday paper, and the emergency plumber, £37 call-out fee,

£15 per hour or part thereof, whistles cheerfully in the bathroom and wonders how long he can spin this ten-minute job out while his mate, who sensibly filled the kettle before they turned the water off, mentions to Wendy that it is coffee time.

'Is it really?' she asks: 'Fancy that,' and John gets up and boils the kettle.

He knows he is being ripped off, but part of him doesn't mind. He hugs the irrational hope that if the plumbers punish him Wendy won't.

He takes a mug from the draining board and wipes it with a tea towel calendar, 1980, the year of their marriage. He pokes July into the pot cylinder, using their wedding day to wipe that awkward join between the side and bottom of the mug. He dries the second mug. 'Do you want coffee, love?' he calls.

He waits for a reply. 'If you're making it.'

He puts the mugs down by the kettle. The kettle is beginning to make noises. He needs two more mugs from the cupboard above the fridge. They hang by their handles from hooks like the dumpy round bags with big handles the men in white jackets take bowling. John and Wendy rarely have guests. Their friends and colleagues are spread across London and the commutable south-east. When they socialise they meet in pubs by convenient stations, drink up in time for the last train. Dave lives in Essex, on the Southend line from Fenchurch Street; Wanda lives in Bedford, travels from St Pancras; Mark Robbins is in Crawley, goes south from Victoria. No one comes back for coffee. He unhooks the mugs. There is a dead spider in one of them.

John rinses it under the tap. The tap spits a gout of water and makes a prolonged whine. He remembers the water is off and shuts down the tap. 'Water's off!' calls one of the plumbers. But there was enough to shift the dead spider. Incey-wincey spider, wash the spider out. It revolves in the steel bottom of the sink, pirouettes indecisively at the plug-hole edge, makes its mind up and goes down the drain.

5

Chapman folded the newspaper. There was nothing he wanted to read, nothing he wanted to do. No, he acknowledged, that's not true: I want to talk with Jennifer.

Were she buried he might visit her grave, think a conversation to her headstone. As it was it was as if she were nowhere, in a limbo more absolute than Purgatory. He had a sudden ill-fitting wish to have been to church that morning, said a prayer for her. He had made prayers on occasion, prayed once for the health of a broom in the garden and often for Jennifer's health, but he was a conventional man and these prayers did not count for him. Real prayer was something for church, and he had not been to church since the army. He had a sudden guilty sense that a real prayer, a church prayer, might have saved her.

Jennifer had no time for God. Yet he recalled something she had told him. 'There's sense in what Pascal said. "If God doesn't exist, and I believe in Him, there's no real loss, but if God does exist, and I don't believe in him, I'm in trouble." ' She had asked for a Christian burial. He thought about this, then realised only seven days had gone by since her talk of Pascal; the realisation was more immediate, more painful, than any thought about God.

A week ago she was alive. Three days ago she was alive. It was not right; it did not make sense to Chapman. The calendar might count off the days, yet between then when she was alive and now when she was dead was much more than a calendar can record.

Yet her death took no time at all. Moments, fractions of moments, that's all; the fluctuating graph by the bedside was stilled; there was someone in the room, and then there wasn't. Absolute precision about the moment of death depends on which of the body's functions are considered, but whichever way it was measured the clock continued to tick. Jennifer was alive at eight in the morning; by ten o'clock she was dead. At some moment or fraction of moment between those two times she died. The clock continued to tick.

Death took no time at all. Yet death lasts for ever. And the moments, minutes, hours are irrelevant. A week ago she was alive; three days ago she was alive. Yet her death, which lasts for ever, lay between then and Chapman, a wedge thrust into his calendar, awkward, unfathomable, there.

Then his head was in his hand and he was crying, his eyes squeezed tight, squeezing out useless tears. He had no control, no need for control, no one to impress. She is dead. The hand moves over his face, tugging at his hair, distorting his nose and upper lip, clenching, unclenching, writhing. His whole body is writhing. He is abandoned, abandoned in his grief, to his grief. There is no dignity to grief. It empties him like a wound. His stomach is hollow, his chest is a husk. She is dead. Greasy sobs work his nose and his throat. His hand clings to his thinning hair. She is dead, and the for ever of death outweighs him. He is unmanned and denied. He is nothing. And this room is nothing and this house and this world, emptied, squeezed tight like his face, wrung out in the flow of his tears. She is dead.

6

Alan lies on his bed, looking at *Literature in the Age of Certainty*. 'The will left by Casaubon in *Middlemarch* is, at the level of plot, a device to keep Ladislaw and Dorothea apart. At first sight it can also seem to emphasise Casaubon's selfishness and pettiness: disappointed in his hermetic ambition to devise a Key to all Mythologies, he obtains a perverse revenge by thwarting his widowed wife. Yet this is too narrow a view. After all, Casaubon was right, and Ladislaw was unsuitable for Dorothea.' Alan, who has never read *Middlemarch*, is uncertain what is meant by 'hermetic' in this context and cannot remember where Casaubon's will fits into the argument he had been reading the night before, returns the book to the bedside table and rolls on to his back.

The Key to all Mythologies: an attractive notion. Physics is full of similar notions, Great Universal Theories or GUTs, superstrings and quantum gravity, ideas that are meant to resolve all the problems, iron out all the discrepancies, elegantly answer our ultimate questions. But so far the attempts have failed. Quantum physics refuses to integrate with Einstein's relativity: there is one law for the very big and another for the very small, which offends. And Heisenberg's uncertainty principle puts a limit on our knowledge: we can know where a particle is or we can know what it is doing but we can't know both.

In classical physics the observer is irrelevant. The apple falls from

Newton's tree whether Newton is there or not. But quantum physics elevates the role of the observer; in quantum physics the act of observation actually effects a change. Quantum theory is essentially practical, an empirical system which successfully explains and predicts atomic and sub-atomic events. Yet it poses as many questions as it answers.

There is a well-known thought-experiment known as 'Schrödinger's Cat'. Schrödinger had devised an equation which describes the quantum state of a wave/particle duality. Schrödinger's equation holds good so long as no measurement is made: once a measurement is made things change drastically. This is weird, as Schrödinger recognised. He imagined a sealed container. In the container is a cat, and also a radioactive atom. There is a fifty-fifty chance of the atom decaying; if it does it will release a gamma ray, and the gamma ray, we are asked to imagine, will trigger a device that emits cyanide. There is therefore a fifty-fifty chance the cat will live. Outside the container is a physicist. He cannot observe what happens inside the container, and therefore, according to the rules of quantum mechanics, nothing happens. Schrödinger's equation holds and the wave does not become a particle. It would appear that the cat survives. But Schrödinger's equation actually contains the possibility – a linear superposition – of both the event taking place and not taking place, with the same fifty-fifty chance, and where does that leave the cat? According to the physicist the cat is in a linear superposition of being alive and being dead. This is not a medically recognised state.

It gets worse. Nothing happens until it is observed: from the physicist's point of view the decay that releases the gamma ray cannot occur until the box is opened; for an observer inside the container, such as the unfortunate cat, the decision between death and survival is made much earlier.

Can this be right? Death takes no time at all; death lasts for ever. But there is surely a moment of death for all that, and that moment is irreversible, that moment is absolute.

Schrödinger accepted this. His interpretation was that reality at the quantum level might be influenced by the observer, but that as things get bigger this ceases to apply, and by and large physicists go along with this. Schrödinger's equation, according to this view, does not apply to something as big and as complicated as a cat.

I suppose, thinks Alan, that most of philosophy has been about this: is reality inside us or outside? mind or matter? subjective or objective? Classical physics worked on the premise that reality is entirely external, out there, ready for us to examine and measure, analyse and explain. Quantum physics denies this. At least at the quantum scale, the observer is also creator; and of course, if this applies to things as fundamental as quantum particles, the things from which everything is made, it has implications for everything else.

Alan closes his eyes.

That peculiar construct we call reality is all to do with where things are, placing them and fixing them in space. That copy of *Literature in the Age of Certainty*, for instance, disloyally discarded by the side of my bed: it is real and fixed in space. Moreover, any attempt to communicate or translate that reality is doomed to failure. However closely I describe that book, open at page 86 but face down, so that the pages on the left are a pile 86 deep and the pages on the right a fatter pile, and with its dust jacket, a rather staid cream with the title and author's name in once-fashionable sans-serif lettering, standing slightly proud of the orange hard cover, I cannot compete with reality. I can develop my description *ad infinitum*, notice for instance that the dust jacket has a flaw down its back where it was creased once and straightened, and that the spine, exposed to sunlight, is a paler cream than the rest, or observe the way pages are not only split left and right, either side of the page I am on, but are also individualised, none quite the same size as its neighbour, so that the piled pages are also layered. I can describe all this, thought Alan, and not even come near to the reality. Apart from anything else, reality is apprehended simultaneously, whereas my language and therefore my description is linear. I can animate my description with resonant and startling words, use similes and metaphor, describe the pages as layers of stairs, expand as Cruso might, draw in the Battleship Potemkin and a pram cartwheeling down the wide steps of Odessa, or stick to naturalistic comparisons, note that the dust jacket, flattened because the book is open face down, raised above the hard cover, has the exact shape, seen end on, of a wire coat-hanger, but when I do this my representation, though more lively, moves further than ever from the thing as it is.

This is because, Alan concludes, my apprehension of the object corresponds, in Heisenberg's terms, with the 'where it is' side of quantum measurement; my representation is the other measurement, not 'where it is' but 'what it is doing'. My representation is a fiction – it can't show the thing as it is, in all its dimensions and its complexities, but it can say something of what it is doing. My fiction cannot compete with reality, but it is the other measurement and therefore just as valid. And that is why fiction is so important. That is why fiction is so necessary.

7

'What are we going to do this afternoon?' asked John: 'Love?' The word was a noun and a hopeful verb.

'I've my marking to do.'

'How long'll it take?'

'How should I know? If you're bored go for a walk or something.'

John looked out. His hope was broken. The winter sun stencilled the shadow of trees on the walls of neighbouring houses. 'Why not?' he said.

He walked between short gardens, parked cars, lamp posts and turds. Bay windows jutted towards him, their angled glass reflecting his approach, watching him pass, seeing him off. As his reflection disappeared from one window it appeared in the next, and the rhythm was repeated – ahead of him, alongside him, behind him – as though he were tagged by a team of experts. Some houses had kept the original Victorian panes that distorted his image and reduced him to pools of identity that shifted at his approach. Other windows had been replaced. Double-glazing ghosted his ghost, mock-Georgiana anatomised him, silly bottle-bottomed panes spun him as though on a centrifuge, splitting him to his constituent parts. He walked by the park. A low stone wall was studded with the remains of iron railings, but the railings had gone in the War Effort; behind the railings a weave of plastic-coated wire sagged where children climbed.

He turned at a gap in the wire. A short path of mud led into the grass. Its margins were littered with cigarette stubs, crisp packets, crushed polystyrene takeaway boxes. He felt the sun now, and saw his long shadow. There was a slatted bench nearby. It had once been gloss-painted and green, but now one end was blackened with fire and the rest carved or spray-painted. Tribal initials, lovers and teams, sprawled across the wood, and the top slat at the back was missing.

John sat down. He put his hands in his overcoat pockets. His green scarf hung loose either side of his neck. A group of skinny girls, curly hair and straight noses, went by, noticing him ostentatiously and giggling. Melancholy suited his dark features, which wasn't much consolation. Don't we ever get to make love these days? I'm sorry about the tap but don't we ever make love any more?

He stood and walked again. It was getting cooler now. He wandered towards the soccer pitches. A match was finishing and the players, muddied in scarlet and blue, walked to the cursory changing rooms. Two boys, sons of the players maybe, took possession of the ball and the field. One tackled the other and fired a wild shot that landed at John's feet.

John trapped the ball without thinking. The boys, separated by fifteen yards now, clamoured for the pass back. He feinted at the boy at the left and side-footed the ball to the boy at the right; the boy at the left made a challenge and the boy at the right returned the ball to John. Again he trapped it. The challenger turned to face him. John balanced himself carefully, weight slightly forward, ready to respond. The tackle came from the left; John saw it coming, slid the ball between his opponent's stretched legs, and was round him. The second boy now came for the challenge and John held him off too. 'Where's the goal?' he asked.

'Either end.'

'I'll take this one then. Hang on and I'll take off my coat.'

There were no showers in the changing room and the players were soon coming out. It was too early for the pub. They saw the lads playing football. John lent the game a kind of respectability. 'Pass, mate!' called one and John passed.

Soon they were divided in teams. John played hard. He was rusty but skilled in the air, and the diving header that scored the first goal was worth the stain on his jeans.

They played until dark. John went home, tired and content. 'Where on earth have you been?' Wendy asked. She saw mud on his face and his clothes. 'Are you all right?'

He could have made something of the moment of her worry. Instead he was happy and honest. 'Playing football,' he replied.

'Playing football!' Wendy was aghast. He really was a jerk.

He ran himself a bath. No water leaked from the tap. This was a good thing, he supposed, but in a way was not. He would have liked the leak to continue, to have confounded the experts, to prove it wasn't just him couldn't fix it. But what the hell. He felt good. Weary but good. He splashed herbal bath oil into the waters and lowered himself in. What the hell.

As a boy he played football a lot. It was not just the game, the victory and defeats. It was what boys did to make friends. He had always been bright and his parents ambitious. His dad had been a printer on the *Standard*, his mum had cleaned houses sometimes. They knew exactly what an education was worth: education wrote the words Dad printed, lived in the houses Mum cleaned. Mum and Dad bought him *Treasure* and then *Look and Learn*, intellectual papers for the intelligent child, no *Wizard* or *Beano* for John. And later of course *The Times*. He had respected them for it and known they were right, but this wasn't much help at school. At school being bright won little reward except from the teachers, and you weren't allowed to care what they thought. The Body Shop herbal bath oil reached under his skin. He remembered Israel Heath. Israel had been bright, played chess, worn glasses, been bullied. John had never helped. He knew he should feel shame about this, but some boys got bullied and others didn't. Israel was one of God's Chosen – God's Chosen Victims. John had liked him, sympathised with him even. But when Izzy hanged himself, aged fourteen and four months, John had felt bad about it but not guilty. Some boys got bullied, some boys wore glasses. The skill was to avoid the bullies, to do without glasses. The skill that counted was to play football well.

And John had been lucky. Healthy – his parents made sure he ate well – and quick on his feet, he had been centre forward of every school team for as long as they had played in teams. His parents even watched him play, Mum every week, Dad when it was a Saturday morning game and he wasn't working, which would have been embarrassing if they hadn't been such good people. Everyone liked his mum and dad. Andy Johnson, the skinhead on the side, who hated everyone, still used to talk about the Rangers with Dad; Roger Southall, Sooty, who was black and a winger and once did a trial for Arsenal, used to tell John how much he liked to talk with Mum; Dave Geary, who had signed with Chelsea and still played professional football somewhere, Wigan or Bolton or somewhere up north, listened to Dad's advice about early passing like it was Don Revie talking, not Dad.

And why not? They were good people, my mum and dad. Good people. The best.

He was lying with his mouth absently below water, breathing in through his nose and blowing out bubbles. They were the best parents in the world. They really were. They looked after me, encouraged me, laid down an example of work and good behaviour.

And Wendy? We met in 1978, just after my father's death. We shared a kind of mourning, for she still missed her father. But her father had left her mother and left her. My dad was with us till the end, and when Mum died within a year it wasn't to desert me but to be with him: I know that at any rate. And Wendy?

He climbed out of the bath, towelled himself, put on his Marks and Spencer towelling gown. Poor Wendy: he felt loyal and that she needed his loyalty. He went through to the living room. She had finished her book and was watching TV. He made to kiss her and she ducked irritably. 'I'm watching telly,' she said.

He watched too. Nothing happened.

8

Chapman went to church. The church was three-quarters empty. A tune rumbled through the organ. Chapman found a pew at the back and waited for the service to begin.

The last of the day came through the windows, and the stained glass transformed the light as music transforms sound, making it ordered, elusive, spectacular. Chapman wore his black tie. The stately graph of organ pipes was the colour of bone. Chapman copied what his neighbours did and knelt. The hassock resisted his

weight. On the shelf in front of him were hymn books, prayer
books. He needed something to say. 'Our Father which art in
heaven,' he began, mouthing the words but making no sound,
'hallowed be thy name. Thy kingdom come. Thy will be done, on
earth as it is in heaven.' The words, learnt in childhood, came easily,
but they meant no more to Chapman than other words he had learnt
at that age – Polly put the kettle on, once I caught a fish alive, went to
sea in a baked potato and all fall down. He looked round. Some of
the congregation were sitting up but most were still on their knees.
The organ rumbled through a tune. He opened the prayer book.
'The days of our age are threescore years and ten; and though men
be so strong that they come to fourscore years: yet is their strength
then but labour and sorrow; so soon passeth it away, and we are
gone.' Chapman was fifty-eight. He turned more pages. It was
getting dark. He thought he was looking for references to death, for
a prayer for the dead maybe, some standardised expression of his
woolly desire to do the best he could for Jennifer's soul. But perhaps
he was looking for distraction. 'Thou art a Priest for ever after the
order of Melchisedech,' he read, and the wonderful word pleased
him.

Artificial lights were switched on; the organ became insistent and
the congregation stood. Bridget fitted the last piece of her jigsaw.
The choir began to sing. 'Done,' said Bridget. Alan and Ernest came
over and looked. The church was full of music, the harmonies of
grace. A silver cross led a procession of blue cassock, lace, the
peeping toe-ends of comfortable shoes. 'Beautiful,' said Ernest:
'Fifteenth century?' Jennifer stood at the gates of heaven and St
Peter wouldn't let her in. 'Fourteen-nine,' said Alan, reading the
box; 'I thought as much,' said Ernest.

'Anyone want a cup of tea?' asked Bridget.

Alan and Ernest admired the picture and in the kitchen the kettle
boiled. 'Does it say how big the original page is?' asked Ernest. Alan
consulted the box again. 'Forty by thirty centimetres,' he said. 'This
must be full-size then,' said Ernest; 'Must be,' agreed his son. 'It's a
lovely picture,' said Ernest. 'Must have been a devil to do.'

Bridget returned, with the teapot under a cosy and cups and
saucers on a tray. 'Help yourself,' she said. She lifted the jigsaw on
its board and tilted it toward the box. The picture began to slide; at

the edge of the board it buckled and broke. Heraldic pennons tumbled. Ornate scrolls of leaf and stem became cardboard shards, rattling in a cardboard box. The picture shattered slowly, heaven's gate opening on to the pinholed backing sheet of Ernest's old drawing board, the Latin text crumbling, becoming fragments in a heap. Some pieces were face up, brilliant, the rest face down and grey, leaves from a tragic fall. Chapman straightened his back, straightened his tie, and sang. 'Who's going to pour?' asked Bridget.

And outside it was cold and dark. I think of Cruso's description from *Orchestra without Violins*. The moon was lost in cloud, and then the moon had won, frost haloed, a blessing, while beneath its fond light the landscape was dark and a polka of dots, dots of life, dots of light, spreading unevenly in every direction. Houselamps, headlamps, streetlamps: a demography pricked from the darkness, clumping densely for the towns and cities, scattered over fields and parishes. Car-lights sprayed hedges and corners. A revolving blue flash scudded toward the hospital. Spotlit belltowers reared up between tower blocks that were random brightness between illuminated stairwells and television masts winked warnings to planes. The planes climbed high, became no more than lights themselves, lines of lighted windows and sparks of colour on the wings, then sparks of colour only until they reached the swollen clouds, where the last of the lights was lost and there was only the gathered dark. And then the plane came through the clouds to the stars. Once people saw men in the stars, Orion and sacred twins, but our terms of reference have changed and now the stars are inverted cities, eternal cities, hanging in the darkness above us, following us in our flight.

Anne-Marie's plane was coming down, landing at Heathrow. The descent hurt her ears and her jaw. A jumbo jet, the plane jerked slightly as it touched the runway, and the reverse-thrust whined. Just as it seemed to be stopping the engine note fell away and they taxied toward the terminal. Hello England, thought Anne-Marie. It started to rain.

Chapter Eight

ON THE TWENTIETH CENTURY
Which is surprisingly concerned with Love

I

It started to rain, slow fictional rain that bounced noisily on the roofs of the plane and banded in the gutters at the runway's edge, hard imaginary rain that made a pox of illuminated spots on the mean aircraft window, dull fictitious rain that was drops of brightness descending yet made the dark night darker.

These are words to invoke the rain: in an earlier century I might have been thought a witch, dangled on a ducking-stool in the Wye at Bakewell, dipped like a teabag until I was done. Instead I am here in the comfortable bed, and my suffering and its cause are not so very different.

I suppose I'm trying for humour, but my jokes are bitter these days. Ask the doctor. Still, it will give them something to tell one another; 'Kept a sense of humour to the end,' they can say. They like to have something cheerful to say, the ones who are left, the mourners.

2

The word 'fact' comes from the Latin *factum*, a neuter form of *facere*, to do or to make; combined with the Portuguese *feitoria* it also gives us the word factory. So when Mr Gradgrind claims that facts alone are wanted in the industrial age he may display his prejudices but he also shows an instinctive grasp of etymology. 'Fact' = to make.

The root of 'fiction' is not dissimilar. It is derived from the Latin *fictilis*, the fashioning of pots; it probably reached us via the French *fictif*, or not genuine. 'Fiction' also = to make.

Not that this means much. The derivation of words is a parlour game; it has little to do with what words come to mean. 'Quark', a term used for the sub-sub-atomic particles which make up a sub-atomic particle, is a literate joke by Murray Gell-Mann: 'Three quarks for Muster Mark,' says Joyce in *Finnegans Wake*, but, since Gell-Mann made his joke, theory has required a fourth quark. 'Fascist' comes from the plural of the Latin *fascis*, bundle; Mussolini used it first as a symbol and only later as a name; somehow the English equivalent, bundle-ist, does not have the same ring. 'Epicurian' meant one of simple tastes; only irony has given it its current meaning. So the fact that the original meaning of fact is much the same as that of fiction, though useful to my argument, is not necessarily significant. Current meanings are what count.

What are facts? Fact is indisputable. The Second World War began on 3 September 1939; Alan Gruafin was born on 1 September 1961. These facts are verifiable; they cannot be challenged.

But facts depend on your point of view. Einstein's theory of special relativity demonstrates that what time it is depends on where you are and where you are going. For you and me, on this earth and going this fast, relativity is not a problem: we can agree about the time. But photons, whizzing about space at the speed of light, could never agree; their clocks would all be different, to mine, yours, and one another's. The Germans invaded Poland on 1 September, so for a Pole the war started earlier; Alan was not born on the twenty-second anniversary of this event because he is a figment of my imagination.

It would be wrong to be over-reductive. There are facts. Auschwitz happened and so did Hiroshima. Thackeray wrote *Vanity Fair*. The most wonderful history since Gibbon is Fernand Braudel's *Civilization and Capitalism 16th–18th Century*, a book composed almost entirely of authenticated evidence. But bare facts tell us so little. Primo Levi's description of Auschwitz is more immediate, and therefore more real, than the facts or the statistics. His was not a typical experience. For one thing, he survived. Induction, expanding from the small to the big, from Levi's experience to that of all the prisoners of Auschwitz, would give a most inaccurate picture when set against the documented evidence. Yet Levi's description beggars all other description.

Likewise *Vanity Fair*. The reality of *Vanity Fair* lies between the covers. Neither the bleak facts of its date of composition nor Jennifer Fox's exegesis can compete with Thackeray's novel. And so also Braudel's history. It is a historian's duty to start from the facts; it is a historian's genius to extrapolate from them.

Gradgrind never existed. He was created by Charles Dickens. Yet he exemplifies better than any factual character a factual attitude to fact. If facts alone were wanted we would be quite different creatures. We need our stories as well.

3

We need our stories as well, but there are fashions to the way we tell them. The form of the European novel known as realist has a number of characteristics. It shows a cross-section of society; it takes place in a world as close as the author's pen can describe to the world where the author lives; it refuses to sentimentalise. Realism is a quintessentially nineteenth-century phenomenon, and quintessentially French; that century's material confidence and spiritual despair, mirrored magnificently in Stendhal's *Le Rouge et le Noir*, combined with that unflagging advance of 'progress' which could be measured in statistics or in flags on the world map, created both an interest in the world as it was and a faith in exposition. But, as the nineteenth century eclipsed nature and turned romanticism into an indulgence, so the twentieth century denied realism.

There were undoubtedly many reasons. The defeat of the French armies at Verdun made the world-as-it-was a less attractive place; the discipline of sociology, with its aggregate approach to society, made the novel an unscientific medium for describing the human condition; the new science of psychology, and the development of relativity, suggested that objectivity was beyond human capabilities. But surely the fundamental reason realism petered out was that it could not keep up.

'I wonder if perhaps our whole generation, and maybe the one before as well, has felt something a bit like that,' wrote Jennifer Fox: 'That the world is going too fast.' New methods of transport, first the train, later the aeroplane and automobile, demanded new methods of exposition. New methods of warfare, aerial bombardment, the machine gun, seemed too quick and comprehensive for conventional description. And new methods of recording – the camera, and then film and magnetic tape – made the written word seem redundant.

Nor was literature the only medium to suffer. All the arts suffered similarly. Paintings retreated into abstraction; music into noise. There was a general and not unreasonable feeling that the traditional methods of representing the world simply could not cope with the twentieth century: modernism was a collapse of confidence in the means of representation.

The very best, of course, retained their confidence. Picasso was challenged by the twentieth century but he was not intimidated; his constant innovation was a result not of despair but of certainty; he never doubted his art was capable of expressing his age. Unfortunately, his stylistic innovations were easier to imitate than his confidence: novelty became more important than quality. There are a number of reasons for this. The best painters, Picasso, Matisse, Gris, made experiment seem not just respectable but also essential, while denying objectivity seemed also to deny objective criteria of quality; the apparent inability of the arts to capture the world as it actually is made novelty the best many dared try for. And the twentieth century encouraged – expected – innovation. As planes got bigger and cars got faster, buildings taller and bombs deadlier, artists looked for an art that would reflect not stasis but change. Jennifer Fox called it *The Age of Uncertainty*, but this is a simplification: in its expectations it was an age of enormous confidence, and it took enormous cataclysms to knock that confidence – two world wars, two atom bombs, Auschwitz, Suez, Vietnam and global warming.

For music the situation was in many ways similar to that of the visual arts. Again, traditional methods did not seem adequate to cope with the new age, and again novelty was given a spurious authority. In the twentieth century, however, two things distinguish the history of music. One is the development of new recording and broadcasting techniques, which made music available to all and gave it a central position in the life of the century. The other is that though the harmonies of classical music may have seemed irrelevant to the discordant modern age, an alternative tradition, less developed maybe, but certainly vital, was available: jazz.

A suggestion. The appeal of music is that it operates in the same way as the brain. The movement of thought, in the form of electrical charges, through the synapses, shares with music both its linear quality and its multiplicity. The mind can keep up with the theme on the horns whilst the violins play another tune because the mind is designed that way: music is modelled on the mind.

And if music mirrors the workings of the brain, jazz mirrors the mind when stimulated, by drugs or drink or sex. Jazz could not encapsulate the whole century, maybe, but at last it provided a viable accompaniment to our methods of escape, and because of that it could never be redundant.

Literature too did not suffer quite as much as the visual arts, but unlike music this was not because it found some new direction. On the contrary, it was writing's inability to find new directions that proved its salvation. Abstract music is noise, abstract painting is shape and colour, but there is no such thing as abstract literature; literature was prevented from disappearing up its own backside because it uses words, and words resist abstraction. It is possible to avoid an association between a noise, a shape, or a colour and the concrete world, but words do not have this quality. Abstract formations of letters can of course be created easily enough – esabalob, gry-thumkyn, abooo – but these are not words.

Ernest, knowing the artist, once bought an abstract painting. To him it looks a bit like a hammer; Bridget, who dislikes it, calls it 'that bloody blue tree'; one of Alan's friends once described it as 'a headless monk waving his arms about', which is how Alan still thinks of it: none of these descriptions is definitive but all are valid. There is no literary equivalent.

One abstract formation of letters amongst a page of conventional words might suggest something: possibly onomatopoeia or association could dig out some meaning for esabalob or abooo. But if this happened then the word would no longer be abstract. And imagine a page of such words. Unlike Ernest's headless monk waving his arms about, which is at least readily assimilated, such a page would be well-nigh unreadable, and without the slightest claim on our attention save a soon-lost novelty.

But what then should the artist attempt? The notion of artist, in the sense we now use it, is essentially romantic. The romantic artist is more than a dedicated craftsman: the romantic artist is creator of something which is of greater value than the material world. Indeed, the stereotype romantic artist eschews materialism, lives in a garret, dies young of consumption, is appreciated only when dead. According to the romantic ideal, it is that artist who provides the symbols of the age and the essence of humanity. But the icons of the twentieth century – despite 'Guernica' and *The Waste Land* – have nothing to do with romantic artists. The twentieth century is to be found in the Empire State building, the mushroom cloud, the view of the earth from Apollo 11, that searing photograph of the naked Vietnamese girl fleeing a napalm attack. Nor should this surprise us, for such symbols of earlier ages as the pyramids or the medieval cathedrals are equally anonymous. Perhaps it was romanticism that was the aberration, and now the romantic artist is finished, gone the way of the steam train and the biplane, becoming like them the province of enthusiasts only? Am I, pen in hand, trying to compress a world into words, outmoded? Modernism, with its lack of confidence in traditional means of representation, suggests as much. I sit up in bed, my notebook open. The twentieth century bangs shut like a stable door. I struggle to turn my perceptions into ideas, my ideas into arguments, my arguments into words. I often feel I am wasting my time, my strength, and God knows I have little enough of either.

I often feel that way, yet still I carry on. In Islam first there is marriage, then there is love. In the West it is the other way round. Yet we know, we have always known, that romantic love is a chimera. It has no foundation in reality; we create it in our heads. It is based on such slight things, the way someone laughs at our jokes, the way they incline their head. Romantic love is ephemera and delusion.

Yet rationality offers no solace. Our reasoning is always reductive. We cannot reason a reason for life. Life is nasty, brutish and short. We are born, if we are lucky we reproduce, and then we die. Reason will uncover no meaning.

So we might as well stick with romance. I am not a Muslim, I am a fond and foolish lover, loving the world in which I live for no better reason than that it is there to be loved, aware that I have created that world in my head and therefore desperate to write it down, give it substance. And because I am a lover, fond and foolish, and know a little of love, I can see the world in these terms too. Romanticism and classicism, romance and rationality, individualism and collectivism, invention and reality, the world inside and the world without: they are fond and foolish lovers, inextricably, inexplicably entwined. I write in despite of reason, I live in denial of death.

And who am I? In conventional mathematical notation i is the square root of minus one. A minus cannot have a square – any number multiplied by itself gives a positive – and therefore the square root of minus one is purely conjectural. Yet despite this our imaginary i has tangible uses. It is part of Schrödinger's wave equation, describing the behaviour of unobserved sub-atomic particles; it is used in Euler's formula, which is the basis of trigonometry; it is an element in the equation which gives us the amazing Mandelbrot set, that astounding computer-generated figure which reproduces its details at any magnification and which, for all its genesis in mathematical conjecture, is undeniably, reproducibly *there*.

Perhaps it doesn't matter *who* I am, it only matters *that* I am. I AM!

Chapter Nine

AS YOU LIKE IT

*In which Alan thinks of Anne-Marie
and Chapman views a corpse*

I

Anne-Marie took the underground from the airport. As a student she had sometimes played her flute in the tiled tunnels, Mozart and Haydn usually, enjoying the enamel acoustics and the reward of copper hitting copper in her case. There are no seasons on the underground, she knew, nor is there day and night: time is slow periods and rushes, the first train and the last. But the indicator boards were blank and her watch still set for Tampa, so she felt as if she had ducked right out of time. The train could be seconds or hours away. It could be any hour of any day of any year. Other passengers waiting for the long ride from the airport to the city shared her jet-lag and dislocation, but shared nothing else. Anne-Marie knew they were fellow travellers for each stood in a mound of luggage. Businessmen in business suits, lightweight Arabs, flamboyantly wrapped Africans, tourists slung with cameras: the only conversation came from a conference of labelled Japanese, speaking amongst themselves, animated and incomprehensible. Limbo was international as well as timeless, she decided, which was an orthodox eschatology.

The train arrived, ploughing a push of air that chilled the platform and shifted the garbage. The carriages plugged the gaps in the platform and gave the station function. She stood at a pair of doors; they waited long enough to be inhospitable, not long enough to be downright rude, before opening. An African, his skin burnished a noble colour that was almost purple, followed her in. The train left the way it had come. The African sat down and read a newspaper in French; Anne-Marie had a copy of the *New Yorker* she had bought in Islington for the journey out. She had read it four times, cover to cover. She still did not understand the cartoons.

2

'You don't need the car today?' asked Wendy. It was the first thing she had said since they got up; John was looking forward to getting to work.

'No,' he said. At least at work he felt useful.

'Good. We'd better get off then. Finish your toast in the car.'

Yes miss, thought John.

They locked and left their flat. Wendy drove John to the station. 'Anything special happening today?' he asked her.

The question irritated. It always did. 'Not that I know of,' she replied. What did he expect to happen? If I'm lucky we might have a fire alarm to break the routine, if I'm unlucky 2H will arrive from swimming in dribs and drabs and the lesson'll get off to a lousy start. 'You?'

'Not really. I've got to check Siobahn's sorted Cruso's schedule, and I've lunch with Malcolm Dormie. There's a photographer from the *Sunday Express* of all papers wants to get some shots of Malc, so we've got to run over to a studio in Earls Court. And Robert's got a manuscript he wants me to look at, see if I can see an angle.'

'Tough day,' she said.

'No more than usual,' he replied, missing the sarcasm.

'That reminds me,' she said. 'Has Robert looked at Jim Hamilton's stories yet?'

'I've no idea. I'll mention it if you like.'

'Do.'

They reached the station. She stopped the car. He leant over and kissed her. 'See you tonight.'

'Okay. Bye.'

'Bye.'

He really has no idea, she thought: he really has no idea how much I envy him.

She was right. She was a decent teacher, John knew: no crises in the classroom, no riots or major rows; she was a teacher, and he never questioned what that meant to her.

John was neither insensitive nor foolish, but his parameters were different. John's parents, ill educated, respected education. John had been brought up to look up to teachers. His own job was ephemeral, a source of income. He was a seller of books to the trade. A teacher was someone special.

Teachers were viewed differently in Wendy's family. Teachers lived in semis, and Wendy's house was detached. She had never desired to teach. Teachers weren't special at all. But Wendy liked books, read English at university, and afterwards, newly married, had needed something to do. A year's teacher training was not unattractive, a way of postponing the decision about her future, but once there, having been swept into the competition to find teaching posts, she had got herself a job. And that was that. She couldn't stop work: it seemed hard enough to make both ends meet on two salaries, and what else could she do? She sometimes wondered if John could find her a job in publishing, which she was sure she would enjoy, but she never asked about it. To ask would be to admit to John that she had made a mistake. She hated admitting mistakes.

The tube rattled south, went underground. Wendy turned into the staff car-park. It must be nice being a teacher, thought John.

3

Professor Jardine turned the clipped pages of his Filofax: 'Obit – Jenny. Contact Williams, Extr.' It was nine o'clock, a little early to phone Dr Williams. He went through to what they called the computer room, where two cheap Amstrads and a BBC computer were stationed, to write the obituary of Jennifer Fox he had promised the *Independent*; the novelty, and flattery, of being asked to write for a national newspaper had worn off, and now, with the term starting next week and a desk full of problems, he regretted taking it on. Still . . . He took a disc from his briefcase and put it into one of the Amstrads. The venetian blind of green and black stripes fell, announcing the disc was being read, and then the start-the-day menu came up. He changed discs and pressed the *f1* key; at once the new menu came up. The document he wanted was called JENFOX. He pressed the E key and entered the document.

The basic information was there: date of birth, graduation, fellowships, honours and publications, taken from the staff files. Having nothing yet to write, he read; ingenious interpretation was his job, and he looked through the dates for some key to what he might say. BA (Oxon.) 1943; D.Phil. (Oxon.) 1952. Oxbridge graduates are promoted to MA twenty-one terms after graduation – an automatic bonus Jardine, whose Scottish MA had been earned with an extra year's study, resented – but there was no record of Jennifer Fox having received hers; neither did Jenny seem to have a B.Litt., the usual preface to research at Oxford. This seems a bit unconventional, thought Jardine, but then Jenny could be unconventional too: I might be able to use this.

He thought again. He supervised graduate students: some of them wanted to base their theses on this kind of speculation; Jardine was a better scholar. He needed evidence, but was too young to know the facts. Perhaps in those messy post-war years it wasn't at all unusual to go straight into a doctorate. How should I know? he asked himself: I was still at school when Jenny became a D.Phil. Or perhaps she just didn't bother mentioning an MA and B.Litt. on the accurate grounds that both were subsumed in her recorded degrees? Jardine sat back. He had recently had a student who, looking for evidence that Virginia Woolf had been molested as a child, had uncovered a bit of doggerel:

> There was a girl in a mountain pen
> Had it off with a fountain-pen,
> And they called the bastard Stephen,
> They called the bastard Stephen
> They called the bastard Stephen
> Because it pissed out blue black ink.

According to the student's account, this was a reference to Woolf's half-brother G. K. Stephen, his penis a 'fountain-pen' because he came from a literary family; she used it as testimony to Stephen's notoriety. But Jardine had been in the St Andrews First

XV: he had sung the same song in the bath after matches, although with slightly different words, and knew they called the bastard Stephen 'Because that was the name of the ink'. The student was too young to remember Stephens ink, maybe: on such are reputations won and lost, and though he was impressed by the student's inventiveness he was depressed to realise that there must have been several similar occasions when he had failed to spot such errors; on bad days he suspected the whole of literary criticism might be based on cunning fancy.

To his annoyance he realised he was dwelling on this incident because he felt like questioning Jennifer Fox's famous book, *Shakespeare's Great Theme*, on similar lines. An obituary is no place to ask questions: what was wanted was a brief summary of her career and her significance. The cursor flashed its question at the top of the screen: I'm ready, it told him, so what do you want to say? He scratched his neck through his beard and thought.

The argument of *Shakespeare's Great Theme* was plausible enough, he decided. She had begun with two characters, both called Antonio. One is the sea captain in *Twelfth Night* who risks his life for his friend Sebastian; the other is the merchant in *The Merchant of Venice* who nearly loses a pound of flesh. Both are selfless characters; at the end of each play, neither receives much in the way of reward, or even acknowledgment, for their sacrifice: it is always others who win the girl.

From this she went on to look at the character of the narrator of the Sonnets. The Sonnets are often seen to be Shakespeare's most personal work, and Jennifer went along with this interpretation. The Sonnets describe, through cameos rather than coherent narrative, how the writer loves a boy and has a 'dark lady' as his mistress; eventually the boy wins the dark lady, and the author retires with regrets but good grace. The boy is out of his reach because of his sex – these are not homoerotic poems, and the author wishes the boy were a girl so their love could be consummated, rather than wishing for sodomy – and the dark lady is – reasonably, in the narrator's judgment – dazzled by the boy. In this view, then, Shakespeare loses twice, and Jenny drew parallels between this situation and that of the two Antonios, suggesting Shakespeare identified more closely with them than with any other character.

Next she looked at the name Antonio. St Anthony was attacked by temptation, and survived; the Roman Antony was lover of the most famous dark lady of all. It's a good argument, Jardine conceded, and according to Jennifer's version *Antony and Cleopatra*, about a man who fails to do his duty because of love, contains another, rather hyperbolic, identification between Shakespeare and an Antony, and a warning about what might have happened to Shakespeare's career had he continued to pursue the dark lady. Renunciation, giving something up, is essential to happiness.

Jardine had doubts, though the argument was robust and the writing persuasive, about the *Antony and Cleopatra* theory: although he was no Shakespeare expert, he rather suspected that *Antony and Cleopatra* was simply a jobbing playwright's inevitable sequel to his successful *Julius Caesar*, and though to some extent Jennifer had pre-empted this criticism by drawing attention to the undeniably great stylistic differences between the two plays, he was still sceptical.

Shakespeare's Great Theme then continued with an examination of the major tragedies in the light of the notion that 'renunciation is essential to happiness'. She noted how King Lear has to give up everything – first the power of kingship, then its trappings, and finally his sanity – before he can be reconciled, albeit briefly, with Cordelia; she showed how Macbeth is at his most sympathetic and memorable when he relinquishes his pretensions in the 'Tomorrow and tomorrow and tomorrow' speech, and how Othello too wins the audience's sympathy with his beautifully understated 'I have done the state some service'. *Hamlet* she treated differently: *Hamlet*, she suggested, was a play about wasted potential, inspired by a different autobiographical experience; *Hamlet* was a response to the death of Shakespeare's son Hamnet.

Her final study was of Shakespeare's final Antonio, in *The Tempest*. This Antonio is the schemer and traitor who usurped the Dukedom of Milan from his brother Prospero; he is far from the self-effacingly generous Antonios previously encountered. Yet according to the thesis of *Shakespeare's Great Theme*, he too is more closely identified with Shakespeare than is any other character in the play: he is observer and planner; his intellect, unlike that of Gonzalo and, even more obviously, Prospero, is of a practical nature. *The*

Tempest, in this view, is something of a summation of Shakespeare's career: Shakespeare was a man of vision, a conjurer, a man of words; he was also a practical man, the successful plaintiff in several attempts to enclose the common land, the man who left his wife his second-best bed. In *The Tempest*, according to Jenny, Prospero and Antonio represent these sides of his character: Prospero gets the plaudits and the best lines, but to redress the balance somewhat the usurper is given Shakespeare's favoured name of Antonio. At the end of the play Antonio gives up his authority as Prospero gives up his magic.

The book concluded with the statement that 'Giving something up is a rehearsal for death': this, according to Jennifer, was Shakespeare's Great Theme.

Oh, it all hangs together, thought Jardine. I just wish I liked it: I can't help feeling this biographical account would either work better if we knew more about Shakespeare, or would fail altogether; the amount of information we have permits all manner of speculation and no certainty. It would certainly have helped her argument had Shakespeare had a brother. I wonder if Jenny had her doubts too: it's strange that after the success of *Shakespeare's Great Theme* she didn't concentrate on Shakespeare, develop her reputation and expertise; instead she moved on almost at once to nineteenth- and twentieth-century literature. Perhaps she wasn't happy with *Shakespeare's Great Theme* either? Still, I'll give Jenny her due: at least she challenges the big issues, in this and all her books; too much criticism is about pettyfogging details or pettyfogging authors. It's the fault of the doctoral system, I suppose: the student has to engage in original research, which nearly always means something so trivial it hasn't been done before; to get a grant he or she has to give a description of the results expected from the next three years' research, which rather negates the point of the research in the first place; to get the degree the student is examined by people who, simply because the doctorate must be original, cannot know as much about the subject as the student does.

The worst thing is that, once embarked, there is shame in admitting a mistake. I've known at least a dozen students who have produced perfectly plausible proposals that have come to nothing. Usually the problem is the 'influence' question. One student, one of my colleagues', actually, rather than one of mine, wanted to do a doctorate on the influence of Post-Impressionist painting on Virginia Woolf – it's funny how Woolf's name crops up so often with dodgy doctorates, almost as if the student attracted to her is naturally muddle-headed – and spent twelve months discovering that, although her great friend Roger Fry had organised the first Post-Impressionist exhibition in England, and although her sister Vanessa, her sister's husband Clive Bell, and her sister's lover Duncan Grant had all been intimately involved in it, Woolf's own sense of art appreciation never got beyond the 'but I know what I like' level. The student was in a mess. If she abandoned the thesis there would be disgrace and even the possibility of having to pay back the grant; none the less, she had proved something useful, which is that writers are influenced by what they read more than by anything else. Unfortunately, the latter conclusion, though unimpeachable, was insufficient for a doctorate, so she did what the system demands: she bullshitted, and passed. I knew what was happening. I was head of department; it was my job to know. But I turned a blind eye. The whole system is geared to bullshit. If some real criticism gets done, some real scholarship, it's more or less by chance.

Jardine looked at his watch. Christ: half-ten! And I still haven't written a thing. But it isn't easy. I don't want to mention my reservations about *Shakespeare's Great Theme*, but on the other hand – I come to bury Caesar, not praise him – I don't want to give the impression I endorse everything she wrote. It's hard.

It was not as hard as he thought. Had he written for a national paper before he would have lost this sense of a waiting world ready to pounce on his every word. A daily paper is an ephemeral thing; yesterday's newspaper is yesterday's news. He need not have worried so much.

He got up from the keyboard and went into the secretaries' office. 'Any coffee on, Ann?' he asked.

'Oh, you were in there. I've been trying to get hold of you. There's been a couple of calls. Dr Williams phoned from Exeter.'

'About the conference? I'll get back to him straight away. I've got his number. What was the other?'

'A man from Lanchester Press wanted to know the time of Dr Fox's funeral.'

'You told him?'

'Yes. Poor Dr Fox.' Ann got up and turned the kettle on. It was a squat, old-fashioned kettle, the kind that doesn't switch itself off. 'If it'd been term time we could have had a collection, got some flowers,' she continued as she spooned instant coffee into mismatched mugs.

'That would have been nice,' agreed Jardine. 'She'd been here a long time.'

'Longer than any of us, I expect.'

'I know.' Jardine rubbed his beard again; Ann thought it a rather silly gesture that made him look like he had nits. 'We really ought to arrange something for her I suppose, but there's been no time, with the vacation and everything.'

'What sort of something?' From the moment he had arrived Jardine had cultivated good relations with the office staff: they knew the place better than anyone. 'A wake?'

The kettle boiled. 'I was thinking more along the lines of a memorial lecture,' said Jardine.

Ann stopped pouring hot water and raised her eyes to his. 'I think she'd have preferred a party,' she said.

The disadvantage with his policy was it cost him authority; the advantage was it kept him in check. 'I expect you're right,' he said. 'Though I suppose we could always do both. The lecture could be an annual thing. Perhaps Convocation would give us the money: there must be thousands of graduates Jenny taught out there.'

'I suppose,' said Ann. She stirred the coffee and handed it him. 'It's not exactly the way I'd want to be remembered though.'

'Ah,' said Jardine triumphantly. 'But then you're not a scholar, are you.'

4

The Gruafin family was drinking coffee too. 'You did bring a suit, I hope?' asked Bridget.

'Yes, Mum. My grey one.'

'Good. And a black tie?'

'Mum!'

'You must wear a black tie. I'll ask your father if he's got one spare.'

She did not need to ask him. He was in the same room. 'I haven't, I'm afraid.'

'I'll get you one,' she told Alan. 'I've got to go into town anyway.'

Alan looked at Ernest. Ernest said nothing.

Bridget took the packet of cigarettes from the mantelpiece. 'I don't know who else will be there,' she said. 'We're her only relatives, after all.'

'I expect someone'll come from the university,' said Ernest.

'Well, let's hope so. She worked there long enough. But she was hardly there at all last term, and you know how quickly people forget.'

'I don't think Jennifer was so easily forgotten,' said Ernest.

Bridget paused, to consider this, to light her cigarette. 'That's true,' she said. It was an unexpected concession.

Ernest picked up his coffee. 'I'll be in my study,' he said. He always felt in the way. The daytime house was Bridget's; only at night was it theirs to share. When he had first retired she had found him things to do, and he had been amazed at the number of things that needed doing. The garden for one: he spent hours a day in the garden, whereas before it had been just a couple of hours a week; it was odd how it looked no different for the extra attention. There were little jobs too, taking out the rubbish, defrosting the fridge, sorting the washing. He'd had no idea that two people generated so much washing. And now he looked for things to do, to keep him from under her feet, to keep things as they had been. His study was his refuge. He had always had a study, somewhere to do the work he brought home, with a desk and a drawing board. The drawing board had gone now of course, and he had redecorated. The room had become more like a library than an office, a place to keep his art books, Gombrich and Lord Clark, and his histories of architecture, his Pevsners and his Bannister Fletcher. The books filled a wall, unsystematic but familiar, arranged more by size than subject. A magisterial volume on the great gardens of Britain was next to a bookclub edition of the works of Leonardo; a paperback on the pyramids of Egypt abutted *The Penguin Dictionary of Arts and Artists*. He sat down in his armchair. Alan had made the coffee. The sugar was wrong again. Still, it was nice of him to try and help.

Alan drank his coffee and looked at his mother. He was bored. He wanted to talk to her, perhaps explain what had happened with Anne-Marie and why he had stayed away at Christmas, but could neither think how to begin nor predict how she would react. She had only met Anne-Marie once, after all: she didn't know her. And the two women hadn't got on well. They were both rather intolerant, he thought, and thinking this made him realise that they were alike in other ways. It was an observation that both amused and worried him. He thought about them, finding similarities he had never noticed before. It was the way they treated him, mostly. For one thing, neither of them was ever wrong. When Alan burnt a shirt with the iron it was his fault, naturally; when Anne-Marie did the same thing it was his fault for leaving it with the thermostat too high: 'Can't you ever do anything right?' He couldn't imagine his father doing the ironing, but he could imagine parallels. And for another thing, neither of them seemed to appreciate his poetry, nor to consider it as important as the things they did – Anne-Marie's flute or his mother's acting. Perhaps there was something oedipal in my relationship with Anne-Marie, he thought, knowing that he couldn't have thought this if he believed it to be true; it wasn't Oedipus, he decided, so much as training. I'm used to being put in the wrong. In fact, I'm so used to it that it doesn't bother me. When Anne-Marie blamed me for letting her oversleep her rehearsal I didn't answer back because I didn't need to; we both knew I'd woken her up on time, and she'd gone back to sleep; if she wanted to take it out on me that was her business. A weak attitude, he accepted, but what the hell? Anything for a quiet life.

Or was that why she left? The thought pulled him up abruptly. Did she go because I was too passive, too bland? When she provoked me was she really wanting me to assert myself, giving me a chance to prove I was a man? Now I come to think of it, I suppose it wasn't so much that Anne-Marie was like Mum as I let her treat me as Mum did. Mum never wanted me to answer back – or at least, I never got the impression she did. But Anne-Marie? Maybe it was different with her.

It was certainly different to start with. Do you remember how we met? he wondered, addressing her in his head. Of course you do. I was in the music library at King's. It was a daft place for a physicist to be but I was looking for the score of *An American in Paris*; I'd just bought the Labeque sisters' version for two pianos and I was intrigued by the idea that it had been un-orchestrated. And you were there with your flute case. You always had your flute case in those days, like some women have handbags. I couldn't find a full score – maybe someone had it out – but I found the parts score in a file, pulled it out, and spread Gershwin all over the floor, un-orchestrating it even more thoroughly than the Labeques. You helped me pick it up. I explained about un-orchestration; you laughed and let me buy you coffee.

God, you were sweet then. You soured later. Did I sour you?

The reminiscence came to a halt. It was safer that way. Her departure had been too recent, too sudden. It hurt to face it.

Bridget finished her cigarette and waited for the pressure on her bowels. A cigarette and a cup of coffee, and then she went to the toilet. Almost everyone has such rituals, I suppose; I suppose also that my current situation makes me more aware of them.

Actually, there is a paradox about this situation of mine. From one point of view here I am, betrayed by my body. I have always relied on my brain more than my body, I suppose, and looked after it better, exercised it more, but never have I relied on it to this extent. Thinking is my only escape. But from the other point of view I have never been so aware of my body as now it is letting me down. Little things I had never much considered, such as the state of my bowels, suddenly assume a new importance. After all – and this is a desperate thought – a good bowel movement is about the only physical pleasure of which I am still capable.

I've just had a good bowel movement, and today is a good day.

The bowel movement is one of the most important movements in history. It is an underground movement, of course, its secrets rarely discussed. It is like the very sewers that take away the shit: accepted yet unacceptable. Coprophilia has never been my line, but I find myself wondering about this shit business. I have spent my life thinking about thought, looking at history in terms of intellectual movements, yet bowel movements are just as important. A thorough history of mankind would surely have to acknowledge the body as well as the mind. I almost wish I had thought of this before: it might have made a fitting climax to my career. *A History of Defecation*, perhaps, to lie alongside Foucault's *History of Sexuality*.

Foucault, of course, died of AIDS, which is carrying research too far. At least I can guarantee I won't die of that, though for the same reason it is too late to start a new project. Still, I have just had a good bowel movement, and today is a good day; I am in the mood for a *jeu d'esprit*. God knows it is a rare enough mood.

The extent to which history has been moulded by the ability to shit to order or otherwise is debatable. Records are copious but unclassified. It is perhaps easier to look at the figures of speech defecation has provided. Prime amongst these is the verb 'to purge'. Standard etymology traces this word to the Latin *purgare*, to purify, but this is incomplete: the popular meaning of purge, to clean out the bowels, was established before the sixteenth century; though 'purge' has come almost full circle, and means again 'to purify', its current usage is figurative. When the Party is purged it is purified, but by means of a laxative.

Similarly, there is a curious association between the bowels and compassion, which dates back at least to the gospels. John wrote of the 'bowels of compassion'; the phrase recurs in many forms, most famously in Gay's *The Beggar's Opera* when Macheath cries 'Have you no bowels, no tenderness?' A revealing version comes from Cromwell: when he wrote, 'I beseech you, in the bowels of Christ, think it possible you may be mistaken', he is at his most human, and so is his Christ: perhaps the association comes about by reference to our common humanity.

The history of a figure of speech is often fraught. 'Writer's block' is a case in point. I have no authority for the suggestion, but I suspect this is a reference to constipation: writer's block is mental constipation. Blockages take other forms, of course, but none so immediate to our experience.

Constipation is probably the aspect of this issue that has had most effect on our history. Luther's constipation is famous; the economy of the eighteenth-century spa towns depended on it. The problem of constipation, however, has been marginalised in official histories; it is to diaries we must turn to learn of its impact. One of my favourite diaries is that of Elias Ashmole, a seventeenth-century alchemist, whose daily entries are full of references to purging, followed inevitably by looseness. Ashmole sums up a universal human trait: we are fascinated and repulsed in equal measure by the actions of our bowels. It is, I suppose, a kind of alchemy, a transmutation of matter. In one end goes all manner of shapes, colours and flavours; from the other end, with remarkable consistency, comes a single shape, a single colour, a single smell. Our gut is a sort of philosopher's stone, though not one with much commercial value. In China human excrement is a valued fertiliser but I know of no European equivalent. We tend to keep quiet about the whole business.

On one hand this silence is understandable. The smell is not pleasant. Bedpan-bound, I have had to grow accustomed to it; I have not yet grown to like it. Auden once wrote that secretly every man likes the smell of his own farts; perhaps so, but it does not apply to me. The consistency too is repulsive.

On the other hand, we all shit. Swift's wonderfully ironic recognition of this fact has never been surpassed:

No wonder I have lost my Wits:
Oh! Celia, Celia, Celia shits!

And I think again of Cromwell's letter to the Church of Scotland: 'I beseech you, in the bowels of Christ, think it possible you may be mistaken.' Helen of Troy shat, Leonardo shat, even Christ did if Cromwell is to be believed. I wonder if all megalomaniacs are constipated: I gather that both Napoleon and Hitler were. This makes sense. Shitting brings us down to earth; shitting reminds us of our own weakness. Perhaps only someone who doesn't shit could think themselves a God. I wonder what Cromwell's bowels were doing? Constipated mostly, I imagine, but the day he wrote to the Church of Scotland was a good day.

We all have them from time to time. They do not last. Ask my doctor. Ask King Charles.

Bridget was in the toilet, Alan was alone in the living room. The sky was grey and so was the garden. He went to the door of his father's study and knocked. 'Come in, Alan,' said Ernest. Bridget never knocked. 'Can I help?'

'Just looking for something to read.'

'I thought I saw you with one of Auntie Jennifer's books.'

'I know it sounds terrible, but I really can't get on with it. It's a bit too specialised for me, I suppose. I was all right with the early part, the general stuff, but now it's just lots of ways of looking at books I've never read. I wondered if you'd read anything interesting recently.'

'I'm glad you asked!' said Ernest, and meant it. 'As a matter of fact there's this.' 'This' was George Lesser's book about Chartres Cathedral, *Gothic Cathedrals and Sacred Geometry*, volume three. Ernest looked through in search of a page. 'It could be right up your street: it shows how Gothic cathedrals used Pythagoras to establish their proportions.'

'The square of the hypotenuse of a right-angled triangle is the sum of the square of the other two sides?' asked Alan.

'There's a lot more to Pythagoras than that, as you should know.'

'It's all I can remember,' admitted Alan. 'I can give you the proof of the theorem if you like.'

'No thank you. Take the book, read it, tell me what you think.'

He had nothing better to do. 'All right,' he said. 'Thanks.'

'Are you doing anything today?' Ernest asked.

'Not a thing. Why?'

'Why don't you come down to the club with me at lunchtime, have a game of snooker?'

'I haven't played in ages.'

'It's only for fun. Come on, it'll get you out of your mother's way.'

'Well, thanks very much then. What time do you go down?'

'About one usually. I have lunch here first then get out of your mother's way.' The repeated phrase was insistent.

'That's fine.'

'Oh. And Alan?'

Alan was turning to go. 'Yes?'

'Thanks for the coffee.'

Alan left. Ernest returned to his chair, to his thoughts.

5

Wendy was marking 2H's work. 'My bog is a ditch,' she read. She looked again, then laughed. She had been wrong in the car: the day had its rewards after all. 'My bog is a ditch!' It was the best example of dyslexia she had seen.

There was neither malice nor mockery in her reaction, just relief from the tedium of marking. Thirty-two similar essays with thirty-two similar mistakes – apostrophes, there/their/they're, of/off, now/know – can dull the mind. She turned to her staffroom colleagues. 'Just listen to this,' she said. They shared the labour; they deserved to share the joke.

6

Chapman was puzzled. Jennifer was in hospital for two weeks; for years before that she was going to work most days. I never had any trouble filling the days then: why is it so difficult now? It was a relief when the telephone rang.

'Chapman,' he said.

'Hello, Mr Chapman. Ormond and Gullick here.'

The undertakers. 'Yes?' he said cautiously.

'We're just confirming tomorrow's arrangements. Cars at ten-twenty all right?'

'Yes. I expect so.'

'Good. And you'll be wanting to view the departed?'

Chapman had not given it a thought, but he felt he could hardly answer no. 'Yes,' he said, as cautiously as before.

'Excellent. Three o'clock suitable?'

'Oh. Fine.'

'Good. We'll expect you. Will there be any other mourners accompanying you?'

'No. No, I don't think so.'

'Three o'clock it is then. Goodbye.'

Chapman put down the receiver. Oh Jennifer, Jennifer, what have you let me in for? He had a nervous desire to laugh. Viewing the corpse! The notion was bizarre as well as morbid. But, if that's what's expected, he thought. He was a very conventional man.

For a moment he let his mind wander, wondering what she would look like now she was dead, but the thought was unrewarding, unpleasant. He could not imagine: he could only see her as he had seen her in the hospital, before they had driven him away and then wheeled her out in the canvas-topped tin box. She had been so white then, and her eyes had been open.

The box had bothered him. He had not expected that. He had been standing in the corridor, awkward, knowing the worst yet not admitting it, while the doctor pronounced her dead and filled out forms. I signed one of the forms, he remembered, but he had not read it, had no idea what it said. He suddenly worried he might have signed away her kidneys or her heart.

His thoughts kept returning to the box. It was a very ordinary box, two yards long, eighteen inches deep, made of galvanised steel that was regularly embossed with small four-pointed stars. Over the top, held in place by studs and eyes, was a sheet; inside was all that was Jennifer. He had the sudden clear thought that some day he too would lie in such a box, be wheeled from a hospital bed, undignified and dead. It was an impossible thought to face. Death did not seem likely for him. He was the mourner, the one who survived. He had been blown up by a mine in Korea, had been there when Jennifer died. His role was to watch over the dead, remember them and preserve their memory. It wasn't part of his role that he should die.

But death was a galvanised box, a canvas lid. Death was tangible in that form, undeniable. One day he would lie in that box. He imagined it cold and uncomfortable. But of course, he thought, that doesn't matter when you're dead.

What's it like to be dead? he wondered. The voice in his head asked Jennifer, but if she knew she didn't reply. The dead can tell us much about what it is to be alive, but they say nothing of what it is to be dead. And what if I did sign away her organs? Nobody could need them less than Jennifer did. Or is that blasphemy?

7

The sports club was even quieter than usual. 'Have you met my son?' asked Ernest. 'Madge, I'd like you to meet Alan; Alan, this is Madge.'

'Pleased to meet you,' she said. 'What are you drinking?'

'The usual for me. Alan?'

'I'll have a half of bitter, please.'

'Fine. Peter not been in yet?'

'Haven't you heard? His wife's taken badly. She's in hospital.'

'Oh dear. No. No, I'd no idea. When did this happen?'

'Friday. Just after he left here. Dennis told me.' She lowered her voice. 'She's not expected to last the week.'

'Oh God. How awful.'

'Isn't it.'

'Is there anything?'

'I expect Dennis'll be in later,' she said. 'He'll know.'

She put the drinks on the bar and Ernest paid. He picked them up and took them to a table. Alan followed and sat with him. 'How awful,' Ernest repeated. 'And Jennifer too.' There was a pressure on his ears. Perhaps it was the sound of his blood. Can you hear blood? he wondered.

Alan had nothing to say. They sat in silence for a while, then Ernest puckered his lips ruefully and took a drink. He was drinking lager. The head clung to his upper lip. 'It makes you think.'

'It's funny how these things – ' began Alan but he did not know how to continue.

Ernest followed his son's thoughts. 'I know. First one, then another.' He took another sip. 'They say these things come in threes.'

'I hope not.'

Ernest shook his head. 'Old wives' tale,' he said. 'Doesn't mean anything at all.'

Alan was glad to agree. It seemed a good time to change the subject. 'I'm sorry about Christmas, Dad,' he said. 'About not making it home and everything. Was Mum annoyed?'

'She wasn't pleased. I expect you had a good reason.'

'Do you want to hear about it?'

'Do you want to talk about it?'

'Anne-Marie's left me.'

'Oh. I'm sorry to hear that.' Like his wife, Ernest had met Anne-Marie only once. It was not his habit to judge people. 'Are you upset?' he asked, feeling his ground.

Of course I'm bloody upset, thought Alan, or we wouldn't need to talk about it at all. 'I suppose so,' he said.

'Recently?'

'Middle of December. She's been gone for a month, just about.'

'You spent Christmas on your own? In the flat?'

'I couldn't face coming home.'

'Alan!'

'It's true. I'm sorry. I know you'd have been ever so nice, but either I'd have told you and had to answer questions, or not told you and pretend everything was all right. I really couldn't face either.'

'But you're here now.'

'Auntie Jennifer is dead.'

Ernest drank his lager. 'Another drink? Shall I get a snooker ticket?' he asked.

'Good idea.' Alan went with him to the bar. 'It's really quiet in here today. I thought we'd have to queue for a game.'

'It's never really busy at lunchtime. Well, it was busy over the holiday of course. But the rest of the time!'

Sometimes Alan thought he heard his Jewish grandmother in the way his father spoke. Or more precisely, as he had never met his grandmother, his father's Jewish blood. Can you hear blood? 'Isn't it my round?'

'Don't worry,' said Ernest. 'You just set up the balls.'

The snooker system was simple. Any member of the sports club could buy a numbered ticket, which entitled him to a game; the games were played in order, but no one was allowed to play with a ticket in his pocket; Ernest bought ticket number one. Alan picked the balls from the gullies beneath the pockets and rolled them towards the spots while his father paid for more drinks. He racked the reds and placed the pink and the black; he was glad his father arrived in time to position the yellow, brown and green because he had forgotten the order they came in.

'Call!' said Ernest, putting a coin beneath his hand.

'Heads.'

'Heads it is. Do you want to break?'

'You can.'

Alan was hopelessly out of practice and dwarfed by the table. Ernest built up a steady lead. They exchanged conventional comments: 'Hard luck', 'Good shot', 'By a mile', but there seemed little time for conversation.

Alan potted the last red, which doubled his points. 'Well done,' said Ernest. 'What next?' They circled beneath the bright lights.

'Pink.'

'Where has Anne-Marie gone?' asked Ernest.

If it was gamesmanship it was both blatant and uncharacteristic. Alan missed the pink and decided his father would never deliberately put him off: Dad's more disappointed when I miss than I am. 'I don't know,' Alan replied.

'You haven't heard from her?'

'She went abroad.' The table was green, a vast map.

'Abroad? How do you know?'

'Well, that's what she said she was doing. She packed her bags, took her passport; she said she'd had enough of England and was getting out.'

'You can't just up and go like that. There are formalities, visas.'

'I know. Perhaps she went to an EEC country. She speaks French.'

Ernest potted the yellow. 'I think you need a few snookers,' he said. 'You don't think she was making it up? About going abroad? It seems a bit drastic.'

'If she said it she meant it.' Alan surprised himself by potting the green and the brown at the same visit to the table. It was too late to do him any good but he felt better.

Ernest sank the blue and the pink. 'That's it, then,' he said. 'Thanks for the game.'

'Well played.' Alan tried for the redundant black but missed. 'I'd better get some practice in before next time.'

'Sign of a misspent youth,' said Ernest. 'Or a misspent old age, in my case. Still, keeps me out of your mother's way, I suppose.'

'It really is my turn to get the drinks.'

'Do you want another one?' asked Ernest. 'Or shall we get back?'

'I don't mind. I've nothing else to do.'

'You've twisted my arm,' said Ernest. 'I'll have a half.'

Ernest went to sit down. Alan watched his father as Madge poured the drinks. How well do I know him? he wondered. How well does he know me?

Ernest had been a pleasant enough sort of father to have, but not a very obvious one. An offstage presence really, paying the bills and going out to work. I remember him most from holidays, weeks in Scarborough when I was little, France when I got older. He liked France: he was sure that the name Gruafin was French, but we never found another, no distant cousins or family vaults. Is that why I suggested Anne-Marie might be in France: to make him like her too? And if so, what's the point? What's it matter if he likes her when I'm trying to forget that I do, forget her altogether?

It is not easy to forget. It was as if his thoughts kept crossing a neuron marked Anne-Marie. He held a silly, potent association in his head between Anne-Marie and a treble clef. The treble clef has a woman's shape, a woman's voice. Anne-Marie was slim. She did not have the full, pregnant curves of the treble clef. Her flute would have made a more accurate visual image. Yet still he thought of the clef when he thought of her, and it hurt.

Ernest was thinking about Alan. I wonder how much she meant to him; I wonder how much she still means. I was married at his age, and Bridget and I had been courting for years. It seemed easier in those days: when a couple liked one another they got married, and being married they stayed together. Though Jennifer and Chapman never married, of course, and they stayed together. They're the exception to prove the rule: I still think it was easier, by and large; you got married, raised a family, and a sort of family loyalty held you together. I don't pretend my marriage to Bridget is ideal: if it was I wouldn't be here now, keeping out of her way. But as a partnership it seems mostly to have worked. We're not lovers any more, but we are family, blood. That's what counts.

Alan came back with the drinks. 'I had a look at that book,' he said, sitting down. 'Fascinating. Do you remember when we went to Chartres?'

'That was a long time ago. Seventy-five?'

'It was later. It must have been seventy-six; I did my O-levels in seventy-seven.'

'That's right. The hot summer. It was hot too. Do you remember where we stayed?'

'Madame Robert's!'

'That's right. Even your mum said the cooking was wonderful.'

'She liked Chartres too.'

'Who couldn't? We've got some photographs. I haven't looked at them in years. We ought to get them out.'

'I'd like that,' said Alan. 'I'd like that a lot.'

Family, that's what counts. Family. Blood.

8

Current styles suited the funeral parlour. The inappropriate modernism of its original 1960s' design had been replaced by heavy curtains, heavy colours. Everything was velvet and oak, crimson and brown. Before the changes the emphasis had been on a kind of efficiency. Carpet tiles made an ochre and black chessboard of the floor; the chairs were low-slung and businesslike; the light was bright. But death is efficient enough, it needs no assistance, and the comfortable plush of the new look, its heavy fake Victoriana, its slightly ponderous dignity, seemed appropriate, correct. It also made it look like a bordello, but perhaps that was appropriate too: the association between sex and death is an ancient one.

Chapman stood with his hat in his hand. He had hardly worn a hat in thirty years. But somehow he felt he needed a hat, a hat to take off to show his respect, and had bought a trilby along with his black tie. On his head it felt awkward, but it was useful in his hands, something to hold, something to tap against his hip when he was nervous. He was tapping it as he waited. A suspiciously young receptionist looked at him through blue-lined eyes. 'Mr Chapman? Our Mr Ormond will be with you in a minute. Would you care to take a seat?'

'Thank you.' He recognised the receptionist, but it took a second to work out where he had seen her before. Behind a bar! That was it: behind the bar of the Castle at the end of the road. Had she changed her career, or did she moonlight in the bar when she had finished at the undertakers? First he was intrigued, and then he realised he did not really want to know. He had been a customer of hers before, ordering G&Ts for Jennifer and himself, but that was a different life, a different world, and it was right the two should be kept apart. She probably felt the same, he reasoned: an evening with the living after a day with the dead. Just because she works in a funeral parlour doesn't mean she's morbid. It must be a funny place to work though. I mean, there can't be much variety really, lots of bodies and grieving relatives, it must get very familiar. But you can't let it look as if you're bored, you've got to pretend that each death is special. Because, for someone, each death is.

It came as a shock to him to realise he would not mind being an undertaker. It would be nice to help people through their grief. He shook his head rapidly: if the receptionist noticed she said nothing, for she was used to the behaviour of the mourners, always subdued, often odd. Chapman shook his head but could not dislodge the thought. I am good at mourning now, he thought. I was no good at it at all when my father, my mother, died. Maybe I was too young, death too far away. But I am good at mourning now, he thought, and the thought was a guilty comfort.

He needed what comfort he could get.

Mr Ormond came into the room, elderly, the sagging creases of his face laid out professionally, solemnly. 'Mr Chapman. My deepest condolences. You are a relative of the deceased, of Dr Fox?'

'Not exactly. We were friends. Very good friends.'

'I understand,' said Mr Ormond, and perhaps he did. He must have seen much of life, this expert in death. 'Shall we go through?'

Conducting relatives to see the corpse was Mr Ormond's speciality. The funeral arrangements he left to his younger colleagues, the accounts to his partner. Mr Ormond showed the dead to the living, with great discretion and tact. He held the door open for Chapman, said nothing but followed him in. Discretion and tact: they were the keys to this business. The younger fellows, they could handle the cars, shoulder the coffins; they could deal with the dead. It was the living that proved the real problem in this job, and only experience could deal with that.

Chapman walked into a darkened room. His thoughts, which had been gibbering, seemed to slow down now. The coffin, lidless, was on a covered table and lit by discreet spotlight. He paused. His feet seemed as slow as his mind. Mr Ormond nodded encouragingly. Chapman approached, uncertain what he would see. They never know what to expect, thought Mr Ormond.

201

Chapman looked into the coffin. Jennifer lay peacefully in the silk. Her hair, though thinned by treatment, was clean and carefully combed. Her eyes were closed as in sleep. She wore a long black dress Chapman did not recognise, and her hands were crossed at her breast. Chapman stood a long time looking. His thoughts were hopelessly hackneyed: she was there, yet she wasn't. She looked so serene. It's good you're at peace, he told her. It's good. She was there, yet she wasn't, which was how she would always be. Mr Ormond watched the mourner carefully, tracing emotions he knew well, watching trepidation turn to relief and then waiting as relief turned, as it always did, to a kind of embarrassment. When he saw the embarrassment, the uncertainty about what to do next, Mr Ormond coughed. He always coughed, once, into his hand. The mourners appreciated this cue that their time was up. They appreciated all the guidance he could give, as long as it was accompanied by discretion and tact.

Chapman took one last look. She looks beautiful, he thought. He turned to Mr Ormond. 'Thank you,' he said, his voice low. They never know what to expect, thought Mr Ormond, but they always say thank you when they leave.

9

It was gone four by the time John got back from Earls Court. Janice was at the reception desk, sorting letters for the post. 'Ah, you're back,' she said. 'Robert wants to see you.'

'Now what?'

'Nothing much. He's going away for a day or two, some funeral in the north. He needs to rearrange a couple of things in his diary.'

'Okay.' On his way up the stairs John remembered Wendy's request. He knocked on Robert's door and went in. 'Hi!'

'Good. You're back. Still loyal to the old firm?'

'I'm still here,' said John, slightly embarrassed by the question.

'That's good enough. I've got to dump a couple of things on you, I'm afraid, as I'll be away tomorrow. Jennifer Fox's funeral.'

'Jennifer Fox's!'

'Don't sound so surprised. Jennifer was one of my first successes. *Shakespeare's Great Theme* is still in print today. Not bad after forty-odd years.'

But *Literature in the Age of Certainty* and *Literature in the Age of Uncertainty* bummed, thought John. Still, a funeral's a good excuse for a day away from the office. 'Okay, so what do you want me to do?'

'Just a couple of meetings.' He looked at his diary. 'I've cancelled Terence Walters: no problem there. And Janice is rearranging Clive Thompson.'

'Sounds like a good idea,' said John.

Robert laughed. 'He can't help being a prat. So was his father. Anyway, what I've got for you is someone from JD Distribution at eleven, which should be right up your street.'

'Agreed. And?'

'Penny Gough.'

'Robert!'

'I know she's a pain, but she is her husband's executor. We've got to humour her.'

'You know she'll want us to publish that last book of his. What was it, *Hoping for Winter Rain*? How can I humour her? Tell her we're going to do it, or tell her the truth: that it's a load of crap and we suspect she finished it for him anyway?'

'Just charm her a bit. You don't have to admit to anything. That's my job.'

'And that's why you're away for the day. Oh well, I'll just refer her to you every time she asks a question, and take her out for a meal. That okay?'

'Fine. I'll be back on Wednesday. I'm sorry about this.'

'So you should be. Anyway, you can do me a favour in return. Some friend of Wendy's has sent us a manuscript apparently, and is getting a bit desperate to hear from us.'

'They all do.'

'Yes. Well, you can have a look at it while you're away. Give you something to read on the train.'

'I'm not short of things to read.'

'And you're not having to face Mrs Gough! Go on, quid pro quo, as the rock band ticket tout said.'

The only rock bands Robert knew were the Beatles and the Rolling Stones; Status Quo was beyond him, as was John's reference. He shrugged it off. 'All right. Let's have the title and author's name.'

'Jim Hamilton's the author. I don't know the title. Short stories.'

'Just what I need. Unsolicited short stories. Has he got an agent?'

'How should I know! I've never even met the man.'

'Worse and worse. Still, I'll see if we can find it. When did he send it in?'

'About nineteen seventy-eight if Wendy's to be believed. I don't know.'

'The things I do for you,' muttered Robert, but he wasn't serious.

'The things I do for you,' said John, and he was.

10

Professor Jardine felt tired but pleased. He had somehow condensed Jenny Fox's career into 400 words and it seemed quite an achievement. He phoned the number he had been given.

'Copytakers?'

'Oh, yes,' said the professor.

'Give me your number, I'll phone you back.'

Jardine gave the number and the extension. He put down the phone and waited. As he waited he read through the obituary again. He was aware of a childish excitement: this is Keith Jardine phoning his copy in from Sheffield; hold the front page! The telephone rang. He quashed the fancy. 'Jardine?'

'Ready for your copy. It's for?'

'Gayle Wallace. Obituaries.' He heard a typewriter keyboard clatter down his words.

'Yes,' said the copytaker.

'Dr Jennifer Fox,' said Jardine.

'Yes.'

'Jennifer Fox, who died on Thursday.'

'Yes.'

'Is perhaps best remembered.'

'Yes.'

And so on, a summation of a lifetime. Jardine read through, spelling out the awkward names, getting used to the rhythm of the keyboard at the other end of the line, and approached the end. 'Her most famous line was.'

'Yes.'

'Open quotes, capital, Renunciation is a rehearsal for death, full stop, unquote.'

'Yes.'

'But Jennifer Fox renounced nothing, comma.'

'Yes.'

'And fought right to the end. That's it.' He was exhausted. He wanted to ask the copytaker's opinion but suspected the copytaker would have none.

'Thank you,' said the copytaker. 'Goodbye.'

Jardine put down the phone again. He revived the excitement.

11

Anne-Marie was tired of walking, and tired of ringing the flat. Where can he be? she asked herself: I didn't really want to arrive back unannounced, but it's getting dark.

She caught a bus up to Hornsey. She was surprised nothing had changed, then surprised at her surprise. I was only away a month, she told herself, so what did I expect?

Now there's an interesting thought, she decided. What *do* I expect? Alan to hug me to him, smother me with kisses, forgive me for having gone away? Or recriminations, violence, the works?

She got off the bus and crossed the High Street. There were no lights on in the flat. Is he still out? What on earth can he be doing? She still had her keys. She let herself in through the communal door, climbed the stairs, opened their door. The door shoved a couple of bills and a free newspaper aside. He's gone away, she realised. Good grief.

There was nothing in the flat to eat except half a stale loaf in the cupboard. She turned on the television, caught the local news. She watched Wogan, interviewing a celebrity author. 'And tell me, you don't need the money' – that cheeky smile – 'so what makes you write?'

'Everyone has a book in them,' said the celebrity, answering smile for smile.

'But not everybody can get it out,' said Terry happily.

She turned off the television, went into the bedroom. The bed was unmade: it's a bachelor flat again already, she thought, and the thought troubled her. Where was he and who was he with?

On top of the wardrobe was a pile of sheet music. She looked at it a while but could think of nothing she wanted to play. She went back into the kitchen and picked up the post. Telecom and the Gas Board. That'll be nice for him. She put them on the table and went out.

For a while she walked without purpose. She walked up Crouch Hill, past better-quality houses, past where Wendy waited for John, and walked back down again. There was still no light in Alan's flat. She crossed the road and went to the pub where, mindful of her condition, she drank only lemonade.

12

He arranged the side plates first, inserting a triangle of paper napkin between each and lining up the points of the triangles one above the other, neatly, unimaginatively, making a tower of white china and pink paper on the dining table. On the dinner plates he put doilies, and on the doilies the food. Sausage rolls, mince-pies dusted with icing sugar, salmon sandwiches, mushroom vol-au-vents, fairy cakes, cocktail sausages. He put clingfilm over each plate before taking it to the dining table. An eggcup was filled with cocktail sticks. He straightened the edges of the table-cloth, creasing the corners military fashion; he polished the crystal fruit bowl and the glasses. Knives and forks would not be needed, but he put the coffee spoons on a tray in the kitchen and added the cups and saucers. He took oranges, apples and grapes from the grocery store bags and put them on the fruit bowl. He stood back. Jennifer had never had much time for fuss, but Chapman enjoyed a loaded table, light on cut glass, the delicate shades of piled fruit. He tidied the kitchen. Before going to bed he trimmed his moustache. He tried not to think much at all.

13

Bridget and Alan struggled with the screen while Ernest plugged in the projector. The screen was obstinate: they had managed to assemble the telescopic framework but each time they tried to hook the unrolled white screen up the telescope collapsed. When the third attempt failed they started to giggle.

'What are you doing?' asked Ernest. 'Here. Let me try.'

He hooked the screen on to the still collapsed frame, extended the telescope, and it clicked into place. 'Clever clogs,' said Bridget.

'Natural talent,' corrected Ernest. 'Can you switch off the lights, Alan? I think everything's ready.'

The lights went out. 'Action!' said Ernest, switching on the projector. The first slide came up. It showed Bridget and a teenage Alan in front of the Arc de Triomphe, and was upside down. 'Technical hitch,' said Ernest. 'And stop laughing.'

But he was laughing too. Family, blood, that's what counts.

14

It grew late. John got home. Wendy had finished *Aesthetics of a Gumtree* and was watching the television. John moaned about Robert and microwaved his tea. They watched television. She told him about the bog and the ditch. He laughed and they went to bed.

The Gruafins watched their slide-show and afterwards, unexpectedly, had a drink together, cream sherry for Bridget, whisky for Ernest and Alan. Chapman did not try to sleep. He sat in the living room, smoked a couple of cigarettes, kept a silent vigil for Jennifer. And Robert finished his hotel cognac and went up to his room. The journey north had been tiring. He sat on the bed and looked at his briefcase. I've still got that bloody manuscript to look at. I could leave it till tomorrow, read it on the train back, read it tomorrow night for that matter. Unsolicited short stories! A publisher's nightmare!

He stretched. The room was comfortable. That was about all that could be said for it. What time is it? he asked, and checked his watch. It was later than he had thought. He turned on the television, changed through the channels, switched it off. He lifted the phone and asked for an outside line, woke his wife with his call, spoke briefly to tell her he had arrived, put it down.

He was not tired. He wondered if the bar was still open and took the lift back down. The bar was still open, but a delegation of civil servants on a conference was in there, celebrating their break from home, and he had no wish to join them. Nothing else for it, he thought as he returned to his room: I'd better see what Jim Hamilton's like.

The manuscript was in a loose-leaf folder; the stories had been typed on several machines. There did not seem to be a title. Robert started to read.

Chapter Ten

RHETORIC

Which is concerned with the Telling of Stories

C lassic rhetorical composition involves three stages: *inventio*, the finding or discovery of an idea; *dispositio*, or arrangement; *elocutio*, the way of telling.

The first of these is the *inventio*, which in storytelling means the subject. The desire to tell a story is stimulated either by the (historical) wish to record or the (imaginative) question 'What if . . .?' Often a single scene, a static picture, is enough to begin with. A seaman on a sinking ship taps SOS on a broken radio. A car crashes but the radio plays on. A masterpiece hangs, unseen, behind a soiled sheet. Someone screams in the vacuum of space. A condemned man in his cell writes a manuscript no one will read. What if . . .? What if . . .? What if . . .?

The scene must be developed, however: stories are about change because in life things always change and stories are about life. This development, *dispositio*, is the plot. There are five basic types of plot. The most common by far is the gratification-through-adversity model: the protagonist wants something – to avenge his murdered father, to return home from Troy, to live secure from the clutches of the workhouse or Fagin; a series of obstacles must be overcome before this ambition is realised; finally the progatonist achieves gratification.

The failed-gratification model has the same elements, but this time the protagonist, who wants to kill the white whale or defeat Richmond at Bosworth Field, does not achieve his aim. These two models are so universal that they are almost a definition of a story. There is a subject-object-verb kind of logic here. The subject of this kind of story, the hero or protagonist, has an object in life which can be achieved only by action, overcoming an obstacle or undergoing an ordeal: the action, the verb part, is generally what we enjoy most about such stories, and our pleasure comes from the skill with which the storyteller balances the strengths of the protagonist and the obstacle so that we are never quite confident of the outcome; the 'With one bound he was free' solution to the protagonist's problems is rightly despised because it takes away that enjoyment.

A third model is that of spoilt-gratification, in which the protagonist, who wants the crown of Scotland or that all he touches should turn to gold, gets what he wants but finds the victory hollow. I have a particular liking for stories of this type.

There is also the synecdochal model. Synecdoche is a rhetorical device by which a part can represent the whole: to write of fifty sail when meaning fifty ships is the Oxford English Dictionary's example; Dickens is playing a game with synecdoche in *Hard Times* when he notes that the factory workers are known as Hands, and that it would suit their employers better were they indeed no more than hands. The synecdochical model, using a part to represent the whole, is the basis of satire, allegory and utopianism; it is oblique, so that a description of a decaying house, for instance, can represent a dying woman.

Finally there is the contemplative model, sometimes known as stream of consciousness, in which the narrator reveals something of him or herself, sometimes accidentally, through an apparently unstructured overspill of thought.

The baggy novel, unlike the leaner short story, generally combines a number of these models.

The *dispositio* also involves the arrangement or dynamics of the story. There are several standard arrangements: the episodic, one event after another linked more by common characters than common themes; the parabolic, in which all the events are cumulative, one leading to another so that the characters' fortunes might be charted on a graph; the baroque, in which embellishment is as important as narrative thrust; the misleading, which has an unexpected twist at the end. In a baggy novel it is even possible to introduce a hiatus, such as this chapter, before a significant event.

The final category is the *elocutio*, the way of telling. Some of this area is called 'style'; it also concerns such decisions as the choice of first- or third-person narrator or the choice of tense. Most stories are told either in a disengaged third-person voice or an involved first person, but there are alternatives. The Sherlock Holmes stories and *The Great Gatsby* are told in the first person, but the narrator is more an observer than a protagonist; *A Portrait of the Artist as a Young Man* is told in the third person, but the narrator is intimately involved with Stephen. Most stories, likewise, are told in the past tense, but a number take advantage of the immediacy of the present historic.

These are descriptions. There is only the one commandment, which is to be interesting: the breaking of the usual ten is the storyteller's meat and drink. Interest is vital. The earliest stories survive only because they were interesting enough to be remembered; printing is no excuse for being boring. Length is important: all stories have a natural length, and while many can be shortened few can be extended. Trust is also important: the audience must trust that the storyteller will keep them engaged, forgiving the digressions in the belief that the end will make it all worth while.

In his hotel room Robert reads the manuscript. A seaman on a sinking ship taps SOS on a broken radio. A car crashes but the radio plays on. A masterpiece hangs, unseen, behind a soiled sheet. Someone screams in the vacuum of space. A condemned man in his cell writes a manuscript no one will read. What if . . .? What if . . .? What if . . .?

2

THE FIRST STORY: THE SHARK'S HEAD

They rarely land sharks on this coast. I could not pass up the chance. It cost a lot of money but I bought the head. I lied: I told the fishermen I wanted a trophy.

It had started so long ago, but my memories were vivid. How could I forget! The bomb had landed square in the aft hold, blowing a hole in the hull, and the blast had ripped through the superstructure. Shipshape and Bristol fashion we'd been, but now it was a different ship. Smoke billowed from the hold, and where the smoke parted red flames made ugly shadows in the night. I'd been on the foredeck, supervising the Bofors, and as I made my way aft I could see the ship was finished. We were already listing to port, and the bosun was trying to organise the life-boats, but it was going to be a difficult job. The port boats swung out of reach, and the starboard boats rested unlaunchably against the tilted hull.

'Anyone seen Captain Williams?' I asked. Nobody had. I climbed to the bridge. The windows were out and the radio mast had fallen through the roof, but the walls were sound. The metal was hot. I pushed at the door. It opened a few inches and jammed. I pushed harder, till I could squeeze through. There was enough light through the broken roof for me to see the mess. The mast had crushed most of the navigation gear. I could make out the wheel, broken beneath the wreckage.

I struggled over the twisted debris and on to something soft. It was Hibbert, second mate, and he was past caring that I stood on his chest. Even in the dimness I could see his white face and the dark mark of blood on his forehead, so I carried on, feeling my way and calling. I heard a groan in reply.

The ship gave a sudden lurch and I lost my footing. Not much time, I told myself. I found the captain next. He was alive, pinned to the deck by a leg of the mast. 'That you, Peters?' he managed to ask.

'Sir.' I tried to pull him free.

'Are we going down?'

'Yes sir,' I said, gasping as I tugged at the metal.

'Did Sparks send out a distress signal?'

'I don't know.' I couldn't shift the mast at all, and I suppose the captain knew it.

'Stop messing,' he said. 'There's no time. Check we sent out a mayday.'

I didn't like to leave him and told him so. 'For Christ's sake, man,' he said, 'I'm ordering you.'

'Yes sir.'

The ship lurched again.

The door to the wireless cabin was broken down, as was the roof. Through the opening I could see smoke between me and the bomber's moon, and Sparks, slumped over the radio set. I tried lifting him but his neck was broken and fell back, impossibly long and white, like a gull's.

The set had its own batteries and seemed to be working, but the mast was down. I tried anyway, tapping out a brief desperate 'Save Our Souls' and trying to estimate our position. My finger worked automatically, but could anyone hear? I did not dare ask.

Captain Williams called. 'Peters! Leave it now! Abandon ship before it's too late.'

He was right of course. The list was appalling now. I made my way across the desperately sloping deck back to him and in the hope I might save him. 'I told you,' he said. 'It's no use.'

'What are you going to do, sir?'

'I'll go down with my ship.' His voice was calm. 'As is my duty and my right.' But then the ship lurched again and I was able to pull him free. I would to God now I had let him have his way.

Half dragging, half carrying him, I left the bridge the way I'd entered. It no longer felt the same. The ladder wasn't vertical any more, and instead of deck beneath us there was water. I held him as best I could but it was hopeless. I dropped him and he fell into the sea. The rungs were truly hot now. My hands couldn't keep their grip and I fell too.

I was winded but my Mae West kept me afloat. I caught my breath through the waves and struck out from the ship, kicking my seaboots off. I needed to be clear when the ship sank or I'd be sucked down with it. When the swell lifted me I could see two life-boats, but in the troughs I was alone. I headed for the life-boats. Behind me was a slow gurgle, the sound of a ship as it dies, and then I was hit by an unnatural wave, washed forward and pulled back. It was all I could do to keep my mouth above water, and by the time I could look the ship had gone, leaving flat, oily water, floating barrels, and a pall of smoke beneath the fat, round moon.

One of the life-boats was heading back, circling for survivors. The other was out of sight. An oil drum floated near me. I tried to raise myself from the water on it, make myself seen, but it rolled me back to the waves every time.

There was a sudden bang as something hit the drum. I turned to see teeth in a vicious pink mouth, and then the shark was past me, his dorsal fin proud of the water. My stomach rolled. He had missed. He would not miss again.

I unsheathed my bowie knife. I had to hope the shark would attack on the surface again, for if he came from beneath I was done for. I was probably done for anyway. I watched the silent fin arc through dark water. The swell was not much but it was enough to hide the shark for a moment, and then he was on me, fast, his white nose tipped upwards like a cheeky schoolboy's and his arc of teeth like the mouth of hell.

I had one chance and half a moment to take it. I thrust at one of his eyes, eyes without life or feeling, and was lucky. The knife entered. It wasn't enough to stop the shark's run, and he hit me squarely and smashed me into the drum, but it was enough to save my life. The shark didn't close his mouth on me.

The life-boat pulled me from the water. They told me later they had seen sharks thrashing, and had been amazed to find me alive. I was amazed to be alive. I had several broken ribs, mind, and one had punctured my left lung slightly, which made me cough blood till it healed, but this didn't trouble me till later. At the time all I cared was to have survived. I asked about Captain Williams but he hadn't been found.

A hot day dawned over the South China Sea. There were eight of us on the boat, Chambers, Walters, Jim Bridy, Hanson, Knowles, Knox, the Chinese cook and me, and several of us were in a bad way. My injuries you know about. Hanson had what was probably a fractured skull, Chambers had been badly burnt, and Knox had a broken leg. Chambers died first, on the third day. We threw his body overboard, knowing the sharks would eat him, and the Chinese cook surprised us by reciting some of the service of burial at sea: 'We therefore commit his body to the deep, to be turned into corruption, looking for the resurrection of the body when the Sea shall give up her dead.'

Food was running out. We had water still, thank God, or I wouldn't have made it, but we needed to eat too. There was a gaff in the life-boat. Sharks followed us all the time, often coming close, occasionally nudging the boat. These were blue sharks, maybe ten feet long, not enough to sink us but enough to keep us nervous day and night. Jim Bridy had worked on whalers before the war. On the fifth day a shark came in close, and Jim hit it with the gaff.

The blow didn't kill it, though it made it bleed. Sharks have no swim bladder. We watched it sinking through clear water. The other sharks tore it apart.

Another day passed before Jim got a second chance. This time he was quicker, and anyway we were desperate. My condition was getting worse. I couldn't help, but I watched as they hauled the shark aboard. The mouth came first, closing on the wooden side of the boat, and Walters and Bridy struck at the head. Even then it probably would have survived had other sharks not attacked its tail, ripping it off and making it lighter. The men got the shark aboard.

Jim tried again later, but he was tiring. The gaff impaled the back of a shark all right, but the shark sank before he could pull it out.

The night was spent stripping the shark. The stench was awful, even to men in our condition. I suppose I passed out.

I was in fever much of the time from then on, but there were lucid moments. I remember the cook feeding me something raw, grey and disgusting. 'What is it?' I asked. The cook laughed. 'Brains,' he said. 'From the shark.' Walters was watching me oddly, and he laughed too.

Hanson died round about then. I remember that. Blood ran from his ears. He knew he was dying and his eyes begged our help. But there was nothing we could do. The cook made the suggestion: 'We'll have to eat him.'

'No!' I said. 'We're Englishmen!'

For some reason the others just laughed at me.

I don't think they ate him, but I can't be sure: I don't like to think they ate him. But I had passed out again, and when I came to I was being shaken. Walters was over me, and a man in a white uniform. 'Captain Peters?' asked the stranger. His accent was Australian. So was the uniform when I got it into focus.

'Mr Peters,' I corrected him. 'First mate.'

He raised his eyebrows. 'Walters told me your name, but I thought by your cap you were the captain.'

'Cap?' I reached up and there was indeed a captain's hat on my head. It was bloodstained. There was a label inside: Captain Williams. 'I don't understand.'

Walters looked at me that same odd way. 'Bit of a joke,' he said. 'We reckoned you'd earned it.'

'You found Captain Williams?' I asked. He had been a fine man.

'We found his cap, sir. In the belly of the shark.'

The Australian cut in, telling Walters I needed to rest. Which I suppose I did. Walters left, laughing.

It took me a while to work it out, and even then I wasn't sure. Walters had a strange sense of humour. He would have enjoyed baiting me. That was why I had to have that shark's head. I took it home. It took an axe to get through it, and inside there was nothing at all like the grey stuff I had been given on the boat. I knew the worst. The shark had not only eaten the captain's cap. The shark had eaten the captain's head, and so had I.

3

THE SECOND STORY: CRASH REPORT

1. A neon sign winks and the wreck is punched with light/lost in shadow/punched with light.

2. The car is a Cadillac, New Hampshire plates. The fender is bent almost in two, like it tried to embrace the billboard. All the lights are out and glass is strewn on the sidewalk. The impact has shoved the hood sideways, twisting it, and where it twists it flakes skyblue paint.

3. The chrome is still bright.

4. The radio still plays.

5. The windshield is badly cracked. The cracks seem to focus on a single point in front of the wheel. At this point certain shards have been pushed aggressively forward, stabbing at the billboard. There is blood, and something else, on these shards.

6. The blood is red when the neon shines, black when the light is off.

7. The radio still plays. It is playing rock and roll.

8. The driver is sitting back in the seat, but had apparently been thrown forward at the moment of collision. His eyes are open. Severe damage at the joint of the frontal and occipital bones has caused irreparable damage to the cerebrum.

9. Most of the blood comes from his nose. It trails down his cleanshaven upper lip, skirts his mouth, and has dripped on to the collar of his shirt.

10. The radio still plays and the music is relentless. Elvis sings: I got a whole lot o' livin' to do.

11. The shirt is white, good quality, and recently pressed. He wears a pair of light grey Brooks Bros slacks and a darker reefer jacket. In his pockets there is $45 in bills and three dimes, one a 'Lucky'. He carries a New Hampshire licence and wears a fraternity ring. Contusions to his chest, especially in the region of the *pectoralis major*, indicate he hit the wheel as well as the windshield.

12. The radio still plays and Elvis still sings. O the moon is big and bright/In the Milky Way tonight/But the way you act you never would know it's there.

13. There is no moon tonight.

14. The seat right of the driver is empty but on the floor in front is a bunch of roses. The roses have been damaged by the collision. The radio still plays – You're the prettiest thing I've seen/But you treat me so doggone mean – and the rose petals look black in the night.

15. The radio still plays.

16. I got a whole lot o' livin' to do,
    A whole lot o' lovin' to do.
    Come on babe, to make a party takes two.
    I got a whole lot o' livin' to do.

17. One rose has been separated from the bunch, though the base of the stem is still entwined with the rest. The stem is badly bent some four inches below the flower, and several petals have come loose.

18. One petal has landed on the lap of his light grey Brook Bros slacks.

19. The neon winks and the wreck is punched with light/lost in shadow/punched with light.

20. I got a whole lot o' livin'/A whole lot o' lovin' to do.

4

THE THIRD STORY: THE VECCHIO CARTOON

'It is neither my habit to explain my actions, nor my intention to justify them to you, here or at any time. But it is clear from our recent conversation that your investigations have brought you close to the truth: rather than be the subject of further speculation I therefore append my own account of my brother Edward's demise.

'You have learnt I employed a certain Felix Rubbia as my agent, commissioning him to establish my brother's whereabouts, and to establish also what cause had kept my brother from his family for almost four years; you know also, I believe, I received a fateful telegram from Rubbia which, reaching me at the House, precipitated the sad events I now relate, though I do not believe you know the contents. A terse and painful note, it informed me that my brother had been found, dead, in a rooming house in Florence. The cause of death was not given.

'I had been on the point of leaving for luncheon at my club but my appetite quite vanished upon receipt of this sad and painful missive; I excused myself of my companions and returned at once to my town house, in search of solitude and the opportunity to consider this unfortunate circumstance. The thoughts which troubled my mind sprang not only from that natural sense of grief all must feel at the loss of a relative so close, but also from more worldly concerns. I had not seen my brother Edward in four years, and we had never been intimate, he being much my junior, and my sense of loss was coupled with a yet deeper sense of misgiving. For though I knew not what enterprise my brother had undertaken, I never doubted but that it involved some dark and dangerous dealings. News of Edward's death could not be kept long from the world; I resolved at once that I should embark, *incognito*, for Italy, and pursue the matter there.

'It is a reflection of my state of mind that, for the first time since the disaster of the last election, I was grateful my party was not in government. No matter that the ship of state was steered by incompetents; I had the leisure to investigate my brother's death and perhaps prevent the foul breath of scandal. I telegrammed Rubbia with instructions to inform no one of my brother's fate nor make any move, and to anticipate my imminent arrival in Florence . . .

'My affairs being well ordered, I was able to leave the next day. I travelled without pomp and with only one manservant, crossing the Channel at Dover and reaching Paris by nightfall; at Paris I eschewed my habitual haunts and stayed instead at an hotel near the railway station, ready to recommence my journey at dawn. Paris is the city of carefree youth, quite unsuited to the mood of these my middle years.

'Such is the quality of the railway system even on the Continent that I arrived in Florence within five days of receipt of Rubbia's telegram, and upon my arrival in that city I lost no time in hunting that gentleman out. I found him at his hotel. He was much as I remembered him: a small, dark, intelligent man, in whom were combined the manners of a gentleman and the spirit of a mercenary; he was not a man with whom one might choose intercourse, perhaps, yet he was ideally suited to my purposes.

' "Have you notified anyone of my brother's death?" I asked him as soon as we were alone together.

' "No one, I assure you."

' "And the corpse?"

' "Remains where I found it. Nothing is disturbed, Your Grace."

' "I am travelling under the name of Davenport," I informed him curtly. "I ask you to remember that."

' "Certainly, Mr Davenport." I suspected insolence yet said nothing; I needed this man's help, and his silence.

' "Take me to this boarding house at once," I instructed. "You can relate all you know on the way."

'It was a short journey, and his a shorter tale. Rubbia, upon receipt of my commission, traced my brother by means of articles, bearing the family crest, deposited at various pawnbrokers. The trail took him first to Rome and then to Florence, where for a while he lost the scent, until he heard of a solitary Englishman living in extreme poverty in the poorest district of that city.

' "You were certain that man was my brother?" I asked.

' "Not at first, but I showed the picture you had given to me to his landlady and, with the inducement of a certain amount of money, she recognised it at once. More money won me the key to his mean room. He was dead, exactly as you shall find him today: I have obeyed your instructions to the letter. There is no doubting it is he: despite the poverty into which he had sunk there is ample evidence of his identity. I took the precaution of removing that evidence, incidentally, in case another found the body." He handed me a monogrammed notecase, a loosely bound manuscript, and a bundle of letters.

'I could not fault the man's conduct thus far, yet I felt foreboding. He was a man of intellect and such men are dangerous. None the less I was obliged to trust as well as thank him. "And that is all you know?" I asked. "You do not know the reason for my brother's poverty, nor for his death?"

' "Both, I think, shall be apparent when we reach the room."

'This we soon did. The house was as Rubbia had described it, a once-prosperous merchant's mansion gone to seed, the façade cracked and crumbling, the shutters hanging awry. We entered surreptitiously, Rubbia having taken a copy of the keys. Dry plaster from crumbling ceilings powdered the bare boards; the walls were marked with grime; an evil smell of neglect and worse seemed to cling to the very air. What destiny had brought my brother here?

'Rubbia took me to a rank corridor. The windows were filthy, and no light penetrated save where panes were cracked and broken. He led me to a door. Only in so foetid a place could that foul odour of decay have gone long unremarked.

'He opened the door. The putrescence released almost overpowered me. "I do not vouch for his condition," my companion remarked.

'We entered. The room was bare save a miserable mattress and a chair. On one wall a dirty sheet was hung. Another sheet concealed a bundle on the floor. Rubbia lifted the second sheet. For a moment I thought I was victim of some dreadful deception. The corpse on the floor was that of a Negro. But then I realised the mistake was mine. Though blackened by the marks of death, the face was undeniably that of my brother, Edward.

'I stepped back in horror. The cheeks were sunken, the swollen black tongue protruding, the staring eyes an awful white. But the features were unmistakable. "How?" I gasped. "Why?"

'In answer Rubbia walked to the wall and drew back the second sheet. "I changed only one thing in this room," he said. "I thought it better this was covered." The condition of my brother's corpse had disconcerted me, but at least I had been prepared; nothing could have prepared me for what lay behind that sheet.

'I know not how long I stood stupefied. It was Rubbia broke the silence. "Superb, is it not?" he said.

'I could not deny it. "You know what it is?"

'"Your brother's notes confirmed what I already suspected. It is the lost cartoon of the battle of Anghiari. I gave you the notes: you should read them. The story they tell is quite remarkable."

'"I must sit down," I said. The solitary chair was placed directly in front of the panel. I sat and stared at Leonardo's lost masterpiece, the chalk cartoon he had made in preparation for decorating the walls of the Palazzo Vecchio. How can I describe such magnificence? Two stately stallions, their muscles highlighted in firm white lines, reared in the foreground as their riders fought. One rider held a slashing sword, the other a spear. From the expression on the swordsman's face one could sense his exultation: he was about to deliver the *coup de grâce*. And perhaps a premonition of his fate had reached the other, for his face was resigned and his eyes bright with the pity of it all. In the background were other figures, entwined in combat, and beyond them a roughly indicated landscape of wide valleys.

'I turned to the manuscript Rubbia had presented me. I do not believe I have to describe to you the details of Edward's painstaking research and how he eventually discovered the cartoon, unidentified, in a dusty corner of a disused monastery: it is clear from our conversation that you retraced my brother's steps with commendable thoroughness. Nor do I need tell you how the recovery of the cartoon became Edward's obsession and only goal, nor yet how, having achieved his goal, and displayed the masterpiece upon the wall of that dingy room, he never once moved away from it. As to his state of mind, of course, we can only guess what mania prevented him leaving its sight for a moment, so that in time he died of hunger and thirst. Perhaps your friend the physician knows of similar cases, but certainly this is unique in my experience.

'Clearly, however, for all your knowledge, you are mistaken in one respect. For I do not possess the cartoon.

'My family, as you are certainly aware, is one of the oldest and most distinguished in the realm. For eight hundred years we have served our country. In return we have received many honours: my own dukedom dates back only to the reign of Queen Anne, but the earldom I bear was granted by the Conqueror himself. Yet such distinctions, welcome as they are, are mere trifles beside the family name. My brother bore that name. We had not, as I have said, been intimate. Yet still he was my brother, scion of my noble house. He deserved better than this anonymous death in a foreign land, this mean death in a meaner room.

'It was expensive to persuade Rubbia to assist me, but that is of no matter. Together we wrapped Edward's corpse, awkward and stiff though it was, in that magnificent cartoon, and in silence I lighted one corner. We watched as the flames consumed both corpse and cartoon, until the fire spread to the floor and walls and we were driven out. There are those who would call the destruction of such a masterpiece a sacrilege. I am not interested in their opinions. This man had been my brother, and this was a fitting end.

'I do not believe you would find it easy to press charges. Few knew of the cartoon's existence, and though your client has, I gather, prior claim to its ownership, he is welcome to whatever is left. The proprietor of the boarding house was more than happy with the compensation I gave: I blamed my brother's carelessness for the fire. Likewise I am steadfast in my right to dispose of my brother's body as I thought fit. And finally, of course, your absolute inability to find Rubbia weakens considerably any case you may have.

'In other words, Mr Holmes, your cleverness has been to no avail.'

He ceased to speak. His secretary, recognisably the same man who had taken his Grace to the squalid Florentine room, laid down the pen. Together they walked to a corner of the spacious library. This corner was an interesting detail, a priest-hole, though of ample proportions. The duke opened the secret door. No natural light entered. The two men lit lanterns and went in. One wall was hung with a blood red curtain. 'Pull it back, Edward,' said the duke, and his brother was pleased so to do. They laughed, and gloated as they laughed.

5

THE FOURTH STORY: FROM THE ORBITING STATION

They thought of it as below, for they had gone up; they were used to changes down there. Cloud patterns altered constantly. The colour of the sea changed too. These things came and went. But one day they noticed that things only came. That brown smudge over Africa continued to grow. The green stain in the sea off Holland turned ochre but refused to disappear. A second brown smear developed over South America.

To begin with there was still contact. They heard from base; they heard radio stations and TV shows. But one by one the shows went off the air. They did not need the infra-red to know: 'It's getting hot down there,' said Denisov. Base was last to go, and that day the ice-cap went too.

They were trained, they were professional; they were the élite survivors of the toughest of regimes. But when they passed into the shadow and saw each time fewer lights, until one time there were no lights at all, they felt bad, they were unable to cope. 'There's only one thing for it,' said Dupont. 'I'm going home. You coming?'

Denisov and Donlon looked at one another: 'Why not?' they answered.

They put on their space suits for the last time; they opened the airlock and left. They could leave only one by one. By the time Denisov, who was last, emerged, his colleagues were being drawn by the earth. First they were silver glows as the sun caught their suits, and then they were briefly red as they burnt upon re-entry.

They were trained, they were professional, yet still Denisov screamed. Sound is the vibration of air recorded on the inner ear. In space there is no air. And in all of space, in all the universe, there were no longer any working inner ears.

6

THE FIFTH STORY: THE MAN OF LAW'S TALE

I cannot understand their minds. When I asked for pen and paper they were embarrassed, their demeanour implying that even by making such a request I contravened some law of decorum. *Of course you can have pen and paper*, their faces suggested: *We are not barbarians*. Yet they are frightened of what I might write, and being thus frightened, why do they not deny me? At least in such matters the Reich was consistent.

But their attitude over this pen and these sheets of paper is, if not consistent, at least characteristic. The mock legality and affected humanity of these entire proceedings is as offensive as the hypocrisy by which I am condemned by one legal system for upholding the statutes of another. I have been found guilty of 'crimes against humanity', of 'war crimes', a *post facto* description of my actions which bears no relation to justice but only to my status as one of the defeated. I am condemned for having done my duty; I am condemned for being on the losing side. It appears that Cicero's tag *Silent enim leges inter arma* – laws are inoperative in war – still applies, for my accusers ignore the dubious moral basis of their position and concentrate entirely on the fact that they hold me captive; yet, if Cicero was right, as he appears to be, the very category of crime for which I am accused ceases to exist.

Do they not understand that their position is untenable?

Let me begin with a confession. I confess that, as charged, I signed the death warrants of slightly more than one hundred thousand individuals found guilty of crimes against the Reich. I also admit that there will be relatives and friends of that one hundred thousand who would wish to see me dead. The German state lost the war: I am the captive of those I sought to destroy. I accept that I will die: natural law, the acceptable demand of those I harmed for revenge, would demand no less. But I do not accept, nor can I accept, either the particular case brought against me or the terms in which it is framed. Were I being charged for my actions by my victims or anyone who spoke for my victims I should naturally have to accept their judgment: they would establish that my signature had indeed condemned all those people to death, and then they would tear me to pieces. But I am not being charged by those relatives and friends, nor by anyone who speaks for the victims. Rather, I am being

225

charged by the victors. And I should rather be torn to pieces, be subject to violence in return for violence, than have my victors sit in judgment over me.

For that is what they are doing. They judge me, they weigh my soul and find it wanting, and thus I am sentenced to death. I was never so confident in my judgments. We relied on strict biological and racial criteria to lead us to our conclusions, and recognised that our right to judge derived solely from our strength. Those who have judged me are less honest. They believe that they are in the right. Yet the same essential formula applies in this court as in the courts of the Reich: the judged are weaker than the judge.

I must go carefully however. I shall not die tomorrow, but it could be the next day or the day after, and though I have counter-charges to make against their court, there are other things I must first say. First, I shall demonstrate that, as a functionary of an established legal system, I cannot have committed any offence by upholding that system's laws. In this process I shall argue that the law permits no contradictions, and, indeed, that the elimination of contradiction is a major function of the law. Therefore, if the laws I upheld were internally consistent – and I shall demonstrate that they were – then for me to have challenged those laws would be *ultra vires*; it would be beyond my legal position and would place me beyond the law.

Secondly, I shall challenge the assessment of a just or unjust law, and establish that any such assessment must be entirely subjective; I shall then determine objective criteria by which to evaluate laws, and prove that the system I upheld conforms to any objective test.

Finally, I shall show that the court which has sentenced me has offended against the law, and against humanity, because it has denied the basic principles of both the most sophisticated, and the most simple, of legal systems.

To recapitulate a little on my own position, I was, as I have said, a functionary. I entered my present position within the legal community, indeed, before the last government, and though the Reich extended my powers my role remained essentially the same: I was a prosecutor, and it was my job to establish the guilt of the accused. That under Weimar the accused were tried in open court and that under the Reich – for reasons of economy – guilt was generally decided in committee is irrelevant: my position and function remained the same. It was my job to evaluate the evidence and to present the case against the defendant; it was not my job to examine the correctness or otherwise of the laws I was called upon to uphold, nor should it have been so. This 'war crime' of which I have been accused, this 'crime against humanity', seems to be that I did my job, yet my job was the same under Reich or Weimar: there is an inconsistency here.

I shall not, however, take the easy way out and base my defence on this alone. Why should I? For their arguments do not topple as a line of dominoes but rather fall discretely, each of its own weakness.

I reiterate my position once again: I was a functionary. My job itself was not illegal; the illegality must therefore reside in the laws which I upheld. But can a law break a law? This is a difficult question, and if the answer is *No* then I am already discharged, because there is no charge to answer. But we will assume that the answer to this question is *Yes* – you see once more how I refuse to take the easy way out, such is my confidence I can refute them – and that *a law can break a law*. Indeed, we can see this if we think of a simple law which, for instance, prevents gambling in any place which sells intoxicating liquor, contradicted by a different law which is the product of a different generation and which says that the function of the bar-room in a gentleman's club is gaming and drinking. When this sort of contradiction occurs, it questions the validity of one or both of the laws; no such contradiction occurred in the laws I was asked to uphold. On the contrary, those laws were based on a simple and logical system, with readily established evidence of a biological or racial kind to determine when they were contravened. That some might find this sort of evidence distasteful does not negate the legality of the process in any way: evidence, particularly in cases of sexual deviation, is frequently distasteful.

The purpose of a legal system is to regulate the behaviour of individuals for the well-being of society: the definition is my own, but I believe it to be accurate and appropriate. Except in cases where the laws challenge themselves, such as in the case above where there is a distinct anomaly, it should not have been my role to question the law. Rather, it would have been the converse of my role, for my function was to maintain the law. For me to have taken any course other than the one I took therefore would have demanded that I question the law – not any specific law, but rather the whole fabric of the law, since there was no internal contradiction within that fabric – and thus, challenging the fabric of the law, I should have put myself in a position beyond the law. It is not possible to challenge an entire legal system without denying oneself the benefits of that system; equally, to do so would be impractical and indefensible, since society cannot function without the regulating action of the law, and neither can the individual flourish. Only in a state of anarchy would it be permissible to challenge the laws with impunity, and in such a state there would be no laws to challenge! This last is a joke, yes, but it is a Teutonic joke: it has its serious side.

For if you are to deny the legitimacy of my laws, the laws it was my function to uphold, you are also denying – because there is no inherent contradiction in those laws which I call mine to render them vulnerable to attack – the supremacy of the rule of law. Yes, we can dismember the legal system and the legal apparatus, and the result will be anarchy. And yes, if that is what we want, we must do this and accept the consequences. But that is not, apparently, what those who sat in judgment over me wanted, for they have simply replaced one legal system with another. The method by which this has been achieved is brute force, and the right by which it has occurred is the right of conquest. Yet they still do not admit this, and claim instead that their justification is their superior morality!

But again my desire to voice my dissatisfaction with the court which tried me has interfered with the logical progression of my ideas. I have jumped ahead, although in a way which is not entirely irrelevant. All I have said so far has ignored the question of 'just' or 'unjust' laws, a question which I expect will be of paramount importance to those who read this in a critical way, with the desire to maintain their condemnations of my actions and myself. (And if I am honest I must acknowledge that no one but those who have condemned me, and seek to keep me condemned, is likely to read this.) So I must turn my mind to the question of justice.

Again, this is not a simple question. It is certainly the duty of a court of law to put the law into practice without prejudice or malice – in other words, to administer the laws justly. This is a pragmatic point: the court must be impartial. But can laws themselves, framed by society and according to society's requirements, be impartial? It would seem not. The law deals, as Aristotle told us, not in equality but in equity. It treats equals as equals. But it is society, rather than the courts, which defines who is equal. In most legal systems money can buy the best advice and the best defence. Therefore these systems tacitly acknowledge that our most frequent criterion for judging who is equal to whom, and who unequal, is financial. This is not, generally, seen as unjust; it applies the notion of equity and does not seek to impose any spurious or controversial notion of equality; this inequality is accepted in a capitalist system because in such a system money is seen as a primary distinguishing feature; only an idealist would deny it exists, and the law is a pragmatic rather than idealistic institution, reflecting rather than imposing society's values. Under National Socialism the primary distinction was race, and though each analysis, each method of dividing society, may be imperfect, at the same time each at least recognises that an attempt to pretend everyone has parity is doomed. Were we all the same, then absolute equality before the law would be a simple matter; as we are all different, then the best that can be done is to devise a system whereby there is at least equity, equality between equals. (Incidentally, it is perhaps worth noting that the National Socialist system, unlike many competing systems, did aim towards some ultimate equality; its method, of course, was the very process of elimination for which I am now sentenced, and once again the poor logic of those who have judged me is evident.)

There are certain demands we can make of the law. That it is consistent is one. That it treats equals equally is a second. Further to this we can expect the law to be intelligible and widely promulgated, to avoid making impossible demands, and for there to be a congruence between its declared aims and actual practice. The laws I upheld contravened none of these requirements. Consistency was a principal feature, for the laws were entirely consistent not only in whom they affected but also in the actions they took against that group. It is likewise evident that equals were treated equally: the race laws differed for different groups within the Reich, but within those groups the laws were applied even-handedly. That the laws were intelligible and widely promulgated is certain: indeed, the groups singled out for special treatment were identified well before the treatment was put in practice, and made to wear distinguishing marks such as the yellow star. The laws were operable, obviously: had they not been I would not be here condemned. And that there was congruence between declared aims and actual practice is apparent from even a cursory reading of the Führer's speeches.

I have by now demonstrated the fallacy of the arguments used against me. To summarize: it was my duty and function to uphold the laws of the land, unless they failed to conform to specific criteria; the laws I was required to administer did not fail to comply in any way with any of those criteria, and therefore had I contemplated any action other than that which I took I should have contravened the law. I cannot be charged with an action for which the alternative was illegality. Nor can I be accused of injustice, or of unjust practices: each of those warrants was signed only when infringement of the laws had been established beyond reasonable doubts. The case against me collapses.

Finally, however, I wish to present counter-charges against the court which tried me. I am tired and must be brief: none the less these are important issues and such is my feeling on these matters I must drive myself on.

For the offence of that court is greater than any with which I have been charged. (Forgive me if my English grows more stilted as I tire.) That court has adopted a position which is untenable by all the criteria I have laid before you. It does not treat equals with equality: for instance, I, an officer of the court, am treated as though I were some truncheon-wielding sadist from the Sudetenland. Secondly, the laws by which they have attempted to convict me are retroactive: they were not even in existence at the time of my so-called transgression, much less promulgated and intelligible. Thirdly, they are inconsistent: some of these inconsistencies I have demonstrated, and result from the speed with which these laws were devised and executed; others, such as the court's reaction (or lack of reaction) to the way the Russians treated their prisoners, are the product of wilful blindness. Fourthly, they make impossible demands, in that one cannot be expected to conform to a law that did not exist until after the event. Fifthly, they are not operable, except insofar as they will result in my death and that of a few hundred other individuals, for they pretend to be 'international' laws (the only way they can be used against citizens of the German nation state) yet have no international jurisdiction: I have mentioned the Russians' treatment of their prisoners-of-war; there is also the case of the American South, and of the concentration camps in British South Africa; if the laws by which I am tried do not operate even in the nations that devised them, then what chance do they have of being truly international? And finally, they are the product of a mock moral superiority which is subjective and has no place in the process of the law. My trial was a sham, by any standards. My trial was the intervention of a third party in a dispute which was already settled; it was the blatant attempt of the victors to place the burden of the war on the losers. Versailles crippled the German economy for two decades, by making us pay for the last war in cash; Nürnberg and these other so-called trials will cripple the German spirit, by making us pay for this war in guilt. We are the scapegoats for the victors, and their standards are double.

I am confident of my arguments, yet less confident of my expression. I intended to be resolute and rational, yet my feelings have infiltrated my ideas. But what reaction do you expect to injustice? How else can I respond? It is not the fear of death which makes me feel so strongly (and write so badly), it is my hatred of those who mock the law. I do not think I am afraid of death.

I am afraid of dying.

I saw once the oven doors opened, and the guards tossing out the dead. My attention was directed to the corpses' damaged and bloodied nails. I had known of course that men would fight against their death, yet I had not known how hard: they had torn at the walls, the air-tight doors, and at one another; not only their fingers, but also their toenails, were ripped and raw. Some of the nails were torn completely off, which must hurt very much.

It is this that frightens me; death does not. When the air is clear the bodies are removed, piled into heaps, bulldozed away. Limbs detach frequently. The bodies are rolled into trenches and covered. These are not people, they are corpses. They are beyond our laws and our sympathy; they are beyond our understanding.

I have worked hard all my life and have done my work with efficiency; I have few regrets. I shall naturally miss my wife, and my grandchildren, and the retirement we had promised ourselves in Rügen, and I am sorry I have never read Goethe's *Faust*, but these are feelings I should have had if a heart attack had finished me, and are not responses to the current situation. There is only one cause, one particular, that makes me cavil at my fate, and that is that all my adult life I have spent upholding the due and correct process of the law and am sickened by the false court and the false laws by which I am condemned.

Sickened.

7

A SIXTH STORY

Jennifer Fox is laid in the earth. Her soul goes up to heaven.

Chapter Eleven

A WINTER'S TALE

*In which Jennifer Fox
is Laid to Rest*

I

Pastel day, flat cloud hiding the sun. Colours are denied; everything is muted, faded, tactful.

They climb the hill in careful cars, turn left to the cemetery gates. They stop a while. Chapman and the Gruafins sit in the same car. It is the second car in the procession. The first car is the hearse. Alan and Chapman face backward. Ernest and Bridget face forward. There is plenty of opportunity to exchange comments or glances but no one does. They sit in solemn silence, out of respect for death and perhaps for Jennifer.

Chapman has his hat on his lap. He holds it with both hands. He looks through the side window. His view brushes Ernest, who sits opposite, but he looks neither at Ernest nor at anything beyond. He is trying to remember the last words he spoke with Jennifer, and cannot. They swapped words in a hospital room, and then there was a hurry of doctors and nurses. Everyone was busy in the hospital. Even death. He is grateful he viewed the body, glad to have seen her in tranquillity after her messy clinical death. It helps. The reality of dying is the hospital, perhaps, the washed-down walls and scrubbed floors, the efficient steel box for the removal of bodies; all the rest – the silk-lined oak coffin with brass handles, the serenity of the prepared corpse, the ceremony of this funeral – is just theatre. But it seems to Chapman that though dying is a routine thing, a medical opinion and a signature on a form, death itself is different. Death needs the theatre, the ritual. He has seen the reality of dying, the pain and the functional steel box, and can neither ignore nor forget it. But he has also seen Jennifer laid out at rest, at peace with

235

her death and the world she has left, and that is part of death too.

Alan would make a poem of such thoughts. He is looking for a poem. He is looking through scrupulously clean windows for a poem, and has not found one yet. The wait at the cemetery gates gets longer. The churchyard had been filled a century ago, save a few family spaces, and a new graveyard had been opened by the council. The council cemetery is next to the council estate. There is a sign outside, white lettering on a pointed blue board, which bans dogs, glass bottles and cars without permission: West Derbyshire County Council reserve the right to close the cemetery to the public without notice. There is a poem in that perhaps, but not the poem he requires.

Ernest finds he wants to fidget. This pause is disconcerting. There seems to be some administrative problem to sort out with a man who has come from the gatehouse. The sexton? The gatehouse is substantial, with a conservatory and a garden full of cold-frames. The winter cold-frames are empty and look abandoned.

Bridget looks at the gatehouse too, at the conservatory and the cold-frames. She wonders if the sexton supplements his income selling flowers. Doubtless, she thinks, he finds a ready market.

Whatever the problem was it is solved. Ernest wishes he knew more about funerals. He blames his ignorance on his Jewish mother, who kept him cut off from the rites of the Anglican Church. But none of them knows much more than him. Bridget, thinking about the sexton, was deciding that funerals are the province of experts. The undertakers take the responsibility, the vicar the best lines. All the mourners have to do is mourn, and even in this they are assisted, given acceptable ways of showing their grief, acceptable ways of accepting their grief.

The procession begins again, driving along a tarmac track between tombs. The oldest graves are nearest the gate; to reach Jennifer's plot they must drive the length of the cemetery, the length of the century. The graveyard is longer than it is wide, and is built, as all Derbyshire is built, into the side of a hill. A slice has been taken from the hill, Ernest notes, in an effort to reduce the gradient. He wonders about drainage. He does not know much about funerals but he does know about drainage.

Bridget looks beyond the graves. A steep precipice to the north drops through unkempt woods to a line of semis; on the other side there is a lane, colonised at one end by a few houses, and beyond that farming land. Ahead too, over the boundary hedge, are fields, and at the far side of the fields the land slips away to the Wye valley. Haddon Hall is somewhere over there, hidden in the trees; the land rises again, and further away, out of sight, is Chatsworth.

Ernest is thinking about a more modest architecture. There are two chapels in the cemetery, similarly ugly buildings which, despite their gothic inspiration, seem to lack the aspirations associated with gothic architecture. No spires here; no reaching for the heavens: these chapels are grounded in the earth, almost crouching, and their silly flèches prod the sky apologetically.

They move on. Bridget too looks at the chapels. She wonders why there are two of them. Do so many people die in Bakewell they need a second chapel of rest? Do so many people live in Bakewell? She thinks about the ugliness of the chapels, the proximity of the council estate: though she knows there is no choice, no space in the churchyard, she feels there is something proletarian about being buried here, away from the feudal grandeur of the church, before deciding the thought is uncharitable. After all, she decides, this is a pleasant enough place to lie. The views are good, though presumably unappreciated; the grass is well tended; the leaves swept regularly. The wind is a little strong, that's all.

The cars pass the first chapel, approach the second. A spray of roses in a perforated stand catches Ernest's eye. Even their bright colours are faded in the listless light of this day. Ernest has a rose bush in his garden which, in this mild, carbon-dioxide laced winter, has flowered unexpectedly and rather well. These roses, however, are past their best, and petals scatter prettily on a gravel of marble chips. The marble chips are the colour of sugar crystal. The rose petals lie discarded across the marble. At this distance they could be toffee wrappers, thinks Ernest, which is odd, because if I discovered they were toffee wrappers I would think them ugly, disgraceful. Toffee wrappers would be litter; rose petals are poignant.

The cars come to a halt outside the second chapel. The driver gets out first, opens the doors for them. The priest is waiting, a black hood hanging over his white surplice. He offers a consoling smile to the mourners as they get out. Alan returns the smile nervously, habitually, as if uncertain which convention to obey.

The third car draws up, carrying Robert and the professor. It is easier for them, thinks Alan. They represent institutions; their grief is not meant to hurt. They can concentrate on the performance, the studied solemnity. They need not test their expressions against their emotions as I feel I must.

The coffin is lifted carefully from the hearse. Fat wreaths, like life-belts that came too late, deck the coffin. Six strong men lift it easily. The weight is all in the wood. They carry it into the chapel. The vicar follows, and Chapman follows the vicar.

Robert envies Chapman. Robert represents an institution. He need not test his emotions. Yet neither can he show them: that is not his role. He remembers the manuscript of *Shakespeare's Great Theme* – a fat heap of bank paper, a carbon copy of the original, hole-punched holes bound with a pale blue ribbon. He liked the ribbon, the frivolity of it, the femininity. He liked the manuscript. It was the first really good manuscript he had handled. The King was dead, the Queen uncrowned. He remembers the Skylon, the Festival Hall, the youth of it, the promise. Death is an unsubstantiated rumour when you are young, he thinks. The war was long enough ago to be history, recent enough to make peace seem worth while. Death was something that happened elsewhere. There were crises and bomb tests, atolls and iron curtains. They did not stop me being young.

He remembers the proofs, vast sheets meticulously revised, and the best of the reviews. 'Exactly the study of Shakespeare needed', was the *Manchester Guardian*'s verdict; 'The most refreshing insight I have seen for a long time', said *The Times*; 'Destined to be a classic', said *London Magazine*. Jenny was my first success, he thinks, and I miss her. This is why he envies Chapman. Chapman was her lover; Chapman is allowed to show grief. But who am I? Her publisher: representative of an institution. I mourn her, my youth, myself, yet I am not allowed to grieve. Lord knows there is plenty to grieve for.

They enter the chapel. Candles would be nice, thinks Ernest: it is a shame there are no candles. A candle for Jenny Horse-face; a candle to light her to heaven.

Six people to see her off, thinks Jardine. He is embarrassed none of his colleagues has come. Their excuse is the vacation. He has another embarrassment. He had parked outside Jenny's house without thinking, composed his face, greeted Chapman; Chapman, deferential, had asked him to move his car. 'The cortège,' he had said, and Jardine had cursed himself for not thinking of this: 'I'm so sorry; I'll move it at once.' So clumsy; so stupid; so me.

His obituary was not in the *Independent* this morning, which worries him too. I should have got it done over the weekend, he tells himself, and though he knows the answer he asks himself why he didn't. Busy, he reminds himself, but he knows this was not it. He had been scared – scared he was writing her off, suddenly aware how little he knew her, suddenly aware how little he knew. He has written two books on Yeats, knows the poems and the alterations the poet later made, knows the hermetic system which informed the poems, knows the background, Maud Gonne, the Celtic Twilight, the Troubles, knows it all. Yet what do I really know? He stands in the chapel. Electric bulbs hang from the ceiling, concealed in black iron lanterns. They are suspended from metal chains. Each link in the chain is a diamond-shaped spike and the diamonds, though all the same size, alternate so that one points up and down, the next side to side. Round the spiked chain is the flex, off-white, cruelly twisted. What do I really know? Jenny had seen Death's Angel. What do I know of that?

And without that, without some sense of the mystery that lies beyond the world, what can I know of Yeats, of any poet? All my life I have thought Yeats's mysticism no more than an heuristic device, a slightly batty notion which inspired some marvellous poems. That's how I treat it in my books: of interest for the poems it produced; of no interest in itself. Yet what if Yeats was right? Who am I to say he wasn't? With the benefit of my rational education, secure in my knowledge that mysticism is an elaborate hoax, I never thought to wonder . . .

To wonder what?

Nothing. That's the point. I never thought to wonder.

And now here I am at Jenny Fox's funeral, making a prayer to a God I deny. I do not want my prayer answered, thinks Jardine. I do not even want it to be heard. So why do I so much want to make it?

The priest starts to talk about Jennifer's life. He calls her a scholar and an inspiration. Ernest accepts she was a scholar. He is less certain that she was an inspiration. He remembers first meeting Bridget. He was in the second year of his course, a diligent student, and there had been an evening lecture on proportion in early medieval secular buildings. His diligence made him attend, but he had been the only student there and the lecture inaudible and incomprehensible. Afterwards there had been a discussion but he had nothing to discuss. He sat through it blankly.

There were still trams in Sheffield then. After the lecture he was crossing Glossop Road when the girl who crossed next to him tripped on the sunken tramlines. He helped her up. She thanked him. She was catching the same tram: he was going to his lodgings in Crookes; she was going further, to her parents' house in Fulwood. They exchanged this information as they waited, though they had not yet exchanged names. 'You're a student?' she had asked. 'You should be talking to my sister then. She's the clever one in our family.' And he remembers how he rebelled against this, resented this clever unknown sister who made this pretty girl think she was stupid. A scholar, yes. But not an inspiration. A weight.

The priest continues his peroration, remarks how she will be missed in Bakewell, her home for so many years. Funny how no one from Bakewell's turned up then, thinks Bridget: except Chapman of course, and he's hardly here as a neighbour.

She finds herself thinking kindly of Chapman. This is unexpected, and in a way unwanted. There is still some monkey business about the will to sort out. But I have to admit he's doing this well. He misses her, but there is dignity in his loss. She realises she has been watching him all the time, since they arrived at Jennifer's house and he greeted them: she has been waiting for that contemptible little man she knows is there to show. But it hasn't shown. She expected him to be pathetic, probably embarrassing, and instead he has been admirable. She looks at him. He sits listening to the vicar, his shoulders slightly bowed though his back is straight, his face composed though his lower lip, drawn in, registers his grief. She finds she is copying his position, his expression, using him as a model for her mourning. This disconcerts her, yet fascinates her. How well he bears up, she thinks with deliberate irony, but irony does not really suit her mood. I can see what Jennifer saw in him, she thinks.

She jerks her head, violently enough for Ernest to notice, but she does not see his concern. She has suddenly realised that this is the first time she has given Jennifer a thought all day. Ernest sees her blanch. He gives her his hand and she takes it, squeezes it, returns it.

Alan sits next to his father. He has few memories of Auntie Jennifer, none at all worth holding. He finds he is tapping his fingers on his lap. This irritates him. He did not mean to be bored. Boredom is irreverent, and he has no wish to be that. Yet he is bored none the less, and relieved when the vicar stops speaking.

There is another prayer. Chapman closes his eyes tight. He is speaking to Jennifer, not God. And then it is time to go outside. Alan is relieved. In a way they all are. Ernest supports his wife's arm.

The day is brighter than Alan remembered. Rooks' nests knot the branches of elms. They follow the coffin to the freshly turned earth, the open grave. The coffin is placed on tough black ribbons. Ashes to ashes, dust to dust. Time, which for all of them had been so slow, suddenly speeds up. Like at a concert, thinks Alan. You sit through hours of dreary twiddling and then along comes the tune you recognise, and all of a sudden things seem to get moving. Ashes to ashes, dust to dust. The coffin is lowered into the ground. A cold breeze blows from the hills, wraps round them as they stand, heads bowed, hands clasped, looking into the grave's narrow mouth. Chapman is aware of a kind of weariness but he does not close his eyes. He watches a token shovelful of earth scatter on the coffin lid. Ashes to ashes, dust to dust. Forasmuch as it hath pleased Almighty God of His great mercy to take unto Himself the soul of our dear sister here departed, we therefore commit her body to the ground; earth to earth, ashes to ashes, dust to dust; in sure and certain hope of the Resurrection to eternal life. Alan shivers slightly in the cold. Robert turns his eyes from the grave, looks at the clay that smears his black shoes. There is silence, time for thought, then slowly they turn, slowly they walk away. Leaves rustle, rooks creak in the trees. Their silence stays with them, and a different silence clings to the grave.

2

Afterwards, the drinks at the house. No one particularly wanted to stay, but there were too few of them for anyone to leave discreetly. Chapman handed round cream sherry in the pleasant living room. 'No books?' asked Jardine.

'The books are upstairs,' said Chapman. 'In Jennifer's study.' Only it was no longer Jennifer's study, and they were no longer Jennifer's books. 'Perhaps you'd like to look through them,' he said. 'If there are any you want I'm sure no one would mind.'

'I couldn't,' said the professor. 'I mean, that's terribly generous.'

'I don't suppose they're really mine to give away,' said Chapman. 'Jennifer didn't leave a will so it seems everything goes to Bridget, as her nearest relative. But I'm sure Jennifer would like to see them go to a good home.' He turned to Bridget. 'If you've no objection. There are rather a lot of books.'

Bridget said nothing; Jardine was flattered and slightly moved. 'Thank you,' he said, but he did not go upstairs.

Alan registered what Chapman had said. 'Excuse me.' Apart from a brief good morning earlier that day it was the first time he had spoken to Chapman in years. 'Did you say Auntie Jennifer didn't leave a will?'

'It never turned up?' asks Bridget.

Chapman shook his head. 'No.' He smiled at them. 'I'll move my things out as soon as possible. Now, does anyone want anything to eat? There's some food in the dining room.'

'You can't move out,' said Alan. 'That's ridiculous. This is your home.'

Bridget pulled Alan to one side. 'Don't be hasty.'

Alan spoke equally softly. 'Why didn't you warn me? I mean, we can't turf him out of his own home.'

They were too few for secrecy; though his voice was low all heard what was said. 'It's not my home,' said Chapman. 'It was Jennifer's. Now it's yours. Or your mother's at any rate.'

'Alan's,' said Bridget firmly. 'I've already got a home.'

'So've I,' said Alan.

'A rented flat in Hornsey!' said Bridget. 'What about when you get married?'

'Dad!' Alan appealed.

Chapman looked at them. 'Your mother's right,' he said.

Robert and the professor looked at one another uncomfortably. Alan looked at Ernest. 'Dad!' Alan said again.

'I don't know,' said Ernest. 'If Jennifer died intestate then I don't know how her estate gets divided up. I'm not a lawyer. I'm sorry.' The last remark was lame, and he realised as much. 'But I don't want to see Mr Chapman kicked out of his house,' he added, more strongly.

'Neither do I!' said Bridget.

'Well then,' said Ernest.

'But,' said Bridget, 'the house belongs to us.'

'Exactly,' said Chapman.

'Couldn't you contest this?' asked Alan. 'I mean, you live here. How long have you been here?'

'Thirty-five years, more or less.'

'Thirty-five years! You must have some rights!'

'Jennifer didn't leave a will. It would have been different if we'd been married of course, but we weren't.'

'Why not?' asked Ernest. It was not the sort of question he would normally have asked; this was not the sort of conversation he would normally have had.

'I never asked her,' said Chapman simply. He had been wondering about this: it had never occurred to him until it was too late that she might have wanted him to ask her; now it had occurred to him, too late, he wondered if she was deliberately punishing him by not leaving a will. In which case, he reasoned, he deserved to be kicked out.

'This is ridiculous,' said Alan, sticking with the only adjective that seemed to suit.

Robert and Jardine felt increasingly awkward, but no opportunity to leave presented itself. The professor decided to invent one. 'I really must be off,' he said.

'Me too,' said Robert.

'Are you going back to Sheffield?' asked Jardine, finishing his sherry.

'To the station, yes.'

'Would you like a lift?'

Robert would indeed.

'It was ever so good of you to come,' said Chapman. 'Thank you so much. I'm sure Jennifer would have appreciated it.'

Damn the man, thought Bridget. Why can't he grovel? Why can't he be abusive? Why can't he be pathetic? If he insisted we eat the food he's prepared, if he forced his pathos upon us, everything would be all right. But instead he's being so proper, so nice. 'All right!' she said. They all turned to look at her. She had the feeling they expected a speech. She had no speech to give. 'We can't expect you to leave your own house. You've lived here long enough, for goodness' sake. I mean, legally it doesn't belong to you.'

'No it doesn't,' agreed Chapman.

She had not finished what she wanted to say; she was getting infuriated. 'Look. Do you want to leave here? Or do you want to stay?'

'Well, I've been here a long time.'

'Exactly. So you want to stay.'

'Well, I suppose so. But it isn't my house.'

'Bugger whose house it is!' said Bridget. Alan and Ernest looked at her. Neither had heard her swear before. 'You can stay.'

There was a brief pause, then Robert began to clap. Jardine, Ernest and Alan joined in. Bridget turned on her son. 'I don't know what you're looking so pleased about!'

'That's extremely nice of you,' said Chapman, 'but it wouldn't be right.'

'Will you stop doing the decent thing for one moment please, and let me for a change?' asked Bridget.

Chapman looked at her, then held out his hand. She looked back, first at his face, then at his hand. She nodded. She shook his hand.

'Well, I really must be off,' said Jardine.

'Yes, me too,' said Robert. 'It really has been lovely to meet you, even under such sad circumstances. I'm so glad everything has been worked out for the best.'

'Sentimentalist!' said Bridget.

'There's nothing wrong with a bit of sentiment now and then,' said Robert professionally. 'It makes a pleasant change.'

Bridget was still facing Chapman. 'I presume you'll pay rent,' she said.

'Mother!'

'I'd be glad to,' said Chapman. He still had his pension; he suspected the DHSS might even help with the rent.

'Good.' She turned to her family. 'Everyone happy? Then we might as well leave too.'

'You must stay, have something to eat,' said Chapman.

Ernest, though a step behind his wife's moves, knew her well. 'I think we'd better go,' he said.

'If you insist.'

'I think we'd better.'

They went outside together. Ernest's car was parked by Jardine's, a little way down the street. 'Well,' said Chapman. 'Thank you again. For everything.'

'Don't mention it,' said Bridget, and she meant it.

Robert and Jardine left first. Neither spoke until they had turned the corner, reached the bridge. 'All's well that ends well,' said Robert.

'That was a relief,' said Jardine. 'I thought it was going to be nasty. Fancy Jenny not leaving a will. It seems out of character.'

'Who's to say?' said Robert. 'I haven't seen her in years but I used to know her well.' He remembered her typescripts, her meticulous proofs. 'She wasn't a careless woman. Perhaps she wanted things to turn out like this?'

'Perhaps,' agreed Jardine. 'Who's to say?'

The Gruafins got into their car, exchanging farewells with Chapman. 'We must meet again soon,' Chapman said.

'We will,' said Ernest and Alan. Bridget said nothing. She said nothing all the way home.

'What a charming man,' said Ernest as they too crossed the bridge. 'I'd never realised. He was always so much in Jenny's shadow.'

I can understand that at least, thought Bridget. God knows I can understand that.

Chapman cleared the glasses, the untouched food, and sat down with a cigarette. He watched the cigarette burn down in his hand. The smoke tufted and curled, a turbulence of blue. He inhaled and blew out a different texture of smoke, finer, more purposeful, less pretty. He addressed Jennifer in his head again. Thank you, he told her, and then: Thank you all.

3

'You're sure you'll not stay another night?' asks Ernest.

'I'd better get back,' replies Alan.

They shake hands, something they have never done before. There's nothing wrong with a bit of sentiment now and then, remembers Alan: it makes a pleasant change.

He takes the train back to London, dozes a little, sketches a poem:

Death is no confinement; despite
the rigid oak box and the sheer-sided trench
to die is to spread across heaven and earth,
across memory.
Death is redistribution.

It is nine-thirty when he gets back to his flat. He climbs the stairs and lets himself in, drops his bag and sits in the kitchen. He feels strange, rather wistful. He picks up the phone and dials the number Wendy gave him. Why not? But he is glad it is Wendy who answers: after all, there are reasons why not, even if he chooses to ignore them. 'Wendy? Alan here. Alan Gruafin.'

'Hello!' she says. She sounds pleased to hear from him.

He is pleased she is pleased. 'I wondered if you'd still fancy a drink?'

'Sure.'

'Tomorrow night?'

'That'd be lovely.'

'There's no problem is there?' With your husband, he means.

'No. That'd be fine. Where and when?'
'Somewhere local? I haven't got a car I'm afraid.'
'The Old Dog?'
'Great. Nine o'clock?'
'Great. I'll see you then. And thank you for ringing.'
'Thank you,' says Alan. 'See you. Bye.'
'Bye.'
He puts down the phone and sees the bedroom door open.
'Girlfriend?' asks Anne-Marie.

4

When the mourners have gone the gravediggers return. They fill in
the hole. The earth bounces heavily on my coffin to start with, and
then the soil piles up and the noise is increasingly muffled. In time
my coffin will decompose and the worms will eat me, I suppose. At
the moment there is just the silence that clings to the grave.

Chapter Twelve

AFTER THE FUNERAL

A Grammarian's Funeral at that

'Grant I have mastered learning's crabbed text,
  'Still there's the comment.
'Let me know all! Prate not of most or least,
  'Painful or easy!
'Even to the crumbs I'd fain eat up the feast,
  'Aye, nor feel queasy.'
                    Robert Browning:
                    'A Grammarian's Funeral'

I

So there you have it. You guessed, or maybe you didn't? It doesn't matter – I gave clues to my identity, but there is no stigma to not working out that I am Dr Jennifer Fox. And there are still things to explain.

First, this is not a ghost story: I am not you and I am still not dead, not yet. Rather, as I explained to Professor Jardine, I toss my death like a pebble into the lives of my characters and watch the ripples move forward, backward, sideways in time.

There are a number of reasons I have done this. I am not you, and I am not dead. But the cancer is real enough, and the pain and the confinement.

I write this in defiance of death, and in defiance of Death's Angel. It is a piece of bravura, an attempt to confront the worst.

I write this to make sense of my cancer, to make sense of my death. I want to rationalise my death; I want something of me to survive. I try to imagine what it will be like. The details may be inaccurate: it is surprisingly hard to get a straight answer to questions about funeral arrangements or legal niceties while on a terminal ward; they are embarrassed either by me or for me, I do not know which.

And I write to make sense of my life.

This doesn't explain everything, I know. In particular, it doesn't explain the discrepancy between my name and the name on the cover of this book. I will come to that. Before I do, let's think about reality.

2

◗ Though the human mind is incapable of absolute objectivity, it is capable of degrees of objectivity.[1]

◗ Objectivity is the area of agreement between the sensory organs of different humans. It occurs within fixed parameters, defined by the limits of those sensory organs; it is restricted to the visible spectrum, to certain audible wavelengths, to a certain number of chemicals that act on our senses of smell and taste, to a degree of refinement in our touch, and to operations that occur within time.[2] If a human being is given a substantial dose of radiation the five senses will be unaware: none the less there will be objective results that can be measured in time.

◗ Reality should not be confused with objectivity. Any objectivity attainable by a human being is confined, for instance, to electromagnetic wavelengths of a few thousand angstroms, the visible spectrum. Reality involves all wavelengths, all spectrums.

◗ Though absolute reality is beyond the reach of our senses, we each make a representation of reality in our heads.

◗ This representation is a transaction between objectivity, which is confined to electromagnetic wavelengths of a few thousand angstroms, and subjectivity, which isn't. Subjectivity is the welter of experience and assumption we bring to bear on our perceptions. The results of this can be positive, as when by analogy and connection we increase our understanding, or negative, leading to prejudice and inflexibility.[3]

---

[1] I reject the idealist argument on the grounds of modesty and practicality. I do not believe I have created all I perceive; even if I do believe it I find it makes not the blindest bit of difference.

[2] It can be argued that time is subjective, and certainly our perception of time can be coloured by subjectivity. The existence of time, however, is objective according to the definition of objectivity given here; it is an essential component of being human, of the process of birth-life-death we all register. Notice however that objectivity ≠ reality (see ff.); time need not be a component of absolute reality.

[3] Does this mean that some people's representations are closer to reality than others'? Of course it does. A Muslim believes in Mohammed's version, a physicist in Einstein's. The difficulty is finding the criteria by which to establish whose representation comes closest.

▶ Thus is absolute objectivity beyond us, for we each filter objective experience through our subjective minds.

3

The name on the cover of this book, you will have noticed, is 'Richard Burns'. Richard Burns is a novelist, a professional storyteller. He has written a number of books. Perhaps you've read some? I think this his best, but I am biased.

I could describe Richard Burns for you, illustrate him in a sentence or two – has too many children, for instance, and not enough money; he is five foot eight; his eyes are blue – but there is little point in this. Any description I give is bound to be provisional. All our objective observations agree: Richard Burns is getting older; Richard Burns is going to die.

I find this fascinating. Not his death, which frankly doesn't interest me one way or the other, but the fact that, though I am every bit as good a writer as he is, he can describe me yet I cannot describe him.

The reason for this has to do with the nature of art. Richard Burns is a novelist, but all art forms follow the same rules of representation. Standard representation, by which I mean that representation of reality we construct in our heads, is a combination of the objective and the subjective. Artistic representation, on the other hand, does not need to rely on objectivity to nearly the same degree.[1] Because reality is not the same as objectivity a work of art conveys a greater degree of reality than a purely objective description. This is why art is so important. This is why art is so necessary. Richard Burns can describe me not because he invented me – I resist the notion that he invented me: I have a reality of my own – but

---

[1] The conventional way of describing the degree of subjectivity in a work of art is to refer to realism or abstraction, but obviously in this context 'realism', at best a relative term, is inappropriate; even 'abstract' is not entirely satisfactory, because many abstract artists of the twentieth century could claim with some justice – and perhaps some cynicism – that they used abstraction to objectify the speed and violence of their age (cf. Chapter 8).

because he is not restricted to objective phenomena.[1] Were I to describe him I would either have to limit myself to objective phenomena – height and weight and bank balance, which is itself transitory –; or else I would have to include my subjective apprehension of him – whether I like him, whether I agree with what he says and does – and therefore to an extent fictionalise him.

This is why I approve of the way he has constructed this novel. He could have narrated it himself, of course, but even if he had the narrator would still have been a fiction.[2] This would have been acceptable, though I have my reservations: this book does not intend to blur the line between fiction and reality, but rather to show it is blurred. Equally, he could have chosen a different narrator, a less intrusive one, and told the events surrounding my death through the mouth of Chapman, perhaps, or Alan. This would have limited his scope, perhaps, and his opportunity for presenting different views of the same event, but would have been more conventional. In doing neither of the above he is, if I understand him correctly, attempting to exploit and examine the ambiguities and opportunities of fiction. What better guide to a fictional world than a fictional narrator? What better guide to death than a narrator presumed to be dead?

Sophistry? Possibly. And now my charms are all o'erthrown. I have written myself into your life, I write myself out again; Richard Burns has written himself into your life, and writes himself out again; he has written me into your life, and I cannot be disposed of so easily. For, make no mistake, there is more reality in your apprehension of Jennifer Fox, who never lived, than in your apprehension, even should you know him, of Richard Burns, who did.

---

[1] Think of the trouble Alan had in describing even something so simple as the cover of my *Literature in the Age of Certainty*.

[2] For instance, the narrator of a book is oblivious of the death of the author: the narrator, therefore, could not strictly *be* Richard Burns, who will some day die though this book will continue to exist.

4

And now I must finish my story. I am weak: the fictional cancer of a fictional character is no less dreadful than any you might suffer; the treatment does no good. The cancer is inoperable; chemotherapy makes me sick and I believe they administer it only that they may be seen to be doing something. In the 1940s a woman called Helen Lane died of cancer. The cells from her cancer were preserved and persuaded to reproduce in petri dishes. These so-called HeLa cells survive. Rationality is no help to me here. Rationality tells me that the preservation of the HeLa cells, to study, to help find a cure for cancer, is reasonable, commendable. Yet Helen Lane is dead and the rebellious cells that killed her live on, and I am appalled. I know I shouldn't be. I know I should welcome any measures that will help cure cancer. But I know too that when I die I want the cancer within me to die too. It is the only revenge I can have. Sometimes it seems I imagine what my death will be like in the hope it will be better than living like this. But then I think of Helen Lane. Death's Angel still lurks beyond the venetian blind. The nearer death comes the more fond I am of life.

Which is why I end this story the way I do, choosing the happiest outcomes. These outcomes follow reasonably enough, I hope, but they are not inevitable results of the situations I have created; they are inevitable given the situation I am in. The nearer death comes the more fond I am of life.

Chapter Thirteen

ALL'S WELL THAT ENDS WELL

*In which the Rule of Three is implied
and a Book that began with a Death
is made to end with
the promise of
a Birth*

I

She waits till after midnight, till after they have gone to bed, till after they have made love, then tells him. 'Alan,' she says. 'I'm going to have a baby.' It is a simple statement, an obvious way of expressing the facts, yet she has agonised over it, sought alternative ways to put it, sought somehow to break it more gently. She has wondered about not telling him at all for a while: telling him first that her period is late, and then perhaps that she feels sick in the mornings; letting him work it out for himself. He is a man of course, and men are slow about these things, but surely he would get there in time. Yet she has to tell someone, and no one has more right to know.

'My God,' he says. A rush of confused thought threatens to immobilise his mind. Is it mine or did it happen while she was away? Is that why she went away? What am I meant to do? What can I do? Is she keeping it? If it is mine do I want her to keep it? He wants to ask these questions, yet holds back. They are impertinent. He changes his mind: he does not want to ask these questions after all. He just wants the answers.

She makes a pattern of the moles on his chest, a star chart, a private constellation. 'It's yours,' she says.

'I know,' he says, and it is true. He did know. Of course he knew. He puts out a hand and strokes her hair. He still feels confused, and even a little angry – how could she let this happen? – but he is aware both that it has happened and that she did not do it on her own. 'What do you want to do about it?'

'I'm going to keep it.'

'That's not what I meant.' But: what did he mean? Anyway, he is glad she has made this decision, though he also knows that an abortion would remove the problem, and that if she had decided, on her own, that she wanted an abortion, then he would be free of all blame. And then he realises he can never be free of all blame: this embryo, this cell that splits and multiplies within her, is his as well as hers. He can never be free of all blame. 'I meant: what do you want me to do?' he asks.

The question is clumsily phrased. It annoys her. 'Do what you want!' she says. She remembers why she left.

He is silent, thinking: she has come back; we have made love; we are going to have a child. But she did leave. Why did she leave? Did she know she was pregnant then?

His silence softens her. She rephrases her reply. 'What do you want to do?' she asks.

'I don't know,' he says. But this is inadequate and not quite true. 'I want to be a father.'

The line is out and he regrets it. He regrets it because it commits him; he also regrets it because he has a sense that it was a good line to say, appropriate, dramatic, the sort a scriptwriter or novelist would give him, and he is not yet certain it is true. But he has said it, and he has committed himself.

'I want you to be a father,' she says, and it is another good line, unassailably the right reply, and therefore as suspect as his. Are we playing out roles, he wonders, or do we mean all this?

She is less critical. She has had time to get used to the notion. She has decided she wants the baby. It is enough in itself: she is pleased he wants to be a father, but it is not an essential decision for her. The essential decision was that she wanted to be a mother. A father is a useful accessory to a mother; he is nothing on his own.

It is a man's curse that he cannot bear children; it is a woman's curse that she can. 'Let's go to sleep,' she says. It has been a long and tedious day for her. She is tired.

It has been a long day for him as well. He has lost a house and gained a child. He has the sense he has lost control of his life, and the equal sense that perhaps he never had control, that any impression of control was false. It is a disturbing thought, a kind of quantum thought. Until quantum physics, scientists had steadily increased their understanding, their ability to predict how things would behave. But quantum particles cannot be predicted. The odds on a certain behaviour can be calculated, but as any gambler should know, odds are not certainties. There is absolutely no way of knowing what an individual quantum particle will do. No mathematics, no computation, no sophistication, can overcome the Uncertainty Principle.

But so what? he asks himself. Was it ever really expected that everything could be explained? How could it be, when life is so peculiar, so much out of control?

In the dim light of their midnight room he sees his lover's face. Her eyes are closed. He does not know if she is asleep; he finds it hard to believe she can sleep when he feels so awake. I'm going to be a father, he thinks.

A whole new set of worries hit him, a list:

we can't live here
what will Mum and Dad say?
I can't tell them
what if there's something wrong with it?
we ought to get married
how do I tell Mum?
what are we going to call it?
when were we so careless?
I might not like her when she gets fat
'Mum, Dad, you're going to be grandparents.'

He sees the list in his head. It looks like a poem, a comic poem with him as the butt. Trivia; inevitabilia. A week ago I was worried I couldn't write any more, couldn't think of a thing to say! No shortage of subjects now. It has been a long day. It has been a long week. He goes to sleep.

2

It has snowed in Sheffield, a thin surface snow that covers everything yet will not last. Jardine looks through his window at the whiteness of his lawn. The sun is a cold disc behind the clouds. It is more white than yellow. He looks at it: how can it be more white than yellow without being cream? He does not know. Would science have the answer? Probably: science is good at explaining the objective world. In fact science is good at enlarging the objective world: if objectivity is the area of agreement, then better instruments, better theories, make it easier to agree. First the sun was a god that circled the world, and each tribe had a different god, and men fought to assert the god of their people; then it became the centre of the universe, around which we travelled, though men were imprisoned and ridiculed for saying so; now it is a nuclear reactor in the sky and, having discovered the force that powers the sun, mankind has used the knowledge to make bombs.

And what will it be next, he wonders, when the ozone layer has been peeled away and it bombards the earth with radiation, our civilisations are destroyed and we are at its mercy.

The earth goes round the sun; the sun is just one star among a lot of stars. But as he looks at it, rising over the distant hills, the council flats and the water tower, it still seems it moves round the earth. And as he watches it, flat and cold behind cloud, it seems it is still a god.

His thoughts move, without effort, to Jenny in her coffin. Knowing that it isn't really Jenny in there, that Jenny has ceased to exist, that all that is left are the molecules that were Jenny, doesn't change much. He still thinks of it as Jenny boxed in underground, can still chill himself with the thought of the earth falling over her, burying her.

'Penny for them?' asks his wife from the bed. It is a good, comfortable bed, a cocoon.

'I was thinking about Jenny,' he replies.

She stretches in her cocoon. With the children out of the house – Sarah married in Epsom, Mark skiing with his school in Austria – there is little urgency about her mornings. 'Morbid,' she remarks. 'What's worrying you?'

'Nothing much,' he says: 'Death.'

She does not want to get involved in a discussion. 'Your turn to make the tea,' she reminds him.

He recognises her reluctance and understands it. 'Don't worry,' he says. 'I'm on my way. And it's funny, I feel much better about her death today. It was that business about the house, after the funeral. It was right Chapman kept the house. We forgive life a lot when things work out right.'

'A clumsy epigram, Professor,' says his wife.

'All right,' he says, dismissed. 'I'm getting the tea.' In his field he is eminent, in the house he is second among equals. This suits him really.

The post has come, and the paper. The post contains nothing of interest: a late Christmas card from a colleague in New Zealand and another invitation to subscribe to the *Reader's Digest*. The paper contains the obituary. He reads it through greedily, critically. They have cut his final line. He is disappointed. He felt the notion that Jenny had renounced nothing had rounded the piece off nicely. But, he thinks as he boils the kettle, warms the pot, perhaps it wasn't right. Death is when you renounce everything; who am I to know how much or how little she'd chosen to renounce?

He puts the teapot on the tray and goes back upstairs. Mary is sitting up in bed, her reading glasses on. 'Anything in the post?' she asks.

'Christmas card from Jim Kirkby.'

'Good heavens. I've taken all the cards down.' The half-moon glasses make her look severe, a magistrate.

'He is in Auckland,' says her husband.

'Even so. When did he post it?' She is not really severe; she is in a good mood. The children are away and safe. The bed is warm. 'Anything else?'

'My obituary is in the paper.'

'*Your* obituary. Well fancy that. And I didn't even know you were dead.'

3

'How do you feel this morning?' asks Wendy.

'Knackered.' They sit in the kitchen, in the cosy smell of warm toast. 'I'm sorry I was back so late. Did you find anything to do?'

'I phoned a friend,' she says. 'I had an early night.'

'Good for you,' says John. 'Bloody Robert's fault.'

'How was it, being chairman for the day?'

'Lousy.' But it is nice she asks.

'Good practice,' she says. 'If ever you get the chance to do it full time.'

'That reminds me,' he says, not so much reminded as seizing an opportunity. 'I've been meaning to tell you, waiting for the right moment. Only somehow we don't seem to have had much chance to talk recently.'

'Yes?'

'I'm leaving Lanchester. I've been headhunted. I'm going to Incorporated Publishers.'

'Incorporated.' A dull, unromantic word.

'Why not? Look. I get a lousy fifteen grand where I am, and work my rocks off.' Facts that were impressive when he rehearsed them in his head sound defensive now he speaks them aloud. 'Incorporated offer twenty, a car, and a team to back me up.'

'A car? How nice.'

He knows she is being sarcastic yet cannot respond to the sarcasm. 'Jenny Green had a Peugeot 405 when she was with them,' he tells her.

'Super.'

'We'd better get off,' he says, 'if you don't want to be late.'

'Why?' she asks. 'I can afford to lose my job now you're working for Incorporated.' She sees his face and relents a little. 'I was only joking,' she says. But she hates his new job.

John knows this. She'll come round, he persuades himself. When she thinks about it.

4

Chapman washes dishes. He has the radio on Radio 2. A band plays 'In the Mood'. He swishes water in time to the swing. I used to enjoy dancing, he thinks. Jennifer didn't dance, of course, and anyway when we'd met I'd trouble enough just walking. I can't say I missed it especially. But it would be nice to go just occasionally to a dance.

He does not acknowledge, even to himself, that at a dance you have a partner, but there is a flourish to the way he washes the last plate before putting it neatly on the rack.

5

Bridget hears Ernest hunting through the hall cupboard. 'What are you looking for, dear?' she calls.

'My galoshes.'

'In a plastic bag, hanging from the door. What do you want them for?'

'I just thought I'd clear the drive.'

'Don't be silly. There's not enough snow to bother with, and the sun's coming out. Besides, we're not going anywhere are we?'

'I thought I'd pop down to the club, if that's all right, find out how Peter's wife's getting on.'

'The snow'll have gone by then.'

He doesn't reply, but she hears him struggle with something, the galoshes presumably, and then go out.

She is right, he recognises when he gets out: there really isn't much snow. Still, all the more reason to get it done.

The house is south-facing; the drive is in shadow most of the day. It is cold. Despite his gloves he feels the cold, trimming his finger-nails, numbing the pads of his palm. He goes into the garage and gets his shovel. He could do with a snow shovel: all he has is an old-fashioned coal shovel. Still, he thinks, the work will keep me warm.

6

Alan and Anne-Marie get up late. 'Shouldn't you be at work?' she asks him.

'No,' he says. 'Shouldn't you be practising?'

'What for? I'll not be working for months. It's a good job my subs are up to date: at least I'll get a maternity allowance.'

'Play anyway. I expect the baby'll like it.'

'Come off it,' she says, pushing the bedclothes back to expose her flat stomach. 'There's nothing there yet. Ears and things don't develop for ages.'

'Even so, there is something there. Play it a tune. It can't do any harm.'

She is happy enough to please him. She gets up and opens her flute case, fits together the pieces of the flute, gets back into bed. 'It's a cold morning,' she says. 'What do you think it'd like?'

He lies back in the bed and smiles. 'You'd better ask it. You're the one in touch with it, remember.'

'All it tells me so far is to feel lousy or to go to Florida.'

'Oh,' says Alan. 'That's why you went. The baby wanted to go. What is it, an embryonic coke dealer?'

'Alan,' she says sweetly. 'Fuck off.'

'Well, you can't blame the baby.'

'Why not? Pregnancy does funny things to the hormones, it screws up your emotions. I've been reading about it: I'm not the first woman who has done something barmy at the start of a pregnancy. It's worse when you don't know what the cause is. I didn't know I was pregnant; all I knew was that everything you said and did used to drive me mad.' She gives him the same sweet smile as before. 'It still does.'

'Are you going to play that thing or what?'

She touches him with the tubular tip. The metal is cold and the cold makes him recoil. 'Okay. Tune for an Unborn Child.' It is rather a lovely title.

She begins to play. The tune is haunting and familiar, though she embellishes it with trills and short runs. He does not recognise it at first, then catches on. 'Rock-a-bye baby,' he says. He rests his hand, gently, on her belly.

7

Just before lunch Wendy has a fifth-year class. It is their discussion
session: once a week they talk about some controversial issue that
they can write about for homework. Not all the pupils do
homework, but that is a different discussion. Today, in the first
discussion after Christmas and the New Year, the subject is drink.
The usual points are raised: the dangers of drinking and driving, the
curious licensing laws. The last get several of them indignant. 'It's
not fair. There's lots of ways the laws discriminate against us, miss. I
mean, we're allowed to get pregnant and get married at sixteen, and
we can go into a pub, but we can't drink till we're eighteen.'

'Yeah. I'm joining the army next year, miss. I might get killed but
I can't have a drink legal. Not till I'm eighteen, miss.'

'And we can drink at home,' says the next speaker. 'I bet everyone
here's got drunk plenty of times. So why'd they keep us out the
pubs, miss?'

There are answers, Wendy realises, but none that will be
acceptable. She tries anyway. 'One: adults actually like the fact that
there are no kids in a pub; it gives them a break. Two: the law allows
people to drink but it doesn't encourage them; if you were allowed
to drink at sixteen you would.'

'We do anyway,' says one of the girls.

'And what difference does it make if we wait till we're eighteen to
get plastered, miss?'

Wendy does not bother trying to answer. 'And three, all right
you're discriminated against a bit maybe, but it's a discrimination
you'll grow out of.' Not like being a woman, which is something
I'm stuck with for ever. 'Childhood, youth, whatever you want to
call it: it doesn't last, you know. When you're older and can drink
legally you'll wonder what all the fuss was about.' My husband gets
a new job and I'm meant to be happy! 'Time changes the way you
look at all sorts of things.' Like my marriage and my husband.

She smiles wryly. 'Miss, this is *serious*, miss,' says one of the boys,
pained she can carry their worries lightly.

'Of course it is,' she replies. You must never patronise in this job, never forget that for a youth the priorities of youth are the right priorities. They need to understand as much as they can at this age: there'll be plenty of time for them to learn how much remains incomprehensible when they get older. 'I was just thinking about something else. My husband has got a new job.' They like it when she mentions her life outside school. She has a reputation for strictness. That she has a life outside school humanises her.

The class are not slow to take advantage. 'What kind of job, miss?' They did not mind talking about drink, but are happier talking about things off the GCSE syllabus. There is honour to be gained by distracting a teacher, and they know it.

Wendy accepts the distraction. She tells them about John's work, and about Incorporated Publishers. She drops the names of the film-stars and royalty Incorporated publish and, as she intended, they are impressed. They have heard of these people, read about their private lives in the *Sun*, seen them on *Wogan*. 'You must be real proud of him, miss.'

'Oh I am,' she says. Are they old enough to appreciate irony? She doubts it. 'But let's get back to the subject. You've still got to do a homework assignment on it, remember.'

'Aw, *miss*.'

8

It is twenty past twelve. Bridget goes into the study. Ernest is reading. 'I thought I didn't hear you go out. There's nothing wrong is there?'

'No. No, nothing. I just thought I'd give the club a miss today,' says Ernest. 'If you don't mind.'

'Of course I don't mind. Are you sure you're all right?'

'I'm fine. I'm just not in the mood. You know, Jennifer, Peter's wife.'

She accepts this. 'All right. But I've not much in for lunch,' she warns. 'I expected you'd be going down to the club.'

'I'm not hungry anyway,' he says. 'Touch of indigestion.'

9

Chapman is in his improbable apron. There is a large grinning orange cat on the apron which I always thought of as the Cheshire cat. Apparently I was wrong about this; apparently it is a cartoon character called 'Heathcliffe', of all names. I expect I was wrong about many things. Chapman only wears the apron when he has serious housework to do. He goes upstairs to Jennifer's study.

He starts at the desk. He begins by emptying the drawers. He finds matches from the days when she smoked, old stamps, odd postcards, anonymous telephone numbers. He has with him a large black plastic bin bag. He starts to fill it. This is the drab detritus of a bookish life, these reinforcement rings, ranks of linked staples that crumble at the touch, rubber bands, bottles of Stephens ink crusted at the neck like old port. There are paper-clips here and ring files, each with a purpose once, and old essays that should have been returned, odd notes that she wrote to herself. Some of the notes are important insights into an aspect of literature. Others say Bread Marge Bootlace. They go into the same bag.

When the drawers are cleared, so that only the few things worth preserving remain – a virgin bottle of ink, stamps that are not out of date, binders in decent condition – he starts on the desk top. He makes neat piles of paper, bond paper, bank paper, yellow copy paper. He returns glossy thin sheets of carbon paper to their narrow box. He uses the binders to organise the papers. He is uncertain what to do with papers with writing on.

The desk is straight now. The ballpoints are laid out by the side of the typewriter, the typewriter's carriage is centred. It looks rather splendid now that the desk is cleared, he thinks, a kind of museum piece, black and noble, upright and confident. She called it her 'tripewriter'.

He goes downstairs and returns with the vacuum cleaner. The floor is bare board and rug. He vacuums the rugs carefully, standing on them to stop buckling in the suction. They could do with a beating but that can wait till spring. The floor needs a good scrub too, and that can also wait for spring.

Next are the books. There is no order he can discern here. There *is* no order. This was a study, not a library. He does not know what order to adopt, but where the books go is anyway conditioned to a certain extent by size. Somehow it seems right that the paperbacks should go on the DIY shelves, on their aggressive modern brackets, the hardbacks in the glass-fronted cases. Some of the hardbacks are leatherbound, dignified. He sorts these out first. *Vanity Fair*, *Bleak House*, Carlyle's *French Revolution*, a copy of *The Origin of the Species*, Tennyson's *Idylls*. He begins to find large numbers of Loeb Classics, mostly without their dust jackets, red for Latin authors, green for Greek. He discards the last of the dust jackets and arranges them alphabetically in coloured blocks, Accius to Virgil, Aeschylus to Xenophon, on the shelf beneath the leather books. They look good. He finds volumes one and three of Braudel's *Civilization and Capitalism* and hunts out volume two. The black spines look noble together. A different collection of black spines are the Penguin Classics. Again he arranges them alphabetically, irrespective of any other logic. Tacitus lies next to Tolstoy. He starts to recognise certain names. Here is Euripides again, in several volumes, and here is Plato. He finds other Penguin Classics, an older edition, the spines cream, and topped and tailed with blocks of colour. The colours signify the original language – brown for Greek, purple for Latin, green for French; to his annoyance, there is an inconsistency about the lettering on the spines, for some read left to right, others right to left, and this spoils his patterns.

Other paperbacks are even less consistent. Slim volumes of Faber & Faber come in various sizes and colours. He puts them together anyway, along with fatter Faber volumes of prose, George Steiner's *Death of Tragedy*, Auden's *The Dyer's Hand*, the essays of T. S. Eliot. He finds a second copy of *Death of Tragedy*, identical to the first, and puts it to one side; he does not mind repeats in different editions, but exact duplicates seem redundant.

Auerbach's *Mimesis* is there, and Abrams's *The Mirror and the*

Lamp; she has both the Norton and the Oxford anthologies of English literature, one volume of the Oxford in hardback and the other in paperback. He dusts the shelves before replacing the books.

In time the patterns begin to emerge. They are specious patterns, perhaps, patterns of colour rather than function, coincidences of design rather than content, but the room looks better for them. He starts to take a bibliophile's interest in things, and even a biographer's interest: he notes a number of recently acquired paperbacks on quantum physics and relativity, and a group of antiquated school primers in Latin and Greek, evidence of shifting tastes; he finds a miscellany of works on Shakespeare, all from the early 1950s; he finds copies of her three books. There are carved bookends, redundant where they stand on the shelf. He puts them on the desk, uses them to prop up the six editions of *Shakespeare's Great Theme*, the one edition each of *Literature in the Age of Certainty* and *Literature in the Age of Uncertainty* (but there are five copies of the latter, as though she found it hard to get rid of). He works until it is dark outside, and until he is satisfied, and when it is done the room looks good.

It has lost its purpose. It is no longer a working room. The books are a collection now, rather than an aspect of study. But it makes a better monument.

Chapman stands by the door. His arms are folded. He looks at the tidy desk, the ordered shelves. Death is a rearrangement, of molecules, of books. Individuality, not being you, not being dead, is lost. But something always is preserved.

10

Robert is in a different roomful of books. 'I want your opinion,' he tells John. 'I know you'll not be with us much longer and all that, but perhaps that'll make you more objective. I'd like to reissue Jennifer Fox's books, in a uniform edition, something to remember her by.'

'I don't know,' says John. '*Shakespeare's Great Theme* maybe:

it's never gone out of print. But the other two didn't do half so well. I was looking through them. *Literature in the Age of Uncertainty* never even made a second edition.'

'I know. But that might not have been Jennifer's fault. She was out of phase with the times. *Age of Uncertainty* came out in sixty-eight. It didn't seem like an age of uncertainty then: peace marches and flower power and sit-ins and love-ins, all the paraphernalia of a brave new world. But maybe now she'd get a better response.'

'It's a tall order. It wouldn't work. No one's going to review a reissue of a twenty-year-old book. I haven't read it but I suppose you might be right, there might be a market for it now that there wasn't then. But you'll have to spend a lot of money finding that market. You'd do better trying to get them into paperback. The Shakespeare book is in paperback already, of course, Penguin do it. Why not see if they'll take the other two?'

Robert smiles. 'I was on the phone to them this morning. Nothing.'

'One phone-call? You must be getting old. Since when has one phone-call meant anything? Persevere.'

'I know I'm getting old. Nothing like a funeral to remind you. It's probably time I dropped out of this game. I don't mean retire, just take a back seat. Are you sure you want to go to Incorporated?'

John reaches for the implications of this. 'Why do you ask?'

'Somebody's going to have to take over here.'

'Do you mean what I think you mean?'

'The job's yours if you want it.'

'Hey, look. I'm flattered. But I'm a publicity man, not an editor. What do I know about editing books?'

'As much as anyone, I should say. A damn sight more than I did when I started. And you know the company. You don't have to make a decision straight away. Talk it over with Wendy – and by the way, those stories of her friend's aren't bad, you can tell her I've not made my mind up yet but that I am interested.'

'It'd mean letting Incorporated down.'

'They'll survive.'

11

After dinner they stay at the table. Bridget smokes a second cigarette. 'I wonder how Chapman feels now he's got what he wanted.'

'You mean the house? I don't think it was what he wanted. He was reluctant enough.'

'That was for show. He wanted to stay well enough.'

'I was proud of you,' says Ernest.

She blows smoke across the empty plates. 'I didn't seem to have much choice.'

'It was the right thing to do anyway,' he insists. 'We couldn't turn him out, whatever the law.'

'I know.' She blows out more smoke, a curling cone that disperses according to complex laws of turbulence over plates still smeared with gravy, smudged with the odd leaves of Brussels sprouts. 'I know.'

He looks away from her. His indigestion is still there, a rough-edged ache in his chest, a tightness at the base of his ribs. He feels too warm. 'It's a bit late in the day to mention this,' he says, 'but I still love you, you know.'

'Sentimental old duffer. Are you feeling all right?' she says dismissively, though she is delighted. She looks at him, stubs out her cigarette. His hair crinkles across his scalp in tight grey waves. His face too looks grey in this light. 'Are you feeling all right?' she asks again, more urgently.

'I'm fine,' he reassures her, reassures them both. 'A touch of indigestion. It'll pass.'

12

John lets himself in. Wendy is home first as usual. 'Hi, love!' he calls as he closes the front door behind him. He has a bottle of champagne, wrapped in green tissue, in his hand. He goes into the living room. Wendy is marking books. He brandishes the champagne. 'A celebration,' he announces.

'Oh yes? What are we celebrating?'

'My new job.'

Champagne! she thinks. 'John. I'm not interested in your new job. And I can't drink. I'm going out later.'

'Going out? Where?' He refuses to be deflated; his interrogation is intended to show an interest in her life.

'Just out. Does it matter where?'

'No.' No, of course it doesn't. I don't pretend I own you. Only I thought you might like some champagne. 'Only I thought you might like some champagne,' he says.

'Well,' she says. 'Now you know I don't.' She shifts the pile of exercise books from her knee. 'You've been celebrating already,' she observes.

'Robert and I went for a drink after work.' He mimics a shamefaced, caught-red-handed look. 'We've already had one bottle,' he admits.

'Robert? I'm surprised. Not your new friends at Incorporated then? I thought the champagne was their style: brash and ostentatious.'

He feels as if the champagne he has drunk already has done something to his face, exaggerated his expressions to those of a cartoon character. When comprehension dawns he expects lightbulbs to appear in his eyeballs. 'I think we're talking about different jobs.' How could she know? he chides himself.

'What do you mean?' She is bored with this. She picks up the exercise books and starts towards the kitchen. She used to like it when he had a drink inside him: it made him playful, ingenuous; it made him that East End boy who couldn't believe his luck. That was a long time ago, she thinks.

'Different jobs,' he repeats. 'Robert's offered me his.'

She stops in the kitchen doorway. 'Pardon?'

'Robert's retiring. He wants me to take over. He'll still be chairman, of course, but I'll run the firm.'

'Good grief. Are you sure?' There's a stupid question, she thinks. He can't fix taps but he isn't an imbecile. 'I mean, what did you say?'

'I said I'd think about it.'

'John!' He couldn't throw this away. Could he?

'But I've been in touch with Incorporated, told them I'm no longer available.'

'John!'

'No Peugeot 405,' he reminds her.

She goes through to the kitchen and puts the books on the table. I don't believe this, she thinks. Robert's job!

'Well?' he asks. 'What do you think?' He really wants to know. She *seemed* pleased; he wants confirmation.

She *is* pleased, but it takes her a moment to be sure. 'You'd better open that champagne.'

He goes over and kisses her on the forehead. He says nothing. He has a shrewd suspicion that this is wisest.

He unwinds the wire that confines the cork. 'I'll get some glasses,' she says. She puts two wine glasses on the kitchen table and he fires the cork inexpertly into the ceiling, spurting wine on to the floor as he watches the ricochet.

'Get it poured!' she encourages.

'To the Lanchester Press!' he toasts.

'And its new boss,' she replies.

'Robert'll still be chairman,' he repeats. 'I'll just be doing all the hard work.'

'I know.' She smiles at him. 'The commissioning, the approving, the deciding. The hiring and firing. It'll be hell.'

'Absolute agony,' he agrees. 'What's for supper?'

'I thought you'd had a liquid meal.'

'Let's go out. Let's celebrate in style.'

'I've got a better idea,' she says. 'Let's stay in.'

'Suits me,' he says, and it does. It suits him fine.

'Pop out to the wine shop,' she says. 'Get another bottle. Or two. I'll get something to eat. We've plenty in: I went to Sainsbury's on Saturday.'

'That's right. And I fixed the tap.'

'No you didn't,' she says, and they laugh. But Sainsbury's has reminded her about Alan. 'I'd forgotten. I was meant to be going out tonight.'

He is immediately deflated. 'Oh.'

'It's all right. I can cancel it. It doesn't matter. I'll give him a ring.'

'Him? Secret admirer?'

'One of the Crouch poets.'

'Oh.' He has met the Crouch poets. Jim is pleasant and hairy, Ted a bit of a wimp, Crabcalf a pretentious twit. He dismisses them. 'Right. Some more champagne for madame?'

'Please. You'd better go down to the wine shop before you have any more though. I'll be on the phone.'

She goes through to the living room, takes Alan's number from her handbag, phones him.

13

They are on their way out when the telephone rings. 'Ignore it,' says Anne-Marie.

'I'd better answer,' says Alan. He returns, picks it up. 'Gruafin?' Anne-Marie waits in the doorway. 'No. No, that's fine. No, absolutely not. I haven't decided about tomorrow night yet. No, something's come up. Yes, I'm sure we shall. Well: thanks for calling. Bye.' He puts the phone down. 'Christ,' he tells Anne-Marie. 'I'd completely forgotten.'

'Your date for tonight? I'd remembered.'

'You could have reminded me.'

'You poor innocent.'

'I wouldn't have ditched you if you had, you know. I promised you a meal out, a meal out you shall have. A celebration.'

'You're sure you want to celebrate?' Every so often a serious sentence slips into their conversation like a bill through the door.

'Sure I'm sure.' They go down the stairs. 'After all, it's the first time we've been out together, the three of us, as a family.'

Family, blood, that's what counts.

They go outside. A Fiesta XR2 is parked illegally on the pavement and its owner buys champagne on his Barclaycard. They do not see him. The sky is clear. Despite London's glow there are stars visible, little gods, a spreading heaven. We make meaningless patterns of the stars, organise them according to the designs we see from the earth, irrespective of the real distances between them, the real relationships they have to one another. Alan puts his arm protectively round Anne-Marie's shoulders; she stiffens against this, against his maleness, his dominion, and then relaxes. He has his arm around her, and this feels right. We make patterns of the stars; the stars make patterns of our lives, patterns for those with a will to look, patterns otherwise unnoticed and maybe never there, patterns for poets and fond lovers to find. The XR2 drives off. Messages from the stars twinkle childishly in the frost. Anne-Marie relaxes her shape into Alan's. On the road the traffic parts to let an ambulance through. The XR2 waits with the rest. The ambulance assaults the night with streaking blue light and is gone. 'Not an accident, I hope,' says Anne-Marie.

Alan squeezes her shoulder. 'Someone having a baby,' he assures her. The ambulance passes them, its revolving light splashing the shadows. For a moment they are brightly lit, brilliant, and then the light leaves them; when it returns the ambulance is further away and they are lit obliquely, bleakly this time, a man with his arm around a woman, dwarfed by their own shadows. And the light strikes them a third time, more faintly yet; they are touched with brief St Elmo's fire, a fringe of glimmering blue, before the ambulance is gone and the last of its light with it. Alan and Anne-Marie stand by the roadside, dim shapes in the dimness, insubstantial figures on a London street, insubstantial, enduring as fiction.

A NOTE ON THE AUTHOR

Richard Burns is the author of *A Dance for the Moon* (one of the winners of the 1983 Cape/Times Young Author Competition); *The Panda Hunt*; a thriller, *Why Diamond Had to Die*; and two fantasies, *Khalindaine* and *Troubadour*. He reviews regularly for *The Independent*.